CHRISTA WOLF

Childhood

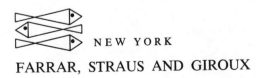NEW YORK

FARRAR, STRAUS AND GIROUX

English translation © 1980 by Farrar, Straus and Giroux, Inc.
A Model Childhood was originally published in German
under the title *Kindheitsmuster*, © 1976 by Aufbau-Verlag,
Berlin und Weimar
All rights reserved
Published simultaneously in Canada by McGraw-Hill
Ryerson Ltd., Toronto
Printed in the United States of America

FIRST PRINTING, 1980

DESIGNED BY HERB JOHNSON

Library of Congress Cataloging in Publication Data
Wolf, Christa. A model childhood.
Translation of Kindheitsmuster.
I. Title. PZ4.W8532Mo   [PT2685.036]
833'.914   80–13601

The translators wish to thank Bruce Benderson for his
intelligent, sensitive collaboration.

Where is the child I used to be,
still within, or far away?

Does he know I never loved him,
or that he never loved me?

Why when we grew up together
did we later grow apart?

Why when my childhood years were dead
didn't each of us die too?

And if my soul fell from my body,
why does my skeleton remain?

*

When does the butterfly in flight
read what's written on its wings?

PABLO NERUDA, *Book of Questions*
(TRANSLATED BY MARGARET SAYERS PEDEN)

A Model Childhood

1

What is past is not dead; it is not even past. We cut ourselves off from it; we pretend to be strangers.

People once remembered more readily: an assumption, a half truth at best. A renewed attempt to barricade yourself. Gradually, as months went by, the dilemma crystallized: to remain speechless, or else to live in the third person. The first is impossible, the second strange. And as usual, the less unbearable alternative will win out. Because of what you're getting ready to begin on this dismal day, November 3, 1972. You lay aside stacks of tentatively filled pages, insert a fresh sheet, and start once again with Chapter 1. As in so many times during the last eighteen months, when you were forced to learn: the difficulties haven't even begun. As always, you would have ignored anyone presumptuous enough to tell you so.

The present intrudes upon remembrance, today becomes the last day of the past. Yet we would suffer continuous estrangement from ourselves if it weren't for our memory of the things we have done, of the things that have happened to us. If it weren't for the memory of ourselves.

And for the voice that assumes the task of telling it.

Back in the summer of 1971, you agreed to the proposal to drive to L., now called G. Although you kept telling yourself that there was no need for it. Still, why not let them have their way. The tourist business to hometowns was booming. People who had gone came back praising the friendliness of the town's new inhabitants, and describing the roads, the food, the lodgings as "good," "fair," "adequate." You listened without any particular emotion. Topographically, you said—partly to give the appearance of genuine interest—you'd be able to rely on your memory completely: the houses, streets, churches, parks, squares, the entire layout of this ordinary town was forever preserved in your head. You had no need to visit the sights. Still, said H. Whereupon you began conscientious travel preparations. Visas were still required, but regulations had already become very relaxed, and the noncommittal reply "to see the sights," given under "purpose of trip" in the duplicate application forms, met with no objection. The true answer—"research" or "memory test"—would have raised eyebrows. (To go sightseeing in one's so-called hometown!) Unlike the officials at the People's Police, you thought your new passport photos didn't look like you at all; in fact, you thought they looked positively awful, because you looked older than you felt. But you thought Lenka looked great, as she always did. She rolled her eyes, to avoid commenting on her photographs.

While the applications for exit permits and the requests for currency exchange with the Bank for Industry & Commerce were being processed, your brother, Lutz, took the precaution of wiring for hotel reservations—in the town which appeared bilingually on your application forms, under two different names, as L. under "Place of Birth," and as G. under "Destination"—because in your hometown you didn't know a soul with whom you could stay overnight. You received your identification papers and your three times three hundred zloty promptly, and you didn't give yourself away until the eve of the day set for the departure, when your brother, Lutz, phoned to say that he hadn't had the time to pick up his papers. When you couldn't have cared less that the trip was being postponed by one whole week.

Thus your departure was fixed for Saturday, July 10, 1971, the hottest day of that month, which was in turn the hottest month of the year. Lenka, not quite fifteen and accustomed to traveling abroad, declared politely upon questioning that, yes, she was curious, it would be interesting, yes, certainly. H. took the wheel, as you were still half asleep. Your brother, Lutz, stood waiting at the Schoenefeld station. He took the seat next to H., you sat behind him, with Lenka's head in your lap, a leftover habit from her baby days. She slept as far as the border.

Previous drafts had started differently: with the flight. When the child was almost sixteen. Or with the attempt to describe the working process of memory, a crab's walk, a painful backward motion, like falling into a time shaft, at the bottom of which the child sits on a stone step, in all her innocence, saying "I" to herself for the first time in her life.

Yes, most of the time you started with the description of this seldom-remembered moment, which you were able to summon up after some thought. Yours is an authentic memory, even if it's slightly worn at the edges, because it is more than improbable that an outsider had watched the child and had later told her how she had sat on the doorstep of her father's store, trying the new word out in her mind: I . . . I . . . I . . . I . . . I . . . each time with a thrilled shock which had to be kept a secret, that much she knew right away.

No. In this case there are no outside witnesses who so often supply us with our childhood memories. The stone step (it exists, you'll find it again thirty-six years later, lower than expected. But who, in our day and age, doesn't know that childhood places have the habit of shrinking?). The irregular brick pavement that leads to the door of her father's store, a path in the shifting sand of Sonnenplatz. The afternoon light is falling onto the street from the right, and is reflected in the yellowish fronts of the Pflesser houses. The stiff-jointed doll Lieselotte with her golden braids and her eternal red silk ruffle dress. The smell of this particular doll's hair, after all these years, so distinctly, unpleasantly different from the smell of the short, dark-brown, real hair of the much older doll,

Charlotte, which had been handed down to the child by her mother, bore the mother's name, and was loved the best. But what about the child herself? No image. This is where forgery would set in. Memory hovered inside this child and has outlasted her. You'd have to cut her out of a photograph and paste her into the memory, which you'd spoil in the process. Making collages can't be what you have in mind.

Everything would have been decided behind the scenes, before the first sentence. The child would follow the stage directions: she has been accustomed to obedience. Whenever you'd need her (first drafts are always bungled), she would crouch down on the stone step, take the doll into her arms, and, on cue, express amazement, in a preconceived interior monologue, at having had the good fortune to have come into this world as the true daughter of her parents, the storeowner Bruno Jordan and his wife, Charlotte, rather than as, for instance, the daughter of that ominous Herr Rambow, who has a store on Wepritz Boulevard. (Herr Rambow, who sold a 38-pfennig pound of sugar for a half or a whole pfennig less, to undercut the competition of the Jordan store on Sonnenplatz: the child has no idea why Herr Rambow seems so ominous to her.) At this point, the mother would have to call the child in for supper, from the living-room window. For the first time we hear the name by which the child will be called in these pages: Nelly! (And thus, quite incidentally, the baptismal formalities have been taken care of, without dwelling on the tedious search for a suitable name.)

At this point, Nelly has to go inside, more slowly than usual, because a child that has felt the first thrill of her life at the thought of I . . . me . . . can no longer be pulled in by her mother's voice. The child walks past the corner window of her father's store, which may be featuring a display of small packets of barley coffee or cereal soup, and which today has been expanded (as you know since that Saturday in July 1971) into a garage, where a man in a green work shirt with rolled-up sleeves was washing his car as you pulled up at ten o'clock in the morning. You concluded that all the people who now live on Sonnenplatz—including those in the newly constructed houses—do their shopping at the cooperative down on Wepritz Boulevard, the former Rambow store. (Wepritz has become Weprice, which was probably what it had been called initially.) The child Nelly rounds the corner, climbs the three steps, and disappears behind her front door, Number 5 Sonnenplatz.

You've got it, then. She moves, walks, lies down, sits, eats, sleeps, drinks. She can laugh and cry, dig sand pits, listen to fairy tales, play with dolls, be frightened, happy, say mama and papa, love and hate and say her prayers. And all with deceptive authenticity. Until she strikes a false note, a precocious remark—less than that: a thought, a gesture—exposing the limitation for which you had almost settled.

Because it hurts to admit that the child—aged three, helpless, alone—is inaccessible to you. You're not only separated from her by forty years; you are hampered by your unreliable memory. You abandoned the child, after all. After others abandoned it. All right, but she was also abandoned by the adult who slipped out of her, and who managed to do to her all the things adults usually do to children. The adult left the child behind, pushed her aside, forgot her, suppressed her, denied her, remade, falsified, spoiled and neglected her, was ashamed and proud of her, loved her with the wrong kind of love, and hated her with the wrong kind of hate. Now, in spite of all impossibility, the adult wishes to make the child's acquaintance.

The tourist trade to half-buried childhoods is also booming, as you well know, whether you like it or not. The child doesn't care why you've become involved in this mission to find and salvage her. She will continue to sit and play with her three dolls (the third doll, Ingeborg, is a hairless celluloid baby in a sky-blue flannel playsuit). You're familiar with the various stages of childhood development. Any normally developed three-year-old severs himself from the third person in which he has thought of himself up to that point. Why then the shock, caused by the first conscious thought of "I"? (One can't remember everything, but why this particular incident? Why not, for instance, the birth of one's brother, shortly thereafter?) Why are shock and triumph, thrill and fear, so intimately linked for this child that no power in the world, no laboratory, and certainly no soul-searching can ever separate them?

You can't answer that. All the carefully researched stacks of material won't tell you. Still, don't say that you wasted the weeks which you spent in the State Library, looking through the dust-coated volumes of your hometown newspaper, which turned up in the archives, to your and the helpful librarian's incredulous amazement. Or the time you invaded the strictly sealed-off room in the House of the Teacher, a pedagogical center, where the school books of your childhood lie stacked up to the ceiling, quarantined, removable only by special authorization: German, history, biology.

(Do you remember what happened when Lenka looked at the pages of *Tenth-grade Biology*, which depict members of inferior races—Semites, Middle Easterners? She said nothing. Wordlessly she handed you back the book she had secretly borrowed and expressed no desire to look at it again. You had the feeling that she was looking at you with different eyes that day.)

Memory aids. Lists of names, sketches of the town, scraps of paper with sayings, typical family expressions, proverbs the mother or the grandmother were fond of using, first lines of songs. You started sifting through photographs, which are scarce; the subsequent inhabitants of the house on Soldinerstrasse probably burned the fat brown family album. Not to mention the material readily accessible from books, television, old films: surely not all of it was useless. Just as it isn't useless to sharpen one's focus on "the present."

It is interesting that we either fictionalize or become tongue-tied when it comes to personal matters. We may have good reason to hide from ourselves (at least to hide certain aspects—which amounts to the same). But even if there is little hope of an eventual self-acquittal, it would be enough to withstand the lure of silence, of concealment.

At any rate, there are still all kinds of harmless details that call for description. Like your Sonnenplatz, a name you recognized not without emotion in its Polish translation on the new blue street signs. (You were delighted every time you saw something that had remained stable, especially names, because too many names, like Adolf-Hitlerstrasse, and Hermann Göring School, and Schlageterplatz had been changed by the town's new inhabitants.) Maybe the square had always looked a little shabby. After all, it lay on the town's periphery. The two-story housing project of the COHORG (a magic word, the decodification of which—Community Housing Organization—was a disappointment to

Nelly) had been built during the early thirties into the white sand of the end moraine—the geological equivalent of the Wepritz Mountains. A windy business—the mother's term—since the desert sand was practically always on the move. Every grain of sand that gets between your teeth makes you taste the sand of Sonnenplatz. Nelly often baked it into cakes, which she ate. Sand cleans the stomach.

On that blistering Saturday in 1971: not a breath. Not a speck of dust was stirring. As you used to in the past, you had come from "below," meaning from the boulevard, with its impressive linden trees, the terminal of the municipal trolley line Number 1, whose old red-and-yellow cars are still in service. You had parked your car in the street along the south side of the Pflesser houses—whatever their present name—a gigantic square with 650-foot-long sides, enclosing a very large inner courtyard, through which you had the familiar view into the vaulted doorways on your walk up Sonnenweg: old people sitting on benches, watching children at play. Scarlet runners and marigolds.

As before, in the days when Bruno Jordan's poorly paying customers lived in these houses, it was forbidden to walk through one of the doorways, to enter one of the courtyards. It had been established once and for all that no COHORG child could set foot on Pflesser ground with impunity: it was an unwritten law which nobody understood and everybody obeyed. The ban had been broken, the hatred between children's gangs had subsided. But the catcalls and thrown stones of the "Pflesser gang" had been replaced by the silent eyes of the old people on the benches, guarding their yards against outside intrusion. The old urge to sit down on one of these benches, just once, was as unattainable now as before, though for different reasons.

Interestingly, your brother, Lutz, your junior by three years, not only understood your reluctance, but seemed to share it, since it was he who stopped Lenka when she casually headed for one of the archways, drawn by the music coming from the courtyards, by a desire for companions her own age. Never mind, Lutz said, stay here. But why? Why can't I go in there? Better not. As you walked on, you figured out for him that he was exactly four years old when he left Sonnenplatz, and had never gone back since, having had no reason to go back. Yes, he said, without going into an explanation of how he knew that no one was allowed to enter the Pflesser courtyards.

Not that opportunities had been lacking. Nelly could easily have entered every single one of the evil-smelling hallways and every single yard with its padding of scarlet runners, on Sunday mornings, at the side of her father when he went debt-collecting, armed with his fat black ledger. Unlike her mother, he favored giving her an early look at real life. But out of an exaggerated feeling of embarrassment—which she had inherited from her mother, in the unanimous opinion of all Jordans—she flatly refused to accompany her father on these errands; just as she stubbornly resisted any suggestion that she deliver flower pots and congratulations or condolence cards to their customers on occasions of christenings, confirmations, weddings, and funerals.

Memory, according to today's interpretation: "The preservation of previous experience, and the faculty to do so." Not an organ then, but a process, and the capacity for carrying it out, expressed in one word. An unused memory gets lost, ceases to exist, dissolves into nothing—an alarming thought. Consequently, the faculty to preserve, to remember, must be developed. Before your inner eye, ghostly arms emerge, groping about in a dense fog, aimlessly. You have no way of penetrating all the layers systematically; you're wasting your energy, with no more result than fatigue; and you go and take a nap in broad daylight. Just then your mother comes in, even though she is dead, and sits down in the big room, something you had always secretly wanted. The whole family is gathered, the living and the dead. You alone are able to tell one from the other, but you have to go to the kitchen, to wash all those dishes. The sun is shining through the kitchen window, but you feel sad, and you lock the door so that no one can come in and help you.

Suddenly, a shock that penetrates even the roots of your hair: in the big room on the table lies the manuscript, with, on the first page, only one word, "MOTHER," in large letters. She'll read it, guess your purpose, and feel hurt.

(There's your start, advised H. But you didn't want that; let other people give themselves away. That was in January 1971. You attended every board meeting, council meeting, work session, administrative gathering, which seem to burst into feverish activity at the beginning of every year. Dust accumulated on your writing desk; of course there were reproaches, which you could only counter with a long list of undeniable obligations.)

So far as you know, Sonnenplatz has never appeared in any of your dreams. You've never dreamed that you were standing in front of the corner house, whose number 5 is indicated twice now, in keeping with the needs of the time: the old well-known weather-beaten 5, cemented onto the house wall, and, immediately beside it, the new white enamel plate with the same number in black. You've never dreamed of the red geraniums which bloom or bloomed now as then in front of almost all the windows. Only the white shades behind the windowpanes are unfamiliar. Charlotte Jordan had bought modern net curtains for her living-room window. No memory as to the curtains in the parents' bedroom. The nursery had a blue-and-yellow-striped curtain that filtered the morning light in a way that made Nelly wake up full of expectations. Except when, as during Nelly's fifth year, a murderer crept into the room, in precisely that half light, a crooked little man ("I'm going to my little room to eat my bread and jelly; there stands a little crooked man, with half inside his belly") bending over the head of baby brother's crib, holding a shiny knife in his hand, with the tip about to pierce baby brother's heart . . . Unless, at the very last moment, his sister, Nelly, stops pretending that she's asleep and gets up enough courage (by God! she's doing it!) to creep slowly, slowly, carefully, carefully past the murderer's back, out into the hall to alert their mother, who is coming out of their bathroom in her petticoat. Disbelieving, laughingly, their mother shakes the pile of clothes on the chair in front of baby brother's bed, where it had bunched itself into a hobgoblin. (Could that be her first memory of her brother?)

Better not tell how the mother pats Nelly's cheek, saying half-pityingly what a "good girl" she is, being so fond of her little brother, to worry so; Nelly bursting into tears, even though "everything was all right now." How could everything be all right, when she knew what a bad girl she really was?

You didn't go inside the house. Without any obvious reason you stopped on the left of the stoop, right next to the rotting low wooden fence, behind which the remains of a garden were struggling for survival. The woman with the child on her lap, who was sitting on the top step of the stoop, would not have barred your entry. She may have guessed why you were standing there, talking softly in a language that was foreign to her, snapping a couple of photos, in which you now can count the number of steps that lead to the reddish-brown door: five steps. You can also, if necessary, determine the type of car that is being washed in the former store window, which has been expanded into a garage: an old Warszawa, with the number ZG 84–61 on the license plate; and—although the photo's background is less sharp—you're able to guess the Polish spelling of the word Sonnenplatz on the street sign on the wall of the house: Plac Słoneczny, which you couldn't decipher if you didn't know some Russian.

You look as though you are standing motionless; meanwhile, you're working on the furnishings in the parlor-floor apartment on the left, but despite concentrated effort, only a partial image emerges. Visualizing the insides of houses has never been your strong point—until the crooked murderer of your brother appeared and drew you into the nursery, with your brother's bed to the right of the door, the white chest on the left, past which Nelly creeps, out into the hall, where a yellow light is falling from the bathroom door diagonally across the way.

And so on. You won't have to bother the woman on the stoop. How does one say good morning in Polish? As you give in one more time to the surge of past passions, you're able to sneak unseen into the forgotten rooms and to determine the layout. You'll see what the child saw when she was three years old, and five, and seven, when she trembled with fear, disappointment, joy, or triumph.

The test: the living room. At the end of the hall, that much is certain. Morning light. The wall clock is on the right, behind the light-brown tile stove. The hour hand is moving toward the ten. The child holds her breath. As the clock begins to strike, with light, hurried strikes, Nelly makes her most hideous face, hoping and fearing that Frau Elste's threat will come true, that "one's face freezes" when the clock strikes. They'd all be shocked and horrified, especially her mother. Suddenly they'd be begging her for her real face; and then, when nothing worked, they'd put her to bed and telephone Dr. Neumann, who'd come flying as fast as the wind her real face; and then, when nothing worked, they'd put her to bed to study her frozen face, and look astounded; he'd take her temperature and prescribe sweat packs to induce a thawing of the face: Chin up, homunculus, we'll fix it. They were not able to fix it, however, and they had to grow used to the fact that her soft sweet obedient face stayed hideous. Man is a creature of habit, Frau Elste said.

The clock finishes striking. Nelly rushes to the mirror in the hall and has no trouble making a different face. (The white coat rack with the square mirror must have been in the hall at the time.) She is no closer to an answer to the burning question: doesn't love get smaller when it is divided among a number of people? Little dum-dum, says the mother, I have love enough for you and your baby brother. But when she sold butter at the store, there wasn't enough for everybody: Lieselotte Bornow ate margarine on her bread.

Nelly is standing at the kitchen table (you could see inside the kitchen, the table in front of the window is covered with a green oilcloth), she's biting into a big yellow chunk of butter, she feels the lump melt in her mouth, she feels the soft greasy rivulet run down inside her throat; another bite, she licks the remainder off her fingers, licking and swallowing until it's all gone. But the happy illusion doesn't last: she hasn't become tall and strong, an instant grownup. She feels sick. The fabulous yellow greed was interpreted as a fat deficiency, and broken up into many repulsive slices of bread and butter. She was made to eat them all, while Frau Elste ironed the laundry at the nursery table and showed her how to fold men's handkerchiefs: Like so, and so, and so, and so; there. Whenever Frau Elste sang: "Dawn-red sky-y . . . dawn-red sky-y, still so young, yet I must die-ie . . ." her soft brown eyes automatically took on an alarming bulge and the tennis-ball-size growth on her neck performed the strangest dances, unexpected even to Frau Elste.

The layout of the rooms behind those three parlor-floor windows has been established more or less; anyhow, we can't go on standing here forever. Slowly you set yourselves in motion toward the Wepritz Mountains. Snakes! Did someone say snakes? The Wepritz Mountains are supposed to have been crawling with snakes, if you took Frau Busch's word. (The Busches! For the first time in thirty-six years, Ella Busch's chatty mother comes out of the Pflesser houses, a mocking smile curls her lips: Nonsense, girl, these snakes aren't dangerous!) But it never occurred to these people that they had never seen one of the snakes, let alone held one in their hands. There was only one obvious explanation: snakes were fairy princes in disguise, who balanced delicate little golden crowns on their finger-thin heads, calling lispingly, with forked tongues, to their equally enchanted lovers. That they slithered in the grass wasn't treachery, it only showed how desperate they were. They did remain invisible, but that was altogether understandable. Nelly herself longed for a cloak of invisibility which would help her escape monsters, evil people, sorcerers and witches, but most of all her own persistent soul. Which was pale, appendix-like, ordinarily located near the stomach, but would hang suspended in the air, deprived of the body, naked and alone, exposed to maliciously mocking eyes.

Perhaps the fire department would come to catch the fickle soul, like Frau Kaslitzki's escaped parakeet. Everybody would go in search of the body in which the soul belonged. But Nelly would send her soul to the bewitched snakes and leave it there to its desolate fate, while she herself lay in her bed, as this very minute, freely thinking wild, strident, forbidden thoughts. From now on, nothing would twitch inside her when she lied, nothing would shrink or squirm with anguish when she had to feel so unbearably sorry for herself, because she might have been exchanged in the cradle after all: an ugly duckling, homeless, unloved, despite all protests to the contrary. (Even if she had scribbled over the page in the fairy tale where Hansel and Gretel's parents plot their scheme to lead their children into the woods: every word of the monstrous conversation reverberates inside her, so that she strains to listen, in the evenings when the real life of the grownups begins, to hear what is perhaps being said in the living room.)

Yes: to be rid of your own soul, to be able to look your mother boldly in the eye as she sits on the edge of your bed in the evening, wanting to know if you have told her everything: But you must tell me everything. To lie brazenly: Everything, yes! When you know deep down: not everything, not ever again. Because that's impossible.

A reasonable child forgets her first three years. Out of the fairy-tale thicket filled with glowing figures she steps prissy-faced before the camera. Somewhere along the road she has learned that obey-

ing and being loved amount to one and the same thing. Disfigured
by a hairdo known as "the doughnut," sporting the red department-
store sweater, positioned next to her brother's baby carriage. A
silly grin, the grimace of sisterly affection. When prodded properly
(that is, without being threatened by punishment or even a feeling
of guilt), your memory yields incidents of sibling rivalry, sisterly
betrayal, and fratricide, but it would rather be caught dead than
come up with the image of your pregnant mother, or of the new
child at your mother's breast. Not the slightest recollection of your
brother's birth.

What do you know, here comes tailor Bornow walking across
Sonnenplatz. The new houses are suddenly gone; instead there lies
the old weed-covered desert, trodden paths, sand hollows. Children
and drunks have their guardian angels, tailor Bornow doesn't trip
and fall down. Even the black visored cap with the cord stays on
his head. A song, emanating from tailor Bornow, penetrates the
square. It would be altogether wrong to say that tailor Bornow is
singing. Because on his tailor's table or in the family circle, he
never sings; that would be unthinkable, as Nelly's girlfriend
Lieselotte Bornow reluctantly admits. It's King Alcohol that
makes him sing, makes him into a laughingstock, says Nelly's
mother. Nelly has her own notion. Every Saturday, she thinks, the
singing waits for tailor Bornow down on the boulevard outside the
corner tavern, to alight on him, only on him, as soon as he steps
outside the tavern door—a large heavy bird, whose weight makes
Herr Bornow sway and teeter, while it wrings the song out of him,
always the same song: "You can't be true to me, you don't know
how to be, although your lips declare the truest love to me." A
lament that touches Nelly deeply and places this song forever
among the tragic classics. The sun was shining on Herr Bornow,
remember, and he began to talk and to curse loudly, and Lieselotte
Bornow came running out of Number 6, with her thin braids sticking stiffly away from her head, and pulled her father into the house
by a sleeve, without as much as a glance in the direction of her
girlfriend. "Your heart is wide enough for many more than me,"
Lieselotte's father sang, and the grief that made him sway on
schedule every Saturday afternoon also clouded over Nelly.

No, Lenka can't remember when she saw her first drunk. You're
nearing the end of the short block of COHORG houses, the limit

of the inhabited world, then as now. You recognize the sensation that surged inside Nelly whenever she set foot beyond this limit: a mixture of daring, curiosity, fear, and loneliness. You ask yourself if Nelly would have missed something if she had grown up in the middle of things; would the need for the sensation have made her create a world boundary? Lieselotte Bornow is the first child who is ashamed of her father, although she is too proud to admit it. She gets into moods, becomes demanding, greedy for exaggerated proof of friendship, only to call off the friendship the moment Nelly gives her the proof, and then suffers over it, as does Nelly, but she can't help herself. My first memory? Lenka remembers her terror at the sight of her face upside down in the concave mirror of her baby spoon, when no effort could turn it back right side up. H. refuses to commit himself. At best, domestic scenes in the morning, his parents fighting over eggs too hard-boiled or over misplaced collar buttons; his mother's sigh of relief once his father was out of the house and she could sit down at her sewing machine. Your brother, Lutz, who is neither used nor willing to plumb the depth of his memory, says only one word: measles.

But you were already three and a half then, you said. And Nelly caught the measles from you, it was shortly after the roof-raising celebration at the new house, and you really should remember something else, something earlier than that. Sorry, said Lutz. He had no touching details to offer his esteemed sister.

This is where the famous Wepritz Mountains begin, you then said, with just enough irony in your tone to prevent anyone else from becoming ironic. Today, a jarring stretch of concrete highway will lead you directly to the nearby chain of hills. It would probably make little sense to go tramping into the sand hills. Gorse grows in lots of places. You had seen enough. Besides, you cared only about the three acacias: if the three acacias were still standing. Locust trees, H. suggested tentatively, people are forever mistaking locusts for acacias in these parts. Acacias! you said. They ought to be there still.

Do you mean that thing over there?

Of the three acacias under which Nelly raised her dolls and learned her first English song, one is still standing. And it is a locust, which H. does not point out. The days are long gone when he used to brag about his knowledge of botany. Two totally different images emerge simultaneously from different periods in your life: the sweetness of the juice sucked from the funnels of acacia blossoms, and your sulky silence during an early stroll with H., because he caught you—who took great pride in your love of East Prussian pine forests—mistaking pine for spruce.

You told Lutz that your first memories of him involved unfairness, murder, and quarrels.

So what, he said, but then he reminded you of the tremendous to-do which appeared in the family chronicle under the heading: How Lutz Got Lost and Was Found Again. The horrible hour, during which Nelly, first by herself, then with her mother, her white store smock flapping, and finally with a group of neighborhood children and women, went looking for the little brother, in the streets, on Sonnenplatz, in the COHORG courtyards, all the way into the Wepritz Mountains, experiencing every degree of worry from anguish to hopelessness to desperation, while one sentence kept running through her head: If he's dead, it's my fault.

(This is the first recorded incident of Nelly's "voices of doom," a tendency she inherited from her mother. To Bruno Jordan, who didn't share this particular bent, it meant dwelling on unfortunate future events; and he kept telling his wife all her life: Stop having these black hunches. If only you didn't see everything so black.)

Only after one full hour did it occur to someone to pull the table away from the sofa in the nursery, where the little brother was found lying in his red knit rompers, and everybody crowded in and laughed uproariously about the sleeping Lutz, who didn't wake up in spite of all the noise and who derived no pleasure from the fact that the neighbors were toasting his reappearance with schnapps, and the children with lemonade. But Nelly neither laughed nor drank. Her persistently miserable face began to annoy the others, and when her mother explained how attached the girl was to the little boy, how conscientious she was, Nelly crept away and bawled. Her brother's being well and happy instead of dead in no way canceled the fact that his sister had forgotten all about him while she was doing her homework, that she had barely looked up from her books and indifferently told him to "get lost"; but he had not, contrary to everyone's assumption, toddled off all by himself.

But she knew only too well that the confession which would have changed the loving dependable sister into a little monster would never cross her lips. That was why she cried. In the evening, she didn't want to say the prayer "I'm tiny still, and do God's will" any more. She insisted on "Now I lay me down to sleep"—the song Heinersdorf Grandmother sang after she'd put on her long white nightgown, let down her thin gray braid, and placed her teeth in a glass of water. The second verse contained lines which were important to Nelly that evening: "If I did wrong some time this day, please look, O Lord, the other way . . ." Because, in all truth, she could hope for little else.

Nelly as a schoolgirl; that's running ahead. Still, it would be a mistake to hope that fratricide could be dismissed once and for all. Later it no longer comes up, perhaps—but that may be a misleading assumption—it was after Nelly managed to injure her brother, when the grownups finally had to take her deed seriously: Lutz, moaning dully, his right arm packed in pillows, while, across from him, Nelly softly implores him to stop hurting.

Their mother, clad in her white store smock, as always during childhood crises, reaches for the scissors without saying a word and starts cutting the sweater and the shirt away from the boy's arm, exposing a swelling elbow. Rushing to the telephone, a few brief words, the frightening word "hospital" among them, drives Nelly from the nursery into the living room, where she throws herself down on the couch, on her stomach, her hands over her ears. Her mother comes in, taps her right shoulder with two hard fingers, and says one of the exaggerated sentences that were her tendency even then: It'll be your fault if his arm stays stiff.

Since then, guilt has always been a heavy hand on her right shoulder and the urge to throw herself down on her stomach. And a white-frosted door behind which justice—her mother—disappears, and you can't follow her, and say that you're sorry, and be forgiven.

Now the last gap was closed as far as the layout of the COHORG apartment was concerned: the parents' bedroom, reached through the living room, through the very door behind which the mother is hurriedly getting ready for the drive to the hospital, refuses to let itself be conjured up; next to the door, the glass cupboard begins to emerge, filled with the softly clinking cup collection. Memory becomes helpless when you hit its sore spot; it produces the entire living room, piece by piece: the black buffet, the plant stand, the sideboard, the high-backed black chairs, the dining table, and above it the lamp with its yellow silk shade—a lavish setting for a child that needed but a chair to sit on for one whole afternoon, praying that her brother's arm would not stay stiff, since she couldn't bear to feel guilty for the rest of her life. But a misdeed without consequences is no longer a misdeed. That same evening Nelly laughs until tears come to her eyes. Her mother is relieved, and therefore in an excellent mood. She imitates the young intern who reset the brother's arm with two or three deft gestures, all the while addressing her, Charlotte Jordan, as "madam." You should have been a nurse, madam. Quite a reckless young man, that son of yours. Not a word is said about the culprit who caused the dislocation. Nelly is alone with her parents' good graces. Her anguish is being rewarded with cocoa and hot buns, while Lutz, the absent victim, has to stay in the hospital for observation. She quickly learns the lesson: to rejoice in undue praise. She catches on.

It is right here under the three acacias that Anneliese Waldin, Police Chief Waldin's oldest daughter, condescendingly taught Nelly her first English song; to Lenka's amazement you still know it by heart, and you sing it for them in a childish tone of voice, with dreadful pronunciation: *Baa, baa, black sheep, / Have you any wool? / Yes, sir, yes, sir, / Three bags full.*

There are more words to the song. Is Lutz aware that their mother always wanted to be a doctor? Or at least a midwife? Yes, he is. She repeated until her dying day: Something in the line of medicine would have been just right for me. I bet you anything I'd have been good at it. You always agreed that she would have been good. Of course, your father always scolded her for building castles in the air: Can't you ever be satisfied? Neither of you told her: Why don't you do it, then! Children don't like their mothers to change their lives. In 1945 she might have had the opportunity. In 1945 they would have trained even a woman who was no longer young to become a midwife. In the village? says Lutz. Well, no; that's just it.

It was under the three acacias that Nelly experienced her first betrayal, and of course by none other than her best friend, Helmut, Police Chief Waldin's youngest son, 5 Sonnenplatz, first floor on the right. The subject of "friendship and betrayal" rouses the interest of Lenka, who thereby gives herself away. For weeks her girl-friend Tina has been staying away, and Lenka has avoided her on every occasion, but you begin to worry only when Lenka doesn't go horseback riding, since horses are her passion. You've learned that Lenka never answers a direct question unless she wants to, and you're secretly hoping that you'll find out about Lenka by way of Nelly.

If the traitor is a child, she needs others to put her up to the treachery. Yes, Lenka says. The others don't care, it may amuse them for ten minutes; strange, isn't it? Lenka says nothing. In Helmut Waldin's case it was his three older brothers who put him up to it.

It all started harmlessly enough. Franz threw a stone which accidentally hit his little brother. It might just as easily have hit Nelly, who was crouching next to Helmut on the plaid blanket, playing house with her dolls. Helmut screamed. When he told his brothers about the stone, they were baffled: a stone! None of them had thrown a stone, not at their little brother. But he had been hit by a stone on his shoulder; and there was the small piece of flint, the proof, lying on the blanket, prompting the question: Who threw it? It had to be somebody close by. That was logical, right? Well, who was close by, except the three of us of course, huh, what do you say, Pee Wee? Nobody? Aw, our Pee Wee can't see, lend him your glasses! Naw, he can see all right, he's just a little slow in the head. We've got to teach him who it was that almost cracked his noodle.

Lenka seems to understand completely why Nelly didn't run away. She seems to know from personal experience that certain occurrences become believable only after one has witnessed them with one's own eyes. Consequently, Nelly is forced to look on as the big brothers drive Helmut toward the third acacia, with punches and laughter, until he is standing with his back against the trunk, while they—only for fun, of course, they're laughing all the time—keep asking him over and over who else, besides them, is nearby. But only she is nearby, Nelly, and she didn't throw the stone, they all know that, and Helmut knows it, too. That's why it's all in fun.

Lenka says, in her opinion it's sometimes just plain envy if they need traitors. You exchange a slightly astonished look with H., which she catches. Meanwhile, one of the brothers—it's Kutti now, the youngest one—is holding the tip of a small stick against Helmut's throat, to make him stop pretending. They don't want to hurt their little brother, all they want is for him to tell them who threw the stone. Well? Who? Nelly can't believe her ears when she hears Helmut say her name: her own name. He's crying, but he's saying it: Nelly.

Sooner or later everybody hears his own name as though for the first time. And as the small stick is taken away from his throat, Helmut shouts the name quickly once more, because his brothers are now asking who threw stones at him. Nelly! shouts Helmut, at first in tears, but then, as his brothers chummily punch his ribs—Okay, Pee Wee, there, you see!—he goes on yelling, Nelly, without being prodded, five times, ten times. When he yells it for the last time, he's laughing.

Lenka seemed to know the way they laugh after they've betrayed someone. Let's go, you said. Back on the path, along which Nelly ran home, crying. Past the small piece of windowless wall against which Nelly doggedly practiced volleyball until she became unbeatable. Past Number 5—this time without stopping—where Nelly has arrived way ahead of you, and is calling for Herr Waldin, who finally peers out over his red geraniums, buttoning the top of his uniform, but who instantly slams the window shut when Nelly tries to accuse his sons.

Instead, the nursery window opens in the parlor-floor apartment on the left. Charlotte Jordan calls her daughter into the house and stands waiting for her behind the door, armed with the carpet beater, and beats her without listening to what she has to say, beside herself, screaming, for the disastrous first and last time in her life (a slap in the face every now and then doesn't count), while Nelly remains mute, as always when she is unfairly treated. Who taught you to be a tattletale, who on earth, who? Then Charlotte drops onto a chair, bursting into tears, hands to her face, and says, weeping: Do you have to get us on bad terms with that man, of all people?

What next? The bead.

(The understandable but perhaps dangerous desire for associations, against which H. warned you from the beginning, not in words so much as by the expression on his face. He distrusts anything that falls into place.

On your way to the mailbox after dinner you saw the Big

Dipper and Orion in the clear starry sky; you had to admit that the feeling that star formations were somehow relevant to you had still not completely vanished from your mind. H. tried to convince you that it was precisely this factor that made it harder for you to find a form in which it was still possible to express yourself. You are completely disenchanted; under the circumstances, despair would have a rather comic effect.

After midnight, the stupid phone call from a person who introduced himself as a student and asked about your "new work" in a rude, pushy tone. You hung up, pulled the phone cord out of the outlet, but were too indignant to fall asleep. All of a sudden, sentences began to form which you thought were usable beginnings; you'd be saying "you" to someone. You had found your tone. You refused to believe that you'd have to start all over again, but in the morning the sentences still held up—although they had to be taken out later, of course—but the tone remained. Still refusing to believe, you started one more time. You felt that you were now free to control your material. But at the same time you realized in a flash that you couldn't expect any fast results, that it would be a long period of plodding and doubt. That this was it; not your next book, but this one. Good, you thought.)

It must have been shortly after the incident with Helmut Waldin that Nelly stuck the bead up her nose, despite frequent warnings not to. A small yellow wooden bead, of the kind that people give children to string into necklaces, but which refuses to come back out of one's nose no matter how hard one snorts and blows. Which seemed to be climbing higher and higher, perhaps all the way to the spot where one's mother said the brain was, and where a bead would have reached its point of no return.

Nelly touched off the customary emergency system: Frau Elste, mother with flapping white store smock, frenzied fingers, the telephone, the streetcar. A woman on the seat across the aisle pushed tactlessness to the point of thanking the good Lord that the child had not put a pea up her nose, which would promptly have begun to expand; then kiss the world goodbye.

Nelly would have preferred to leave the good Lord out of this. She wasn't eager to have him read the thoughts in her bead-threatened brain and find a kind of wish among them: the criminal wish to scare her own mother to death by inflicting damage to what the mother held most dear: her daughter.

The doctor, who couldn't imagine the little girl's intricate wickedness, made her sit down on a leather hassock, made disgusting noises with metal instruments clanking against enamel basins, eventually inserted one of the instruments into Nelly's right nostril, inside which the instrument expanded supposedly according to the umbrella principle, making the inner nose space so wide that the bead finally had no choice but to shoot forth in a gush of blood and roll onto the doctor's shining linoleum floor, with a clicking sound the doctor answered with a matter-of-fact "There we are!"

No, her mother had no desire to take the bead of misfortune back home with her, that was the last thing she needed, but she hoped from the bottom of her heart that the whole calamity had taught the child a lesson. A hope shared by the doctor with practical amiability, after accepting a ten-mark bill and warning both mother and daughter against small buttons, beans, lentils, peas, flower seeds, and pebbles. They had, however, no desire to visit the doctor's collection of similar foreign bodies extracted from other noses and ears—to which Nelly's bead was now going to be added.

A slap, a harsh word, even a walk home in silence would have been the proper thing at this point, in Nelly's opinion. Instead, Nelly was told that she had been "brave." No complaining. No tears. Nothing. Mother seemed to derive satisfaction from calling her daughter "brave." She had no desire to find out about her daughter's inner self.

Nelly had the disconsolate feeling that even the good Lord insisted on the brave, truthful, intelligent, obedient, and most of all happy, child she pretended to be during the day. Words like "sad" or "lonely" have no place in the vocabulary of the child of a happy family; as a result the child starts early to assume the difficult task of sparing his parents. To spare them misfortune and shame. Everyday words dominate: "eat," and "drink," and "take," and "please," and "thank you." Sight, hearing, smell, taste, touch, the five healthy senses, they're what make for good common sense. For instance, I believe that five pounds of beef will make a good broth, provided you don't add too much water. The rest is fantasy.

On the walk to the car you remembered the game Nelly made Lieselotte Barnow play, way before their eventual break-up. They called it "hexing," and it consisted of changing oneself into a repulsive creature, on the word "go," in the light-yellow sand of

Sonnenplatz: into a frog, a snake, a toad, a bug, a witch, a pig, a newt, a slug. Never a higher being, always vermin, living in filth and mud, fighting each other tooth and nail. Scratched up and filthy, they'd come home in the evenings, let themselves be scolded and told to stop. The parents of the Frog Prince had also sat by and watched their beautiful golden-haired son turn into a slimy disgusting frog under their very eyes—which the son must certainly have wished to do, deep down. Such things happen.

Lenka has a grateful look for the car waiting outside the former Rambow store. Twenty-six years and six months ago, on January 29, 1945, when Nelly left her town by the same road on the flight from approaching enemy troops, in a straight western direction, she did not, so far as you know, give one thought to Sonnenplatz, or to the child who may have been more deeply hidden under the thinner layer of years than she is today, as she begins to stir, independent of certain promptings. To what end? The question is as ominous as it is justified. (Let the dead bury their dead!) The feeling that overcomes any living being when the earth starts moving underfoot is fear.

2

Who wouldn't wish to have had a happy childhood?
Anyone who stirs up his childhood can't expect to make rapid
progress. He won't find any department qualified to issue him the
required authorization for this undertaking. He can be assured of
the guilt feelings inherent in actions that are contrary to nature: it
is natural for children to thank their parents all their lives for the
happy childhood they have given them, and not to touch it. Thanking? Language behaves as expected, and derives "thinking," "bethinking," "thanking" from the same root. So that investigative
bethinking, and the emotion inevitably prompted by it, can, in case
of need, also be taken for the "expression of a thankful state of
mind"—though a better term might exist. But then, where is the
authority which would attest to a case of need?
The way Nelly's mother acted in January 1945, during the

"flight," when, at the last minute, she did not abandon her house but rather her children, has of course given you much food for thought. You have to ask yourself whether such extreme situations do indeed reveal a person's greatest values, irrefutably, conclusively. But what if the person didn't have the full information that would have enabled him to adapt his decisions exactly to the circumstances? What if it had not been until after the departure of the truck in which not only her children but all the members of her family were leaving town that Charlotte Jordan realized: Yes, there was no doubt about it, the enemy was only a few miles outside the town; yes, the garrison was pulling out, in a forced march toward the West. Would she not have been the first to take her children to safety?

Furthermore, had she, Charlotte, thought it even remotely possible that she would never set foot in her house again, that she would never again see any of its inventory—would she not have packed the fat brown family album instead of all the junk which they abandoned piece by piece, cast off, lost, until one fine summer morning Nelly owned nothing but her pajamas and her coat, both of which she was of course wearing. At four in the afternoon, the first shots from the edge of town (municipal hospital): by then the Führer's picture in the parlor was already burning in the furnace (that felt good, let me tell you), then the decision that she, Charlotte, would lock the house and leave, taking along nothing but a grocery bag with a few generous sandwiches, a thermos with hot coffee, several packs of cigarettes (for bribery purposes), and a briefcase bulging with papers. The brown album must have gotten lost either during the looting of abandoned houses and apartments (first among them a food store, understandably)—by former neighbors, of course—or else it was burned by the subsequent Polish occupants of the house. Naturally they would hate to be reminded of their predecessors.

But photos that have been looked at often and long do not burn easily. Immutable images, they are stamped into the memory, whether or not they can be used as material proof. One photo, your favorite, is at your disposal on demand, down to the smallest detail: the slender, pale birch leaning slightly to the left, on the edge of the darker pine grove which forms the background. Nelly, three years old, stark naked, as the focus of the picture, page-boy hair, her body wreathed with oak-leaf garlands, in her hands a bunch of oak leaves, which she waves at the camera. The littler the happier—perhaps there's really something to it. Although the richness of childhood everyone feels may only be the result of the constant rethinking we devote to it.

Family life.

The picture—presumably snapped by Uncle Walter Menzel at a family outing to Altensorge on Lake Bestien, for the Jordans didn't own a camera—brings order to the system of satellite figures whose laws are more familiar to you, and more intelligible, than the movements of celestial bodies, which strike you as haphazard by comparison; and so you barely suppress your impatience with the confusion of H., who has to ask over and over: Now, who is he again? And she? For instance, during the ride through the former town of L. on the second weekend in July 1971, you felt compelled to draw H.'s and Lenka's attention to all the homes of every one of your relatives who had lived in the town. Lenka and H. didn't even know the names of some of the nineteen persons—to speak only of the close relatives and of those once removed. The venture ended in failure. Weariness, gloom, boredom, family jungle, said Lenka.

(She simply didn't want to make the effort to keep the general picture in mind. This led to your scribbling a kind of family tree into her notebook; that was yesterday, it is December 1972. After the Christmas shopping, into whose whirl you had once again been drawn, you sat in the café at the Nauen Gate. At this hour, it is filled with teachers-college students, whom Lenka tried to copy. She insisted on getting a vermouth, the same as the student at your table, and did her best to gulp it down with the same scowl on her face. If she personally knew her great-aunts and great-uncles, all of whom are living in the West, the family tree would seem far less absurd to her, you said, because you wanted her to know her way about later. Start with the great-grandparents, you suggested: the Menzels—Auguste and Hermann, Whiskers Grandma and Whiskers Grandpa; and the Jordans—Marie and Gottlieb, Heinersdorf Grandma and Heinersdorf Grandpa. The oldest child of each, Charlotte and Bruno, became the Jordan couple, known as the grandparents. And in addition, as is customary, brothers and sisters and their offspring: Liesbeth and Walter Menzel, Olga and

Trudy Jordan. Stop it, said Lenka. Until recently, she had imagined all grownups to be the same age, all people over fifty to be
ancient. She is sixteen.)

Who is interested in these people? The process of naming them
implies their significance, but also imparts significance. To be
anonymous, nameless, a nightmare. The power you assume over
them by changing their factual names into meaningful names. Now
they'll be able to get closer to each other than they managed to in
life. Now they'll be allowed to lead their own lives. Uncle Walter
Menzel, Charlotte Jordan's younger brother, still aiming his Kodak
at Nelly, his niece. Right next to him must have been Aunt Lucie,
radiantly happy, engaged to Walter—it is 1932—although her
father, a real-estate owner and man of means, absolutely did not
wish to give his daughter to a common locksmith. Then I'll just
move in with Walter, she is supposed to have said, a pronouncement which the Menzels received with mixed emotions. It showed,
on the one hand, how attached she was to Walter; on the other,
such talk revealed a certain recklessness, just as Lucie, pleasant,
neat, and nimble, was nonetheless a little free in many respects. Of
course she had every reason to be happy to have Walter, but then
again, she'd snuggle her pretty well-groomed head against his polo
shirt in public . . . Now she is standing there, waving her white
handkerchief at Nelly: Look up, Nelly baby, here into the black
box, look at the birdie!

To think that they were all in their late twenties, early thirties.
And that there was a time when their life was ahead of them.
When Aunt Liesbeth, Nelly's mother's younger sister, was a high-
spirited young woman who pulled the corduroy dress sewn by
Whiskers Grandma over Nelly's head—the child will catch cold!—
and took her between herself and her husband—Alfons Radde,
who had always had stringy blond hair and those ice-blue eyes, but
perhaps not yet the cold stare—to go one-two-three-hop! all the
way to Krüger's coffee garden. There, another snapshot is taken
of Nelly as she, for the first time in her life, is allowed to have a sip
of light beer from an enormous glass. (The same glasses today sell
as antiques for thirty-six marks apiece.) From behind the glass,
Nelly's famous impish look. The eyes the kid has!

Peace. Bliss. Pancakes.

Alfons Radde is not a family favorite, that's a fact. True, he married Aunt Liesbeth, who is wearing a white dress today, with ruffles around the neck, very becoming. He should idolize her. In reality, however, he is married to the feed-and-grain business of Otto Bohnsack & Co., and is the pathetic slave of young Bohnsack. Alfons Radde, with the large pores on the neck, full of dust. With the monstrous nose. Beauty fades away, arse is here to stay. And our Liesbeth, after all, did want him more than anything, just as she now wants a child more than anything—understandably so, after several miscarriages in four barren years of married life. And when Charlotte, her sister, is already expecting her second. (Unfortunately, no photo of the pregnant mother exists. Uncle Walter made her sit behind the coffee table before he took her picture.) Instead, Aunt Liesbeth makes a fuss over her niece: Blond fuzz on the arms, Nelly, that means a rich husband, sure thing! Then Alfons, her husband, says: Now, don't put mouse shit in with the peppercorns. Not one to mince his words, Uncle Alfons. Those who live long enough will get to hear what Charlotte Jordan thinks of him, which she has to keep to herself for now—when she does say it, they will no longer be in the so-called Neumark, in the pine woods on Lake Bestien in Brandenburg, but, unforeseen by all, in the hallway of a Mecklenburg farmhouse. He, Alfons, will get back at his sister-in-law in no uncertain terms, he'll call his mother-in-law a "Polack," and will give his niece Nelly, now sixteen, occasion to warn him that she will not let her grandmother be insulted.

And so on. That's how it is when you're in the picture. The spoilsport who always knows beforehand what comes next, and how it is going to end: Whiskers Grandpa has thirteen more years to live, Whiskers Grandma twenty more, counted from that gaily animated summer afternoon of 1932. But their gray-haired, long-haired terrier Whiskers, with whom the child Nelly "literally gnawed on the same bone" under the table, will be carried to the Serum Clinic by Hermann Menzel in a margarine crate, blind and sick with old age, as early as 1938, and will be carried back as a poisoned canine corpse; whereupon Whiskers Grandma will not eat, drink, or sleep for three days.

(Why go on with the list of the dead? Why mention now that Uncle Walter Menzel will not have seen his sister, Charlotte Jordan, Nelly's mother, for twelve, fourteen years when she dies, because nothing can drag him into the Russian Zone, and Charlotte, at that time already of pension age with travel permits to the West, has her pride, too, and will not go to see him?) Of the four uncles who will gradually make their appearance, Uncle Walter is Nelly's favorite. By far. He plays cling-clong-clam—we-ride-upon-the-tram with her, and carries her piggyback on his shoulder when they finally walk back to the crossing of the two woodland paths where he left his car.

Pictures mounted on chamois that you don't want to tamper with. The hand which shall wither or grow out of the grave if it is lifted against father or mother. Promptly you dream, exactly and in detail, all the stages of an operation in the course of which your right hand—the writing hand—is being expertly taken off, under local anesthesia, while you witness everything. What must happen must happen. You're not putting up any resistance. But it's hardly pleasant. What do you think when you wake up? In the semidarkness you lift your hand, you turn it this way and that, study it as if you were seeing it for the first time. It looks like a fit tool, but you could be wrong.

What does it really mean, Polack, Lenka wants to know. She's never heard the word "Polack," or the saying "dumb as a Polack" ... "dirty Polack" ... Does she have to know them? Brother Lutz briefly turns around, gives his niece a searching look, and a terse explanation, then faces toward the front again, toward the windshield. He repeats the word "formerly," also "at that time." You catch yourself thinking, "At our time," give a start, postpone plumbing the depth of the aberration. Lenka has thrust out her lower lip. Silence is the sign that there is no need to continue, that she has got it and can do without further explanations. (Will your attitude someday seem strange to her, the same way the attitude of the preceding generation seemed strange to you?)

She has never known Hermann Menzel, Whiskers Grandpa. You describe the willow switches into which he cut the most beautiful designs for Nelly, with his sharp cobbler's knife, usually a serpentine line winding around the stick toward the point in ever narrowing circles. It occurs to you after these many years that he had a thing about snakes. One of the two stories he knew was, after all, the snake story; it may have made a deeper impression on Nelly than the tales of the Brothers Grimm, which certainly were far from tame.

Whiskers Grandpa's stories had the misfortune of being taken for truth. Nelly couldn't bear to imagine the terror of the young woodcutter who is peacefully eating his dry crust of bread, sitting on the leaf-covered tree trunk, drinking water from a bottle (the woodcutter's poverty would not of course permit richer fare), when suddenly he feels the tree trunk move under him with slithery motions, because he's been sitting on a snake, thick as a tree trunk, with a dangerous poison fang, evil and lusting for the fellow's blood. He did well to seek safety in flight. But the really frightening part was that from that time on he was no longer quite right in the head and could not control a recurrent twitching of his whole face. Shuddering at the grimace of Whiskers Grandpa miming the woodcutter's compulsive facial contortions, Nelly nonetheless insatiably urged him to repeat it. It was through him and no other that she first learned the thrill of horror: who could be so audacious as to deny this grandfather's importance to her?

Only much later—exactly thirteen years after the beautiful family Sunday on Lake Bestien that is to end in song—much later did Nelly learn from Uncle Alfons Radde, who by now no longer had any reason to suppress his rage at the disdain with which his wife's family used to treat him, that Whiskers Grandpa, whom she had known all her life as a retired railroad employee, and about whose fate she had asked no questions, because children don't imagine that grandparents have a fate: that he had never risen beyond ticket puncher and that he had been prematurely fired for chronic drunkenness. This, to make the Menzels get off their high horse, and above all to put Charlotte Jordan, née Menzel, the ticket puncher's oldest daughter, in her place.

(Again Nelly is the only one who had no idea. Did she perhaps think her grandfather was Secretary of the Railroad? Or at least an engineer? Fiddlesticks. Not even a conductor. Nelly hadn't thought anything; suddenly she feels sorry for Whiskers Grandpa.)

Here. On this trip, H. depends on your directions, stops on Friedrichstrasse, right at the gasworks, where one can see the flat house with the green shutters. There it is: Number 7 Kesselstrasse, the house in which Nelly's mother, Charlotte, spent her childhood. "House" is an overstatement: one almost feels like calling it a two-story barracks. Dismal would be the only fitting word, but no one says it. Here it was, in one of the certainly squalid apartments, that Hermann Menzel—soused, of course—threw the kerosene lamp at his wife, Auguste, and gave her the small scar on the right side of her forehead, a mark whose origin Nelly had never given a thought to, not until the night Aunt Liesbeth—during the first days of the flight—tried to justify her fits of hysteria with, of all things, having been frightened and scared as a child. If your own father throws the lamp at your mother, you just try to get over that scare, especially if you have sensitive nerves. That's when Whiskers Grandma said to her favorite daughter, Liesbeth: When the grass has finally grown over a dead old story, sure enough a young ass comes along and chews it up again.

These, then, are the voices that come streaming in. As if someone had opened the sluice gates. Always this to-do, said Whiskers Grandpa, always this fuss. (If you really think about it, he probably was a stranger in his own family.) They're all talking at once, some are even singing, as they march straight through the woods toward Uncle Walter's car—a black, square box. Nelly is beheading flowers and blades of grass with her serpentine-decorated switch; Uncle Alfons is singing in a loud voice: "Elmer is my son, tra la, 'cause it happened under an elm, tra la, Anna, Anna hop-la-la, Anna-Marie."

Now that doesn't have to be sung in front of a three-year-old, who knows songs herself and loves to sing with her father, "We are the minstrels of Finsterwalde," or "My hat, it has three corners," and also, "We wander far ahead, a penny's worth of bread." So that toward the end of the very successful outing Bruno Jordan's voice, too, will yet be heard, a voice perhaps kept silent for too long, as though it had nothing to say. But not so. Not that singing was his special strong point: not since they cut into his windpipe in earliest childhood to save him from choking to death of diphtheria, in the process damaging his vocal chords. *Sit down, Jordan. Music: F.* Everything else, incidentally, straight A's. At the head of his class. But "Lippe-Detmold, town of many charms, in it a man at arms . . ." he brings off quite well, especially the "boom boom" after the moving line: "They fired the first shot." "And when they entered the great fight . . . they fired the first shot, boom boom." That was Bruno Jordan's stuff. Nobody could tell him anything about that, nobody, unless he had been at Verdun. And had been buried alive in a foxhole. That had done it for him for life, but completely. Since then, war to him means nothing but one big pile of shit.

Herewith a sample of Bruno Jordan's voice: "Ho, there he lies and yells no more, ho, there he lies and yells no more, the soldier boy is dead, the soldier boy is dead . . ." The child is crying. Crying? What's the matter, for heaven's sake. Because of the dead soldier. She's tired, and that's when she's even more sensitive, you just have to have a feel for what you can sing with her. All four women—Auguste, Charlotte, Liesbeth, and Lucie, in the order of their ages—line themselves up in front of the child. That's it. Get in. Six people into Uncle Walter's al-most-fully-paid-for car. A beautiful afternoon. Let's do it again soon. Gives you something to think back on when times get hard. Not that you want to talk doom and gloom. You really can't com-plain. And so the voices go on in the car, back and forth, become softer, stop altogether in the darkness. What lingers is the smell of her father's gray overcoat, in which Nelly is wrapped, mixed with the smell of Whiskers Grandma's lap, where her head is lying, not by accident. Sleep now, you just go to sleep. (Think and bethink, she would say, if you will and must. And thank if you can. But don't feel that you have to. I'm sure you'll know. Nelly was her favorite grandchild.) Whiskers Grandma has never wanted any-thing for herself. Here, at Number 7 Kesselstrasse, it was she who supported her children by sewing and growing vegetables in the garden plot and raising a goat. Along these edges of the road grew the grass for the goat, and all three children were ordered, under threat of dire punishment, to bring in enough hay for the winter. Here she also sewed the snowy white sheet into the angel dress for her daughter Charlotte, who was allowed to sing "From Heaven High I've Come to Earth" in her clear, beautiful voice at Christ-mas Mass in St. Mary's Church.

Charlotte prefers songs which bring out her still beautiful soprano: "Why weepest thou, oh, gardener's lovely wife," or "One time three young fellows were crossing the Rhine . . ." She had been sent to secondary school by Auguste, as had all three Menzel children, ten marks tuition a month. An absolute mystery where Whiskers Grandma found the money. Charlotte, though, with her achievements, could go tuition-free, but she had to earn it all over again every year. Do your best, Lottie, you know what it's for. You've learned to hold your own.

I sure have, said Charlotte Jordan, not without bitterness. If I've learned one thing, that's it. Although her French teacher had it in for her, supposedly, she now knows how to say in French: the moon—*la lune*, the sun—*le soleil*. And she's able to correct her husband, who learned to say "bread" when he was a prisoner of war in France—*"pang,"* he pronounces it, without the nasal sound. You and your education, says Bruno Jordan.

(If you could ask her, Charlotte would probably say: Do what you must. Not quite the sentence you'd like to hear. Better: Do it, if you must. But how can you know with absolute certainty what you must do?

Perhaps by your growing restlessness. By the nightly stomach pains which, in turn, prompt the strangest dreams. The house of the architect Bühlow, the Jordans' neighbor of many years, is on fire. You run over with buckets of water. Through the window you see the neighbor's wife lying in pain; you know: stomach cancer. She is shrouded in smoke, unable to move. A nurse with a hard, mean face under a winged bonnet comes to the window and declares: No extinguishing needed. There is no fire.)

Days filled with titles, there are such days. Titles, for a long time imaginable only in iambic meter, da-dam, da-dam, then changed into uniambic word formations. "Recalling," for instance, but also its opposite, "forgetting." And the word that makes both possible: "memory."

Memory: a function of the brain "which assures the receptive imprint, assimilative retention, and appropriate reproduction of previous impressions and experiences" (*Meyer's New Encyclopedia*, 1962). Assures. Emphatic words. The pathos of certainty. The inscrutable "appropriate." Memory failure: the blanking out of memory images. Of great importance in memory achievements, besides a number of other factors: the individual design of the cerebral cortex.

The number of other factors defy naming. Questions like these: Why does this particular child forget her earliest years, but remember a single scene which nobody really believes? (But you can't remember that, you weren't even three years old, you were still sitting in your high chair.)

Something is dawning on your mother. Your father doesn't have to remember. He was buried alive at Verdun, he has earned the right to forget. For instance: names. Just don't ask me about names. What's in a name? There are things he does remember:

beatings. And that he was at the top of his class, which was not unrelated. Teacher Rodbeck, called the Rod, used to punish the supervising top student for the ruckus the class made. Nominative: bend over. Genitive: pull your pants down. Dative: ouchouchouch. Accusative: My bottom hurts. All together, everybody! That guy was a real drill sergeant.

The things Nelly doesn't want to hear are the very things that are told over and over. But the important things: plumb forgotten. A round table? That was in the old Fröhlich house, that was on Küstrinerstrasse. The back room of our first store, the room where all three of us had to eat and sleep. Sugar sacks were stacked up along the walls. A white tablecloth? That was white oilcloth. But you couldn't possibly remember.

The picture is mute, its age indicated by the faded colors, growing blurred toward the edges. In the center, the bright circle of golden yellow projected by the hanging lamp (my God! the old wax-paper bag!) onto the white table. The picture is incomplete, so it can't be a photograph. The cup, containing a warm sweet liquid for Nelly, is invisible. (Weak sugared coffee, that was all. By the way, a light-blue cup, an enamel mug, to be exact. No, you can't know about that.) The mother on the right, not laughing: radiant. Of the father nothing but squat fingers red with cold, weirdly foreshortened by the gray woolen gloves with the tips of the fingers cut off. (Good Lord, those gloves you wore in the store when it was freezing, the fingertips bare to count the money.) Poor fingers. The child feels an inordinate, anxious pity for them, what with all the glow of the scene, the joy it emanates. (It's the mixture of joy and pity that will fix the picture in your memory.)

The father's red fingers are counting money onto the white table. The mother's hand strokes the father's coat sleeve. The glow on the faces means: We did it!

A banal interpretation, so many years later: the father put on the table his first week's take from the new store on Sonnenplatz. In the middle of the economic crisis—or let's say, toward its end —Bruno and Charlotte Jordan took their fate into their own hands: opened a new business, in a new part of town, in addition to the modest but dependable store in the Fröhlich house. Carved out a living for themselves. Opened up a future for their daughter, who will forget the back room, who will have a room of her own.

That's the first thing they'll do. As it should be. The new customers
responded with trust. Reason for radiance and happiness.
Tentative titles, while shopping with H. Navel oranges still in
the markets. Zeroing in on the unknown word, seemingly hidden
under a parchment-thin layer, but eluding the brain's antennae.
Basic Patterns, Behavior Patterns, Childhood Patterns. A Model
Childhood, H. said casually, in front of the pharmacy at the corner
of Thälmannstrasse. That took care of that.

A model is used for demonstration. To demonstrate is derived
from the Latin "monstrum," which originally meant "showpiece,"
or "model," which suits you perfectly. But "monstrum" can also
become "monster" in today's sense of the word. Right now, as a
matter of fact: Standartenführer Rudi Arndt (an animal, believe
me, nothing but an animal. A statement by Charlotte Jordan).
Except that this particular animal doesn't rouse your interest half
as much as the hordes of half-men, half-beasts with whom you're
more familiar from within yourself.

"Fascism," writes the Pole Kazimierz Brandys, "as a concept, is
larger than the Germans. But they became its classic example."

And you—among your Germans—will not have the courage to
place the above quotation as your epigram before the first sentence.
But then, if you don't know just exactly how they would react to
this rejected epigram—with indifference, consternation, indignation, perplexity—what do you know about them at all?

The question poses itself. Are they eager for classics? To have
been its classic example? Who can tell? Who can overcome himself
enough to find out the truth?

(One distinguishes the following types of memory: mechanical,
gestalt, and logical, verbal, material, action memory.

The absence of one category is acutely felt: moral memory.)

Of concern here and now is a technical problem: how to transfer the Jordan family—father, mother, child—from that shining
evening at the back-room table, abruptly and without transition—
there are neither photographs nor memories—to the action which
took place in the afternoon in Nelly's new nursery, presumably
during the autumn of 1933. Postscript to Sonnenplatz.

Once again: radiance, serenity, harmony, so soothing to the
memory. And yet you do not want to let the grocer Bruno Jordan
approach Nelly's crib without further ado. He is wearing his blue

peaked storm-trooper cap; she has just awakened from her midday nap and is to participate in the happy event. Above her, her parents' faces glow with the unawareness of innocents.

But they must have read the papers. They must at least have had a subscription to the *General-Anzeiger*, the local paper. They must have had the time to read the papers, even during the years when they spent all their time working. He, Bruno Jordan, always on the go from Sonnenplatz to the Fröhlich store, which they held on to as long as they could; she, Charlotte, alone with the new apprentice in the new store in the new COHORG building. And then—he again—on Sundays all the bookkeeping for both stores. It was no bed of roses, a fact that must be kept in mind.

They were showing *The Big Lie* at the Kyffhauser Cinema, and shortly thereafter *The Invisible Man*, but Herr and Frau Jordan live too far away and are too tired to go out. Besides their small radio, they have only the newspaper; they sit with it at the table after supper until their eyes tire; they try to read at least the installment of the novel *Mail-Order Bride* by Margarete Zowada-Schiller, or the interesting column "Voices from Our Readers." Among them a short, heartrending discourse on "Animals in Distress" from the pen of assistant teacher Merksatz, naturalist and local historian. The statement JUNO SMOKERS ARE OPTIMISTS Bruno Jordan applied to himself. It ran along the bottom edge of the paper for weeks in happy, bold type. He smoked Juno and he was an optimist.

Any other information, however, did not concern them. The curtailment of certain personal freedoms (just as an example), announced on March 1, 1933, would hardly affect their lives, because so far they had obviously not planned any publications (freedom of the press), or participated in mass meetings (freedom of assembly): they simply had not felt the need. And as for the order that "searches and confiscations beyond the limits of legality" were "permissible for the time being," why, that was aimed at a category of people with whom they simply had nothing in common, so to speak, to state things as they were, without any value judgments. They were not Communists, although their thinking was socialist in tendency, and they voted the Social-Democratic ticket, the same as 6,506 citizens of their town. Of the 28,658 votes cast, 15,055 had already gone to the Nazis, but one didn't yet have the feeling that every single ballot was being checked. The Communist representatives, elected by 2,207 diehards, especially in the Brucken suburb, had not yet been arrested (although they were to be, twelve days later), and there were 3,944 unemployed in the town—a number which was to be reduced to 2,024 as early as October 15, 1933. But should one—can one—accept this alone as the explanation for the resounding success of the National Socialist Party on November 13 of the same year, when the town of L., with a voter participation of almost 100 percent and a negligible number of invalid ballots, had the most yes votes in the Ostmark district?

Bruno and Charlotte Jordan had not abstained from voting. That couldn't be done any longer.

Those people were controlling everything now.

(Who are we to put irony, disgust, scorn into these sentences when we quote them?) Whether Charlotte and Bruno Jordan mustered the required abhorrence for the "systematically prepared acts of terror" perpetrated by the Communists, which were said to include "massive poisonings," and about which Reichsminister Hermann Göring could have produced not one or two but "hundreds of tons of material proof"—if such had not endangered the security of Reich and state—is to be doubted. He sure piles it on thick, Charlotte Jordan used to remark on such occasions, but whether she said it at that particular time has not been recorded. Nobody will ever know if they racked their brains about the location of the "vaults and secret passages" in their open town through which the Communists "everywhere" tried to escape the police and the law. Certainly nobody could have objected to the new theme song of the official German radio station: "Trust and honesty every day." It was one of the first melodies Nelly sang in its entirety and without any mistakes, and whose powerful text ("A villain's lot is always hard") reinforced in her, early and ever more firmly, the deeply rooted inborn link between good deeds and well-being: "Then you will walk through pilgrim life as if on verdant fields." A lasting image.

The National Socialist Party has 1.5 million members. The concentration camp at Dachau, whose establishment on March 21, 1933, was duly reported in the *General-Anzeiger* has a capacity of only 5,000. Five thousand derelict elements who are politically unreliable and dangerous to the public. Anyone who later affirmed that he had not known about the concentration camps had completely forgotten that their establishment had been reported in the papers. (A bewildering suspicion: they really had forgotten. Completely. Total war: total amnesia.)

Any exchange of ideas about news of this kind which may have taken place between Charlotte and Bruno Jordan—at the Hamburg Harbor concert, with real coffee—remains undescribed, being inaccessible to the power of imagination. A description will be given, in due course, of the look of the concentration-camp inmate at the campfire at Schwerin in Mecklenburg in May 1945. The look behind the strong glasses in the bent steel frames. The shaved head and the round striped beanie. The man to whom Charlotte said, giving him a generous share of her pea soup: Communist? But just because you were a Communist they didn't put you in a concentration camp! And his reply: Where on earth have you all been living.

He wasn't asking a question. He didn't have the strength for one. In those days, a marked lack of strength and trust and insight —not only in Mecklenburg—may have rendered certain possibilities of German grammar temporarily inoperative. Interrogative, declarative, or exclamatory sentences could no longer—or not yet —be used. Many, Nelly among them, lapsed into silence. Many muttered softly to themselves, shaking their heads. Where did you live. What did you do. What's going to happen now—things like that.

One and a half years later Bruno Jordan returns from Soviet captivity, changed beyond recognition; with shaved head, he sits at the table of strangers, ravenously slurping up the proffered soup. What have they done to us, he says, shaking his head.

(Lenka says: She can't understand it. Sentences like that. Said by people who were there the whole time. She does not wish—not yet—to hear how one could be there and not be there at the same time, the ghastly secret of human beings in this century. She still equates explanation with excuse, and rejects it. She says: One must be consistent. She means: uncompromising. You are very familiar with this need and ask yourself when your uncompromising severity began to disintegrate. A process later known as "maturity.")

In the late summer of 1933, SA Standartenführer Rudi Arndt stepped into Bruno Jordan's store in the Fröhlich house. Nelly gets her first account of the scene when she is eighteen years old—when the Jordans have long since left the town which meanwhile has been given its Polish name, when the Fröhlich house has long since been destroyed (but not yet been replaced by the new concrete building you see on your ride through the town), and when her father brings himself to discuss with his grown-up daughter, during a long walk along the south slope of the Kyffhauser, whether or not any human being can be turned into an animal. He tends to think: Yes, that's possible. He has seen too much in his life. Twice in a war. Twice in captivity. Not to mention Verdun; the French in Marseilles with their "Boches, Boches" shouts, throwing stones at defenseless prisoners. And in his last captivity, his own comrades beating Alex Kuhnke, the assistant teacher, almost to death over a piece of bread.

And in between, Arndt. That Hun. That animal. Enter the monster in the brown uniform of the SA Standertenführer, with leggings polished to a sheen. Casually. Just to hear the retail dealer Bruno Jordan answer in a few words whether or not he has been aware of the "scuffles between political adversaries" which had recently taken place on Küstrinerstrasse, and had even made the *General-Anzeiger*. The answer was plain. No. Because said incidents—in the course of which a shot had been fired—had taken place, as was common knowledge, in the late evening, at a time when he, Bruno Jordan, had long been peacefully asleep in his bed on Sonnenplatz. Aha. Then how did he know about the shot? The shot? Well, hadn't it been in the papers? That would really surprise the Standartenführer. This is where Arndt was wrong, or, more likely, where he was bluffing. The shot had actually been reported in the paper. Amazingly enough, from the perspective of today. Equally amazing is the report of the opening of the first concentration camp, or the reprint of a talk which the Standartenführer was to give soon after at the Weinberg Inn, or the advertisement he had placed—not at his own expense, certainly—shortly before, during the time of the boycott of Jewish businesses: Attention HAVA! The prohibition to shop at HAVA has not been lifted, since this is a proven case of Jewish profiteering. Leader of Unit 48, Rudi Arndt, Standartenführer.

The horribly clear consciences they all had.

Bruno Jordan knew who was standing in his store. He knew: That man has it in for me. A regrettable rumor had filtered through to the ears of Rudi Arndt: the wives of certain Communists had unlimited credit with Jordan. That was the first Bruno Jordan heard about it. They all get it on the cuff, Herr Standartenführer, and especially those who are out of work, naturally. But unlimited? What businessman can afford that? And how should he know what party his customers belong to? Unfortunately, he didn't have his ledger handy at the moment.

The Standartenführer did not insist on seeing the ledger. He had seen lists which had just by accident come into his hands during the liquidation of Communist locals. Did the fellow German Jordan by any chance know how much he had spent on so-called Red Help during the past years? No? Well, he, Arndt, could tell him, down to the last penny. No cheating with us.

Bruno Jordan's store never had a chair. No place to sit when the knees start shaking. One could only—like a hypnotized rabbit, let me tell you—stare into the gimlet pupils behind the pince-nez. One had to be glad when an offer was forthcoming, after the appropriate pause. All right, all right. No need to make a big fuss about everything right away. A Standartenführer, too, can forget—numbers, lists, all sorts of things. Under certain conditions. Half a sack of flour, half a sack of sugar for the SA district meeting, Sunday after next in Vietz. That's fair and square, and in keeping with the times. Which didn't mean that he'd be averse to a few extra packs of cigarettes thrown in. And in the future, the fellow German Jordan might pay a little closer attention to the proper observance of the Hitler salute in his store.

Those weren't interrogative sentences either, by the way.

Yes, darling daughter, that's a Hun for you! A statement made by Bruno Jordan fourteen years after the personal appearance of the animal, the monster, in his store and in his life. His only listener his thank-God-grown-up daughter, Nelly. Who grew up with the Hitler salute, and painstakingly had to learn to say "hello" and "goodbye" two years ago. "A German's greeting without fail / at all times should be Hitler Heil." It was the faulty rhyme that bothered her, not the substance of the verse. She may even have tried to improve it, since she was good at improvising rhymes on occasion. Which she doesn't tell her father. She withholds comment on his question: Is it really possible to turn every human being into an animal? If you rough him up enough . . . Because fear is . . . Well, you know, fear is . . . Nelly has become a little distant. A little reserved. She probably thinks too much, it's hard to say about what. Charlotte Jordan, who knew the drawer in which her daughter kept her diary, might be better informed. But what she read there she'd hardly discuss with her husband.

Nelly heard the words "concentration camp"—or rather: "concert camp," as it was commonly called—when she was seven. It's hard to say whether or not that was the first time. Customer Gutschmitt's husband had been released from concert camp, and he didn't speak a word to anyone. Why not? Probably had to sign something. (According to Heinersdorf Grandfather.) But sign what? Never mind, child.

What do I know.

Not an interrogative sentence, either. Nor a sentence that permits a question. But before you get involved in the prehistory of frustrated, unasked questions—a hopeless task—you'll finally finish the scene started earlier, whether you like it or not. The parents are still standing at Nelly's bed. She is to take part in a happy event. Nelly is looking straight into their faces, which were, to repeat, "shining."

Normally, her father would not have worn the blue peaked cap in the nursery; he had put it on especially for Nelly. It wasn't that much different from the cap of his rowing club "Speedy Team," but it could be fastened under the chin with a leather strap. The father demonstrates. (It can be checked in the *General-Anzeiger* at what time the sports clubs of the town were taken over by corresponding branches of the National Socialist Party. The death blow to the German club mania!)

So far, as usual. But who was it that said to Nelly in a happy voice: See! Now your father is one of them, too.

Always assuming that this is not a grave case of misremembering, the overflowing happiness of the parents—overflowing onto Nelly—must have been composed of the following elements: relief (the unavoidable step has been taken without having had to be taken on one's own); a clear conscience (the membership in this comparatively harmless organization—the Navy storm troops—

could not have been refused without consequences. What consequences? That's too precise a question); the bliss of conformity (it isn't everybody's thing to be an outsider, and when Bruno Jordan had to choose between a vague discomfort in the stomach and the multi-thousand-voice roar coming over the radio, he opted, as a social being, for the thousands and against himself).

Thus Nelly becomes acquainted with the composite feeling of thankfulness, not unlike the kind that overcomes her at night when her mother recites at her bedside: "Heather, favorite of bees, bleeding hearts and peonies . . ." She preferred not to ask if this could truly mean that her heart might start to bleed.

One and the same feeling—thankfulness—can thus be applied to totally different causes. Belated insight into the economy of feelings.

But now for the assembly report from the *General-Anzeiger*, which the local reporter had inserted in the paper on June 2, 1933, under the signature of A.B. This is what Standartenführer Rudi Arndt had declared in public the night before: The insurance clerk Benno Weisskirch had not died of physical abuse inflicted by men of his SA storm troop, but of the effects of a heart attack. Nobody ever died of a little beating. (Quoted verbatim.) Weisskirch, who refused to break off his race-defiling relationship with a Jewess, had tried to elude the wrath of the people by escaping in the direction of the commons, without thought of his obviously weak heart. The National Socialist conscience of the Standartenführer is clearer than clear.

Nelly learned to read in 1935, and from 1939–1940 on she was interested in newspapers. This past year, 1971, in the cool, special reading room of the State Library in Berlin, announcements like the following caught your eye for the first time. (They are texts which defy the imagination.)

The slogan: "Community interest comes before self-interest" is already popular when the boycott of Jewish businesses and professions begins on April 1, 1933. In L.—today Polish G.—nine physicians (one veterinarian) and nine lawyers are eligible for this boycott, in addition to a larger, unspecified number of businessmen. While SA guards in pairs move into position outside their doors, keeping patients and customers from entering waiting rooms and stores (although at that time the localities in question had already been closed voluntarily by their owners), other citizens of Nelly's hometown are sitting in their houses, at their kitchen tables, their dining tables, their desks, composing announcements for the *General-Anzeiger* on the following day.

They inform each other that they—and their fathers—were Prussian citizens by birth, and that they have never been members of the Workers and Soldiers Council. Signed: Johannes Mathes, Friedrichstrasse. They declare that their yard-goods business is a purely Christian enterprise. They unite as Christian shoe merchants: For your information, the Shoe House Conrad Tack is not a Christian enterprise, despite the fact that it has turned its deep-pink wrapping paper inside out. Only the decadent will carry shoe cartons in such wrapping paper in public. Please take special notice of this. Signed: The Christian Shoe Merchants of L. One of the town's two dancing teachers assures the other publicly that he is a wartime aviator of proven excellence and comes from a first-class German family of dancing teachers. He himself is first lieutenant in the reserves, ret., 54th Field Art. Regt.

The district leader of the National Socialist Party personally makes it known: "The boycott of Attorney and Notary Dr. Kurt Meyer in L., 2 Friedebergerstrasse, initiated by the SA on Saturday, was based on error and is revoked."

Other news: The Jew Landsheim has filed a complaint against SA Unit 48. April 28, 1933: establishment of a department of state secret police. Bombs over L.: aerial display of the SA air squadron.

Windows open, spring is here—by car, the distant will come near!

When the librarian came to your seat to lend you a pencil, you quickly covered the announcement page with a sheet of white paper. She expressed surprise that you felt warm when she herself had to wear a sweater inside the thick walls even in the summer. At one point, you jump up, turn the volume of newspapers in for safekeeping, take a long run through the streets, Under den Linden, Friedrichstrasse, Oranienburg Gate, and stare into people's faces. Without result. You're thrust back on the transformations of your own face.

Now: preliminaries to the theme of faith.

Nelly never saw the Führer face to face. Once—it was on Sonnenplatz, Nelly wasn't going to school yet—the store stayed closed in the morning. The Führer wanted to pay a visit to the Ostmark district. Everybody ran to Friedrichstrasse, under the tall lime trees, at the last stop of the streetcar, which was of course not running because the Führer was more important than the streetcar. It would be interesting to find out how the five-year-old Nelly did not only know, but felt what the Führer was. The Führer was a sweet pressure in the stomach area and a sweet lump in the throat, which she had to clear to call out for him, the Führer, in a loud voice in unison with all the others, according to the urgings of a patrolling sound truck. The same truck which would also broadcast where the Führer's automobile would arrive. The people bought beer and lemonade at the corner saloon, shouted, sang, and obeyed the orders of the restraining police and SA cordons. They stopped, and stood patiently. Nelly could neither understand nor remember what was being talked about, but she took in the melody of the mighty chorus, whose many single shouts were building up toward the gigantic roar into which they were meant to break, finally, in a display of powerful unity. Although it frightened her a little, she was at the same time longing to hear the roar, to be a part of it. She longed to know how it felt to be at one with all, to see the Führer.

It didn't come about, after all. Because fellow Germans in other towns and villages had been altogether too enthusiastic over him. It was a great pity, and yet they had not spent the long morning in vain, standing in the street. How much more beautiful and better to be standing in the street with all the others who were just as excited than to be all alone in the store, weighing flour and sugar, and shaking the eternal dust cloth out over the geraniums. They didn't feel cheated when they dispersed and ran back to their houses across the still-open grounds, where new blocks stand today and where Polish women call to one another from balcony to balcony in a language that can, unfortunately, be understood only by people who know Polish.

But you don't know Polish, and therefore you can't discover the purpose of the brand-new concrete-and-glass building on Küstrinerstrasse, where the old Fröhlich house used to be. Nothing has as yet been said about long-term and short-term memory. You still remember every single detail of the Fröhlich house, destroyed twenty-seven years ago. You'd be at a loss if you had to describe the new concrete-and-glass building you carefully looked at just a short while ago.

How does memory function? Our knowledge—incomplete and contradictory in itself—insists that a basic mechanism is at work according to the system of gathering-storing-recalling. Furthermore, the first, easily erasable track is said to be recorded by the cells' bioelectrical action; whereas storing, the changeover to long-term memory, is probably a matter of chemistry: memory molecules, fixed in permanent storage . . .

By the way, according to the latest research, this process supposedly takes place at night. In our dreams.

3

A longing for permanence—as an excuse or the motivation? The prerequisite: a refusal to compromise which impairs everyday life. Close to the surface lies the fatal suspicion that daily chores will never condense into significance. The dozens of faces across from you, in the train, on the bus, are sterile from lack of mystery. But the mocking eyes of the girl with the rounded forehead meet yours. And the young man by the window, in the hooded jacket, with his lecture notebook, his rimless glasses, presses his fingertips to his eyes, not to avoid looking, but out of fatigue. The dark-haired woman whose face tells of disappointments, and of her struggle not to succumb to them, is reading voraciously. As if it were your duty to bring at least these three together, to have them meet, these people who by chance and perhaps only this once are sitting in the same bus, one behind the other, each unseen by each. The flat land glides past, very familiar, strange beyond recognition. It is the hour between day and evening, the invisible sunset is mirrored in a high strip of red cloud. It is one of those rare moments when you think you know what to say and what not to say, and how to go about it.

It's impossible to create the high temperatures it would require to melt down the years. The child refuses to talk. Let's hope that whoever gets hold of her will not exploit her helplessness, as so easily happens. Beyond the mountains, the chasms, the deserts of the years . . . Your heart is pounding. You realize to what extent your century has revived the old invention of torture, in order to make human beings talk. You're going to talk. Every sentence, almost every sentence, in this language has a ghastly undertone which the heart, that simple hollow muscle, signals obstinately.

You were aware that the journey to G.—formerly L.—was in reality a return. Journeys come in pairs. A return within ten days entitles one to a reduced fare on certain stretches of the German Railways. For instance, when you were a child, a Sunday round-trip ticket connected your hometown, L., with the Reich's capital, where they had a castle and a cathedral with green-shimmering towers. A second two-way trip took Nelly—together with Lutz—to the small stop after Brandenburg which today still houses the general repair shop for the German Railways where her great-uncle worked as a saddler. Until she was fifteen, Kirchmöser Lake was the westernmost body of water she had seen. The Elbe River, the last hurdle of the refugee trek, was still a long way off, not to mention the Seine or the Hudson. It is hard to decide whether the latter lies to the west or really to the east of the Oder.

A third two-way journey—her fifth and sixth crossings of the Oder at Küstrin (Kostrzyn)—was a free round trip to a training camp for the Jungmädelbund—Hitler's young girls' group—near Frankfurt. The seventh crossing of the river took place on January 29, 1945, in the back of a truck, return not guaranteed. Nelly wanted to look at the river in spite of everything; it was frozen and indistinguishable from the snow-covered land beyond its banks. A new two-way journey is being undertaken twenty-six years later, from the opposite direction. Suddenly you felt that the trip could not be postponed one more day, despite the papers' warning about the heat wave: not every circulatory system would react with equanimity to temperatures over 85 degrees, and an increase in the number of accidents was to be expected. There was some talk about collisions and overheated tires later, but you neither saw nor were involved in any accident. It didn't take long to get to the Schoenefeld Cross and onto the autobahn to Frankfurt (Oder), heading due east, the sun in front of you, and not too many vehicles in the opposite lane. But for a stretch of forty miles, at least three, four stumps of destroyed bridges, still in ruins. Hackenberger, Lenka said. At each destroyed bridge she mentioned Hackenberger, whom her Uncle Lutz didn't know. Lenka told him that she'd known Sergeant Hackenberger records for ages, Willy A. Kleinau, as the incarcerated, soliloquizing, mad sergeant who boasts about the bridges he blew up in the last hour of the war, and about his shrewd trapping of recalcitrant recruits with their own recalcitrance: Mouth it, but don't sing.

Lenka has a talent for imitating even male voices.

In quick succession you pass Königs Wusterhausen, Storkow, Fürstenwalde, Müncheberg, Müllrose; parts of the large forests between towns are military-training areas in whose vicinity it is forbidden to take photographs. Occasionally, a clear still lake comes surprisingly into view. The last gas station before the border. Gas is cheaper in Poland, but your supply of zlotys was not generous. The clearance at both border-control stations goes smoothly.

There were as many cars from the West as there were from the East. In silence, the passengers sized each other up. Behind the wheel sat those who had been children at the same time as you, in Küstrin, L., Friedrichswalde, Friedeberg, Schwerin, Posen. In back of them, the young of today, raised in Cologne, Bochum, Hanover, Potsdam, Magdeburg, or Halle. Ten minutes in bumper-to-bumper traffic, side by side with a Porsche from Düsseldorf. In front, two men between thirty and forty, in white nylon shirts. In the back, a woman of about forty and a fifteen-year-old girl with dark frizzy hair. After Lenka had studied her for a while, the girl pulled out a lipstick from a bright-red patent-leather pocketbook—at the exact moment when their papers and yours were being returned through the rolled-down car windows—and painted her lips. Squares, Lenka said.

Frankfurt (Oder) and Slubice are connected by the reconstructed Oder Bridge, from which one has a view of the Oder River, losing itself in meadowland and thickets of willow, an eastern river, wide, untamed, and silted up; quiet, beautiful water that you joyfully recognized. Trees that may once have marked the banks seemed to be standing in the middle of the river. It is the same river which the child Nelly crossed seven times, at different spots. Her mother, Charlotte Jordan, affirmed that one could tell if a person had spent time looking at a river as a child. It changed one's outlook. The Vistula! she said, now, there's a river for you! when they stood on the embankment of the modest Warta and looked at passing rafts. "Raftsman, whence comes the wind so wild? From out of the asshole, m'child . . ."

Oh, but the Vistula! The rafts glided by proudly in the middle of the stream, and your voice couldn't reach them. Behind the children—Charlotte and her sister, Liesbeth, and her brother, Walter—Grandfather Johann Heinrich Zabel mowed his patch of meadow. That, and his tiny cottage, entitled him to enter his name in the church register as "landholder," although he couldn't possibly have lived off his land. He had to work as a track walker for the railroad, walking the track between Schwetz and Grutschno, in the Kulm area on the southern edge of the Tuchel Heath. Till the end of her life, Charlotte Jordan preserved the image of her grandfather: disappearing into the forest, reddish hair and beard, in his right hand a sturdy stick, in his left a red-checkered cloth bundle into which his daughter, Aunt Lina, had wrapped bread and a slab of bacon. The children were allowed to walk along with him as far as the first trees. They'd watch the pine thicket swallow him up. Sometimes he'd walk in the direction of Therespol, sometimes in the direction of Parlin.

This was what Charlotte Jordan wrote in her gray notebook, on seven pages dedicated to her grandfather, when she was gripped by a longing for permanence toward the end of her life. You are reminded of the dream which she told Nelly, thirty years after she dreamed it for the first time. She is a child again, spending her vacation at the frame cottage in the village of Wilhelmsmark. On every Sunday, she is called upon to sing her song. The pine floor has been scrubbed white with soft soap and strewn artfully with fine sand, the table has been covered with a square of plush and a runner, and on a raised stand rests the Bible from which her grandfather has finished reading the Sunday Gospel to himself, his family, and a few neighbors. It's the girl's turn. Charlotte gets up, full of good will, to sing her song, the only one she knows: "From heaven high." But she can't remember it. Her grandfather knits his brow. They're all afraid of him. Today he'll feel no need to nudge his daughter Lina after the service: Lina, a cookie for the children! Today he has to get into the act himself, he has to cue his granddaughter, he even has to sing, to show her how. The shame. No one has ever heard him sing. He confuses the songs, he sings quaveringly. She can't sing along, although she feels terrible about it.

No, Charlotte says, intimidated, but her grandfather takes it as a refusal. In a rage he gets up and walks out. They all follow, and have to watch sadly as he pulls the straws out of the thatched roof with his own hands. He who'd rap the knuckles of anyone who'd touch his roof, because he lived in constant fear that it might wear thin and start to leak. But that's not the end of it. He walks down the road to the village. What is he looking for? It's terrible to say: he's looking for the gambling money, the pennies he won last night at a card game in the tavern and which he always scattered over the meadow during the night with the cry: Gambling money!— devil's money!— Now, accursed, he is picking them up again. There he goes, the righteous man, to the tavern for a beer in broad daylight on a Sunday morning. And it is she, Charlotte, who is to blame for everything.

She told Nelly that she always woke up thinking one thought, which must still have been part of her dream: It's all wrong. In addition, the deep shock made the dream significant for her to the point of tempting her to get up in the middle of the night and write it down. But how can she get up in the middle of the night, she, a grocer's wife, and write down a dream? How could I? Charlotte asks her daughter thirty years later, when it is no longer a question. The daughter has no choice but to agree: Of course you couldn't; how could you have.

On the road from Slubice to Kostrzyn—a good, though narrow road—Lenka brought up the subject of the belief of the Tasaday, a tribe of twenty-four people who were discovered on the Philippine island of Mindanao, according to what she had read in the paper. In the course of six thousand years, she said, they had not devised even the smallest of inventions, and do you know what they believe? They believe that white teeth belong only to animals, and file theirs down almost to the roots, and dye them black with plant juice. After all, H. said, you were talking about all kinds of ways of distinguishing animals from humans. You have to start somewhere, don't you?

After that, you were silent for a long time. By all kinds of detours your thoughts turned to the maid Elvira. Did your brother Lutz remember Elvira? Elvira with the permanently offended smile.

Why?

Because Elvira came from a family of Communists. Lutz hadn't known this. But Elvira had told eight-year-old Nelly, on a hot summer afternoon, while a grid of sunlight fell on the kitchen table and the linoleum through the closed blinds. It was then that Elvira, the maid, told Nelly that all of them—her father, her mother, she herself, and her two brothers—had stayed home on the evening they burned the Communist flags on Hindenburgplatz, four years before. They had cowered in their basement apartment next to the slaughterhouse and witnessed the whole thing as if they had been present. And they had wept. Wept? Nelly asked. But then—Were you really Communists? Yes, Elvira said, we were Communists, and we wept.

Nelly kept the story to herself, although she didn't forget it. She felt uneasy. Communists were people whom SA men knocked down in the streets or mowed down with sniper bullets. "Comrades, the Red Front has been shot dead . . ." Communists raise their fists, shouting "Red Front!"

Why did Nelly not tell anyone what Elvira confided in her? Did she fear for Elvira? This time you've got to find out what the child is up to, impossible though it seems.

First the facts.

Did the flag burning actually take place in L.? The *General-Anzeiger* leaves no doubt: "A thorough clean-up on Hindenburgplatz!" Date: March 17, 1933. "The Communist leaders," so it says, "turned their backs on their party." This is reason enough for the SS and the SA to confirm the final result of their weeks of clean-up efforts in a "triumphant parade" through L. "Standartenführer Arndt will be cheered by thousands." All the windows overlooking Hindenburgplatz have been rented out. Each resident is requested to turn every penny of the money received over to the treasury of the SA.

March 17, then, is the day of the National Socialist takeover in L. The usual breakfast at the Jordans, perhaps they are reading the headline in the *General-Anzeiger* to each other. Charlotte possibly reads a few sentences too many, with the special intonation certain sentences are apt to take on when she speaks. Come off it, Bruno Jordan may be saying. We're not going to cheer, and that's that. The windows on Hindenburgplatz . . . Wait a minute! You think Lucie and Walter . . . ? (Charlotte's brother, Walter Menzel, who lived on Hindenburgplatz with his young wife, Lucie. Would he, too, be renting out his balcony?) Nonsense, Bruno Jordan may have said, you and your notions.

Nobody will ever know if the night of March 17 was the night when Charlotte thought—or dreamed—for the first time, with a shock: It's all wrong. It is precisely this kind of unreported, statistically unrecorded fact which would interest you today. More than the fact that every town experienced the National Socialist takeover. Or that—according to the *General-Anzeiger*—the population of L. stood shoulder to shoulder along the main streets, waiting for the SS and SA torchlight parade to approach during the eighth hour of evening. From the direction of the Adler Garden. March music and song. Waving banners. The upward thrust of hands. Known gestures, known all too well. What were the thoughts that went through people's heads, that they preferred not to know about: that's what you'd like to know.

Bruno Jordan may have been laid up with a mild case of the flu. Besides, he was not yet familiar with the words of the "Horst Wessel Song," which would surely be sung. Lucie and Walter Menzel watched the approach of the parade from the balcony of their apartment. They saw members of the Red Front Fighters' League of L.—wearing their uniforms for the last time—marching in the parade alongside a float carrying the "Symbols of Communism." They couldn't make out the expressions on these people's faces from their balcony. (But you can imagine them.) Did they rent out their windows to spectators? The question remains unanswered, because Nelly's outgoing Aunt Lucie never said a word about this spectacular people's demonstration.

Now the mayor addresses the citizens. "On the fiftieth anniversary of Karl Marx's death, his ideology is being crushed in the country of his birth." The town-district leader of the National Socialist Party announces that the leaders and members of the Communist Party will burn their flags and insignia themselves.

The Communist youth leader, whose name shall not be mentioned, stresses the fact that his leaders have fled. "Comrades! It is futile to run after an ideal that cannot be realized." (At almost the exact same moment, your friend F., a young Communist who had gone to Moscow, asks the appropriate department of the Comintern to send him to Germany, to work among the young, almost certainly expecting to end up in a concentration camp. Which is what happened.)

"Germany must live, even if we have to die!" the Standartenführer is said to have bellowed before giving the command to ignite the funeral pyre on which the Communist flags have been placed. (Hindenburgplatz is now planted with short tender grass. Along the sides are benches where men play cards on Saturday afternoons; they keep a bottle under the bench to toast one another every now and then.) For the maid Elvira, the time has come to weep. For the reporter of the *General-Anzeiger*, it is the moment to note: "On the anvil, the Communists are smashing their lyres, manifesting their usual delight in destruction." The moment has come for the "Deutschland" and "Horst Wessel" songs, for a forest of raised arms, for ten thousand hearts to beat in unison, and for the shout of jubilation from every throat.

Today, almost forty years later, the time has come for a few questions. Their harshness is based partly on Nelly's innocence: she was four years old. (You can't get around the fact that in this country innocence is almost infallibly measured by age.) Questions like the following: How many residents on Hindenburgplatz turned the received window money over to the SA treasury on the following morning, as they had been requested to do? (Only small amounts could have been involved: a mark or two per standing room, certainly not more, considering the fact that L. was declared a depressed area a few weeks later and people were warned against moving there.) Furthermore, how large a percentage of the population of L. (48,000 inhabitants) wept on this evening—other than the family of Elvira, the maid, whose father worked in the slaughterhouse? A moot question, since no yardstick exists to show how many members of a population must weep, in order to invalidate the laughter of the rest, of the overwhelming majority. Five percent? Three point eight? Or will one single family suffice to save an entire town? Five upright human beings out of fifty thousand?

You tend to set up a counter-calculation: what if only one single person had laughed, only one had cheered and sung at the top of his lungs! (A moral rigor which doesn't help because it remains inconclusive. You suspect that you may be looking for a chance to revitalize faded moral standards . . .)

The number of people lining the streets and Hindenburgplatz (or whatever its name may have been) is also unknown. The distance from Adler Garden to Hindenburgplatz is approximately two to two and a half miles. They were standing "shoulder to shoulder," the paper says. All right. But how many rows deep? One? Or more?

In any case, statistics are too coarse for your purpose. Even in the face of exact figures, you'd still want more information, and it's unobtainable in this world. After the tears you'd want to count the beads of sweat—of fear—on the brows of some in the cheering crowd. The palms that turned moist with disgust. The hearts that skipped as they beat faster. Maybe these details, too, would turn out to be depressing. Perhaps it was true: perhaps they cheered Standartenführer Arndt and would have cheered anybody, regardless of his name, with or without his bowlegged walk, the short arms and legs, and the double chin which the storm strap cut in two. But they had him, none other. And since they didn't need him as much as they needed their cheering, they accepted him and cheered.

Is that reason enough for putting off the journey to the once jubilant hometown you have lost? For you shouldn't feign disinterest. Perhaps you have as little desire as anyone else to cross borders behind which all innocence stops. It is, by the way, remarkable how a single peasant woman with a white kerchief tied in a certain way and a rake over her shoulder can change a familiar landscape. This was after Gorzyca (formerly Göritz), on a road bordered by flat fields on both sides, an eastern scenery that begins to arouse your curiosity. You call out the names of the plants you recognize along the wayside: yarrow, cuckooflower, St.-John'swort, blue chicory, coltsfoot, mugwort, plantain, and shepherd's purse. Those can be found anywhere, H. asserted, and Lenka, who was beginning to side with him, had to agree. There really was nothing special about it. But you saw what everybody should be seeing: that only a road ditch on the other side—or rather, on this side—in any case, east of the Oder, could be covered by this particular mixture of vegetation. Their protest, a trifle too emphatic, was meant to warn you not to become emotional. Which wasn't necessary. Of course you got annoyed that they felt the need to warn you. Never mind, Lutz said. They don't understand.

But you wanted to explain. You didn't claim that you'd never been homesick. Neither would you deny that you had struggled against it ruthlessly at times, and that ruthlessness in emotional matters is always risky as far as possible aftereffects are concerned. But it has been years since the streets of your hometown have appeared in your dreams (unlike before, when you kept dreaming that you were asked to name them but couldn't. As you woke up, you'd rattle off all the names that had eluded you in your sleep: Adolf-Hitlerstrasse and Bismarckstrasse and Schlageterplatz and Moltkeplatz and Hermann Göring School and Walter Flex Barracks and the SA housing project. The network of the streets in your childhood town has been indelibly imprinted on your—and everybody else's—mind as the basic model for the layout of marketplaces, churches, streets, and rivers. Now it exists only in part, modified, in an altered form, because it gives you away too much, points out tracks which must be erased; for you are forced to shuffle the details in order to get closer to the facts). The dream has not recurred in so many years—what better proof of your detachment? Later on it will be asked: What does it mean, that you began dreaming of it again after your visit to the town?

Most of the town's streets were paved, some with cobblestones, but most with large panels of so-called graywacke, an indestructible stone which possibly still remains under the asphalt cover of the modern streets. It's probably still under one of the lanes of Soldinerstrasse, which was later widened into two lanes paved with tarred gravel. Incidentally, the now run-down Adler Garden lies on the left—coming from the town—and some 450 yards farther up the street (it runs uphill) on the right stands the two-family house which Bruno Jordan built in 1936, and in which the family lived for the last nine years, until the flight. It was from the very same Adler Garden—a tavern with a dance hall and a so-called coffee garden: tables and chairs on a gravel court—that the deplorable parade set out in the evening of March 17, 1933, as well as that other one: the marching column of men eligible for military service from Town District Northwest, who were mobilized on the morning of August 26, 1939. Bruno Jordan was one of them. A short week later he marched off to his second war.

Everything in its time. The question was: Why did eight-year-old Nelly recognize that the announcement of the maid Elvira, six years older than she—about their being Communists and having wept—was an important secret which she should keep to herself?

Tentative answer: Because of a feeling of reluctance. (Tentative, because it explains nothing, although it questions the earlier assumption that silence can be a virtue.) Yes—if she had kept silent because talking might have harmed Elvira. This was not the case. It never occurred to Nelly that Elvira and her family had not afterward been converted to faithful supporters of the Führer. No, the thing that mattered was not to protect Elvira, whose spiteful smile often disturbed Nelly. She had to admire that smile because it was a sign that Elvira had access to spheres of life that were inaccessible to Nelly. Perhaps what mattered was to enlarge her own secret realm. Because, unknown to herself, this child's straight, truthful mind—to me, you're as transparent as a pane of glass, Charlotte used to say to her daughter—had designed secret hiding places to which she could retreat alone. Other people's prying is at the root of secretiveness, which can develop into a need, finally into a habit, and produce dangerous vices and great poetry.

You must tell me everything.

Guilt and concealment were forever tangled in Nelly's mind, and furrowed a deep rut studded with glitter words. When adults pronounced them, their eyes began to glitter. One had to watch their eyes, not their mouths, when they spoke, to find out which words one couldn't ask about.

Not normal, for instance. Charlotte's repeated exclamation: I really think you're not normal!

It came to Nelly in a flash that her mother might be right. Not to be normal is the worst thing by far; everybody feels that when they see Heini, who is being pulled along the street in a padded box by his unfortunate mother or surly brothers, his withered hands dangling at wrong angles, his feet jerking, spittle running down his chin, as he babbles his only three words: "Mama poor aunt" at everyone he sees.

Heini is called Mama-Poor-Aunt. He laughs all the time without being happy. He is not normal. But Nelly is healthy, thank God. Thank God, her mind is normal. She will not allow her limbs to flap at the joints—although she secretly tried this out—she will not let nonsensical words slip out of her mouth. Nelly will control herself. That's what every human being has to learn, or else he's no human being, says her mother. One really must learn to control oneself! she says when the Waldins' Anneliese, barely seventeen, takes prolonged evening strolls in the Wepritz Mountains with a baker's apprentice. I'd sure like to see the cookies he bakes for her! The girl is oversexed, even a blind man can see that. Outside smart, inside a tart . . .

Oversexed is a glitter word. Consumption is another glitter word, although a weaker one. One that Nelly seldom has a chance to try out. She is sent out of the room for spilling milk on the breakfast table. Go play outside. Christel Jugow is standing outside with her guilt-ridden pale face and her insufferable wicker doll carriage. You want to play with me?

Not today.

Tears, as usual. But it's you I like to play with best. As if I could help that. Then why don't you play with me!

That's when Nelly decides to end the pitying, hypocritical relationship with Christel Jugow once and for all, now, this very moment. She informs her that her mother, Frau Jordan, has strictly forbidden her to play with Christel Jugow, who has, after all, a whopping case of consumption, and in her lungs at that, which is horribly contagious, as everybody knows.

When Frau Jugow stands outside the Jordans' apartment door ten minutes later, with disheveled hair and her apron strings dangling, Nelly denies every word right to her face and lets herself be called "rotten." To her mother, who pulls her behind the closet, she admits everything readily and without remorse, but refuses to give an explanation for her behavior. She accepts the disbelieving, reproachful look which she had perhaps counted on, which she had perhaps intentionally provoked, and sits down at the window.

But Sundays are long, and Nelly saw her scant supply of self-satisfaction dwindle and wane by the hour, until she had to face the question: Why had she really broken with pale Christel Jugow? Because she didn't want to lie any more—for which she was prepared to lie shamelessly—or because she had for a long time been looking for an excuse to get rid of the boring sourpuss. Whenever she succeeded in clearing herself of guilt, she had to experience a rebirth of the question on a deeper, darker layer within herself. Each time the answer turned out to be different, until all certainty about herself threatened to disappear into a bottomless funnel. A process of eerie fascination which she recognized: On the labels of cans of Libby's milk, a nurse in white with outstretched hand offers the onlooker, buyer, milk drinker, a second can of Libby's milk, on whose label a second nurse, this one quite small, does the same with a third can. And so forth. Until nurses and cans have attained a tininess no brush could paint, but which Nelly's tormented brain can imagine all too precisely, in sharpest focus, until a pinpoint spot above her right eye turns into a red-hot quiver.

What's the matter with you? Is something wrong? What do you mean, a headache? Let me look. Aha, a fever. But the child has a fever. The child belongs in bed this very minute. Now it's as plain as the nose on your face why she acted so funny today. She was coming down with something . . .

Chicken pox, Dr. Neumann said, shouldn't be taken any more seriously than fly shit. Except that our homunculus must show character and not scratch them off.

Nelly was not unhappy that character could be tested only in adversity; that outside, meanwhile, the great COHORG sports contest was underway, to which she had been able to wangle her entry as a participant only by a sizable bribe out of her father's candy jars; that Christel Jugow, so she heard, was now pushing her light-brown wicker doll carriage leisurely across the courtyards in the company of a newcomer by the name of Hildy, who, according to Nelly's mother, also looked like death warmed over; and that she herself was able to crochet a few potholders under Frau Elste's tutelage. Frau Elste, whose chicken pox lay behind her and who could therefore sit at Nelly's bedside without fear and sing, the tennis ball on her neck bouncing furiously, "He walks to muffled drumbeat's roll . . . How long the way, how far the goal . . . Oh, could he rest and find relief . . . I fear my heart will break with grief . . ."

It was then that Nelly, weakened by fever, of course, finally broke down and cried.

Alien blood was another glitter word. Isn't it likely that Bruno Jordan now and then read words such as these to his wife from the paper, words which she herself would never have used? The law for the prevention of genetically unfit offspring. Or sterilization, which, as the paper stressed, was not to be identified with castration.

Bruno! Please. Think of the child. A back-and-forth of expressions, studded with glitter words, among which the highly interesting word "sterile" escaped her mother's lips. Her father's two sisters, it must be said, are sterile, sad but true. And nothing can be done about it. Her father's younger sisters are: Aunt Olga, who lived in Leipzig with her husband, Uncle Emil Dunst (supposedly a cosmetics salesman for a firm of high repute, to which Charlotte could only remark: If he really believes that, I'll eat my hat), and Aunt Trudy, who lived in Plau am See, with her husband, Harry Fenske, automobile-repair-shop owner. Plau am See, if not the most beautiful, then at least the most wondrous, town in the world, where lovely delicate toys were on display in every store window (ballet dancers, for instance, in organdy tutus, which Aunt Trudy brought as a present for Nelly, only to play with them herself all afternoon), where charming people genteelly conversed with one another, and where husbands—especially Uncle Harry, Aunt Trudy's husband—literally worshipped their wives. But how can it be (*It really can't be!*, one of Aunt Trudy's favorite expressions) that the thought of "Plau am See" conjures up ladies with white parasols and white sails on the water, instead of the actual, undistinguished town through which you've traveled frequently since then, and where you have occasionally stopped for an ice cream. Who is to know how that can be possible?

Perhaps anyone interested in proving the power of the unreal, the fantasy, over the real things in life.

So much for now about Trudy Fenske, who was sterile, a word that Nelly was not supposed to hear, or she'd be sent from the room immediately. Aunt Trudy, who one day—after enduring much hardship, even after the husbands in Plau am See have stopped worshipping their wives—will tell her niece the story of Karl the sailor, which is also the story of her sterility.

For the time being, however, Aunt Trudy and Uncle Harry are looking for a child to adopt. An infant, to be exact. Because Aunt Trudy adores babies. Charlotte doesn't want to be a pessimist, but she'd hate to be a baby in the care of her sister-in-law Trudy. Why? Because a small child needs his regularity and, above all, feedings on the dot. And you must admit, your sister is and always was a downright slob.

After three days of observation by a pediatrician, the infant was declared to be not only of normal but of superior intelligence, the child of lower-class parents, who both signed a release and were not allowed to learn the whereabouts of their offspring. Incidentally, the father's Aryan pedigree goes way back, while that of the mother—a housemaid—cannot be traced very far. To put it plainly: the boy's mother, too, is illegitimate. Well, such things happen, of course. But the genes just aren't the best.

What are jeans? Something boys wear, or what?

Nelly was too young to understand. Besides, much too much was being discussed in front of the children. Look at them, sitting there, with such big ears.

And then the newspaper again.

A eugenic way of life. From now on, schools will educate the children in a eugenic way of life.

Now what's that supposed to be?

What do you want it to be? They'll forbid a healthy girl like your daughter to marry a sick boy like this Heini.

But I'd think that that would be obvious!

Look, here it tells you: Forbidden to marry are: persons with venereal diseases, consumption, mental and hereditary illnesses. Four hundred thousand will be sterilized at once.

Bruno, please.

Four hundred thousand, strictly volunteers, of course.

What are venereal diseases, hereditary illnesses?

Glitter words. These are questions one must not ask. Frederick the Great, from the venerable hereditary House of Hohenzollern. A white enamel plate on Richtstrasse: Specialist in Skin & Venereal Diseases. So it could happen that an entire venerable family contracted a hereditary disease and thus became unfit for marriage. Nelly had to tell herself that her family, too, might come down with a hereditary disease, consumption or mental illness. All the Jordans would become ill and go mushy, and she'd be stuck with it. In the end she would be the one who couldn't get married.

More specific details about her family's hereditary state of health could be obtained only from an unsuspecting person. Whiskers Grandma.

Why sure, you may sleep at my house, Nelly child. Let her be. And why shouldn't I cook split-pea soup for her, when she likes it so much?

Whiskers Grandma and Whiskers Grandpa now live on Adolf-Hitlerstrasse. Lord help us, you get used to everything. Sick? says Whiskers Grandma. Us, sick! As if we had the time for that! Or do you perhaps mean my gall bladder? Not the gall bladder, no. After all, that had been taken out years ago. Consumption? Lord, not that I know of. Mentally ill? You don't say! Uncle Ede? Aunt Lina's husband in Grutschno in the Polish Corridor? My brother-in-law Ede mentally ill? Who on earth told you that? I thought so. Your mother sometimes talks as the day is long.

Aunt Lina in Grutschno, she has a husband who's soft in the head, and not just a little either, Uncle Ede.

The news is confirmed by two witnesses who just traveled through the Polish Corridor in order to visit with Aunt Lina and Uncle Ede: Whiskers Grandma's brother Heinrich and his wife, Aunt Emmy, both living in Königsberg (East Prussia).

Oyoyoy, I tell you, the things that go on at Lina's. Nothing good, that's for sure.

In her pajamas, Nelly is lying on her stomach outside Whiskers Grandma's living-room door, listening through the crack about why Aunt Lina—she's good fun, let me tell you, and is she ever fond of kids—has to fear for her life. Not that Ede is a bad sort, he never was; anyone who says that is a liar. It's just that his home brew always goes to his head too fast. And Whiskers Grandma—God be her witness—has told him more than once: Ede, why don't you listen to reason. Someday you'll be sorry, for sure. But Uncle Ede, whom Nelly pictures as a little sad man with a round head, could only reply over and over: Gussie, Gussie, if you only knew ... Nelly wanted to keep this profound remark in her mind at all costs. She heard with uneasy satisfaction that Uncle Ede would come at Aunt Lina with the hatchet when he had his fits, but later, after he came to, he'd put his head in her lap and cry: Looshie, my Looshie.

All these strange goings-on happened in the Polish Corridor, which was never neat, because of the proverbial Polack mess, unlike her own German corridor, in which nobody was allowed to leave his muddy shoes at any time, because you could always tell a housekeeper by the bathroom and the corridor.

The tulip tree in front of the grandmother's house would differentiate it from all other houses on the long street, you thought, and so it did. The tree was no longer in bloom in July. It had grown, and the house in back of it had shrunk. The pale-blue shutters were hanging askew, the doorway was falling apart, a toothless mouth—a fleeting impression, since you were driving past, slowly, but without stopping. Lutz, however, who was four years old when the grandparents moved from here, recognized neither the tulip tree nor the shutters. For the life of me, he said. An absolute blank.

So you kept silent about the snake. But it was here that it had come into Nelly's life—or crawled, or slithered: a loathsome creature. And thick as a tree trunk, for the young woodcutter in Whiskers Grandpa's tale would mistake it for a tree trunk. Here it was, on the brownish-patterned sofa in the sitting room, that Nelly received the tale, for "heard" would be too weak a word. The snake lay next to Nelly's bed from then on, every night. It never as much as got close to her, yet it kept her from getting out of bed during the night. Snakes aren't the kind of animals one bargains or establishes contact with. Silently they take their place at the foot of one's bed, and depend on the clairvoyance of a guilty conscience to interpret the reason for their presence. They can't enter the grandmother's house, because there Nelly sleeps back to back with her grandmother, in a wide creaking wooden bed, her face turned to the wall on which the street lamp projects the leaf pattern of the tulip tree in shadow play. The big white chamber pot in front of the bed can be used without fear, while Whiskers Grandpa's snoring rises loud and persistent from the other bed. Nelly lies awake and tries to catch her thoughts at the moment of their conception. She makes her head empty. Then she makes herself think: It is dark. But each time a kind of inner whispering appears before the fully developed thought and she cannot grasp it.

(Ruth, your older daughter, telephones: She's had a dream

about you. You had swum too far from the shore, on a mirror-smooth water surface, with the intention of killing yourself. Why are you telling me that? you said. Are you trying to give me ideas? One can hardly maneuver more cautiously than I at this point. Perhaps your sometimes senseless fits of courage appear as a challenge to others to annihilate you? Ruth said. So you don't have to do it yourself. Too simple, you say. Because, if there is another shore at the other end of the lake, I'd love to see it. You remember the fears you used to have for your mother, when you were a child. Does everything repeat itself? Must the insight as to how the cycle might be broken always come after the damage has been done, when one is too old to make decisive changes?)

Why was it so important to Nelly to be considered brave? Her Uncle Heinrich from Königsberg, a sarcastic man, guides her right index finger slowly, slowly, through the flame of a candle. Nelly doesn't flinch, though her eyes are brimming with tears, and yet her Uncle Heinrich says: No no, little lady, to be brave is something else. Being brave is if you now tell me that you're furious with me, and that I'm ugly. Uncle Heinrich with his long yellow shiny horse's pate, and the big yellow teeth. Well, are you going to say it? No, Nelly says. There, you see. You may be softhearted, but brave is something else.

The next test followed on the spot. The bell rang. In came, profusely apologizing—Nelly almost thought: At last!—one of those creatures without whom the world wouldn't be what it is, but who have good reason for not showing themselves in broad daylight: a witch. As old as Methuselah, and ugly as sin. Obsequiously ushered in by Uncle Heinrich: Madam here and Madam there. A little cup of coffee for Madam. Now, what's the matter, Nelly child. Let's show a little courtesy. This child is my grand-niece, by the way, very well-mannered, her name is Nelly.

The witch said it was her pleasure, and sucked at the wart on her upper lip. Not that it hadn't struck Nelly that the witch was wearing her wart on the exact same spot as Aunt Emmy, who happened to be absent just then. Nor that she had put on spectacles with pasted-on squinty eyes, from which hung a repulsive red cardboard nose. She did, however, understand: anyone who really wants to deceive won't be so blunt about it. This was one of those sophisticated double tricks that Nelly thought she understood: somebody puts on an ugly mask so that nobody dares suspect how much more ugly he really is. Except that Nelly didn't fall for this ruse, no more than for Aunt Emmy's green shawl, which the witch had wrapped around her shoulders. The witch wanted to be taken for Aunt Emmy playing a trick. She talked the way Aunt Emmy talked when she disguised her voice. But it didn't help her one bit. It's true, for sheer politeness' sake Nelly softly repeated: But that's Aunt Emmy! several times. But from the very start she had no doubt about who it was she was dealing with. Because there are unmistakable signs for telling a witch. A witch is endowed with the ability to change the composition of the air: certain improprieties suddenly appear natural, whereas things that were natural before seem totally ludicrous.

For example: the witch who has instantly seated herself in the place of honor on the sofa has the audacity to make fun of Whiskers Grandpa, who is cutting dozens of one-millimeter-wide gashes into the bread with his sharp knife on his wooden board, so that his toothless gums will be able to grind them down. The witch, who knows neither respect nor compassion, calls him Hermann Sharptooth, haha, and Uncle Heinrich laughs his broad laugh: You're so right, Madam. What's even worse and more improper, Whiskers Grandma, too, starts giggling like a young girl, with her hand over her mouth, and above all, Nelly herself can feel a tickle in her throat. Look at yourself, just look at yourself, says Whiskers Grandma to the witch. She is on familiar terms with her.

After vociferous complaining, the witch has stuffed herself with everything Uncle Heinrich put on her plate. Now she begins to writhe and double up, and to rub her stomach, until—to her own relief and Nelly's distress—she is forced to emit an endless succession of unmannerly sounds. Witches know no feeling of embarrassment and are able to ask a child who happens to be present, in a fake voice: Well, and the little Fräulein? Is she properly disgusted with me? Oh no, not at all, quite the contrary, really. (These are statements which belong to a subdivision of sanctioned white lies, to lies of compassion, which must be directed toward all that is misshapen.) But witches are never forced to lie, they are brazen by profession. Unhesitatingly they take one's lies at face value (this is the second point in which they differ from humans) and therefore begin to pet one's cheek endlessly with a gnarled, wrinkled hand. On which, to her unspeakable annoyance, Nelly notices Aunt Emmy's golden pearl ring.

According to the law of her species, a witch cannot be satisfied until she has turned the people around her into caricatures. She now takes her leave under exaggerated assurances of gratitude. She finally wishes everyone a long life, so that the survivors don't have to worry about what to wear to the funeral, which is always the first thought that comes to mind upon the death of a loved one. For which they later blame the deceased, rather than themselves. But that's the way people are, and that's the way they have to be taken.

What comes to your mind, Lutz, when you hear "Aunt Emmy"? A wart. Königsberg. Knitting. She must have knitted incredibly fast.

Aunt Emmy, as she appears in your memory for the last time, is sitting with her sister-in-law Auguste—Whiskers Grandma—on the stoop outside the front door of the Jordans' new house, on a hot summer afternoon, busily knitting. Nelly is doing exercises on the banister. It must have been 1941 or 1942, after the invasion of the Soviet Union, but before Stalingrad. Aunt Emmy without any disguise. Someone, a female figure, furtively flies up the steps along the side of the house which lead to the second floor and end in the stoop on which the women sit, knitting. Nelly recognizes the faded drill cloth, the white kerchief, the large letter O on the woman's chest and back: "Ostarbeiter" (laborer from beyond the Eastern border). She recognizes the Ukrainian housemaid who works for Major Ostermann's wife. At Charlotte Jordan's special request, she always did the shopping for the major's wife just before store-closing time; she was lodged in the foreign laborers' camp near the stadium. But Nelly has no idea why she dared run up the outside stairs in broad daylight and is urgently demanding to see the "Missus."

Aunt Emmy, barely looking up from her knitting, informs the stranger that the Missus can't take time out from her store. Then she tells Nelly with unusual strictness: Go away. And without transition, barely moving her lips, not raising her eyes and not interrupting her knitting for a second, she switches to a rapid unintelligible mumbling, in a language that was most likely Polish, and in which she exchanges a number of sentences with the

Ukrainian woman for less than a minute, whereupon the woman glides back down the stairs without another word, like a shadow, and disappears as though she had never been there.

What did she want?

That one? What she wanted? Oh, for goodness' sake, what on earth could she have wanted? I couldn't understand half of what she was saying. Some message from the major's wife.

That was a lie, and Nelly couldn't endure it. Only today you wonder why Nelly, with her reputation for nosiness, didn't insist on finding out the truth. She put on "her face," sulked even more because Aunt Emmy paid no attention to her, and withdrew to her hiding place in the potato furrow under the cherry tree to bury herself in her book from the school library, perhaps *The Stoltenkamps and Their Wives*.

Only a few years before, Nelly wouldn't put up with these secrets. She had yanked the living-room door open again, through which she and her brother, Lutz, had just been ousted, to call in: They needn't think that she was stupid. She knew anyhow what they were going to talk about: Aunt Trudy's divorce. Lasting satisfaction with the effect she had achieved.

Had her curiosity meanwhile diminished? Does curiosity diminish if it remains unsatisfied for a long time? Is it possible to numb a child's curiosity completely? And could this perhaps be one of the answers to the question by the Pole Kasimierz Brandys about what enables human beings to live under dictatorships: that they learn to restrict their curiosity to realms that are not dangerous to them? (All learning is based on memory.)

It should be asked: Isn't it the nature of curiosity to be preserved either in its entirety or not at all?

Would Nelly then gradually lose her ability to differentiate between dangerous and non-dangerous subjects—"instinctively," as people like to say, deflecting her curiosity from dangerous areas—and cease asking questions altogether? And was the maid Elvira's announcement—that she had wept, on the evening the Communist flags were burned—perhaps not passed on because Nelly had realized that adults were avoiding sentences containing the word "Communist"? Even candid Aunt Lucie, who gave Nelly helpful hints in another area—sex, which was taboo to Nelly's mother—never mentioned that particular evening, which she had to have witnessed, as a resident of Hindenburgplatz. Aunt Lucie's silence was especially convincing, since her easy manner didn't arouse any suspicion that she might have anything to hide.

This may conceivably have laid the groundwork for the reluctance which would condense into defiance and inaccessibility several years later.

In any case, Nelly didn't learn until long after the war that her mother had gathered up a few linen scraps and diapers and old flannel cloths on that warm summer evening; that Whiskers Grandma had resolutely torn up an old sheet—as she'd done on the day she bandaged Lutz's badly bleeding knee after a fall from his bicycle—and had placed the pieces at the bottom of a basket which the Ukrainian maid of Major Ostermann's wife had come to pick up the next day. Nobody though, not even Nelly's mother, found out if the child lived, after the Ukrainian's friend gave birth in the foreign laborers' barracks, if and for how long it lay in Charlotte Jordan's linen rags, and when it had died (as was only too likely). Great care had been taken to eliminate all signs that might betray the origin of the rags in which the child was to be wrapped. No monogram, God forbid; otherwise, the two gentlemen who came to call on Charlotte Jordan two years before the end of the war would have appeared sooner. One very early morning, Charlotte had found a bunch of field flowers at her store entrance. She never asked the Ukrainian woman about the child, and the woman never mentioned it. Least of all was Charlotte's twelve-year-old daughter Nelly allowed to suspect that a tiny infant was lying in her old diapers in the women's camp near the stadium, and would probably die. Because rumor had it that the Russians in the men's camp, located next to the women's camp, were dying like flies. (The expression was used. Nelly must have heard it: "like flies.") The only reply to this sentence was a dark shocked look from her mother. Not a word. Nelly knows what is expected of her. She plays deaf and dumb.

And that's what she became. Only the memory of her mother's look, a look without a context. The cause for it had been fogotten. You have to wait until you see the stadium again. The tips of the poplars surrounding the stadium appear silvery above the edge of the chain of hills. Contrary to expectation, your first thought is not of the sports contests the Hitler Youth held in the stadium every year, in which Nelly was once among the ten best, in the disciplines of running, jumping, and volleyball. Instead, you think: The camp! The site where the barracks used to stand can no longer be found. The barracks have been torn down. Polish army trucks are standing there, the training field Nelly knew from childhood has been enlarged. Guns under camouflage tarpaulins, shirtless soldiers doing athletics.

Suddenly you know that everyone knew. Suddenly a wall to one of the well-sealed vaults of memory breaks down. Snatches of words, murmured sentences, a look—all kept from re-creating an incident which one would have had to have understood. Dying like flies.

Yes, it was a blistering hot day, like this July 10, 1971. Yes, the air was as liquid as it is today, and smelled of hot sand and mugwort and yarrow, and in the potato furrow Nelly found her body imprint, a mold she had made by lying down as if in a coffin. But twenty-nine years later you have to ask yourself how many encapsulated vaults a memory can accommodate before it must cease to function. How much energy and what kind of energy is it continually expending in order to seal and to reseal the capsules whose walls may in time rot and crumble. You'll have to ask what would become of all of us if we allowed the locked spaces in our memories to open and spill their contents before us. But memory's recall—which incidentally varies markedly in people who seem to have had the exact same experience—may not be a matter of biochemistry, and may not universally be a matter of choice.

If this were not so, some people's assertions would be accurate: documents could not be surpassed; the narrator would therefore be superfluous.

4

During this mild month of January 1973, the news of an impending truce in Vietnam is once again thickening, and you write "4" at the top of a new sheet, bound as you are by your daily work schedule and the arbitrariness of chapter divisions. The President of the United States of America forecasts a long era of lasting world peace. He does this with the brand of hypocrisy which the last third of this century has perfected to such a degree that it goes unrecognized. According to your plan, Chapter 4 will describe a baptism and the legendary occurrence of a wedding: events of 1935 and 1925–26, years during which Nelly did not experience anything at all, or else she was so young that her testimony is hardly valid. We're all familiar with the negligent memory of children; only radiantly colorful events are worth retaining, or else disasters, but not the repetition of daily life.

Today is today, yesterday is gone, there's no doubt about that. In case it's a crime to efface boundaries . . . In case it's a crime to insist on boundaries . . . In case it's true that nobody can have his cake and eat it, too . . .

The thought that there was a time when she didn't exist was always unbearable to Nelly. (This sentence, which may be considered "factual," must be blended with a great many half-true or fictitious sentences, which must, in turn, sound more real than the "true" ones. The arrogance of not wanting to make a mistake leads directly to losing the ability to speak. You've had the experience.)

A forced pause. In February 1971. Hours spent in front of the TV, watching the spaceship Apollo 14 succeed with its sixth link-up maneuver, after five failures. The assurance that astronauts Shepard and Mitchell will land on the moon no matter what. It is obviously a matter of prestige. The kangaroo leaps of the two men in front of the by-now-familiar crater landscape could no longer rouse your interest. An alarming symptom, perhaps, but you were not alarmed.

Whereas you would have been passionately interested in a televised interview with Bruno Jordan in 1934—a truly unrealistic notion—during which the reporter would most likely have asked the retailer's opinion about certain government slogans. What, for instance, did he think of the line: "The new industry regulations have started a general offensive against imported fats!" Or: "The people must be able to buy again. Buying is the main objective."

"Buy now, and help reconstruction!"

"As reichsmarks from the pocket flow, work, industry, and retail grow!"

Exclamation marks to which Bruno Jordan could only have added an exclamation mark of his own. Incidentally, technical progress—for instance, the possibility of keeping anyone's voice, face, and opinion preserved on celluloid for decades—is not always in the interest of the man in the street, in rapidly changing times such as ours. (And still less in the interest of the men in power, as proved two years ago by the TV camera—President Nixon simply refused to comment on the accusations that he was concentrating troops at the southern border of Laos.)

You hit the back of your head so hard against an iron ledge that you lost whole days—or gained them, as you secretly thought—in headaches, doctor's visits, and X rays. Your friend F., who was in the hospital with a heart attack, assured you with a wide grin that you, too, were suffering from heart trouble: something on which he of all people was hardly qualified to pass judgment, having just spent sixty hours on blood thinners. You started to quarrel, which was what he had wanted. And when you both finally remembered the usual recommendations and advice to someone ill, he said a person always has to butt against the sheep pen or else the fence starts growing toward him.

Naturally you had trouble falling asleep, and so tried the Schober method, which, unlike self-hypnosis, consists of exhausting the mind. You force yourself to think of a sentence—any sentence that comes to mind—with increasing intensity, to the point of pain, in order to emergency-brake it at full speed, so to speak, at the point of climax. If you repeat this four, five times, each time with a different sentence, it will induce total exhaustion and thereby guarantee sleep; according to Professor Schober.

Sentences pop into your head: The green tree is already on its way. Sky, I like the way you look. Three more mornings to wake up. Everybody is encouraging me— Then you were cozily ensconced—you thought—in an old house with worn-down furniture. You didn't recognize any particular piece, yet it all felt familiar. Through the door you see a woman who comes running toward you across field and meadow, pursued by a man in a blind rage. With infinite slowness—in slow motion—she comes closer. Help is out of the question, you're barely able to wave to her. Finally she's standing in the door, the man close behind her, his panting breath brushes her neck and your face. Just in time you manage to slam the door shut and turn the key, with your last strength. Outside, the man belabors the rotting wood. He kicks at it and throws his weighty body against it. You two anguished women wonder if the weak bolt will hold.

You awake, lying on your left side, on which you're supposed to avoid sleeping. Your legs are drawn up so tightly they hurt, and your arms are numb, asleep. You spent a long time imagining more secure bolts and sturdier doors. You thought the isolated house should have had an inner double door made of a strong light wood that one could reliably close with a key and an iron bolt. However, H. presented half a dozen techniques to easily pass through any door these days; he recommended renouncing the urge to barricade yourself and preparing for a life with wide-open doors which, things being as they were, would be most likely to guarantee protection of the few secrets worth hiding.

On the same day you found a pretext for not attending the only and perhaps important meeting of the month and began concentrating on your writing for good.

The discovery of the heart, which caused Nelly such unusual excitement, may be reported now as well as anywhere else. The heart was one of the few concealed parts of the body whose discovery was not only allowed but even decidedly encouraged. There was nothing indecent about its name, which one could recite to one's heart's content, and even sing out loud. But most importantly, it could be shown in a picture.

Nelly was lying in her father's bed one Sunday morning when she discovered the fold-out heart in a red booklet from the series "Life and Nature," which Bruno Jordan subscribed to. She made him read her the article that was next to the picture and describe the enormous vital effort of a heart. She understood: there was something inside her that had to beat, or else she'd drop dead. Her father guided her hand until she felt the thudding on the left side of her chest. She had never experienced anything quite so magnificent and at the same time so frightening. She kept her hand on the spot and immediately understood—as the article incidentally mentioned —why there were people who couldn't sleep on their left side, for fear of squashing their heart. From then on, Nelly was one of them.

That much is certain. But it's less certain whether or not she was allowed to go to her cousin Manfred's christening, because the numerous fragments of various family celebrations which the memory preserves only rarely apply to one specific occasion.

I hope he makes it, Charlotte Jordan said that Saturday afternoon, when she came back from the emergency baptism of the prematurely born infant, and simply pulled her white store smock over her black dress with the see-through lace sleeves, something she had never done before, as far as Nelly could recall. Let's hope he does, for Liesbeth's sake, after all these years. If he doesn't, I bet she'll go off her rocker.

Because of all of the above, it is most probable that Nelly forced her parents to take her to the official celebration: nothing in the world could have been more interesting than her newly born cousin Manfred. Therefore you conclude that she was the only child allowed to sit at the coffee table in Aunt Liesbeth's narrow living room (all of Aunt Liesbeth's living rooms were narrow and dark, no matter where she moved) after she had peeked through the bedroom door at the beet-red wrinkled face of a baby. Cousin Manfred did survive, thanks to the devotion of the nurse Maria, who spoon-fed him, but he remained extremely delicate and absolutely could not be exposed to germs. It would be premature at this point to describe how Aunt Liesbeth Radde realized her intention to have a delicate son, and how she managed to keep him in a state of dependence. But Nelly's impression that a baptism was something ambiguous, inscrutable, and depressing, perhaps even a trifle indecent, is important, because it would prove more than anything else that she was indeed present.

One thing is certain: Aunt Liesbeth glowed and sparkled. Activities—or rather moods—no one could have suspected of her during later life. A rather rapid decrease of glow and sparkle set in soon after, and its reason should not conclusively be called by a single name: Alfons Radde. Rather recently, an obviously unproven suspicion tentatively places another name next to the first —although in a totally different, even opposing, sense—the name of Dr. Leitner, Aunt Liesbeth's physician. It was in this capacity that he was, incidentally, included in the most intimate family celebration, seated to the right of the happy young mother, while the husband, Uncle Alfons, naturally sat at the head of the table on her left. An arrangement that immediately struck Charlotte Jordan (with her X-ray eyes) as not quite proper, even though she couldn't have known then that her sister Liesbeth had insisted on Dr. Leitner's presence against the emphatic wishes of her husband. It had been the latter's intention to use the occasion of his son's christening to impress his boss, young Bohnsack (Feed and Grain), and his wife, Elfriede, in his role as father, head of household, and host; with the cup collection in the breakfront, and a slender doll in green and black silk pajamas balanced on the top corner of a highly artistic embroidered pillow.

The doll became engraved in Nelly's memory, which does not prove, any more than the remarkably good butter crumbcake which

Whiskers Grandma used to bake for all family occasions, that the christening actually did take place. Nelly had developed a technique of lifting the top off the cake with a slight leverage action of her teaspoon, and setting it aside on her plate, which enabled her to devour at least ten hoarded squares of butter crumbs all at once, a habit that prompted Charlotte Jordan to wonder if her daughter might be a sensualist.

Nelly's preoccupation about whom she might ask for the meaning of the mysterious word "premature" without exposing herself to a rebuff may, to some extent, have distracted her attention from the afternoon's events. From today's perspective, these events must have been far more involved than they seemed to her at the time. At any rate, according to subsequent indications, Charlotte Jordan must have had to do more than her share to "keep matters reasonably under control," and for once she hardly had the time to pay attention to her daughter's character defects.

"Control" was the natural detachment which a person either did or did not possess. The gypsy woman who entered after a brief imperious knock, when schnapps and cordials were being served, unfortunately lacked the appropriate amount of control. In spite of many obsequious apologies on her part, she nonetheless insisted upon coming in and earning the schnapps she had been handed at the door. What did she mean, "earn"? By reading the palms of the esteemed ladies and gentlemen.

There was trouble in the air. Charlotte's urgent whispers made no impression on the gypsy woman (who was, needless to say, sporting Aunt Emmy's green shawl and Aunt Emmy's wart on her upper lip). Thirty years later, after the most dreadful arguments and the final break-up with her sister Liesbeth lay behind her, and her judgment about her sister and her sister's husband was no longer clouded by false considerations, Charlotte Jordan still sympathized with the excruciating embarrassment of the infant's parents. After all, it had been more than just a family affair; there was Dr. Leitner, a most refined man, really, and especially the Bohnsacks, who had also come, in spite of everything, and who had the reputation of being unable to take a joke, and this monster of a gypsy woman had to go grabbing for their hands first. At least she was polite enough to foretell prosperity and riches for the Bohnsacks—which was, in fact, true for both of them, but: no offspring . . . none . . . Why on earth couldn't Aunt Emmy have predicted children for Frau Bohnsack; it would have lifted their spirits and kept Alfons Radde's rage in check.

Aunt Liesbeth was embarrassed in front of Dr. Leitner, her guest of honor. As far as she was concerned, her husband could have his vulgar Bohnsacks pickled in brine. From behind his elegant gold-rimmed glasses, Dr. Leitner viewed the appearance of the gypsy woman with equanimity, toasted Aunt Liesbeth with eggnog, at her request, and became embarrassed only when she seized the opportunity to thank him for her son's having come into the world, which was all his doing.

An unfortunate way of putting it, according to Charlotte.

Would Nelly have a chance to ask the gypsy woman in private what a premature baby was?

Happy Aunt Lucie's fate was and remained no one other than Uncle Walter, the man of her life. That was good to know, for Walter, too, who would attain his life's goal in his work, his career, which the gypsy woman clearly read in his palm. He'd show them how high a locksmith could rise. Being foreman at Anschütz & Dreissig was certainly something, but only the beginning for Walter (the gypsy woman proved to be right in that respect, although no one could know at the time that Walter Menzel would rise to district director, assistant director, and even director in the company which he had entered as an apprentice, and that his position classified him as "essential" during the war, since Anschütz & Dreissig had begun to manufacture certain complicated parts instead of agricultural machinery, parts whose war-essential destination was unknown even to old man Anschütz—thank God, he said.) Even Uncle Walter, Nelly's favorite uncle by far, could not be asked what a premature baby might be.

The gypsy woman had arrived at Uncle Alfons Radde, the infant's father. Well, young lady? he said to her, which was in bad taste. The sad, indecent part was yet to come. Well, young man? she retorted, and studied his left palm for a long time, while he quickly downed another cognac with his right hand. No stinting on our son's christening, certainly not. Later we'll have champagne.

Aiaiai, young man . . .

Is that supposed to be my fortune? She carries on like a nanny goat that's fit to be tied.

Sure, sure, said the gypsy woman. Just give me a minute. But there was no more. She dropped Alfons Radde's hand like a hot potato, in Charlotte Jordan's opinion. It may all work out, was all she added. But then again, maybe not.

She didn't even want to look at Liesbeth Radde's hand. She merely pressed both of them in her own wrinkled hands and said what everybody knew, anyway: her fate was the little boy in the other room, who would grow up to be strong and healthy and beautiful, and talented besides.

Do you hear that! Aunt Liesbeth cried, sparkling again and ready to throw her arms around Dr. Leitner's neck, a gesture he stopped by rearranging the glasses on his nose. Nelly hadn't thought that a man could blush. This eliminated Dr. Leitner, whose quiet refined air had inspired Nelly's confidence, as a possible source of information about premature babies.

He didn't permit the gypsy woman to pass him by without telling his fortune. Although merely a guest, wasn't he, too, entitled to his fate?

Lord Almighty. Don't ask for it, my son.

Cousin Manfred was baptized in the early fall of 1935. It was the very last month that Otto Bohnsack (Feed and Grain) could afford—after some hesitation and consultation with his wife—to sit at the same table with a Jew. (You must have noticed that Dr. Leitner was Jewish?) The gypsy woman called him "my son," and Nelly decided that that was not in bad taste.

All right, all right, the gypsy woman said to Dr. Leitner, you're not so dumb, my son. You're almost farsighted yourself, so to speak.

What do you mean, Madam?

Dr. Leitner was seriously calling the gypsy woman "Madam." And that, too, was not in bad taste. Nobody laughed.

Well, my son, what do you think? You're a bachelor, now and forever. There's no one to tie you down. You're free to come and go as you please. And as you must, you understand?

But what if one has no desire to go, Madam?

Jesus Mary 'n' Joseph. What a child you are. Desire . . . wish . . . that's youth talking. You'll be wishing to go one of these days. And you'll be on your way. You'll become a wanderer. You'll *have* to want to go. You'll forget worrying about offspring. What does the Wandering Jew need a wife and child for?

Enough of that, Alfons Radde finally said. Enough of that nonsense.

Nelly must have asked for her share of the predictions. That's right: she must have been present at Cousin Manfred's christening, because she never forgot what the old woman said to her, after a serious and prolonged study of her hand: Well, look at the little critter. You have nothing to fear. You're lucky, you were born in a caul, you know that? Nothing can harm you. That's how it was. Ambiguous, impenetrable, and ominous. (And it all came true. Or did it!)

Toward the end it even became indecent. The gypsy woman sat down on her cushion at the end of the table, and soon she was emitting noises that were really in bad taste. Everyone thought so. And Charlotte Jordan said so. Everything must, after all, be kept reasonably under control.

Sure, sure, said the gypsy woman. It's my digestive system, everybody has one, but who wants to admit it.

Aunt Emmy always had a tendency to go a bit too far. The years taught Charlotte Jordan a more mellow outlook—but that afternoon it wasn't Aunt Emmy who was the worst. The whole afternoon, the whole celebration, took place on a razor's edge. The baptized infant's parents had invited his or her own special guests of honor, and there was no telling how they were going to react to each other.

A family, said H. (you're still on the road, still driving toward L.—now G.—when the subject of Cousin Manfred comes up), a family is an agglomeration of people of different ages and sexes united to strictly conceal mutually shared embarrassing secrets. Lenka likes the formula, although she can't agree with it. Or: what secrets are her parents hiding from her? You see: H., too, is pensive. (Secrets do exist, unspoken between you. The problem is to realize and accept them.) Lenka is at the painful age between child and adult; she doesn't wish to live with other people's secrets, but can't live without secrets of her own. She hopes as much as she fears that one cannot know "the innermost thoughts" even of people who are closest. You say: Not everything we keep to ourselves is a secret. But how then does one tell if it's a secret? By the pressure it exerts upon you, you say. And as you say it, you're struck by the change secrets undergo from one generation to the next.

Dr. Leitner's office supposedly was directly above Aunt Liesbeth's apartment, in the center of town. The house must have burned to the ground. (Addendum after the trip: the house did burn to the ground; that section of the street has been rebuilt with two rows of new houses, with large store windows on the ground floors, featuring electrical appliances, refrigerators, washing machines, and kitchen stoves.)

Before the so-called takeover, it was convenient for Aunt Liesbeth to consult this particular doctor and none other: we had nothing against Jews. Her subsequent sickly dependence on doctors may not yet have been apparent, and her husband's occasional fits of rage reflected merely on him, not on her. The fits of rage naturally became more frequent after the first official measures against the Jews, but Aunt Liesbeth remained true to her doctor. That's the least she could do, she probably said in her inimitable tone, against which her husband was simply powerless—even later, when she had begun to suffer from nerves and he was reduced to screaming, in vain.

Charlotte Jordan didn't know how the SA boycott of April 1, 1933, affected the practice of the Jew Jonas Leitner in particular, which means that she didn't ask her sister about it. Most likely a pair of SA men stood outside the door of the house, next to the white enamel plate, and prevented anyone who could not prove that he lived in the building from entering and baring his Aryan body before non-Aryan eyes.

(It is, of course, nowhere on record whether a single patient tried to visit Dr. Leitner on that particular day. Assumption: the two SA men stood idly about and were bored.)

Perhaps Leitner had simply closed his office, as he was wont to do, and had taken the two-hour express train to the capital, where hotel rooms were supposedly still being rented to Jews. (You picture him sitting in the train, a thin smile curling the corners of his mouth at the thought of two strapping SA men standing watch outside his empty apartment the entire day.)

Liesbeth and Alfons Radde moved to another apartment soon after the christening of little Manny, to Ludendorffstrasse, a corner house beyond the municipal park. Nobody knew exactly why. The new apartment was hardly larger, three small rooms, and dark, as already mentioned. Alfons was even a stretch farther away from his "office" (as he called Otto Bohnsack's dirty grain yard).

Dr. Leitner did not consider becoming a wanderer for quite some time, despite the gypsy woman's suggestion. He had been living in this town for ten years. So far, he rather likes it, the town is no worse than other towns; not all the people who used to exchange greetings with him still continue to do so. But there are a few who do, even in public. Dr. Leitner takes off his hat to every beggar; but if he senses from a distance—and he does—that someone who knows him, and may even creep into his office in the evening, would prefer not to acknowledge their acquaintance in broad daylight, in front of the people and the white swans in the municipal park, he quickly takes off his gold-rimmed glasses, turns aside, and polishes them intently with his fine linen handkerchief. Or else he steps up to the edge of the water and throws pieces of bread to the swans and ducks from a small bag he carries with him. Dr. Leitner is what you might call a tactful man. Sometimes, someone may suddenly want to say hello to him again, after having looked the other way for some time. In that case, Dr. Leitner —as you would imagine—is the first to take off his hat with a friendly smile.

You've been told that the municipal park is beautifully kept up. (It's true.) You'll soon have to go there, since you were told at the Station Hotel that you cannot check into your rooms until 4 p.m., and walking around the streets is impossible in the heat. Lutz and you are thinking about a shady bench in the municipal park. (The memories of older people seem proof that the sun shone altogether differently in the old days. Now, however, it becomes evident: in other respects the sun has maintained its quality. Strangely enough, this fact fills you with satisfaction. As soon as the river Oder lay behind you, you were back in your childhood summer, which you had given up as irretrievably lost: the dry continental summer that crackled with heat, you've always had a profound feeling for it and have unconsciously compared all subsequent summers to it.)

How is it possible that you never gave a thought to the weeping willow behind the Café Volney in all these years? The sight of it comes as a shock you had not anticipated at this particular spot, nor actually at all. Thoroughly familiar with many fairy tales, Lenka promptly quoted the verse from "Iron Henry," at your request. You needed only the line about: " 'Tis the band about my heart . . ." Why? she asked. No particular reason.

What more could you wish for? To be sitting in this spot, in the half shade of the willow, which you've always considered the most beautiful tree in the world, behind you the dilapidated former Café Volney and the soft gurgling of the Cladow, whose water level is of course extremely low. You imagine that you're sitting on the very same boards of the very same bench on which Liesbeth Radde and Dr. Leitner sometimes briefly sat at noontime.

Your Aunt Liesbeth no longer consults Dr. Leitner. Her husband finally put a stop to it. Dr. Leitner understands her husband quite well, and he smiles at the baby. He now has the feeling that he, Jonas Leitner, will have to become a wanderer one of these days, before it is too late, thank God. He'll write two or three letters to Aunt Liesbeth from America, noncommittal letters which can't compromise her politically. She'll send him harmless postcards, perhaps with the picture of the swan pond and the weeping willow. (To this day, postcards with views of the park are being sold at the newsstand next to the park entrance; you buy a few.)

Yes. How did Dr. Leitner manage to discover the new address of his former acquaintance Liesbeth Radde after the war?— through the Red Cross, most likely. In the summer of 1936, neither Liesbeth Radde nor Jonas Leitner would have imagined that the eleven- or twelve-year-old Manfred Radde (who was in good health, but still extremely delicate) would live on powdered milk, cocoa, and canned meat that had been sent to him from overseas—to Magdeburg on the Elbe, during the worst years of hunger.

Not even Aunt Emmy would have imagined it, although she always said—and what's more, believed—that there wasn't a thing under the sun the good Lord couldn't do. But it had to be this kind of sun, which stimulated a zest for life instead of tiring one out, and which tore the veil which had imperceptibly and steadily grown denser over the years (despite the unchanging results of clinical eye examinations) and obstructed your vision. Regaining your full eyesight—which was perhaps the most important aspect of the entire trip—happened during the half-hour rest outside Witnica (the former Vietz)—27½ miles from Slubice, 13 miles from Kostrzyn—on the side of the road to G., which is in perfect condition, although it's not one of the major highways. Incidentally, this was the road of your remembrance: on the left, toward the north, the edge of the end moraine, sometimes a gentle pine-grown incline, sometimes a steep, sandy, ocher-yellow slope; to the right, the railroad tracks, and immediately behind them, swampland and shrubbery which, for better or worse, concealed the view of the river. The unexpected thrill of joy at coming home, a paradoxical feeling composed of opposite extremes. You said you were thirsty and insisted on a rest. H. had avoided crossing you during the entire drive, now he immediately pulled over to the side and stopped in the shade of one of the crooked cherry trees that line the road.

The bushes were a few steps away on a path across the field. Flat fields on the other side of the road—fodder grain—and to the right a small cluster of houses. Lenka was drinking iced tea with lemon from the red thermos. H. and Lutz were walking around the car, testing the tires with the tips of their shoes. That's when it happened. Suddenly you were able to see again. Colors, shapes: the landscape, in its composition of colors and shapes. Your joy was mixed with a feeling of shock at the thought that one can suffer a gradual loss without missing what one has lost. But your delight predominated.

The others noticed that you were in a good mood.

Well, what did they think of it?

Not bad, said H. Lenka, whose day it was for concessions, said generously: Neat.

She doesn't remember. She won't deny that she drank from the thermos, the photo is proof of that. You're already dealing with the second generation of photographs; incessantly time transforms itself into the past and requires clues, such as exposed celluloid, notes on all kinds of paper, pads, letters, clippings. A part of today invariably serves to preserve the memory of yesterday. You know, although perhaps not consciously, that your undertaking is hopeless. One can never hope to realize the secret goal, at least not as long as one is still alive: to make time eternal by describing it at the very moment of its passing, of its having passed. But how can you wish for time to stop—unless you want to wish for death, which you cannot? Between two impossibilities as usual the banal path of compromise: to sacrifice a portion of your life—but not all of it—to accept the unavoidable gaps of reporting, the use of crutches. Steps hewn into the unconquered mountain, along which memory can grope its way back.

It is probable that you'll remember this overcast, dismal, clammy Sunday morning when you wrote this page: not because of the wet silvery shimmer on the trunk of the pine outside your window, not because of the thin watery layer of snow under the birches, or the blackbirds that are rustling the old leaves under the snow; nor perhaps because of the news that one hour after the truce in Vietnam became effective, South Vietnamese planes dropped a heavy bomb load on the road to Saigon. But solely because of the strangely enjoyable effort you have to make in order to describe the hour you spent on the bench under the weeping willow, one and a half years ago, as though you were sitting in the municipal park in the noon heat right now; but at the same time as though this hour were one of the many which can be remembered simultaneously, though you're aware of where each belongs.

An abundance of images, some of which are thrust in from the outside, while others rise within as though in a daze. Red green blue yellow. Light bulbs. Chains of colored light bulbs hanging over the skating rink in graceful arches. The cheapest colors in the world, candy colors, which always gave Nelly a pang of delight or of pain whenever they suddenly appeared in front of a black winter sky. A sensation no other colors ever caused again.

Joy, yes, even reverence, admiration, delight. Even the rink phonograph must obey this powerful signal: RED GREEN BLUE YELLOW: Ali, the owner of the foodstand, who rented out skates and sold hot beverages, instantly left his counter and turned on the record "Do you hear my secret calling," and the best skaters formed a wide outer ring and began circling the rink with the most glorious arabesques, with the greatest of ease, as though it were mere child's play, aware of the wave of admiration and burning envy that rose toward them from the inner circle, where others painfully plowed about on their skates. For two years Nelly was among the skaters of the outer circle, and there were few things she would not have sacrificed to hear the waltz under the strings of lights. A stupid, indelible nostalgia remains. Whether absurd or not—it chose to manifest itself on that hottest of days, so close to the original location.

All kinds of people are strolling through the park. A young Aunt Liesbeth, pushing her baby carriage, would not look at all out of place. A thought which must be ascribed to the heat, and the daze of fatigue. Aunt Liesbeth has to be sitting in the West German city, driving her husband—who is once again distributor for the relocated company of Otto Bohnsack, Feed & Grain—crazy with her various imaginary illnesses. The two blond-braided girls beside you on the bench, who are whispering their secrets into each other's ear, since they can't know that you don't understand a word of their language, would probably get up at once if a woman with a baby carriage wanted to sit down; they'd walk off arm in arm, giggling—as they're doing right now—across the small bridge of unhewn birch trunks and past the stern old man in the black jacket and the black hat. Aunt Liesbeth would sit down beside you . . . and that's as far as you dare go, in your daze, your dream state, because your Aunt Liesbeth will never again sit beside you on a bench, you'll never set eyes on her again (never say never!), although she's alive, that's pretty certain. She'll stop sending her yearly commemorative wreath for the grave of her sister Charlotte, who'll have been dead for almost three years on that blistering July 10, 1971.

At the spot where the two lovers are sitting at the edge of the swan pond, or close to it, Bruno Jordan once slept off a hangover. Altogether contrary to other hangovers before and after, this particular one was deemed worthy of becoming family legend, together with the statement (obviously made by Aunt Liesbeth Radde): nothing less than a gentleman would do for Charlotte. Consequently, you ask yourself why Nelly's mother—head bookkeeper at Mulack's Cheese Factory, at the age of twenty-five—had her heart set on a gentleman. Anyone who knew her only in her white store smock, resolutely tackling whatever chore had to be done, dragging sacks of sugar into the storage room, sorting herring, and scrubbing the floor with ammonia, will raise surprised eyebrows, nothing more. But if one confronted her character—which was proud and unyielding—with the circumstances to which it was exposed: not only the poverty. No: also the humiliation . . .

The incident of the kowtow, for instance. Nelly couldn't stand it when Charlotte recalled the incident. Which she didn't do very often. But Charlotte finally wanted someone to imagine the feelings of a child who is being scrubbed clean by her mother shortly before Christmas, together with her sisters and her brother, and whose hair is being neatly braided in order to convey the image of a trustworthy family to Railroad Inspector Witthuhn, the man who had the power either to fire Hermann Menzel, Whiskers Grandpa, just before the holidays, or to let him go on punching tickets in his little ticket house. Frau Auguste had to promise said gentleman with much sobbing that from now on her husband would arrive sober, stone sober, on the job; while, on a signal from their mother, the children silently sank to their knees before Inspector Witthuhn.

The daughter wants to believe that her mother has never forgiven her father for this episode. But she'd rather not talk with her about it. She feels that it is improper to relive the shame of the child who would later become her mother.

On the other hand, when happier events are being discussed, she has to hide her burning envy of occasions in which she didn't participate. You weren't there yet—that's easily said, but hard to fathom. Wherever was she supposed to have been? Everybody isn't there at the beginning, until the parents get married, Frau Elste declared. In that case, it is conceivable that two parents don't meet, that they don't marry, and that a person who was destined to be born simply loses out and doesn't come into the world. But, silly, that happens all the time. Just think about all the children that couldn't be born because their fathers died as young soldiers in the war. What do those children who aren't born think? They think nothing at all. Nothing? Can't you understand: a thing that doesn't exist can't think, or feel, or whatever.

It was the most hopeless thing anyone could have said to her. Nelly had to take serious measures so as not to be destroyed by the thought. She realized that she couldn't push her nightly fantasies to the point where she risked sinking back into the Big Nowhere herself. She felt certain that it was more than a simple transgression. It was a serious crime, the most serious perhaps—having to visualize every limb of her body being led back to nothingness, every night, while a flickering sensation spun in her head and joints that was not at all unpleasant, but in fact rather beautiful as it picked up speed. Rather sweet, delicious, and enticing. The thought of the bang—if she'd still be able to hear it—with which she would have to explode if she only made her spin a tiny bit faster—

The risk was too great. One evening, she threatened herself that she would break a leg the next morning—a terrifying thought: the cracking of bones—if she didn't stop her game. Different thoughts were the only effective antidote. The thrill of self-destruction was balanced by the joy of self-creation. There existed a magic chain, which the good Lord Himself had strung together, link by marvelous link, to pull a child from the Big Nowhere one fine day, a child in whom He took great interest, whose name then became Nelly. For a person He didn't care about, He would hardly have taken the trouble to link two downright infinite lines of the most felicitous coincidences so skillfully that a miracle resulted.

The good Lord had not hesitated to precede the ultimate miracle with a number of smaller ones. Because it was a miracle—Bruno Jordan said so himself—that he had come out of the mess at Verdun; that total strangers, instruments of a Higher Purpose, in the dirt-encrusted uniforms of soldiers, had dug her father—who had as yet not become her father—from the collapsed foxhole in which he lay unconscious; that they dragged him to the field hospital, which saved his life, although not all of his memory; that the two escape attempts from French captivity ended in recapture and solitary without food, but not in death. And that he lived through the first pea soup—doled out to the returning starving prisoners of war, in the Weinberg Inn—on which he had choked, terrified at the thought that his time was up. (At least his family recognized the twenty-two-year-old man who had been cheated out of the best years of his youth, and was coming home; twenty-eight years later, when he came back for the second time, he had changed beyond recognition.)

The task consisted of bringing about a meeting between the saved soldier—who becomes an employee in the office of an industrial company, acquires a cane with an ivory handle and a round straw hat known as a boater, and, thus attired, frequents the city's amusement spots (he was a gay blade, and this was the term he used to describe himself), possessed by the urge to catch up with his bungled youth, as though it were an express train that a good racing car might catch up with—The task, then, consisted of bringing about a meeting between this man and a certain Charlotte Menzel: single, twenty-five years of age, a bookkeeper known for her efficiency and solid principles. A job well done. Nelly is able to begin with the happy ending as she tells the story to herself, and she giggles in her bed. She couldn't have done a better job herself.

Bruno Jordan joins the rowing club. This leads to a friendship with a certain Gustel Stortz, who works at the town hall and is also a gay blade. In turn, Gustel Stortz makes the casual acquaintance (the word casual must be stressed) of Mieze Heese—a sharp operator, who is Catholic, by the way, and therefore devious— assistant bookkeeper at Alfred Mulack's, although not for much longer, because she's after the boss's son, who is going to pot without her help. At any rate: Mieze Heese is still able to celebrate her twenty-fifth birthday in style, God bless her, devious, manipulative, sharp-tongued, man-crazy, and whatever else she may be. She needed two extra gentlemen for her dinner party: her casual acquaintance Gustel Stortz, who must promise to bring a friend, no matter whom—so he was told—as long as said friend could dance. Bruno Jordan. It must be noted that the birthday hostess knows neither his face nor his name. (Paule Madrasch, a clerk at the savings bank, would have qualified equally well, but that particular evening he happened to be "indisposed.") Bruno Jordan, whom Mieze Heese seats next to her stuck-up colleague Charlotte, whom she couldn't get around inviting, even though she can't stand her.

The groundwork has been laid. The good Lord can afford to take a break.

Bruno Jordan arrived in a tuxedo, the perfect gentleman. He brought flowers for the hostess, he rose when his table partner got up, he held her chair when she wanted to sit down: and he served her salad. He danced a great deal with her, and he knew how to bow when the dance was over. All of this must have been balm to Charlotte's soul—she was proud, but not invulnerable—and she had vowed: I don't care what he is like as long as he isn't vulgar. Even drunk—which he became toward midnight—his conduct must still have been acceptable, even if the homemade currant wine went straight to his legs as he stepped outside into the fresh air. He nonetheless insisted on escorting his lady home.

It is surprising that she lets him. But for the good Lord, nothing under the sun is impossible, once He has made up His mind. Nor under the moon. Which is shining down on the stone stoop outside Number 95 Küstrinerstrasse. Which you looked at, as you drove past, because everything is still standing: the stoop, the sparse front garden with its box hedge and its rhododendron, and behind it, the house itself: the archway to the Mulack Cheese Factory, which used to be in the courtyard.

It is on this stoop that Charlotte Menzel leaves her escort, who is smashed, to put it mildly. She herself races to the front door, which she hastily unlocks and relocks from the inside. She flies up the stairs (to the second floor), unlocks and relocks the apartment door—again in greatest haste—and tiptoes hurriedly down the hall to her room, rushes to the window, looks out and sees . . . Well? (Nelly has to crawl under the covers, not to wake her brother with her loud giggling.) Well? What does Charlotte see? Nothing. There's no Bruno on the stoop. A clear pale moonlight is falling onto the stone; nothing else. Until her dying day, Charlotte can't understand how her escort got away so fast.

Bruno Jordan can't tell her, either. Because this is where the other memory gap occurred in her father's life. Nelly believes it fervently. A memory gap of five hours and thirty minutes, because at 6:30 A.M. on the dot, the municipal park guards start their work, in the summer time: picking up litter, raking the paths, emptying the trash baskets, straightening the Keep Off the Grass signs, etc.

It is Park Guard Nante (Nante Red-Nose, Nante the Souse, who used to shoulder his shovel and rush into the crowd whenever he heard his name called: which is how Nelly met him eventually, but she has three and a half more years to spend in the Big Nowhere.) It was Nante, then, who came upon the corpse of a drowned man, lying four yards from the water's edge that early morning. Nante, who felt that it was his duty to shake the corpse by the shoulder, at least tentatively, and watched in terror when the young corpse rose to its feet and walked to the edge of the pond to wash face and hands and smooth down the hair upon which the boater that the perplexed Nante handed him was then neatly placed by the resurrected man, who handed him an open pack of Juno cigarettes, for lack of loose change. An' here I thought you was a corpse, poor Nante is supposed to have muttered loudly a number of times in succession. He was a handyman totally unaware of the Higher Purpose.

But now comes the most important part. At 7:30 a.m., as Charlotte Menzel enters her office, the phone on her desk starts ringing. It's her escort from the night before, wishing her a fine good morning, in the clear, bright voice of a man who has slept his fill. As good manners demand. He thanks her for the beautiful evening she granted him. And then he asks the question—which must have decided everything, considering the tone in which Charlotte repeated it for many years to come—Fräulein Menzel, where do you think I slept last night?

There was something irresistible about the man, even in the opinion of his future mother-in-law, Auguste Menzel, Whiskers Grandma, who spent two weeks in the seaside resort of Swinemünde with the engaged couple and the dog Whiskers (a kind of engagement present from cheese manufacturer Alfred Mulack, who had been given the animal—for which he had no use—by a business friend from the Balkans). The son-in-law, who was more than a head taller than the plump little woman, had photos taken of both of them in front of the wicker beach loungers, his eternal straw hat in his left hand, and his right arm placed ostentatiously around her shoulder.

The photo irritated Nelly every time she looked at it. It was the same irritation that came over her at the end of fairy tales, when the satisfaction that everything had turned out all right and that the heroes had sunk into each other's arms after all the excitement and complicated trials was nonetheless mixed with a barely admitted touch of disappointment, especially at the conclusion: And they lived happily ever after . . . A somewhat dry, banal, frankly unnecessary statement that might have been left out. Just as Bruno Jordan's arm on his mother-in-law's large-flower print summer dress might perhaps have been left out; or at least the straw hat in his left hand. Nelly wasn't sure, and she didn't really want to be sure. Who was she to find fault with the endings of fairy tales? Besides, Nelly's irritation may have been because of the wicker beach loungers. It was as though they formed a chorus behind the backs of the group, whispering: And they lived happily . . . happily . . .

No. It was because of another photo that always appeared in front of Nelly's eyes when she thought of the picture at the beach in Swinemünde: A portrait of her mother, taken by Richard Knispel, 81 Richtstrasse, in 1923. For many years, this portrait hung under glass in Whiskers Grandma's living room. Nelly has memorized it, for moments such as these, when it is no longer in existence. She fully realizes that the soft brown of the overall picture is Master Photographer Knispel's doing. It nonetheless never fails to make an impression on her. But most of all, is it conceivable that her mother knew a different kind of life, when she was able to wear such a brownish dress with a white jabot and a lace collar, and especially such a wagon wheel of a hat (in which she looked wonderful, but since when do mothers pay attention to the way they look?), and walk along Richtstrasse and enter Knispel's photo studio, and order a portrait. With her hat on.

Even a blind man could see that her mother was beautiful, no matter what she wore. But Nelly couldn't say why she derived such infinite consolation from the fact that there had been a time when her mother had wanted to be beautiful. (Not only the hat. No: especially the look, a slanted look from under the hat!) At any rate, over the years this look took on a pained expression that always made two lines of Frau Elste's favorite song come to Nelly's mind, despite herself: "And marble statues gaze with eyes so mild . . . What has been done to you, my poor dear child?"

So much for that, too much perhaps. One more thing, though: it was the memory of the photograph that stifled the daughter's protest many years later, when her mother said to her: You're so much like me, if you only knew! Although the daughter refuses to admit that the compulsion to use her mother's gestures, looks, and words grows stronger as she grows older. She catches herself at imitations she would never have thought possible.

She does not, however, own a photo of herself in a hat.

5

Force won't milk a bull: one of Charlotte Jordan's favorite sayings.

What has happened to reason throughout the decades, reason as grounds for approval. Reason as the damper. A regulating mechanism which, once installed, stubbornly insists on flashing the "happiness" signal only under certain reasonable conditions . . .

A reasonable child gets kissed good night.

Once, Nelly throws all five geranium pots from the nursery window onto the sidewalk, one by one, and then she refuses to sweep up the pieces. She must have lost her mind. Late that evening she is able to explain: she was beside herself with rage, because Herr Warsinski said that the Führer is spelled with a capital F. But, goodness, Nelly, that's the way it's spelled. What do you mean: he told us to capitalize everything in the German language that can be seen and touched. Nelly can neither see nor touch the Führer (this was in 1936, before the invention or, at any rate, before the use of television). Be sensible! You can't, but you could. Dum-dum. Herr Warsinski had also called her a dum-dum. But Nelly can't stand it when her teacher contradicts himself. To test him—not without foreboding—she does not capitalize the noun "cloud" (it can be seen, but not touched), despite her parents' adamant opposition. Teacher Warsinski is no liar. Nor does he forget. But how can Nelly give in when she knows she's right?

It soon becomes apparent that Nelly is the only dum-dum in her class; everyone else has capitalized the noun "cloud." Everyone's allowed to laugh at her, good and loud: One, two, three, laugh! Nelly did take the initiative to capitalize the noun "rage," even though rage can neither be seen nor touched nor heard nor smelled nor tasted. She is finally listening to reason.

Understanding and listening to reason. Thus: to come to one's senses. (Come to your senses!) Throwing down the geranium pots was the last incident you remembered about Sonnenplatz, after you'd all climbed back into the boiling hot car; Lenka showed no interest. Only sometime later—you were driving down the former Friedrichstrasse, Nelly's first route to school—did you realize the repetition, and not without inner resistance: Nelly's rejection of certain incidents her mother used to remember. You began musing about the vicissitudes to which reason can be subjected; reason and irrationality changing places suddenly, in times of upheaval; the enormous spreading of insecurity before each has been re-established and defined. But none of this belongs here; unused reason, atrophying like any untrained organ; the withdrawal of reason, at first imperceptible. One day it becomes apparent—perhaps because of an unexpected question—that important regions of the interior landscape are occupied by resignation, or at least by indifference. (The question, Lenka's question, that is yet to be answered: Actually, what do you all believe in? Not arrogantly asked by the way. She did want to know.) All of this probably doesn't belong here.

A retractable opinion: why should yesterday's (February 20, 1973) statement by U.S. President Richard Nixon not belong here: At no time during the postwar development had the prospects for lasting peace been as favorable as at this very moment. On what grounds can you suppress this suspicion: whether the fact that during the last couple of years you have anticipated catastrophes less and less—confirming that the postwar era is drawing to a close—whether this has influenced the choice of your subject matter. There is nonetheless something arbitrary about timing: should a reporter not hesitate to sever himself from a past that may still be evolving inside him, and can therefore not be mastered? (H. says: Naturally. You can sit to your dying day, recollecting and taking notes, living and reflecting on the process. But that can become dangerous. One has to draw the line somewhere, before one reaches the end of one's rope.

"When lived as the theme for a description, life acquires a certain importance and can make history." You discuss Brecht's theory for a long time and finally reject it. It's not greatness that can be striven for. What is it, then? That's hard to formulate. Understanding, maybe?)

" 'Tis perilous to wake the lion."—Charlotte Jordan knows her poetry. "The Bell" by Schiller is a poem Bruno Jordan knows, too; he was forced to learn it by heart in elementary school, and it has been saved from time, an undamaged chunk of memory. This day, the bell must be brought forth! Onward, workers, to your . . . It is: Briskly, workers, to your tasks. Bruno Jordan: Must you always put me down! Apart from *pain* he knows other things in French, whole sentences. For instance, when the woman in whose house he had been billeted in Versailles discovered that his buddies had stolen the ham she'd hung up to smoke, while he, Bruno, distracted her with card tricks: *Oh, Monsieur Bruno, un filou!*

Must you brag about stealing, in front of the children!

All's fair in love and war, for God's sake.

Almost everything belongs in here: it has come to that. The suction this work exerts is getting stronger. There no longer is anything you can say, hear, think, do, or not do, that doesn't somehow touch this web. The mutest summons is recorded, forwarded, turned up, turned down, rerouted onto tracks that are mysteriously connected, in ways that are unpredictable, out of the range of your influence and, to your regret: indescribable. Of course you have fits of discouragement in the face of the thicket which cannot be disentangled and which devours the very second in which you place the period at the end of this sentence. Reflecting, recollecting, cutting swathes through the jungle with your description (while attempting to report not only what was, but also how it feels)—which requires a certain, readily upsettable balance of seriousness and recklessness. It remains a makeshift solution. A gimmick, which leads to other gimmicks.

The concept is always infinitely more beautiful than the finished product.

Soon a sort of stalemate comes about, composed of equal parts of eagerness and disgust, self-confidence and self-doubt, which looks like laziness on the outside and produces excuses as long as the real reasons for the paralysis remain hidden. Subterfuges. On TV, Apollo 14's three astronauts have just disappeared behind the moon (February 3, 1971; nobody remembers exact dates any more.) The duration of interruption of communication with earth had been calculated in advance, to the precise second. The astronauts had to follow the plan or risk cosmic death. Deviation tolerance plus minus zero. This means that the actual size of all separate parts used in the capsule and in the landing vehicle must be defined within the same maximum and minimum specifications. (Whether you admit it or not, you too have visions of the one and only form of saving grace, slender, beyond reproach, and on target, like those missiles, for which their builders have tender names and tender glances. Technical perfection fills you with cool admiration, perhaps even a certain consternation, which can easily change to disinterest, but when applied to yourself, the possibility of your being too far off the mark of said description is most important to you.)

Precisely on course, *Kitty Hawk* races earthward. There's no one to calculate the ideal curve for you to hold to. Nor would the builders of spaceships conceive of taking their constructions apart in mid-flight, in order to explain how they work, something you foolishly feel compelled to do. But then, no one will die if you fail in your endeavor, and therefore it would not attract attention. (It is certainly no consolation that the names of space victims no longer appear in the newspapers ten days after an accident. You leafed through the papers of July 9 and 10, 1971, which you had taken along, to make sure. The names of the three Soviet cosmonauts who had been "found dead in the landing capsule which had landed on schedule" on June 30 were no longer mentioned. You had to go to the library and check through the bound volume of newspapers, in order to insert the names here, the men whose tragedy had brought tears to your eyes: Georgi Dobrovolsky, Vladislav Volkov, Viktor Patsayev. Any man in the street could more easily name names of World War II, but that's a matter of generations. And the young could give you the names of their favorite rock singers.) Parallel actions.

Friedrichstrasse is a long walk for the legs of six-year-old Nelly. For the car it's no distance. But first of all you want to go to the hotel. You have a parting of ways at the much-mentioned Fröhlich house: Nelly passes it on the left, and goes up Schlachthofgasse, where she has to wait for a herd of cattle to be driven through the gates of the slaughterhouse. To get to Girls' Elementary III (at the beginning of Adolf-Hitlerstrasse), she has to cross Soldinerstrasse and turn into Hermann-Göringstrasse. She is on time, as always. The day starts with religion, with Herr Warsinski. Whereas you drive past the new glass-and-concrete building that has replaced the destroyed Fröhlich house (on your left) and drive a couple of hundred yards along the former Küstrinerstrasse. The time it takes Lenka to sing: "Freedom, oh, freedom . . ." in her high clear voice. To the right, by the way, somewhere behind the first row of houses, used to be Uncle Emil Dunst's candy factory. An uncle who had a candy factory!

"And before I'll be a slave, I'll be buried in my grave . . ."

During the thirties, Uncle Emil Dunst returned to L. with Aunt Olga, Bruno Jordan's sister, with all their possessions, from Leipzig, the capital of Saxony. Broke, of course. Once again dependent on the couple of thousand marks which his in-laws lent him for the sake of their unfortunate daughter, to allow him to make a fresh start and buy the Jew Geminder's candy factory. A sad-looking place, according to Charlotte Jordan; but Emil Dunst and his business partner, who, unlike him, had experience with candy making, bought it cheap, because the Jew Geminder was in a hurry to leave the country. This was in 1937. Unjust gain prospereth not. That's the way Whiskers Grandma saw it. Although any other man might not have paid a penny to the Jew Geminder, who was sitting on hot coals, you might say. Nevertheless, said Charlotte Jordan, who washed her hands of the whole thing, like Pontius Pilate. However, as Nelly had been personally informed by Herr Warsinski in her religion class, Pontius Pilate had delivered the Jew Jesus Christ to the cross. Charlotte didn't like to be corrected by her daughter.

". . . And go home to my Lord, and be free . . ."

Later we'll look for the entrance to Emil Dunst's candy factory, Lenka, and I'll tell you about the festive sensation Nelly used to have, watching the red and green hard candy—freshly cut, still transparent, warm and sticky—come out of the machine, into which it had been poured as a hot viscous mass, from large vats. And how they'd sit in the evenings—Nelly, her mother, Whiskers Grandma, and Lutz, too, on occasion—wrapping candy which Uncle Emil Dunst was to pick up with his three-wheel delivery car in the morning, ready for mailing. Super, Lenka said. Or how brandy-filled pralines, freshly coated with shiny chocolate, six in a row, moved across the production room on a conveyor belt, while they were drying. Then they were ready to be packed into boxes in the next room by two women packers, who could be supervised in their work by Aunt Olga, sitting behind a glass door, enthroned in the office keeping the books—Aunt Olga, who grew fatter and fatter under our very eyes, which was attributed to either the over- or the under-activity of certain unspecified glands; Aunt Olga, who now found herself compelled to hold her chin in a regal posture, while her fingers stayed nimble and slender through the years.

One of the two packers was a Frau Lude, a name that gradually invaded and spoiled the family atmosphere. That Lude woman again . . . He was with that bitch of a Lude . . . Aunt Olga, sitting stiffly erect on the Jordans' sofa, her head regally supported by her double chin, while a single tear, which Nelly will never forget, trickled out from under her rimless glasses and ran down her cheek. Nelly knows that none other than loose Frau Lude is to blame for that tear—that woman whom Charlotte Jordan wouldn't touch with a ten-foot pole, but who has the men eating out of her hand with just one look of her eyes. Because, according to Heinersdorf Grandpa, that hussy's got the pecker showing in her eyes. A statement he is not allowed to repeat, but which Nelly would not have understood even if he had.

"Freedom . . . Oh, freedom . . ."

Later I'll tell you the rest, Lenka, the tragicomedy. At this point you've stopped in front of the hotel that used to be the Station Hotel and which now manages the former Central Hotel on the opposite side of the street, where your brother, Lutz, has reserved your rooms by telegram. The lobby is modest. The receptionist, a friendly middle-aged woman, speaks a little German. She knows nothing of cabled reservations, nor of a cabled confirmation. But that's no reason to panic. She makes a number of phone calls while you look at the pictures on the walls.

A hand-drawn map of the town which, as you instantly realize, does not completely correspond to the map that has been indelibly engraved in your memory. A list of cafés, gas stations. (You suddenly remember the banner with the slogan that used to run across the entire inside wall of the station hall: *Visit the Town of Lakes and Forests!* The station is new; that is, it has been rebuilt differently. The one you knew had supposedly been bombed by German planes shortly after the takeover by the Red Army.) A large photo of St. Mary's Church, another of the municipal theater, in which they used to play *The Frog Prince, Snow White,* or *The Brave Little Tailor,* at Christmastime, when Nelly used to run a fever from sheer excitement and always got sick after the performance; she was allowed to wear her little white fur cape and sit in one of the front rows. The fur—bleached rabbit—and its odor resurfaced in your mind after all these years, just when the receptionist told you that there were two rooms available and that you could check in at 4 p.m.

It was exactly twelve noon.

Did the smile on the receptionist's face mean that she had guessed the reason for your trip (not so difficult to do), that she had understood why you'd spent so much time looking at the photograph of a small-town theater? Besides, she must have read the place of birth on Lutz's and your papers. She and a young assistant copied your data into the registration forms. The woman said that, in Poland, young people didn't receive their identity papers until they were eighteen, not at fourteen, like Lenka. Her assistant nodded.

Nice, both of them, Lenka said when you were back in the street. The sun on the right is now directly above the station clock. The heat has been waiting for you.

Where to now?

Home, Lutz and you said in one breath.

Meanwhile, Nelly—to return to Nelly—has gone inside her classroom. With a feeling of foreboding she walks past objects whose spelling only Herr Warsinski is the authority on. (Since Herr Warsinski's name ends in *i*, certain people think that he might be of Polish descent. If he spelled his name with a *y*, that would not be the case. The hip injury which still makes him limp was inflicted by a Frenchman in the First World War. Every poke a French bloke, every concussion a Russian.)

Nelly loves Herr Warsinski. Undamaged, he rests in her memory in different poses. He enters on command. His face and chest. A wart on the left side of his chin, full, not to say flabby, cheeks; a strand of ash-blond hair sweeps over his right eye, which is watery-colorless. Or his entire figure: in that case usually walking, with a slightly dragging left leg. Speaking: May we have silence, please! And I mean right now! Where do you think you are, in a Jew school! With or without his brown uniform, with or without his belt support across a slight paunch. Anyone who lets me down when we salute the flag is really going to get it. Our Führer works day and night for us and you can't even keep your traps shut for ten minutes.

Herr Warsinski's ten minutes wasn't quite accurate, but that didn't matter at all and is being recorded here only for the sake of precision. On the Führer's birthday, the salute to the flag plus the speech by the principal, Herr Rasenack, took a good twenty-five minutes. Herr Rasenack, principal and SA deputy of the National Socialist Party, is seriously concerned about the Nordic soul. Nelly isn't cold in her gray imitation-lamb coat. She's wearing two pigtails with yellow barrettes. Of course that's unimportant as far as the Führer's forty-seventh birthday is concerned, but Gundel Neumann, the doctor's daughter, has thick long braids, and they're even blond. She succeeds with the greatest of ease in all the things others vainly wish for. For instance, for no special reason Herr Warsinski puts a hand on her shoulder, in passing. The soul is race seen from within. Race is the soul seen from without. Herr Rasenack has a round head, a neat dark brush of a mustache on the upper lip, and a small though gradually expanding bald spot. His kneecap is coming through, as Bruno Jordan would say, if this weren't the principal. Anyone who is genuinely moved surely won't notice the hole in the index finger of his right red woolen glove, which he must get off his hand before the salute to the flag starts and all right hands fly up in the air. Anyone who is genuinely moved surely won't notice the two inches of slip, which are showing on the right side of the skirt of the Jungmädel who has stepped up to the flag; a properly moved person would surely concentrate on the girl's glowing eyes. "My will is your faith" (Adolf Hitler).

Hoist the flag!

And after that, anticipated all the time, the bother about Nelly's right arm. It's true, supposedly, that her arm muscles have stayed weak. Parallel bars and push-ups were out of the question, even later. However, she'd have to hold it stretched forward for one hundred seconds, the time it takes to sing the "Deutschland" and the "Horst Wessel" songs. During "Mass und Memel, Etsch und Belt," it was still all right. "Deutschland, Deutschland, über alles" propelled even lame arms to jubilant heights. But during the repetition of the moving assertion: "Our comrades killed by Red Front and Betrayal . . . in spirit march among us in our ranks," Nelly was obliged, come what may, to support her right arm with her left, and Herr Warsinski never failed to look over at her just that second. "Within a hundred years the swastika will become the life blood of the German nation" (Adolf Hitler). Nelly faithfully obeys the order to exercise her arm at home, and finally she is able to stand through all three verses of both hymns, keeping it raised. Except that, unfortunately, Herr Warsinski never notices. Nor does he ever hit on the idea of having a breath-holding contest in his class, even though such a contest would have revealed that Nelly achieved record times in this particular discipline, a minute and a half or more. Or that she was able to recite the tongue twister "Der Potsdamer Postkutscher putzt den Potsdamer Postkutschkasten" ten times in a row at breakneck speed, without making a mistake. Or that a personality such as Blendax Max was taking a special interest in her. After she had mailed him the required ten Blendax pictures, he promptly sent her congratulations on every birthday. Blendax Max is good and kind,/Blendax kids are on his mind. It would have been unthinkable to use another toothpaste; that would have been treason. Blendax kids afar and near/hold their Blendax Maxie dear.

All her accomplishments mean absolutely nothing to Herr Warsinski, whereas he disapprovingly notices every one of her short-comings. One day, her threes aren't marching straight and erect in rank and file inside the small red boxes on the blackboard, they float above the lines like trusting swallows, and the worst of it is that Nelly can't understand the cause for any criticism, until Ursel's orderly marching column of threes demonstrates the extent of her aberration and Herr Warsinski feels prompted to pose one of his dreaded questions, which she can't answer, neither with a pleading embarrassed smile nor with soothing gestures, least of all with words: he is asking if she is maybe trying to make fun of him?

Why on earth is she unable to assure him of the contrary? Or reach for his hand, as meek Christel Jugow manages to do, even after she has been slapped in the face; he seems to like that, even if he pulls his hand away. Sometimes Nelly thinks he has noticed that she knows something about him. Then she quickly looks down, not to give herself away. Which may look like a guilty conscience to him. Can't you look a person in the eye? Do you have something to hide?

Herr Warsinski notices everything. At one point he wants to know which girls wash their chests in ice-cold water, to steel themselves, as befits a German girl. Nelly is not among those who can proudly raise their hands, and she is scolded: Not you, either? I'm disappointed, especially in you. "The athletically disciplined person of either sex is the citizen of the future" (Adolf Hitler).

Is it a step forward if Nelly distinguishes herself with Herr Warsinski only by the disappointments she causes him? She can't ask her outraged mother these questions. Her mother is trying to prove to her that the water that runs from the tap into the tub is almost cold. Completely cold, in fact. But not ice-cold! So what? Do you have to announce that in front of the entire class? Here, hold your hand under the tap. Is this water cold, or not?

Lukewarm, Nelly says.

More cold than warm.

Not ice-cold, in any case.

Charlotte worries about her daughter's truth mania, while Nelly, perhaps not consciously, increases her efforts to guess Herr War-sinski's expectations of her. It turns out to be difficult to discuss the subject with Lenka. Her attempts to understand this child are bound to fail. The idea that one might crave the favor of one's teacher is simply foreign to her, she considers it the height of insanity. And as to her relationship to truth, it has eased since her early childhood. She's always been able to lie admirably whenever she deemed it appropriate, without ever doubting that she was basically an honest person. She distinguishes between important issues and trifles.

You remembered her outrage when Ruth, her older sister, reported a theory which her German teacher, Herr M., seriously defended in private: that one must be able to improve a weak poem by means of intelligent interpretation, merely because the poem is part of the subject of the final exam. The main point: not to think, personally, that the poem is any good. Ruth's confusion, which outraged Lenka more than the teacher's split personality, could be explained only by the fascination this man held for her. He was able to prove any theory and then prove the contrary in the next class. And he'd smile irritatingly when she wanted to know what he really thought. Then, during German seminar, he insisted on a new seating arrangement. They took apart the conventional rows of benches, which had forced everybody to stare at the back of the head in front of him, rather than look a classmate in the face, and arranged the tables into a square so that the teacher no longer occupied a prominent place himself. Two days after his suicide—Ruth had left the school meanwhile—Lenka found the old established seating arrangement reinstated in German seminar. The cleaning woman had complained. The class rearranges the benches in a square, but is forced to push them back into rows at the end of the seminar. Lenka cries at home. A person is hardly dead, and immediately they destroy everything he's left behind.

At the news of Herr M.'s suicide, it was not Lenka who cried, it was Ruth.

Nelly's classroom. You couldn't describe it. Beige walls, probably. You're sure of the tops of the three linden trees outside the windows. The classroom must have been on the third floor, toward the front, overlooking Adolf-Hitlerstrasse. In the corner, immediately next to the door, an iron stand with an enamel basin: no one ever washes his hands there. It is for the balls of tin foil which were collected during the week for metal recycling. Herr Warsinski's favorite student was allowed to pull the pieces apart during the first lesson on Monday morning (religion). If it happens to be winter, the blue candles for the Association of Germans in Foreign Lands are burning on the benches. Herr Warsinski is convinced that Jesus Christ would be a follower of our Führer were he once again to walk this earth. In passing, Herr Warsinski places his hand on a number of shoulders. On Gundel Neumann's shoulder in any case, but also on the shoulder of Usch Gass, her girlfriend, whose father is a lawyer, even on Lori Tietz's shoulder, the noodle manufacturer's daughter, to whom he recommends a new recipe for the making of macaroni: Simply drill a hole into the air and wrap the noodle dough around it. Never does he lay his hand on Nelly's shoulder. Helping poorer fellow Germans is helping the Führer. The class sings: "Who's knocking there? Two folk in sorry plight. What seek ye here? A shelter for the night. For God's love, do not forsake us. Oh no, no, oh no! Oh, force us not to go. It must be so! Our thankfulness we'll show." For instance, Nelly Jordan's mother has given Nelly's used clothes to Ella Busch's mother; that's a good deed.

Nelly feels like crawling under her bench. Until that day, Ella Busch had pursued Nelly with offers of friendship. For the following noon, at the slaughterhouse, Ella organizes an assault on Nelly with her brothers from Boys Elementary. They've kneaded stones into their snowballs. Nelly knows she's got to get through. She straps her schoolbag across her chest, shields her head with her lunch box, and, screaming hideously, crashes through the barrier. A teacher from Boys Elementary takes down Nelly's name. Three days later, Herr Warsinski wonders in front of his class how a girl like Nelly got mixed up in a fight with boys. Gundel, who is busying herself with the tin foil in the enamel basin, sticks her tongue out at Herr Warsinski. There are always those who can't stop giggling, and others who can't keep their mouth shut. Like that chalk-faced Ursel, the major's daughter. Gundel stuck her tongue out at you, Herr Warsinski. Nelly raises her hand: No, at me!

Gundel is sent to her seat. Nelly is allowed to take her place at the washstand. Behind Herr Warsinski's back, Gundel taps her forehead to show Nelly that she thinks she's nuts. What's more, the place at the washbasin isn't really such a privilege. During recess she assures Gundel that she'd been trying to get her off the hook. Thanks for nothing, Gundel says, and walks off with Usch.

This time, Ella Busch's brothers are waiting outside Boys Elementary to take Nelly to see the witch Snow White. Freddie Schwalbe, nicknamed the "Swallow," is the leader of the pack, as usual.

The witch's tiny house is near the gas works in a small alley which Nelly has carefully avoided up to now, because the witch Snow White might just happen to put a hex on a passing child. But in the company of the Swallow it's a different matter. I take responsibility, he says. The witch's house is lopsided and ugly, it has a narrow wooden door and two tiny window slits, filled with pots of greenery, the kind the witch uses to brew her magic potions. The children gather at a cautious distance. The Swallow starts chanting: Witch, witch, witch, filthy old bitch. Whereupon all the others yell in chorus: Snow—White! Three times. And immediately, a bony old woman comes rushing out, swinging a broomstick. While two heads appear behind the green pots in the window: Idiot Alwin and Stupid Edith, Snow White's grandchildren. Grandchildren! pants the Swallow, when they've all caught up with each other again on Friedrichstrasse, after a frantic escape, and a counting of heads, to make sure that nobody is missing: Grandchildren, my eye! It's as plain as chicken shit that she hexed those two. One of these days I'll raid the place and rescue them.

At home, Nelly crawls inside the cave which her brother, Lutz, has built under the table with blankets. She teaches him a poem, after he has sworn the solemn oath never to recite it out loud: "Did you see the man walk past / in a dark-blue coat / His shirt is bulging from his ass / with a heavy load . . ."

Nelly realizes that she is several different girls, a morning girl, for instance, and an afternoon girl. And that her mother, who has taken the well-scrubbed afternoon girl by the hand, to go to a pastry shop with her, on one of her rare afternoons off, hasn't the faintest idea of the existence of the morning girl. They stop on Richtstrasse and the mother asks her daughter: Can you read what it says up there, Nelly? Nelly knows the name of the coffee shop, and reads—haltingly, for her mother's benefit: Ca—fé Stae—ge. Very good. Nelly's mother and her intelligent daughter seat themselves at one of the small round marble tables next to a wooden tub with a dusty palm; the mother orders eclairs and hot chocolate from Mrs. Staege, who comes to serve them in person. The daughter devours everything as though she'd deserved it.

Charlotte Jordan is never informed of the fact that Nelly proposes "pretending" to Herr Warsinski the next morning, when he asks his class to name emotions, because he finally wants to settle all the nonsense about capitalized words. Herr Warsinski's test wasn't particularly successful. It was to be expected that Gundel immediately hit the nail on the head with "joy." Ursel, the major's daughter, said "obedience," which was a doubtful emotion, while "modesty," suggested by Lori Tietz, the noodle manufacturer's daughter, passed with flying colors. But Ella Busch came up with "poverty." Poverty as a feeling word. Poverty is a condition, not a feeling. Poverty is a feeling, said Lieselotte Bornow, the tailor's daughter; it's something one can also see, smell, and taste. No, dear. Poverty cannot really be seen. Or touched. Nor is it a feeling, but it must be capitalized nonetheless, because it's preceded by an article. Christel Jugow did well with "fear." But Herr Warsinski would have liked to hear "courage," "devotion," "loyalty." That's when Nelly had to come up with "pretending." Another singular disappointment. Finally, Herr Warsinski writes his favorite words on the blackboard, in his own hand, in Gothic script.

Memory probably has its reason for projecting unexpected scenes when prompted by a certain word. The House Game is a proven fact—even Lutz, who was at most four years old when the game was at its high point, remembers it vaguely. But only now do you remember that the game was also known as "Pretending." A regular doll house with four rooms, a living room, a bedroom, a kitchen, and a bath; with curtains in the windows and tiny flower pots in front, with small ceiling lamps and the tiniest plates and cups in a little cupboard, and a pretty little chimney on the red roof. Seven celluloid dolls live in the house. They are elegantly clad in colored scraps and have the fanciest of names: Hurdy-Gurdy, Fallada, Pancake, Holly, Love Potion, Rose Perfume, and Bag-of-Tricks. Presumptuous names, as will be seen in a minute. Because they sit inside their little house, all seven of them, and brazenly sing in their chirpy-thin voices: "Hannapatsy Polar Bear / took a shit and knows not where / A dreadful stench is over there / Where's Hannapatsy Polar Bear . . ."

That's a provocation if there ever was one. Nelly and Lutz rush to the house. The Pretenders have stopped singing, and are going about their usual business, which is pretending. Nelly and Lutz, who know what goes on in the culprits' minds, shake them up and call them by their real names: Spare Rib, Owl Claw, Bat Beast, Stink Puke, Cross-eyes, Mongoltop, and Dung Heap. There is weeping and gnashing of teeth. Their punishment is based on the principle that pretenders deserve to be misled. Their arms and legs are tightly bound with yarn, they're thrown into a corner, Stink Puke's head is pushed into the toilet. All food is removed from the house. Lutz, who controls the batteries, must cut off all the lights. The open back wall of Villa Liars' Den is boarded up with cork boards from Mr. Hammer's Toy Workshop. The windows are hung with black rags. Inside, the incorrigible pretenders impudently sing: "Oh, how lovely is the e-ev'ning, is the e-ev'ning, when the bells are sweetly ri-inging, sweetly ri-inging, ding dong ding dong . . ." while outside the chorus of the avengers howls a hideous: Ye shall repent.

Finally, hours later, the pretenders break down and are tearfully pressed to the heart. At that point, their misdeeds change from open mischief to criminal thoughts, which Nelly cleverly detects as soon as the crime is being committed: You're thinking bad thoughts about me, admit it! Mercy! cry the criminals, who are caught in the act. Lying will get you nowhere! Witch's Paw squirms and writhes, until he finally confesses, lamenting that he had thought Nelly one of them, a pretender. Witch's Paw is condemned to life imprisonment in a shoebox.

Even at slow speed, the ride from the Station Hotel to Gallows Mountain takes no more than five minutes. It took the Jordan family forty minutes to walk to Gallows Mountain for the first time, in the spring of 1935. You're forced to delay the description of this walk to insert a lengthy pause in your fifth chapter, because of the news of M.'s—the German teacher's—suicide, which brings yet another aspect of the word "pretending" to your mind.

It was inherent in the nature of things that M. had to conceal his intention—on Wednesday, January 31, 1973—when he and his girlfriend, a great deal younger than he and a former student of his, paid you a surprise visit to return a book he had borrowed. (Musil: *The Man without Qualities*.) He knew that this was to be the last evening of his life. The letter they mailed to you that same evening must have been in the pocket of the parka which the girl hung up outside in the hall. They couldn't stay long, they had to go to the post office. The last sentence of the letter, which offered no explanation of their act, merely a sober accounting of the money they were leaving, read as follows: "As you read this, we have ceased to live." M.'s interest in your new painting must have been an obvious pretense—if that's the word for it. He rightly called your painting "eerie." This parade of poplars, he said. He briefly commented on the blue, which he knew to be your favorite color also. You speculate about his mentioning Kleist and the TV program the previous evening, which had given a poor presentation of the double suicide of Kleist and Frau Henriette Vogel, all wrong and maudlin. Had he wanted to rule out the suspicion that his act might have been influenced by that particular television show, which had not been to his taste? Or had he wanted to implant a parallel with illustrious models in the minds of persons who would surely later understand his intentions?

He might have miscalculated. This particular piece of your brief conversation had, strangely enough, completely slipped your mind. After you received the news of the double suicide, you insisted for forty-eight hours that there hadn't been the slightest hint as to his intention on that last evening. It wasn't until Monday morning, when you passed the house in which he had rented a room (he, himself, had removed his nameplate from the garden door, on the last afternoon of his life) that Kleist's name resurfaced in your memory, in M.'s dry, mocking voice.

M. had a slight lisp. The pills his girlfriend had probably taken from the hospital where she worked had begun to take effect. From a remote distance he was discussing the psychology of his students, the reasons behind the widespread phenomenon which he called their "reluctance to achieve." Later, you all said: He's got a point, that M., he's really concerned. You couldn't—nor did you want to—realize that that was precisely what he no longer was; that he merely sat there and made comments that weren't going to change him or anyone else. Had he snickered to himself when his girlfriend, twenty years his junior, turned down the vermouth: she didn't drink alcohol? And let's not constantly talk about the school.

Her application to medical school had been turned down for the second time, although she had passed all preparatory exams brilliantly. Both took turns denouncing the admission requirements, mockingly, without emotion. You expressed indignation they no longer felt. No, they weren't going to submit any more applications. They answered yes and no at the expected places, but deep down they may have thought: How dense they are. Or: Those poor people. Or: Those poor dense people.

In the Musil book which he had returned—one of his favorite books—you found several annotations on the second day after his death, terrified at the thought that he might have placed a message between the pages, as a last rescue attempt. A number of underlined passages—only he could have underlined them—among them the following sentence, with exclamation marks in the margin: "There's only one choice: either to play the game of these vicious times (to travel with the pack), or to become a neurotic. Ulrich chose the latter."

You're forced to tell yourself: If you had found this sentence right then and there, it wouldn't have made you drop everything and run the two minutes' distance to his room—sometime on Thursday; there would still have been time, until Thursday night—to keep your finger on the doorbell, to force your way in at any price, ridiculous though you might have appeared, in order to prevent the worst. His pretending was too perfect; its high point was the evening he came to say goodbye. He had kept the book so long, he said, because he wanted to see if he felt like rereading it. There followed a number of ifs. If you had felt the urge, you'd have gone to get it, you said. He laughed a sparing laugh and said in that case he should have waited to see how much more time you'd be giving him. On the stairs he asked you to say hello to Ruth, his former student, whom you'd be seeing sooner than he would. (He, who knew that he would never see her again.)

His pretending matched yours to a T. You made a few playful remarks, thinking that his girlfriend had obviously put an end to his suicide fantasies. He had made you see exactly what you wanted to see, which is the ultimate purpose of any pretending. A person who's not afraid to know the truth can't be deceived for long. But since everybody fears some form of truth, one person's deceit usually matches the other's denials, and that's what we call compatibility. From this point of view, you assume after the fact, these two people were compatible in their quest for death.

M. may not have expected that news like the news of his death would stimulate an eagerness for life, and later anger, after the initial shock. He accurately sensed the difference between your occasional depressions and his uninterrupted incapacity to put up with life. Whenever he came to see you, he'd find your table strewn with newly written pages, while he'd been spending his afternoons in idleness, lying on the couch, listening to music behind the protective shield of earphones. Now you know why he stopped coming to see you. He no longer wished, or was no longer able, to expose himself to the doubt of his desperation. Interpreted today, the smile he gave you when you ran into each other was a smile reserved for a deserter who doesn't stick things out. Pity for someone who can't face absolute insight, who can't respond with absolute unbelief. Without a doubt, he asked himself on that last evening how the event he alone knew about was going to affect you. Perhaps he even admitted that an element of vanity was involved in his exit from a stage that had not offered him a suitable part. Since he was too proud to appeal to the sympathy of others, this may have been his last means to gain mastery over his fate, if only for hours or days. He may conceivably have counted on how a number of his acquaintances would speculate about his thoughts while he dissolved the pills in a glass of water, from which she may have drunk before he did; while he—instructed by her hospital experience—pulled the plastic bags over their heads and tied them under their chins; perhaps nothing more than a practical attempt to hasten death, still, something that increased the horror of all those who heard about it.

Lenka expressed the general feeling when she asked herself: Should she feel sorry for him or not? I don't know . . . The students who had counted on him felt disappointed; his colleagues —most of them younger than he—expressed total incomprehension or self-righteousness; but all of them felt cheated. A proof that one wishes to know those with whom one lives, in order to keep one's own pretenses hidden. You noticed in yourself an increased attention even to trifles during the next few days, especially to people's faces, and to the very first stirrings of life in nature, on the birches outside your window.

At times, you wished for the days when everything was undecided, the days before the beginning, when you could still hope that choosing one of several possibilities would not irrevocably exclude all the others. It's not your task to transfer the news about the supposedly successful landing of the three astronauts Roosa, Mitchell, and Shepard onto these pages, but only the question which occurred to you at the sight of the three, standing bare-headed before millions of onlookers aboard the airplane carrier, murmuring a prayer of thanks. What do the astronauts believe in? Do they believe that they must display piety to the millions who don't know any better? That it was God who had held His hand over—or under—them. The next day you go to the Institute of Radiology, to have your neck X-rayed, finally—because of the persistent headaches after you hit your head on the steel corner of the fireplace. Your name is called out and you disappear behind a frosted-glass partition with sliding doors, which protects you from the eyes but not from the ears of other waiting patients. While your old records were being located in one of the enormous filing stacks along the wall, you went to sit on one of the chairs in the hall, trying, like everyone else, not to listen to the directions being given to other patients over the loudspeaker: Herr A., room 1, uncover your abdomen; Frau B., room 2, uncover your chest; you can't help picturing Herr A. and Frau B. with bared abdomen and bared chest, after they blushingly crept to their rooms; you yourself sitting in room 3—take out all hairpins, take off your glasses—as X rays are being taken of your head, in different positions—and you suddenly find it difficult to follow the instruction not to swallow. During all of these events in which you participated merely as an object, you kept thinking, without getting any closer to the answer: What do those astronauts believe in?

A number of pages were written in this unconcentrated fashion, which is obviously unsatisfactory but still allows you the possibility of rejection and retreat. You intentionally provoked H.'s anger: it wasn't at all that certain that you were going to write this book. Through the years his indignation has become tailored to match your pretending.

Naturally, the house you're heading toward after you pass the settlement of the "Yellow Peril" on the right, and the four Bahr houses higher up on the left, has shrunk and turned much grayer, exactly as expected. It used to be gleaming white, a point which was decided on early in the game, even before the blueprints, while Charlotte Jordan was still hemming and hawing. Build a house!

Are we millionaires! And if so, why in the middle of a desert? People must think we're crazy.

It has already been mentioned that Charlotte had a pessimistic streak. At any rate, she was often sad or obstinate, and she had her "moods." She's simply not in the mood to walk the long distance from Sonnenplatz to Soldinerstrasse on Sunday morning, merely because her husband is hatching a crazy project. First of all, the whole beautiful afternoon is wasted if you eat such a late lunch. Second, she isn't going through another fit with that boy again, Lutz, who screams: Water! Water! at the slightest drizzle, as though he were about to drown.

That does it for Bruno Jordan. If a person uses rain as an excuse on a cloudless fall day, then that does it for him, he'd rather stay home.

But now they're going to go, even if it rains cats and dogs. Papa must have his wish. And we're not going to take an umbrella, either. During the walk, the mood improved, after a bit more bickering. For this is a brisk march of three-quarters of an hour (Nelly is made to read her father's pocket watch, although they have not yet learned to tell time in school). It's best always to be a neck ahead of the others. Punctuality is half of life. Standing still is regression. You've got to make something of your life.

But (did many of Charlotte's sentences start with but, in those days?)—but everybody we've asked advises against it.

You can't scare me.

But we don't even have the money.

You and your ifs and buts.

But what if another grocer takes the place next to the barracks?

You certainly know how to encourage a man.

The ravine, a cut through the hilly chain of the end moraine, links Friedrichstrasse to Soldinerstrasse. The last third of the end moraine, a richly structured but easily scanned hilly landscape, is an ideal playground for children in both summer and winter. This is where Nelly finds out that Germany is going to have soldiers again.

But what if the others won't put up with that?

You'll see, all you need is nerve.

But a girl shouldn't grow up between two barracks. Soldiers have sex on their minds.

Let's be realistic. Soldiers need cigarettes and beer on their day off. And officers' wives like their groceries delivered.

But who's going to deliver them?

Who do you think? We are. Good God in heaven, let's show a little initiative, a little self-confidence!

Charlotte Jordan doesn't allow her husband to put his arm around her shoulders in public. You work your fingers to the bone and run yourself ragged, and along comes another war and blows everything to smithereens.

Sometimes you can really drive a person up the wall.

Nelly heard only the word "war." It's one of those words she could fish out of any conversation. War is when rows of soldiers in spiked helmets—which she knows from her father's old brown album—stick other soldiers in the belly with their bayonets until their intestines hang down to the ground; other soldiers in red pants: Frogs. Actually, that photo has nothing to do with World War I, but with 1870–71, but it was the perfect illustration of her father's close-combat regulation, which he would recite by heart. The conviction that war, fear, and death are one and the same thing was extremely familiar to Nelly, a conviction she had trouble hiding completely from Herr Warsinski, who was, once again, disappointed in her.

Here, you think?

Stop, you told H., who made a U-turn and parked in the shade of the Bahr houses. Since you had nothing else to say, you repeated Nelly's exclamation when her father first showed her the spot on which their house was going to be: But, there's a mountain here!

Well, Bruno Jordan, mover of mountains, is supposed to have replied, well, we'll just have to take the mountain away.

Mountain was quite an exaggeration. The contractors Andersch & Sons, who started digging the foundations six months later, had no trouble leveling the edge of the chain of sandy hills into which the house was going to be set. Since they had to wait for the end of the winter frost of 1936, the brief delay gave Bruno Jordan the time to apply for a bank loan.

Incidentally, just as there is a short-term and a long-term memory, some people seem to be correct now, while others turn out to be right in the long run. Bruno Jordan was among the former: it soon became evident that his house was being built in a favorable location, from a business point of view (between two barracks, one of which, the Walter Flex Barracks, was itself still under construction), and also at a favorable point in time. The number of Germany's unemployed had dwindled to two million, which meant that working families were spending twenty to thirty marks on weekend shopping. The store was booming, the mortgage was practically paid off by the time the Jordans were forced to abandon their house eight and a half years later. A fact Charlotte Jordan never forgot to mention later—just when they had no more debts. (She had turned out to be right in the long run.)

At the time she said: But the soil! Pure sand, for heaven's sake! Well, that couldn't be helped.

She did participate in pacing off the front of the property. But one thing is certain: We'll install an electric mangle. And I want separate cellars for coal and for potatoes. I refuse to start without that.

Granted. And right here, at this corner, we'll plant a poplar.

But the wind is going to break it!

This time she turned out to be wrong. The poplar is still standing. Once a thin switch, today a solid thirty-five-year-old tree, even though lightning must have split the top in two at one time or another; its beauty is impaired by two long uneven tips.

The house, too, is still standing. The war—about which Charlotte turned out to be right—did not blow it to smithereens: the few bombs that fell over the town were dropped by individual planes of the Royal Air Force, out of fear or embarrassment, after German Flak or Jäger units had driven them from their target, which was Berlin. And the battles which destroyed the center of town at the end of the war did not reach as far as the northwest periphery. The arson that occurred was the concerted action of freed Polish forced laborers, under the leadership of a certain Frau Bender, whose attempt to save her dying son with stolen ration cards had landed her in jail. After the end of the war, she had people burn down the houses of Nazis she knew in the neighborhood. That was how the two houses next to the Jordans, those of architect Bühlow and engineer Julich, were burned to the ground. New, slightly smaller houses have been built on their old foundations. They change the profile of the landscape.

Otherwise, however, the inconceivable was accomplished: the sand mountain was leveled and apparently dumped into the deep gap of the ravine, where the dangerous devil's slope used to be, a narrow trail between two humps, which required special skill to ride up and down. All the other profiles are also changed. At the rocky bottoms of onetime valleys lie new meadows, on which crowds of children were playing on that blisteringly hot Saturday in 1971; you couldn't understand their shouts and snatches of song, but they comforted you more than anything had comforted you in a long time, as you stood at the edge of the ravine—at the exact same spot where Nelly used to play Prince and Princess with her girlfriend Hella—looking over to the new blocks of houses crowding the space where the sand mountain used to be: the one-time Gallows Mountain, the top of which had been leveled ages ago, an enormous unbeatable playground five hundred feet in diameter.

You were aware of the aging process of houses, that houses shrink with time. But that makes no difference. You also know that there are certain taboo houses which one is not allowed to enter. The house across from you, on the other side of Soldiner-strasse—familiar, strange, and aged—is one of those that are taboo. But that makes no difference. You can step up to the store window—although that, too, may seem strange—and look at the display: cardboard milk bottles and cardboard cheese packages, advertisements. You could even enter the store and buy a bottle of milk by pointing to it with your finger, but you feel that you'd be confusing the salesman. He'd probably serve you politely, exactly the way he serves his local customers, whose number must have increased with the dense settlement on the sand mountain.

They would move mountains.

While her house was being built in 1936, Nelly discovered the smell of plaster, how mortar is mixed, and how one keeps one's balance on a sloping plank; also—during the roof-raising celebration—how one fishes sausages from a huge vat. All that time she must have been carrying the magic cork around with her. It has to be there when she puts her hand into her coat pocket. She must be able to feel it under her bench in school. It has been studded with small brass nails all around, and when she touches a particular nail she is invulnerable. She no longer fears a look from Herr

Warsinski (or his ignoring her), she solves every arithmetic problem and can stand up to Gundel. Not to mention that she can readily distinguish between transitive and intransitive verbs. As long as her hand is around the cork, she is no longer on the outside. There is only one thing one can't do: one can't deny the cork; then it loses its effect. Although she would have no need of it, if she managed to win Gundel over to her side.

During recess she displays the cork for Gundel to see and to ask what it is. Nelly answers casually: A magic cork, nothing special.

The rumor spreads throughout the class. The cork passes from hand to hand. When the bell rings and Herr Warsinski stands in the door, it has disappeared. Only much later does Nelly see it glisten in the hand of Lieselotte Bornow, who is called to the front of the class to sing a song, though she is absolutely incapable of singing. This time, however, she simply takes her position and starts to sing, softly, and in a quavering voice, but audibly:

> *To market, to market*
> *To buy a plum cake.*
> *Home again, home again,*
> *Market's late.*
>
> *To market, to market*
> *To buy a plum bun.*
> *Home again, home again,*
> *Market's done.*

There, you see. Herr Warsinski has always known: Where there's a will, there's a way. But what's that in your hand?

Herr Warsinski doesn't really want to know. If Lieselotte had simply shown him the cork, without saying a word, if she had just looked guilty, he would have been satisfied. He would have reprimanded her and locked the cork away in the desk drawer, into which all toys disappeared, since a school was not a place for toys. He was actually in a good mood. If only Lieselotte had not claimed that it wasn't her cork, with her usual stubbornness. No? Well, then, whose is it?

Nelly hears her name.

Aha, so it's yours. His voice is still almost neutral, but Herr Warsinski has raised his right eyebrow, which Nelly probably didn't notice. She is strongly tempted to say: Yes, that's my cork, and slip it into her briefcase. But in that case, Herr Warsinski will think that she's playful and have contempt for her. He is saying—and it does sound contemptuous—Well, then, take your cork and put it away. Four or five in the class have begun to giggle. Another minute and the whole class will be laughing at her. At that point she hears herself saying: No, that's not my cork. A significant moment. Nelly is lying, she knows it. She is lying deliberately.

It's a cinch, as a matter of fact. It was a total mistake to believe that a deep ditch separated the realm of truth from the realm of lying. She finds herself in a landscape which looks interchangeably like the other one, except for the light. She realizes instantly that this lost light will survive only in her memory, and feels a deep, defiant longing for it, while she repeats no for several minutes, calmly, not at all stubbornly.

Because Herr Warsinski has become bewildered and wishes to know what is what.

One can be wicked without repenting.

It's child's play, all you've got to do is stick with it, once you've started. Even if the good Lord were to ask her, she wouldn't give a different answer.

How come it had taken her all this time to realize that this was the way to be on top of everybody? To see Gundel embarrassed, Herr Warsinski speechless: A girl of that age, to be lying like that, just for the hell of it—that just doesn't happen. He's pleading with her for the last time: You're quite sure now, it really isn't yours?

It really isn't.

Well, then, we'll just forget about the stupid cork, and whoever would like to have it can come and tell me during recess. And maybe Nelly will now recite for us the poem about the giant toy.

Gladly. She'll recite a poem any time. Cool, calm, and collected, as her mother was fond of saying. Just try scratching at cement. The liar always triumphs.

"From peasant stock almighty / a race of giants rose / a peasant is no plaything / may God destroy his foes!"

I really didn't know that that wasn't your cork, Gundel said to Nelly during recess. For the first time Nelly and Gundel are walking arm in arm. Nelly calmly says: But it *is* my cork, and enjoys the perplexity and admiration of the girl, who is at last strolling up and down the schoolyard with her as though they were friends. All the things that had gone wrong up to then righted themselves if one just held one's own for once and lied.

The good Lord had no objection. He meted out no punishments; if anything, he rewarded you. He did, however, insist that one repeat the feat. That one did it again and again, and always for the same reason: out of pride.

Only now does the reason for the bitter fight between Lutz and Nelly surface, the fight during which she dislocated her brother's arm so badly that he had to spend a number of days in the hospital, as already mentioned, where he caught the measles and couldn't be at the roof-raising celebration of the new house. The reason was a grave transgression against the rules of a game known as Mary's Child. It is based on the well-known fairy tale. Nelly plays Mary's Child. Devoured by an insatiable curiosity, she opens the forbidden thirteenth door in heaven. Her brother, Lutz, alternately plays the Virgin Mary and the Supervising Angel, who tries to keep Nelly-Mary's Child away from the door, with a vehement flutter of wings. She overwhelms him, of course, opens the door, and beholds the forbidden sight of the radiant Trinity. She even touches it, and her finger remains permanently gilded. A tremendous fear grips her, which eventually leads to the confession that saves her at the last moment.

At this point, Nelly outrageously deviated from the story line. She has been tied to the bedpost, a flaming sea of red streamers is raining down on her head; in other words, she is burning to high heaven, her finger is still gilded, but she continues to shake her head: No no no. I didn't do it! She refuses to confess, contrary to the demands of the script. Her brother, Lutz, flies into one of his dreaded fits of rage. To calm him down, Nelly dislocates his arm.

Purged with repentance, she participates in the roof-raising celebration. The bare structure of the house is at the very spot which they paced off a year before. Nelly sits on planks that give, among the bricklayers who are showing her how to drink beer from the bottle, and who call her father "Boss." Her first year in school is also over, and it wasn't that bad, after all. When her parents read her report card, they said they'd always known that they could be proud of their daughter.

The new store opens on September 1, 1936. In a brilliant piece of writing, Bruno Jordan had proved to the municipal magistrate that "The Gallows" is a damaging address for a grocery and is given permission to consider himself a resident of Soldinerstrasse —the same northwestern main artery, now divided into two lanes, on which Nelly watched the columns of soldiers marching out from both barracks, first to maneuvers, then to war, and where she finally saw the treks of refugees.

A photo shows Bruno and Charlotte Jordan, both in white store smocks, outside their new house on the day of the grand opening. Bruno is thirty-nine, his wife, Charlotte, is thirty-six years old, their life is sweat and toil, and their two children, both healthy and bright, are seven and four years old. Nobody—except for Charlotte —makes lavish use of words like "happy"; at most in connection with other words, such as happy-go-lucky, happy birthday, happy holidays . . .

But Nelly felt happy, the first day that she awoke in her new room, on a brilliantly beautiful August morning. The sun was shining on the flowers of the wallpaper which she had helped pick out from the sample book, and which she would be able to draw to this day: that's when she thought—and repeated out loud: Today begins a new beautiful life.

6

It is the person who remembers—not memory.

The person who has learned to see himself not as "I" but as "you." A stylistic particularity such as this can't be arbitrary or accidental. The sudden switch from the third to the second person (which only seems to be closer to the first), the morning after a vivid dream.

It took place—a long time after the summer visit to L.—in a town which wasn't your hometown but was supposed to be your hometown, as you knew it in your dream. You find the town untidy, in a state of turmoil. You buy something, carry it in a shopping net, beautiful golden apples. A man comes and accuses you of having appropriated something that had been entrusted to you for safekeeping. You affirm that you deposited it "elsewhere." The man is not unfriendly, he doesn't wish to humiliate you. He has blond wavy hair. You can't hold it against him that he is suspicious of you. You understand: it's his job. Together you walk through an unkempt wood. A policeman with a white cap is brutally roughing up an old woman who has supposedly stolen some wood, a single stick. Your escort informs you that even a petty theft must be duly and severely punished—how much more so your serious embezzlement! You nod. You lead him into a large square gray house at the edge of the sparse, ravaged wood: That's how the woods looked at the end of the war. In a kind of hallway a woman is talking to another at the top of her voice, about everyday things. She categorically denies any knowledge of the object you're asking about. You desperately insist that you left it here for safekeeping. She finally points to a net which holds a few wrapped little packages and a beautiful slender bottle. That's it! you call out, infinitely relieved, although deep down you know that you'd been looking for something else. Your escort, too, is satisfied. He holds the bottle up against the light: it is pale green and transparent, painfully pure and flawless. You see, the escort says, this was a true memory lapse! You're happy to have an explanation for everything, one that exonerates you and with which you can agree.

The ravine. This hillside, the grassy, lizard-populated slope was once Nelly's playground. She had a tendency to hide herself, to shun places in which one could hope or fear to find her. Now you realize why you hadn't been eager to come here for twenty-six years. Unspoken and unadmitted excuses—the loss of your homeland, the possible pain of recognition—were no longer valid. You shied away from an encounter that would be unavoidable. Perhaps those who haven't experienced it should not be envied: a feeling of embarrassment in front of a child.

You had worked your way through to this spot, up to this house, not in a straight line but in a seemingly aimless zigzag course, in order to "get the feel" of the child—possibly with the help of a memory exposed to the impact of details, one that begins to yield items of astounding insignificance. That's when you had to realize that you could never again be her ally, that you were an intruding stranger pursuing not a more or less well-marked trail but actually the child herself: her innermost secret that concerned no one else.

It wasn't a game any longer, and your heart sank. The child

would come out of hiding if you insisted. She would seek out places where you wouldn't feel like following her. You'd have to stay on her trail, ruthlessly corner her, while your wish to turn your back on her, to disown her, would become ever stronger. The road you had taken was barred with taboos which no one may violate with impunity.

You asked Lutz about the light-meter readings. From this angle they could clearly see how far the split top of the poplar extended beyond the roof of the house, and how thick its trunk had grown. Has it been mentioned that Nelly had been allowed to plant the poplar shoot? Old man Gensicke, nurseries and garden center, lifted the young tree with its root clump off his wheelbarrow and lowered it into the hole himself, but it was Nelly who filled the pit with garden soil and trampled the earth until it formed a gentle hollow, into which she then poured the water she had lugged in the lime bucket, with the help of the young bricklayer's apprentice. Old Gensicke treated everybody to one of his stock-in-trade sayings about the thriving of the tree and the thriving of the person who planted it. And from the cellar, where the construction workers were celebrating the raising of the new roof, came the song "Cornflower Blue." High point of life. Impressions that cannot be erased from any normal memory. As Lenka says, she'll never forget the day when the half-rotted bower in their old back yard was given to the children to do with as they pleased. You ask her: Does the old bower come to her mind when she hears the word "homeland"? No. Then what does come to her mind? "Homeland" isn't a word that means anything to me, Lenka says.

You think about it. It could be true.

"Home," Lenka says, sure. It means a few people. Where those few people are, that's home.

She wonders—almost to her own surprise—if Lutz and you by any chance feel vaguely homesick. Right here, for instance.

You hesitate. After all, so much has changed. But then again . . . Not that you're longing to go back, that's not it.

Lenka says nothing. You tell her that Nelly couldn't imagine ever living anywhere else.

Lenka wants to know more about the games Nelly used to play. Lenka knows that Nelly played Prince and Princess at a certain age, passionately, just as she herself used to do. You remember long walks and rides over the hard grassy soil of this hill, veils and scarves streaming after Nelly in the wind. She is the princess and her new friend Hella Teichmann the prince, adorned in velvet beret and feather, followed by the whole royal household, depending on the headgear they had and the demands of the game. There were always crimes. The horrible treachery of a servant, gruesome punishments—after the discovery and the chase—all executed here, on this sun-drenched sand hill in make-believe caves and grottoes, punishments marked by exquisitely lengthy and torturous procedures. Which Lenka's princess games must have lacked completely. She only knows the dark-green hollow under the elder bush that served as a castle, and the painful failure of many princes who simply couldn't fulfill the three tasks and rescue her.

It was here, too, that Sigi Deicke's great scene took place. The boy, shorter than Nelly, lived in the first of the Bahr houses. He snuck up on them, then suddenly came forward and stood at the very edge of the hill (the place where you're standing), yanking up his right arm and screaming at the top of his lungs in an eerily ecstatic voice: I am your Führer, Adolf Hitler, you are my people and must obey me. *Sieg heil! Sieg heil! Sieg heil!*—He was satisfied when Nelly and her friend Hella joined in for the triple shout, he didn't insist on any stronger proof of their submission.

He wasn't quite right in the head, Lenka said. What do you mean? said Lutz, he only repeated what he'd heard on the radio. Poor kid, Lenka said.

It was the beginning of the period older people still refer to as "times of peace": three or four years which their memory extends beyond measure.

Why has this feeling never returned during twenty-eight years of peace? Are the wars, which have shifted the focus of world history to other parts of the world, undermining the tranquillity of those not involved? That would be a step forward. Or, perhaps more likely, were the tensions on our own continent strong enough to keep an awareness of danger alive in us, even if these tensions led only to the cold and not the hot war?

It was a mistake to chance a winter vacation in this popular resort. To be stuck for two weeks among upper-middle-class people, among families whose fathers are addressed as "Herr Professor," whose mothers wear clothes from the West, who are bored with each other and radiate a lethal sterility. You dream that night that you're driving through a clean, square town in white and red colors, you end up in a dead-end street no matter where you go, you wind your way up mountain roads in deep snow and start skidding: you finally come to a stop with your front wheels in mid-air above a deep gorge.

What is the meaning of such a dream in this peaceful valley among these peaceful people? In the morning you read the death notice in the paper, the notice you'd been expecting—and yet it's too soon. You recall what B., now dead, said to you five days ago. Optimistic grief, she said. Could there be such a thing? You were distracted because you knew that you were seeing her for the last time.

H. agrees to drive into town. He lets you walk off on your own, doesn't say anything about the foolish purchases you've made. A dress, a blouse, a handbag. Your delight to be sitting in an ordinary café. On the ride back, your delight at the infinite shades of gray in the sky. You notice them because you are alive. You fall asleep and wake up with the thought of her death, but you're alive.

Peacetime. When we were doing well. Peacetime goods: wool cloth with no slivers of wood in it. When a pound of sugar cost thirty-eight pfennigs, a chunk of butter one mark, and when bananas were thrown in. When Bruno Jordan's fat account book had dwindled to a thin booklet containing the names of practically no insolvent customers, only forgetful ones. (On May 12, 1937, the number of unemployed in the Reich had gone down to 961,000.) When only pure butter was used for baking.

It has been forgotten that the control of household fats began in deepest peacetime, and the Buying Cooperative of German Merchants—BUCOGEM—which has just elected its trusted member Bruno Jordan secretary of its executive committee, must confer with Party Member Schulz from the main division of the Reich Food Producers on the "created condition" of the fat market. Bruno Jordan gives a talk to the assembled food merchants on questions of the four-year-plan, market regulations, and the trade press—his one opportunity to be mentioned by name in the local column of the *General-Anzeiger*. The winter of 1936–37 was mild, this is a documented fact. Bruno Jordan surely had to go out with his friends and colleagues—possibly even fellow party member Schulz from Berlin—after the altogether very successful meeting of January 3, 1937. Therefore it was not late at night but early in the morning when he stood, slightly weaving, in the door of his bedroom and found his bed occupied by his daughter, Nelly: a precaution taken by Charlotte Jordan, who icily informed her husband that he would find his bedding on the new couch in the living room, and when he tried to give a lengthy explanation, she cut him short with a single word: Derelict.

A derelict she called him, Nelly thought before she fell asleep again, locking the word away from everybody. That's how she kept it in her thoughts. A good marriage Charlotte calls it later, in the first year after the war, when Bruno Jordan is still a prisoner of war in the Soviet Union. Charlotte Jordan shows a family photo in which he, too, can be seen in his uniform as a noncommissioned officer. We had a good marriage. A businessman, my husband, the kind they don't make any more. Whatever he thought up worked out. In the photo, between husband and wife stands the new low coffee table with sixteen inlaid tiles, each corner tile decorated with a sailing ship on a heavy sea. Behind the table the children, stiffly erect on the rust-colored, flowered couch. We always got along well with one another.

Lenka isn't particularly interested in her grandparents' marriage, although she would have pricked up her ears at the word "derelict." But it wasn't mentioned. Not everything can and should be said, let's get that clear. Wherever else this word may still come to light, one shouldn't try to call everything by its name, so as to give purity, awe, and reverence a chance to survive in the realm of the unspoken.

It seems evident that children don't wish to know everything about their parents. Nelly was possessed by a more than average inquisitiveness and was forced during her entire childhood to hide this precious trait, even from herself, to the point where it was in danger of being stifled. But she didn't have the slightest wish to hear anything disparaging about her parents. She suffered when her mother's more and more frequent moods—more and more frequently directed against her father—were noticed beyond the immediate family, where they could still be tolerated and passed over in silence. When—as it happened!—Aunt Liesbeth and Aunt

Lucie fussed over the weeping Charlotte in the Jordans' parlor, while upstairs, at Whiskers Grandma's coffee table, everybody sat waiting for the birthday celebration to begin. She simply didn't come. Shrugging of shoulders around the table, before the coffee was poured, before Aunt Liesbeth, who was still cheerful and natural, encouraged her niece Nelly not to make such a face and to recite her poem. Nelly stood up and launched in: To our Grandma dear, happy sixty-fifth year . . .

She's composed it herself, would you believe it! Charlotte Jordan does not speak a word to her husband for days on end, except for essentials. Business talk in an icy tone that Nelly dreads more than anything. Dozens of mornings before school are spent in this silence, which the parents keep up toward each other but not toward the children, causing them to take sides; when the big scene finally does take place, it's triggered by nothing more than a lost glove, unshined shoes, the messiness of the children; dozens of times, when the front door finally slams shut behind her, Nelly swears to herself that she'll never do this to her own children. (Dozens of times you swallow the angry word that's on the tip of your tongue early in the morning, about the endless and hopeless mess of the children—the word, yes. But not the irritation, which they sense. Against which they, unlike Nelly, can revolt; Nelly could only be silent or become impertinent.)

Why do parents really love their children? Lenka asks. Now, of all times. Here, of all places. You're still standing at the edge of the ravine; four, five minutes, that's all the time that had passed. You notice that H. hasn't said a word. You say: Ask your father. He grabs his daughter by the nape of her neck, shakes her. Out of selfishness, bunny. Sure, but what else? When did those questions occur to Nelly? Extremely late. Parental love was as inviolate as marital love.

Lutz wants to give his niece a historical outline on the development of parental love. Love, he says to Lenka, has a very definite meaning at a very definite stage in the development of the species. We're used to it and take it to be "natural." But don't think that parental love would have developed if it had tended to decimate mankind.

And why do elephants bury their dead in their home grounds? Lenka asks. She's seen it on TV: the herd will drag a dead elephant, often over many miles, to the burial ground of the tribe and bury it there, following certain rituals. For whose benefit? Is this animal behavior, or what? What do elephants believe?

Lutz is convinced that the origin of this particular animal instinct will be discovered someday. Lenka shouldn't get hung up on supernatural interpretations.

Since when is parental love so closely linked with anxiety? Did it start when each new generation felt compelled to refute the beliefs of its parents?

Your brother, Lutz, belongs to the age group that had the unique distinction of not being required to spend a single day as soldiers, and this in the middle of Europe, in the middle of the century. As a member of the Jungvolk, at age eleven or twelve, he practiced shooting at the cardboard heads of Churchill, lord of lies, and Stalin, the Bolshevik chief. But that belongs in another chapter, because for the time being we aren't preparing for the real war; instead, we're fighting the production battle, we're waging the birth war, we're organizing the anti-vice campaign. Battles, wars, and campaigns that one gets used to the way one gets used to the occasional test blackouts. Is our cellar bombproof? Don't be ridiculous. That would cost a fortune!

On German Armed Forces Day, Bruno Jordan treats his two children to excellent pea soup from the field kitchen of the General von Strantz Barracks, but he no longer hits the cardboard figures on the rifle range with the accuracy of twenty years ago, when he was the only man in his company to get three days special furlough for excellence. His eyes have become weaker, especially the left one—an affliction he has passed on to his daughter Nelly, though she won't notice it until she's fourteen.

After the first desperately lonely weeks in the new neighborhood, Nelly opens a school for the younger children of the area "on the barrels," where she introduces them to the three R's, to the words and melody of the English song "Baa, baa, black sheep," and to religion in the form of the Christmas story and the crucifixion. "The barrels" are in reality leftover sewer pipes lying every which way on the open, weed-grown lot between the sand hill and the Jordans' house. One of the most popular games during recess is "London Bridge is falling down . . ." Interrupted, wrecked by Rudi the Bully from Fennerstrasse. Rudi the Bully, who never played with girls, came to the barrel school because Nelly, the stupid ass, made him puke. He said so right off the bat. He barged in on their recess games. "See a pin and pick it up, all the day you'll have good luck." Rudi replaced the last word's *l* with an *f*, he shrieked a song with words which teacher Nelly didn't quite understand, but which she ought to have kept from the ears of her pupils. Which is exactly what she's going to do.

What followed was a red-hot scene—red in spite of the darkness in front of Nelly's eyes—horrid, hoarse howls emanating not only from Rudi, no, also from her, a piercing pain at the root of her nose, and finally, the enraged, mad, lustful pleasure: punching into soft flesh. Then she sits on the lowest step of their beautiful new house, white as a sheet, blood streaming from her nose. Her alarmed mother springs into action—the child on the sofa, flat on her back, a cold cloth behind her neck, cotton pads soaked in vinegar up her nostrils—Whiskers Grandma's gnarled, rough hand on Nelly's forehead: There there, it'll be all right, don't fret.

Nobody understands why she can't be comforted. They don't know what Nelly realized as she blacked out: that Rudi the Bully hates her, that he had come, coldly, calculatingly, to humiliate her and to finish her off. And that she herself had felt the same urge from a clearly definable moment on: to get the better of him! If only she'd been stronger! If only it could have been she who beat the other to a pulp! Then he let go of her. He'd got what he wanted. He had leveled with her.

The school on the barrels would never be the same. Nobody in the world could give back to her the proud feeling that she was different from the likes of Rudi. Although she was now respected, and she no longer had to be an outsider at ball games. Now it was up to her to choose the team she wanted to join, and if she didn't feel like it, she simply didn't feel like it and would, God knows why, race around on her old bicycle, which she had vehemently demanded on the very evening after her fight with Rudi the Bully. Contrary to her usual nature, she was so insistent and demanding that her mother heaved a sigh and went and bought the old rattle-trap from a customer for twenty reichsmarks.

Nelly trained daily until she was in complete control of the vehicle. Now she was free to ride wherever she wished, to stop when she saw children fighting and intervene in favor of the weaker ones, to refuse to give information about her comings and goings, and to sit quietly again with the others on the boulders at the foot of the sand mountain. Or even in Whiskers Grandma's room, when the sun was setting far in back of the ravine, and Whiskers Grandma began to sing in a quavery voice: "Golden ev'ning sunshine, oh, so fair and briiight, I can see your splendor, ne'er without deliiight."

Has it been mentioned that Whiskers Grandma could sing? She and Whiskers Grandpa were no longer living on Adolf-Hitlerstrasse but on the top floor of the Jordan house. Two rooms, a kitchen, a toilet, all stove-heated, for thirty-two reichsmarks a month, which she punctually took to her son-in-law on the evening before the first day of each month, and for which she had him sign a receipt in a small account book.

Last night you finally dreamed of her again. Strangely enough, she was almost blind—much like Nelly's mother (who had finally been diagnosed as having glaucoma, at a time, however, when her terminal illness made any other condition irrelevant).

Blind. She, Whiskers Grandma, who used to do the most delicate stitching for her daughter Liesbeth up until her death. Maybe this dream of blindness only expresses self-reproach, since you failed to take Ruth to see her before her death: Ruth, her first great-grandchild, for whom she had knitted a soft wool baby sweater with a hood, destined to survive its maker by years and to be passed on to all new babies in the family . . .

It's also possible that Auguste Menzel's "blindness" merely meant that she didn't want to look at the place where she lived during her last years, and at its river, the Elbe. My eyes have seen enough, she used to say. The totally unfamiliar apartment through which she took you in your dream is inexplicable, as is the eagerness with which you began to dust the unfamiliar, high-gloss furniture, while she sat waiting in an armchair, idle: an absurd picture. Yet she talked to you quite naturally, and you were happy that somebody who had been dead all this time was still able to carry on a conversation as before, and finally you wanted to tell her that you still missed her. But she didn't give you a chance to speak. She pointed out to you that dreaming about the dead indicated good weather, that one had to dream about the loss of a tooth in order for it to mean death. Most of what she said was lost. You only remembered that she couldn't bend over the steam any more because of her eyes: she whom you'd so often seen in the laundry room standing in a thick cloud of steam. But then you were suddenly sitting—not you: the child Nelly—in your parents' house, in the narrow passage between the electric mangle and the store, on a sack of sugar, and Whiskers Grandma, blind, was standing next to Nelly, leaning very heavily on Nelly's shoulder. You woke up from the pressure. You couldn't shake it off. A German girl must be able to hate, Herr Warsinski said: Jews and Communists and other enemies of the people. Jesus Christ, Herr Warsinski said, would today be a follower of the Führer and would hate the Jews. Hate? Charlotte Jordan said. That wasn't exactly his strong point. In the evening she asks her husband: Don't you think it's pretty strong stuff he's dispensing to the children in religion? Just let him say what he wants. You can't stick your nose into everything!

The Jordans weren't attached to the Church. They were attached to their children and to their business and to their new house. Bruno was also attached to BUCOGEM, Charlotte was also attached to her rock garden. She had laid it out in terraces on a rough slope and had planted it, step by step, so cleverly that it was blooming from spring to fall. My only relaxation from the damned standing-around-the-store, she said. The word "damned" in connection with the store.

Nelly's hatred of Jews and Communists isn't quite as spontaneous as it should be—a defect that must be concealed. An attempt at compensation: instead of a composition on the theme Who betrayed the German people at the end of the World War? she offers Herr Warsinski a poem she has written. What? says Herr Warsinski, whose eyes still don't radiate the proper warmth when they fix on Nelly. You couldn't have written that yourself! You must have copied it from the newspaper! (Beset by foes was the German land / at the world's great conflagration, / but our valorous fighting men / kept safe the entire nation. / Then, by perfidious treason of Jews, / was Germany forced to make peace . . .) Unintentional testimony to the quality of newspaper poems, and to Herr Warsinski's history lessons. (Our memory retains rhymes faithfully and for a long time.) My goodness! Herr Warsinski says. That's quite something. Now come over here and read it to the class. Let that be an example for others.

Nelly is standing underneath a scroll that has been lettered in art class by an older group as an example of Latin script: "We feel as Germans, are of German mothers / Our thinking's German, has been so from birth / First come our people, then the many others / Our homeland first, then the entire earth!" Yes, Herr Warsinski says pensively. We haven't gotten that far yet, not by a long shot. Man isn't made to be perfect. Nelly and her friend Hella Teichmann, who is lucky enough to have a bookseller for a father, make up their minds during recess: they want to live to see perfection. They're not afraid. They want to be the new humans.

At last you get it: the smell. Lutz, what does it smell like here? Lutz grins. I'm way ahead of you. Like it used to. The old summer smell that hung over the ravine and the sand mountain and the Jordans' garden, where Nelly lies reading in the potato furrow; the lizard comes to sun itself on her stomach, and you're thinking, or feeling (at any rate that's what you believe her to have thought or felt at the time): What is now will never come back. If one could describe it, you thought, slowly walking behind the others along the edge of the hill toward the center of the ravine. How much at home she felt here. How often she had run up and down the sand mountain, beside herself with exhilaration. Or to stand at Whiskers Grandma's living-room window when it was getting dark and look at the town for a long while, way down to the river valley. Or to lie on her stomach in a flat, sun-drenched hollow here in the ravine, pressing body and face against the dry crumbly earth and the hard grass that gave out the smell that you've never smelled again since. Or the clouds. To lie on her back in the cornfield and look into the clouds. Nelly's body, feeling unfamiliar to her, nestling comfortably, giving signals to the head, signals that crystallize into the sentence: I don't ever want to leave.

You like it, Lenka, don't you? Oh, sure, yes. The politeness of children.

Where she, Lenka, happened to be walking just now, Nelly had stood on that July night, leaning against her mother, when the Hitler Youth garrison celebrated the summer solstice. Strings of torches along the edges of all the hills, a woodpile suddenly blazing up, and the cry from many throats: "Germany, thou holy word / Full of infinity." (The information about the sequence of events was obtained from the 1936 volume of the *General-Anzeiger* in the State Library; the images—"strings of torches," blazing woodpile—" come from memory.) The motto of the festive hour was: "We want to glow, so that by our deeds we may give warmth to future generations." And the district leader proclaimed that it wasn't enough any more to shout: Germany, awake! We now have to shout: Europe, awake! When Nelly got cold, her mother wrapped her in her own warm jacket. At the end she cried with exhaustion because "it was just too much for her." Otherwise, she rarely cried. A German girl does not cry.

But it's all about whether or not a person can hate. Nelly had to be certain, even if it hurt. Unexpectedly, the evening after the birthday party for Lori Tietz threw some light on the subject.

First: she has to go, although she'd like to get out of it. What do you have against them? They're funny. That's no reason!

The technical details, for one. What should Nelly wear, what should she give her? A book? She doesn't read. Come on now! Nelly noticed of course that the birthday party at the Tietzes' mattered more to her mother than any other invitation, and she also knew why: Lori's father was the only factory owner in her class. Act naturally, just be yourself!

Besides, it had to rain, a fine drizzle. Nelly was pleased to see that noodle factories are ugly. The villa lay in back of the red brick factory, one had to walk through a vaulted archway. Nelly would like to know what makes a villa different from a house. The red stair carpet is fastened with polished brass rods, maybe that's it. And the door was opened by a maid in a little black dress with a little white cap and a little white apron, like the waitresses at the Café Staege. Lori's mother appeared. So you are little Nelly. I've heard so many nice things about you . . . Lori herself with corkscrew curls in a plaid taffeta dress with a large bow. Well, Lori, entertain your guest now. Papa—she stressed the last syllable— has called; he'll look in on us later. Oh, these poor men. Does your poor father work that hard, too? Quite hard, Nelly said. But maybe my mother works even harder. Isn't the child priceless?

The hot chocolate makes Nelly's nose run. Her friend Hella, who can handle difficult situations better than she, asks politely for permission to get her handkerchief out of her coat pocket. They tell her, please, for heaven's sake, go ahead and don't be bashful. Charming! Frau Tietz says to her friends while Hella is outside.

But now Nelly can't get up, too. She also doubts very much if she took the handkerchief along that her mother had laid out for her. She drinks five cups of hot chocolate so she can keep her nose buried in the cup. We're so glad you're so fond of hot chocolate . . .

Frau Tietz starts off the game Telephone with the lovely sentence: All children like birthday parties. Nelly passes the message on to the major's daughter, Ursel: Britta and Sylvia are dummies. Ursel, a girl like a lump of dough, doesn't dare to understand. Hella announces at the end: Let's all go slumming.

Charming, Frau Tietz says. So free and easy, our children today. And now why don't you play Blind Man's Bluff or Musical Chairs . . .

Director Tietz, who actually makes an appearance, is a short, almost rotund man with thin, faded, slicked-back hair and enormous black horn-rimmed glasses. Nelly has never before seen a man wear a ring with a black stone on his little finger, which he sticks out while he drinks coffee, standing up, from a tiny cup; Frau Tietz calls it "mocha." Herr Tietz asks Nelly about her marks and compares them with those of his daughter Lori. He sighs reproachfully and cannot understand why there's such a difference, although the explanation is simple and on the tip of Nelly's tongue: Lori is dumb and lazy.

The realization hits like lightning. Indeed: Lori is plain stupid, and Herr Warsinski, who has noticed it all along, can hint at it only now and then with a glance and with the sweetish tone of voice he uses when he talks kindly to her. But stupid people don't understand glances, that's just it. Nelly, however, perfectly understands the glance which Director Tietz exchanges with his wife before he suggests to Nelly that she come and visit Lori every once in a while, and that they do their homework together on such occasions. Herr and Frau Tietz think that would be lovely. Of course there'd be hot chocolate each time, and afterward there'd be games in Lori's beautiful playroom, which Nelly liked so much, didn't she? Frau Tietz had noticed that right away.

Now Nelly experiences—not for the first time but hardly ever as strongly—that she splits in two; one Nelly is innocently playing "The Jew has slaughtered a pig, which part of it d'you want!" while the other Nelly watches the others and herself from the corner of the room, and sees through everything. The other Nelly sees: they want something from her. They're calculating. They've invited her in order to steal something from her that they can't get any other way.

Nelly, fused into one person, suddenly stands in the hallway and puts her coat on. She feels her pocket, mechanically: Aha. Handkerchief in the left pocket. Nothing escapes Frau Tietz. But, Nelly child, what's the matter? We're still going to have pudding with whipped cream, and after that my friend can drive you home in her car.

Oh no. Nelly is determined to leave. And if she has to be a little impertinent, to fib a little, that's just too bad, but it can't be helped. She just can't stomach pudding, she claims, and whipped cream always makes her sick. Unfortunately. And about riding in a car: Never with a woman driver, no, sir. How very strange. But run along, then, I won't hold you.

That's what Nelly does. Her mother, having been informed by telephone, looks at her critically, even puts her hand on her forehead. Do you think you have a fever? No, Nelly says. I'm not going to go there again.

Her mother makes her a liverwurst sandwich. Suddenly their eyes meet and they have to laugh, at first with a giggle, then openly; finally they scream with laughter, slap their thighs, wipe the tears of laughter off their faces with the backs of their hands. Oh, you fibber, Charlotte Jordan says. Just you wait!

Nelly may stay up for another half hour. Her brother, Lutz, is already asleep, and tomorrow is Sunday. She may switch on the floor lamp in the alcove, may sit in the overstuffed chair, a gift from the Knorr company to her father for his good sales of Knorr products, and she may put her book on her mother's sewing table. In the next room is company: her father's friend Leo Siegmann with his wife, Erna. Leo Siegmann has a high forehead and a bald pate, and an obstruction of the air circulation in his pharyngeal cavity which forces him to produce a clicking sound several times a minute ("to click himself free," as Charlotte Jordan calls it, who respects Leo Siegmann, the bookseller, for his education but for nothing else). He is sitting directly across from the Führer's picture, which hangs above the desk, and which he himself had sold to his friend Bruno Jordan (format 20-by-30, semi-profile with peaked cap, collar of the trench coat turned up, steel-gray eyes gazing into the far distance, behind him a grayish swirling turbulence designed to show—and showing—the Führer "braving the storm"). Behind Leo Siegmann stands the new, high-gloss, multipurpose cabinet, its center still bare of the books Leo Siegmann will gradually supply. This time he's brought *Debit and Credit* by Gustav Freytag, to acquaint you with a man who knew quite a bit about business before you and I were even born, my dear Bruno. Two volumes. We'll put them side by side with *The Battle for Rome*, and for the next time I come I have something in mind that I won't even ask about, it's simply a must: *A Nation Hemmed In.*

When Nelly isn't reading, she can easily follow the conversation in the other room. First: The Siegmanns went on a cruise down the Rhine with "Strength through Joy," all old party members, unforgettably beautiful. Second: National Socialist culture and education, because that's Leo Siegmann's pet topic. He is very much in favor of infusing all technical training with biological thinking, which simply means giving the healthy popular emotions a scientific foundation. As far as he's concerned . . . Suddenly the picture becomes very clear: like the lens of a camera it focuses on a single image: Leo Siegmann, leaning slightly forward, his hand on the wineglass, illuminated from the side by the floor lamp, which creates reflections on his bald pate: As far as he's concerned, in his class, in secondary school—under the Kaiser, you understand!— there was this Itzig, a Jew bastard. To this day he can't say how it started. But anyway, when they'd come to class in the morning, this Itzig would be crouching there at his desk like a sack of wet flour, and each of them would walk by his desk and sock him one. It was instinct, say what you will. He just gave off an offensive odor, or whatever it was.

The Jew boy. Nelly can see him clearly. He is pale, with a pointed face, dark, wavy hair, and a few pimples. For some reason he always wears knickers. He sits at his desk like a sack of wet flour, and everyone who walks by him . . . She, too, has to walk by him. She, too, will "sock him one." Or will she? Because he thinks she'll be chicken. That's what he speculates in. All Jews are speculators. He's found out exactly what it is that makes her so furious with him. She braces herself, she knows: she must walk by his desk, she absolutely must, it's her duty. She's doing her very best.

She makes the film run faster. But never, not once during the whole time, as she becomes well acquainted with the Jew boy, as she begins to know every thought in his head, especially about her, not once does she succeed in getting past him. At the crucial moment the film always snaps. It always turns dark when she stands close to him, when he's ready to lift his head, also his eyes, unfortunately. She doesn't find out whether or not she'd be able to do her duty. What she does find out, but would rather not know, is: she wouldn't want to be in a situation where she must do her duty. Anyway, not in the case of this boy, whom she knows so well and therefore cannot hate. It's her fault. "Blind hate," yes, that would work, would be the only way. Seeing hate is simply too difficult.

The Führer must be able to have blind confidence in you, that's what counts.

An uneasiness you can't explain. You're beginning to watch where you're going: you were walking along the road at the bottom of the ravine, approaching the spot which Nelly could never again pass without uneasiness and never again without haste. One can only guess now why she was going in the direction of the gasworks at all on that late afternoon. One went to the tram stop by way of the ravine if one was heading for Wepritz, but when did that ever happen? What made the man appear to her will always remain a mystery.

"Appear"—the word shall stand, although the experience certainly had nothing of the supernatural about it, rather of the unreal, probably because Nelly didn't understand it at all. Every child knew that one had to beware of the derelicts who often spent the night in the ravine in the summer. But this man . . . He didn't seem to be a derelict. He was well dressed, neat, apparently quite clean. Actually not one of those who sleep in haystacks. Standing at the edge of the former garbage pit, of all places—on the left, before one got to the former railroaders' flats, used to be an illegal garbage dump—he glanced at her with a look . . . Sucking, that's how she sees it today. In any case, Nelly couldn't simply turn around, as she should have done and would have wanted to. This urgent, sticky look dragged her, as though by a string, past this horrible person, who pulled something long and whitish from his pants, and pulled and pulled making it longer and longer, a whitish, disgusting snake that Nelly has to stare at, until she manages ten, twenty steps, and the spell is broken, and she can run, tear, streak off.

Although she wasn't afraid for one moment that the man would follow her.

Nobody knows how she got home. Nor whether or not Charlotte "smelled" something (I can always smell a rat!). The fact is that Nelly said nothing because she immediately filed her experience, which she really didn't understand, among those occurrences that demanded to be treated with strict, absolute silence. Why? That's one of those practically unanswerable questions, because the answer couldn't be supported by anything tangible, it would have to depend on glances, a fluttering of the eyelid, a turning away, a change of inflection in the middle of a sentence, a stopping short while talking, an unfinished or falsely finished gesture: in short, those numerous details which determine more strictly than laws what must be said, and what must be irrevocably held back, and by what means.

Nelly has now become reluctant to hold her friends the lizards in her hands; but she does it until the time when a lizard tail remains in her fingers while the tail-less animal escapes. This is one of the rare occasions when she has goose pimples all the way down her spine, when nausea and horror melt into one. It can even become a problem to touch a spider. She has to do it now and then—although she'll never squash a spider—to maintain her reputation: Nelly can touch anything, spiders, toads, flies—simply anything. So far, toads and flies are exempt from her squeamishness.

(It's a touchy matter to this day to inquire into the connection —it must have established itself at that time—between the nameless Jew boy, whom Nelly has come to know through Leo Siegmann, and the white snake. What does the pale, pimply boy have to do with toads, spiders, and lizards? What do they in turn have to do with the ardent, fanatic voice calling out from the flaming woodpile on that summer solstice night: "We pledge to stay pure and to consecrate ourselves to Flag, Führer, and Fatherland!" Nothing, you'd like to say, there's no connection. That's the only proper answer, and you'd give anything if it were true. You know a man, a contemporary of yours, whose childhood has, in his own words, sunk into "nothingness." He declares: To this day he can't talk to a Jew without a feeling of embarrassment, without a feeling of guilt. You wonder how one can create images—the man is a sculptor—without the knowledge of his own childhood, images for children, for instance. That's not a reproach, it's a question.)

One doesn't know how, then. But it came about that by the blending and fusing of seemingly unrelated components, she, Nelly, could no longer hear the word "unchaste" without having a simultaneous vision of vermin, the white snake, and the face of the Jew boy. We know very little as long as we don't know how these things come about; as long as one can only wonder at the fact that these images didn't evoke hate or disgust in Nelly, only awe—a feeling very close to the first stages of fear.

At any rate, she avoided anything that was unchaste, even in thought, and chimed in loudly, perhaps too loudly, when popular songs were sung ("Ladybug, ladybug, fly away home" or "Cling-clong-clam, we're riding in the tram," or "Happy birthday to you, you belong in the zoo"): "Jew-heads are rolling, Jew-heads are rolling, / Jew-heads are rolling all across the street. / Blood, blood, blooood, / blood must be flowing thick as thick can be. / I don't care a rap about / the Soviet liberty."

Nelly—did she ever see the head of the Jew boy roll, of the boy she had so painfully come to know? The answer is no, and fortunately that is true.

The gable of the Jordans' house appears above the edge of the hill (you had turned around). On the gable, Lenka—you ought to tell her but you don't—Whiskers Grandpa used to hoist the swastika flag on special occasions and on holidays. He stuck it out the attic window and had to fasten it inside with a complicated system of ropes, because there was no attachment for fastening the flagpole on the house. That fact doesn't prove much. Nelly never heard a word for or against the flag. It was simply there—since when, by the way? Someone in the family must have bought it— probably Charlotte, since Bruno Jordan never set foot in a yard-goods store—and must have given the cloth to Whiskers Grandpa with the request to display it on appropriate occasions. The words, Lenka, and the facial expressions on such occasions were quite ordinary, not "tortured," as the pulp writers want to make us believe. The daily life, Lenka . . . But you don't say anything.

The Bahr houses, the "Yellow Peril," the "Red Fort" were

studded with swastika flags, although they had once been a breeding ground of Communism, according to the Jordans' neighbor
Kurt Heese—formerly employed by the savings bank, now trea-
surer of the district command of the National Socialist Party—
who passed this information on to Bruno Jordan during an
occasional chat across the wire fence.

It was Nelly's job to water the tomato plants every night and,
if necessary, to tie them up. She caught hold of the word which
immediately began to work inside her head. The breeding grounds
she knew were: birds' nests (occasionally in the taller grass of the
ravine, usually with empty eggshells, due to the cats), lizard eggs,
and the rabbits' nests in the hutches that Whiskers Grandpa had
put up in a corner of the garden. She knew two apartments in the
Bahr houses: that of old Lisicky, who supplied the Jordans with
asparagus and strawberries, and that of the Puff sisters, Berta and
Martha. Berta, a healer who could also remove warts, proved very
useful in the case of a rash on Lutz's forehead. (It's a fact, Lutz
said, since one could talk about the Puff sisters in Lenka's presence: No more rashes!) Martha, the younger of the two, who
sported an enormous wart on her upper lip, took the orders, led
her sister to the clientele, and took care of publicity and finances.
Nelly knew two apartments in the "Yellow Peril": those of Irma
Huth and of Christa Schadow, who were both in her class. And
one apartment in the "Red Fort": that of the deaf-mute shoemaker who uttered tortured, throaty sounds, and who drank 100
percent booze from a bottle standing next to the table leg; his
barefoot, dirty children made an infernal racket behind his back
with pot lids and sticks. None of these five apartments struck Nelly
as being a "breeding ground." Two of them—those in the "Yellow
Peril"—were accessible by worn-down, scrubbed wooden stairs;
two of them—those in the Bahr houses—by worn-down wooden
stairs covered with shabby linoleum. To get to the deaf-mute shoemaker one had to climb down six stone steps; he lived in the
basement and had a red brick floor. Each scratched-up brown
apartment door opened right into the kitchen, and each kitchen
was arranged pretty much like the others, but their states of cleanliness differed sharply: spanking clean at the Huths' and the
Schadows'; grimy, with herbs hanging everywhere, at the Puff
sisters'; dirty at old Lisicky's, who'd been living alone for a long

time; absolutely filthy at the deaf-mute shoemaker's, whose wife, it was said, lay in their unmade bed all day long and drank.

All of these apartments were more crowded and shabbier than the Jordans'; Nelly felt nervous when she entered them, and guilty when she left. But breeding grounds . . . There had to be some misunderstanding.

Looking back, those years must have been filled with misunderstandings. For instance, Nelly's confused ideas about the origin of babies turned out to be totally wrong. And it was impossible to get information from the family circle. Her experience with the breeding of rabbits hadn't given her any conclusive enlightenment. But her friend Dorie from Villa Pineview, an unpretentious yet mysterious house since it lay hidden from view at the foot of a slope, well set back from the road (where it's still standing)—her friend Dorie directed Nelly's attention to the girth of their neighbor Frau Julich, the wife of the engineer. Normally as thin as a rail, she had to walk around with her coat open because "her time" was soon to come. Nelly, who pretended to understand, ferreted all pertinent information out of Dorie and tried to imitate her crooked, suggestive smile. She also decided to ascertain a few details from Elli Julich, the neighbors' reddish-blond daughter. It turned out that everybody knew what was going on except Nelly. "Junior," the Julichs' reddish-blond curly-haired son and heir—who was, however, not to succeed his father in the engineering business—was the first child with whose birth Nelly associated fairly accurate concepts. That's why she always had a certain liking for him, although the rest of the red-haired Julich family got on her nerves, especially her contemporary, Elli, with her squeaky voice and her watery-blue eyes with their short whitish lashes.

Nobody can choose his looks, Charlotte said. Else there'd be nothing but good-looking people in the world. Nelly couldn't see why that would be so bad.

On the same day when you'd read material on concentration camps (not yet the biography of Rudolf Hoess, that came much later); when you'd seen psychiatric evaluations which characterized Adolf Eichmann—no doubt accurately—as "methodical, conscientious, animal-loving, and close to nature," as "sincere" and decidedly "moral," but above all as "normal" (at any rate, more normal than I, one of the psychiatrists supposedly said; his attitude toward family and friends was "not only normal but most exemplary," and the prison chaplain found Eichmann to be a "man with positive ideas." By the way, not only Hoess, the commandant of Auschwitz, but also Eichmann testified that they were not anti-Semites); on the same day when the repetition of the once respected word "normal" is creating in you a faint but penetrating nausea, as if the body's resistance to a kind of permanent poisoning had very suddenly weakened (you reacted to it with alcohol, which didn't improve your condition)—on that same day you remembered, after so many years, the scene which must have taken place early in the new house, in 1936 or 1937.

Aunt Trudy from Plau am See has arrived. She's brought Nelly a delicate little music box, which she winds up for her ten, maybe twenty times and lets her hear *Ach, du lieber Augustin* over and over again. But by the twelfth time Aunt Trudy begins to sniffle, by the thirteenth she pulls out her delicate rayon handkerchief, by the fourteenth time at last the tears begin to flow. At the coffee table it's up to Charlotte to get her sister-in-law to talk, to put order in her incoherent statements, and to sum them up in the sentence: What! Some bastard is spreading the rumor behind your back that you're Jewish!

Aunt Trudy was never able to take harsh words. Half Jewish, she sobbed; they say half Jewish. That's the same, Charlotte decides. Cutting the slander in half doesn't reduce her virtuous indignation. She enumerates the features that could possibly give rise to this dastardly suspicion: black hair, slightly curved nose, delicate profile. Those idiots, Charlotte says.

True, Bruno Jordan's proof of ancestry isn't yet complete. It does as yet not go back to the year 1838, as it will later; but the last three, four generations, those that count, have been verified as "absolutely pure in every branch," and these findings are at Aunt Trudy's disposal. Whether or not it helps—that's a moot question. Because this is character assassination, and what's behind character assassination is usually something that doesn't meet the eye. Somebody has it in for you, Trudy, and quite possibly somebody close to you. Try to rack your brains!

Good heavens, no, Aunt Trudy says. Impossible! They're all such wonderful people . . .

Nelly flees into the kitchen. She crouches on the coal bin and folds her sopping-wet hands. She's beside herself but doesn't cry. Her eyes become moist only when her mother discovers her. Her mother smelled a rat, of course, and wanted to know what was up.

That's when Nelly utters the remarkable words: I don't want to be Jewish! and Charlotte addresses the no less remarkable question to an unnamed court: How on earth does this child know what Jewish is?

The answer to this question cannot be determined.

7

What does it mean: to change?

Now come the real questions, after the ground plan has been sketched. It almost doesn't matter which side you'll approach them from. Something has gained momentum: later we'll call it the "prewar period." Later, meaning today, August 1973, a time when the postwar period is coming to an end, and not without difficulty.

To change may mean, for instance, to take a new job. Frau Elste, who still helps out at the Jordans', wants to change. She is going to work at the rope and burlap factory on the other side of the Warta River, which is where she lives. But Nelly doesn't want to change. She is happy that her environment (the place where the Jordans are going to live for eight and a half years) seems to be consolidating into a firm, stable foundation. Nelly, conscientious and steady, was attached to her environment. You, however, are unable to realize the full impact of change, since you're used to living from one change to the next; the first indications of permanence spur you to a hasty departure.

It made a deep impression on Nelly when a new girl, who had come to Nelly's town and class from the North German town of Husum, said with her deliberate, North German intonation—while she continually chewed on pieces of bread and cake, crumbs sticking to her chin unnoticed—that she thought this town "boring," even "deadly."

Nelly didn't understand. She found it impossible that the local-history walks Herr Warsinski took with his class—Market Square, St. Mary's Church, heart of the city with ruins of the old wall—shouldn't make an impression on Inge, the new girl. Herr Warsinski read to the class from the writings of a local historian, a certain Bachmann, who said that it was "the wise Ascanian John I" who had founded their town in about 1260. "Protectively surrounded by marsh and water, and equipped with palisades, ditches, and bulwarks because of its strategic importance," it became "a haven of Teutonic life in this area," and "admirably stood its ground against the devastating, marauding invasions of the Poles (1325–26) as well as against the later ferocious assault of the Hussite hordes."

Then followed a quotation from the Sunday poet Adolf Mörner, who had so aptly sung:

> How fair thou art with blossom'd gardens,
> My little town, what lovely sight!
> Never a man whose heart so hardens
> That he won't view you with delight!

"Never say never" was one of Charlotte's stock phrases.

People are there, too. People with memories linked to people, memories whose unreliability could be easily tested; take for instance the word "prewar." What comes to your—or their—mind at the words: "prewar days"?

The answers are imaginary, therefore doubly biased.

Bruno Jordan might perhaps say "Volkswagen." We didn't want to, at first, but then, dumb as we were, we did start pasting in stamps and helping Adolf finance his war: thus Charlotte Jordan in the early fifties, when she decided to burn the stamp booklet with VW stamps worth five hundred reichsmarks.

Bruno Jordan could have said: Peace and order! But then he'd have qualified his words: Something was going on, all right, we just didn't know what.

Charlotte Jordan's answers would have undergone a remarkable change in the twenty-four years that she had left to live after 1945. Prewar times? What happy years! she would have said at first. Later perhaps: A lot of work. And finally: One big fraud. This only to make it clear that memory is not a solid block fitted into our brain once and for all; rather, perhaps—if big words are permitted—a repeated moral act.

(What does it mean: to change?)

Nelly's mental association cued by the word "prewar" would probably be: the white ship.

This calls for an explanation.

Has it been mentioned that this child's memory was preoccupied with eerie, frightening, and humiliating subjects? The white ship is an eerie and frightening theme, but at the same time it's a shining, summery image in your fantasy-memory, which stores matters not really seen or experienced but only imagined, craved, or feared. It is true that the fantasy-memory is even less trustworthy than the reality-memory, and therefore you were unable for a long time to interpret this image. Until you found the explanation in the *General-Anzeiger* of May 31, 1937, which excited you so much that you would have loved to tell it to the friendly librarian at the reference desk. You refrained, though, because there were more intangibles connected with the white ship than could be passed on in a whisper, connections in whose center the white ship stood; "stood" is by no means the right word. The ship was sailing under a cloudless, blue sky in lightly agitated waters, also blue, with a white foaming wake, and it was very beautiful and meant war. And to this day—more than two years have passed since that surprise discovery in the State Library—you're still triumphant about the solution to a puzzle that you had considered unsolvable. You were triumphant the minute you realized that your memory was storing not random nonsense but reality—no matter how intricately coded.

Because it's important to know that the word stimulus "white

ship" not only conjured up fear of war but, more than that: homesickness, unmistakable homesickness, and all of these component
parts simply didn't fit, no matter how you might twist and turn
them. After all, "homesickness" did rhyme with "ocean bigness,"
eight-year-old Nelly's first lengthy separation from her mother.
(Maybe in the summer of 1937 there were little white steamships
running from Swinemünde to other resorts at the Baltic Sea? You
knew deep down you were on the wrong track.)

Nelly entered school in 1935—Easter of 1935, Nelly was barely
six years old and was still the youngest in her class—therefore her
first Baltic Sea trip, which took place in the beginning of her third
school year, must be dated June 1937. Medical reports attested to
a susceptibility to bronchitis, and complicated applications had to
be made to the board of education to have her excused from school.
(When Nelly came back after a two-week absence, it turned out
that she was unable to parse the sentence "All Germans love our
Führer Adolf Hitler," and Herr Warsinski insinuated that her head
was still full of sea water. Her feelings were deeply hurt. Herr
Warsinski simply didn't appreciate it when somebody got special
treatment; he had never seen bronchitis that couldn't be cured by
their good, clean Brandenburg air.)

Aunt Liesbeth and Uncle Alfons Radde had acquired a small
used DKW. The rumble seat was for Nelly. In the open air,
wrapped in shawl and blankets, she rode to Swinemünde, where a
cot had been set up for her on the porch. Sea climate is healthy,
nothing will happen to her, Aunt Liesbeth guarantees it. Nelly
lets the ends of her shawl flutter in the wind, Cousin Manfred—
Manni—who is still very small, waves at her through the tiny rear
window of the DKW, Nelly sings loudly, "Hello, hello, we're riding!" and discovers the sentence "Trees are flying by on both
sides" as a personal experience. Nothing was wrong with Swinemünde. Acceptable lodgings, sandy beaches, pleasant weather.
Nelly throws herself into the waves, she's not afraid of the water.
She also likes to play with Manni. What's ailing her, then?

Nothing, absolutely nothing is ailing her, and she's anything but
an ungrateful child. It's only that she dreams of her mother every
night: her mother lying dead in a coffin. Then she wakes up, of
course, and cries, and can't fall asleep again for a long time. She
can't imagine why she is dreaming this dream of all dreams. Surely

she's not homesick, homesickness is something for little children, and the symptoms must be different.

Aunt Liesbeth and Uncle Alfons got more than they'd bargained for, all out of the kindness of their hearts. But the white ship is more important: it overshadows all other worries. Naturally the children aren't told why there's all this sudden excitement, and what it's really about; but Nelly, quiet as a mouse, supposedly absorbed in the spectacle of the waves approaching her sand castle with never-ending, friendly little whitecaps, Nelly hears the words "ship" and "war" mentioned several times in the same breath, and she also hears Aunt Liesbeth ask if it wouldn't be better to leave, since everything seems to be on razor's edge. (To leave! To go home! To find her mother alive!) But Uncle Alfons, who knows that you should sleep on everything first, makes a condescending face, the kind of face men make when women are afraid of war.

Nelly doesn't know the word "panic."

Nor the word "Guernica." (You heard the word, the name "Guernica," for the first time fifteen, twenty years later, in connection with the painting; its good intentions could not be doubted, but its stark execution gave rise to intense controversy. An unavoidable anticipation in chronology: you looked at the sketches at the Museum of Modern Art in New York—preparatory steps toward the great painting—drawings which clearly showed the development from a naturalistically drawn cow into an animal capable of expressing all creatures' accusation against *homo faber*.) In April 1937 the *General-Anzeiger* spread the news that Guernica had not been bombed but drenched in gasoline and then set afire by the Bolsheviks. No photo, of course. However, the launching of the Strength-through-Joy ship *Wilhelm Gustloff* was photographed, and the *General-Anzeiger* published the picture, which, come to think of it, looks not at all unfamiliar to you. Quite the contrary. A white ship whose smokestack billows cheerful smoke, and whose wake forms a white foaming triangle . . . You turn the brittle pages faster. Is this perhaps where Nelly's white ship was launched?

May 31, 1937. RED SPANISH PLANES BOMBARD GERMAN BATTLE-SHIP!

The name of the battleship: 'Deutschland.' Number dead: 23. In a retaliatory action, German battleships shelled the Spanish port of Almería on June 1—Nelly had left for Swinemünde—and destroyed the harbor installations. The cruiser *Leipzig* sailed for Spain. Vacationers at the Baltic seacoast were gripped with fear of war. A homesick child stores two images: one image of the white ship which she saw in the paper and associated with the wrong news; the other, of the mother dead in her coffin. What else: that there's yellow sand, and that one walks over wooden planks to get to the beach. Nothing else. Nothing, until the homecoming in the evening, her mother's white shining face in the dark window. That, too, remains. Oh, my little dum-dum, whatever gave you the idea that I had died while you were away?

Let everything else be granted, for politeness' sake. Yes, the beautiful sand castle. The good food, yes, the beautiful fresh air. But these things never became memories.

And that's that.

After the important discovery, you turned back the pages of the *General-Anzeiger* of 1937—the paper that Nelly saw daily in the hands of her grandmother, that she saw every night in the hands of her parents. You now proceeded more systematically and started from the beginning of that particular year.

Don't be a fool, use Motorcool!

If you haven't earned your supper, give it back! It's possible to commit mental defilement of the race! True Germans shun the Jewish physician!

Then, in bold type: "Bukharin, the Last of Lenin's Old Guard, Arrested by OGPU."

A few pages later: "Beginning of the Moscow Trial of Radek and Others." Seventeen death sentences.

On May 14 the *General-Anzeiger* announces that Bukharin and Rykov have been sentenced. Stalin purges the sciences.

Although it seemed obvious at first that these reports should be passed over as not pertinent, it now seems necessary to attempt to describe how you reacted to them in May 1971, thirty-four years after the events, at your quiet, secure, regular place in the reading room of the State Library in Berlin, the capital of the German Democratic Republic. Maybe the attempt will fail, and you'd be lying if you said that you were exactly eager to tackle it. But just to give an example, a few weeks later, during your trip to Poland, Lenka—then fourteen years old—asked at dinner in the new restaurant on the market square of G.: Please tell me, who on earth is this Khrushchev! That's when you were startled into the realization that certain duties could be put off no longer, among them the duty to describe what has happened to us. We won't succeed in explaining why things happened the way they did, but at least we shouldn't shrink from doing the preliminary work for future explanations.

On the upper right-hand shelf of the bookcase in the Jordans' living room stood a book, behind glass, a book supplied by Leo Siegmann: *Socialism Betrayed*. Its jacket showed, in color, a face distorted in bloodthirsty rage under a cap with a hammer and sickle, and Charlotte Jordan had declared it a forbidden book.

(Incidentally, what kind of duty, or supposed duty, forces you to spill details of this kind? Responsibility—the only one who could talk about it is the person who knows everything and is able to tell the right thing to the right people. Responsibility can become a formula for acting irresponsibly. What remains: the duty of the writer who has to explain, for instance, what "Red Soldier" meant to Nelly throughout her childhood, and why she had this particular image. Didn't the man on the book jacket have a bayonet between his teeth? But isn't it too early to talk about it? You're watching yourself, as you're looking for reasons enabling you to skip the unfortunately accurate news of the Moscow trials of 1937, in contrast to the report on Guernica.)

A taboo is well-defined. It must not be broken without need. But besides awe, which was one step away from fear, you felt annoying rage. You resented the gloating tone of the *General-Anzeiger*'s reporters. Those people had no right to show malicious pleasure, no right whatsoever, at least not as far as this point was concerned, something which you're unusually sensitive about since it affects you directly. Which means: an obligation to be even more accurate than usual, if possible.

Moscow, June 14, 1937: "Execution of Eight Soviet Generals!" How it came about that you were affected by this news in this newspaper—the generals' remains have long since moldered away —as if it were immediate; above all, as if it concerned you personally, while the newsmen of the *General-Anzeiger* and the people who read the paper, people among whom Nelly grew up, to whom she belonged, were "they" and "those" to her, as if they were strangers (they ought to choke on their own hypocrisy): that would be a different story.

What does it mean: to change? To learn to get along without

delusions. Not having to evade children's looks that are directed at our generation when—rarely enough—the talk turns to "back when": back in the thirties, back in the fifties.

We're dealing with memory here. One pound feeds two persons! Remembered by those who shouted the slogan during choral speaking. Clean workers in clean workshops! Fellow Germans, clean up your attics!

What is the substance that memory is made of?

Without proteins, no memory. On TV the scientist in a white coat believes that he's holding the memory substance, a peptide, in his hand. Peptides are chains of amino acids whose variably linked sequences represent the contents of the information. He injects naïve rats, meaning rats that haven't yet been manipulated and are true to type, with a preparation made of the brains of manipulated rats—scotophobin—which transmits the information: Fear dark places!, causing them, as the demonstration shows, to seek out brightly lit spots, contrary to their nature. This means that the rats have taken over a memory component: fear—usually acquired in painful training—from another group of their species, in the form of a material substance, and without training.

Pies in the sky, Charlotte Jordan would say. As if fear had to be injected!

But did they know fear at all, at that time? (Later, yes. There were certain visits . . . Always two gentlemen, in inconspicuous trench coats, whose appearance made Charlotte's knees shake.)

Spain. (If you don't fight, you rot.) A cue to which Bruno, Charlotte, and Nelly Jordan would react with the same response: Hannes. Uncle Hannes. Her mother's cousin. A great guy, for whom it wasn't difficult to become a member of the new German Luftwaffe, and to bounce his niece Nelly—for convenience's sake, Nelly, you're my niece—almost to the ceiling, even though she'd gotten bigger and heavier each time he came home on leave. Who sent word to them that they shouldn't worry if they didn't hear from him for a while, he was taking part in some training exercises.

Something's rotten in the state of Denmark, said Charlotte, who tended to be suspicious. You always think you can hear the grass grow: Bruno Jordan. Until the glorious end of the Spanish War, when Uncle Hannes, among the other members of the Condor Legion, marched past the Führer in Berlin, jerking his sound legs way up in goose step, of course. He still had both legs then; it was years later that he lost his left leg after a parachute jump over the Mediterranean island of Crete. He tossed his niece to the ceiling —she had become big and strong in the meantime—and beamed at her with his bright-blue eyes in a deeply tanned face. I tell you, the Spanish sun! Up here you've no idea what it's like.

It's a safe bet that no one in the entire family—cousin, son, brother, or uncle—pulled Hannes into a secluded corner to ask him any questions. The Spanish War was enough for them as it had taken place in the *General-Anzeiger* and on the German radio. They didn't suffer from excessive curiosity, although no slogan such as Beware of curiosity! was ever drummed into the people's heads. Not once—not a single time!—were they ever tempted to turn the dial of their new radio in search of forbidden broadcasts, the radio they'd been able to purchase after the last payments on the red-brown living-room set and the bookcase had been made.

Ignorance is bliss.

Their ignorance allowed them to feel lukewarm. They were also lucky. No Jewish or Communist relatives or friends, no hereditary or mental diseases in the family (Aunt Dottie, Lucie Menzel's sister, will be mentioned later), no ties to any foreign country, practically no knowledge of any foreign language, absolutely no leanings toward subversive thought or, worse, toward decadent or any other form of art. Cast in ill-fitting roles, they were required only to remain nobodies. And that seems to come easily to us. Ignore, overlook, neglect, deny, unlearn, obliterate, forget.

According to recent discoveries, the changeover of experiences from short-term to long-term memory supposedly takes place at night, through dreams. You imagine a nation of sleepers, a people whose dreaming brains are complying with the given command: Cancel cancel cancel. A nation of know-nothings who will later, when called to account, assert as one man, out of millions of mouths, that they remember nothing. And the individual person won't remember the face of the Jew whose factory—a small, run-down candy factory, Lenka, a candy shack, that's all it was, certainly not valuable property; and if Uncle Emil Dunst hadn't gone after it, somebody else would have taken it over with the greatest of pleasure and paid less for it—whose factory you're going to look for in G., and finally you find it, in the evening, behind a

closed-up gas station on the former Küstrinerstrasse. Uncle Emil
Dunst may not ever have seen the face of the Jew Geminder, so he
didn't have to lie later when he said in his boastful manner that
he didn't have any recollection of him at all. Just an old man, on
his way out, who was glad to be able to get away. He was grateful
to me, if you want to know the truth, really grateful. Uncle Dunst
was in the habit of repeating important parts of a sentence, like
this: Some things may have happened, they may have, that weren't
quite on the level, but not with me, with me, never. Folks like
us didn't know what was going on, and if anyone has a clear
conscience, that's me, I'm the one, yes, sir.

His conscience was clear when he died in a village near Brandenburg in the late fifties, reconciled with his wife, Aunt Olga;
nursed by her, cared for, buried, mourned, and unforgotten by
her.

Things would be easier if he had only lied. During the night
before your trip to Poland you hadn't been able to sleep: the night
before July 10, 1971—remember? The room that wouldn't cool
off. The mosquitoes. The childhood nights at the end of the long
summer vacation. Sleepless, but as yet without the headaches,
which are now going to attack you without fail. Analgesic caffeine
tablets suppress pain and sleep. My head is splitting—who was it
that always used those words? Bruno Jordan. He takes aspirin. His
wife, Charlotte, oddly enough, never has a headache. Charlotte,
most of whose traits Nelly has inherited, doesn't even know what a
headache is. She's lucky, her husband thinks, his head is throbbing.
He cautiously puts one palm to his forehead, the other to the
back of his head, his face contorted in pain. It obviously wasn't
migraine he was suffering from. Whatever that may be.

Tension, then. A kind of anxiety, admittedly. Possibly a cervical
vertebra out of alignment. Increasing stiffness of the shoulder area
can transfer painful pressure to the head. But inner conflicts, too,
may find no other means of expression . . . Once you were "there,"
it would no longer be a game, you were sure of that. There's no
turning back, nothing that can be undone. Once you've walked the
streets, touched the house walls, seen the hills and the river again,
reassured yourself of their reality . . .

What forces you, you had asked yourself—not in words, that's
rare: in headaches—what forces you to climb back? To face a

child (whose name hadn't yet been determined); to expose yourself again: to the look of this child, to the offended resistance of all those involved, to the sheer lack of comprehension, but, above all, to your own strategies of concealment and your own doubt. To isolate yourself, which is the same as to "oppose."

(After a lecture to employees of a business enterprise, you try to find out if the listeners, a group from the economics division, are interested in that particular time of the past. A young blond girl likes to read books from earlier times because they bring home to her how much better off she is today, and because they help her to understand her parents. Others, older people, occasionally want to read about those times, too, but nothing too heavy, a little humor should be mixed in here and there.)

A woman near you, who is five years younger than you, says frankly: For me, that time is the tertiary. The tertiary: a geological era at whose end the contours of land masses and oceans are already similar to those of the present, the formation of mountains is basically complete, mammals roam the earth instead of the earlier saurians, and most insects and birds are close to their present state. Except that man is still absent.

Why, then, stir up settled, stabilized rock formations in order to hit on a possible encapsulated organism, a fossil. The delicately veined wings of a fly in a piece of amber. The fleeting track of a bird in once spongy sediments, hardened and immortalized by propitious stratification. To become a paleontologist. To learn to deal with petrified remains, to read from calcified imprints about the existence of early living forms which one can no longer observe.

That woman has since died. The night before the trip she was still alive; she had already spoken about the tertiary. Among the last visions which tormentingly appeared and reappeared to her was the image of an imperious blond female in high black boots, cracking a leather whip, followed by her pack of dogs, chasing through the corridors of the hospital where the young woman died.

The tertiary!

A car traveling into the tertiary.

It gives me the shivers, Charlotte Jordan would say. Normally her emphasis was more on happiness. A happy marriage, a happy family. At any rate, my children had a happy childhood. She only had the fear that happiness was all too brittle. It was as brittle as glass. Therefore her children had taken to curing themselves when they were sick, in order to spare their mother the anxiety. Except when Lutz's thick speech gave away his swollen tonsils. An obsession with happiness that was constantly being clouded by the suspicion—as if by a murky sediment—that everything was futile.

Once, when she had lugged pails of water to her rock garden all evening—if it dries up on me all the work will have been for nothing—bluish-green spots appeared and spread on the inside of Charlotte's elbows, frightening Nelly almost to death. With a strange satisfaction, almost as if she'd been waiting for it, Charlotte learned that she had to rest quietly: because of a danger of embolism, because of blood clots that might break loose; perhaps one of them was on its way to the heart even now. You see, my child, that's how fast it can happen, she said, still with the same, almost triumphant, satisfaction that Nelly resented, she wouldn't have admitted to herself why. What child wants to have her mother take death lightly? Is her mother perhaps looking for an easy way to leave her?

This failure of language. Well-lit family pictures without words. Wordless pantomime on a tidy, dusted stage. When did Charlotte reproach her husband for his smoking for the first time, when did she first press her left hand to her barely swollen neck, complaining accusingly that she had trouble breathing? This then became a daily routine at table: the mother gasping for breath, the father fanning the smoke toward the window, carefully avoiding creating a draft: Charlotte was sensitive to drafts. Silent film taking the place of speech. No statements, not even later. We had everything we could ever wish for. To master language was not one of her ambitions. If we hadn't been happy—we would have deserved a good spanking. Anyone who claims the contrary must be out of his mind. Charlotte, her hand on her gradually more and more swollen thyroid, slamming doors, cursing the store, was out of her mind, but she didn't know it and later was to forget it completely in her urgent wish to have had a happy life.

It wasn't until this past night—toward morning, when the cuckoo began to call in the small woods along the canal—that you realized you had to fear memory, this system of treachery; that by seemingly exposing it you'd actually have to fight it. The news blackout hasn't been lifted. Whatever passes censorship consists of preparations, encapsulations, fossils with a terrifying lack of individuality. Ready-made parts whose manufacturing process—in which you took part, you won't deny it—must be brought out in the open.

In the age of universal loss of memory (a sentence which arrived in the mail the day before yesterday) we must realize that complete presence of mind can be achieved only when based on a clear past. The deeper our memory, the freer the space for the goal of all our hopes: the future. (Only it's so much easier, as you realized clearly during the night, to invent the past than to remember it; and the following question dawned on you as a possible objection: Is full presence of mind really necessary, and if so, to what purpose?)

Incidentally, what do words like "deep" and "shallow" mean in relation to our memory? Is it "shallow" to note that a child (let's have the other name; the person whose life will come to your mind like that of a stranger; whom you can manipulate, whom you can penetrate—like a murderer. A doctor. A lover), that Nelly Jordan began to count her steps? Something called compulsive counting. Her walk to school was based on the magic number seven: seven steps from one tree to the next, from one fence post to the next, from one rock to the next; seven steps between two shadows, between two strong heartbeats.

The number seven began to dominate Nelly at about the time Teacher Borchers took over religion. Borchers, a gaunt, dour man who enforced the strictest silence in his classes with every means at his disposal. Nelly, not talkative by nature, broke the iron rule (with a single word whispered to Gundel Neumann, who sat in front of her: Finally!) when a girl from a higher grade came in with a blue folder containing messages from the administration to all teachers.

Teacher Borchers saw everything, heard everything, punished everything. In a severe tone he called Nelly's name, ordered her, scared out of her wits, to step forward. Seven steps to the blackboard, where punishments were pronounced and immediately meted out. Teacher Borchers, leisurely attending to the higher-grade girl; Nelly, her brain feverishly counting to seven over and over, her hands behind her back, in keeping with regulations, her mouth grinning (*oh, make me a mask!*): What is she going to do "afterward"? She knows that a person who has been beaten in public can't go on living. Teacher Borchers, finally turning to her, asks her the foolish question, Had she talked?, which she answers truthfully, though almost inaudibly, with yes. Whereupon Borchers, known for his hard and precise blows, lets one of his pupils, who has broken one of his rules, go unpunished, to the boundless amazement of the whole class: Because you honestly confessed that you had done wrong. The class considers her victorious; she feels beaten just the same (this feeling seems to plague her repeatedly). Doubly humiliated because she was praised for honesty when any denial would have been senseless: certainly she would have lied!

The cuckoo, going on and on. Seven calls and another seven calls. It was getting light. First you counted fifty-six cuckoo calls, a number which, according to folklore, would have given you a life expectancy of one hundred. The cuckoo didn't stop until 142, and you had to laugh at your own extravagance. No death wish here.

Is remembering tied to action? It would explain their loss of memory, for they didn't act. They worked so hard that they sometimes said, with uncanny accuracy: This is more than a human being can take. But they didn't act and immediately forgot their non-actions—sleepers who didn't want to wake up—though they remembered the measured excitements meted out to them. Max Schmeling vs. Joe Louis—everybody remembered that. Nelly just nine years old; they wake her up that night. The armchair by the radio. The blanket in which she's wrapped, the glass of hot lemonade. The radio announcer, his excited voice cracking. The roar coming out of the loudspeaker for thirty seconds. Then the announcer's wail and her father's desperation. He held his head in both hands, something he had never done before. Those Negroes must stuff their boxing gloves with lead in order to k.o. our great German prizefighter. Foul play, Bruno Jordan shouted. Foul play! Foul play!

The airship *Hindenburg* explodes while landing in America: That, too, everybody remembers. A survey of people over fifty might be interesting.

The terrifying lack of individuality.

Not to speak of the invasions. A nation that is becoming accus-

tomed to invading other nations, and to athletic victories. I can't
imagine any country that isn't delighted to be allowed back into
the Reich by our Führer. Herr Warsinski was right again. As
usual. Nelly can't do chin-ups, a damned shame, barely made up
for by her high accomplishments in track. Although she deserved
praise for having learned to swim—as a member of a nation of
swimmers—at age seven, in the year of the Olympic Games: in the
Warta, with old Wegner, the swimming teacher, who used to help
his students by pulling them against the current with a rope even
during their "graduation" swim. Except that Horsty Elste, Frau
Elste's young son, shouldn't have drowned in that very same river,
although it happened near the opposite bank. River is river. No
telling what may drift toward you when you have your eyes open
under water. Unfortunately, Nelly was listening when Frau Elste
gave Frau Jordan a description of the tragedy: how Horsty must
have gotten into loose driftwood along the bank and been pinned
between two tree trunks, how her husband dove and dove after
him until he finally found him, dead; and how she ran along the
bank calling his name. Oh, Frau Jordan, I don't wish that on my
worst enemy!

Now Nelly doesn't want to go swimming in the Warta any more,
oversensitive child that she is. Too much imagination. At Christmas, after she'd been given the accordion and had pretended sufficient surprise and delight (Annemarie, the new maid, had shown
her the black box downstairs in her parents' closet long before, and
Nelly had known ever since that she really didn't much feel like
learning to play the accordion); after the kale, cooked by
Whiskers Grandma, had been eaten (goose giblets, fat pork, a
handful of groats for thickening); after she'd been overcome by
peaceful lassitude, there was one of the frantic alarmist telephone
calls from Aunt Liesbeth Radde concerning her son Manni, now
three years old: Cousin Manni had a fever. Aunt Liesbeth, beside
herself with anxiety, was almost sure that her son had come down
with infectious meningitis. The shock knocked Nelly's legs from
under her. Only yesterday the stricken cousin had been sitting on
her lap. In Nelly's mind rose the specter of her family gripped one
after the other by the contagious disease. Cousin Manni, it turned
out, had a little cold. Nelly had already pictured him dead, as well
as everyone else.

Can it be true that a person's basic makeup is formed by the time he is five? Nobody, says the psychologist on TV, could answer this question with an unqualified yes or no. However, basic traits are engraved early. For instance, one must make oneself likable in order to be liked. In former days, incidentally, the pineal gland was taken to be the seat of the soul.

The basic framework—one might also say, the model of perception—could be visualized, if need be, as a network of firmly connected nerve fibers. This network is in fact being knit in the first months of life; later, the brain doesn't grow any more. It supposedly differs from family to family, from culture to culture, according to the kind and intensity of communication with the outside world, which scientists call "determining." But other than that, the structural model of the ten to fifteen billion nerve cells of the brain (each of which is interconnected with ten to fifteen thousand other cells) is the same in 99 percent of all individuals of the human species. The differences are rooted in the remaining 1 percent.

In 1937, the signal "fear" began to flicker along the entire considerable track of 300,000 miles—the supposed combined length of the nerve fibers between cells, more than the distance between earth and moon—of each individual around Nelly and of herself; but not the reflex "compassion," which we admittedly acquired much later in our phylogenetic development.

What does it all mean?

It presumably means that the reactions localized in the cerebral cortex—especially in the frontal lobes—which we take to be "typically human," will, under certain circumstances, give way to reflexes steered by the brainstem (give way, be erased, be unlearned; to fade, to slip away, to disappear; be outlived, outdated, simply gone: missing. Tertiary). Forget it. Here today, gone tomorrow. Little paper boats on the river Lethe.

(What does it mean: to change? To learn to keep the uncontrolled reflexes of the pre-human brainstem in check without making them malignant by brutal repression?)

Why didn't they suffer? The question is wrong. They suffered without knowing it, they raged against their bodies, which were giving them signals: My head is splitting. I'm suffocating.

("When the functions of the cerebral cortex are blocked, the ability to remember is lost. But a reaction to external stimuli is still possible for an individual thus afflicted. If we prick him, the affected extremity will flinch; if we shine a light in his eyes, he'll close his eyelids and his pupils will narrow; and if we push food in his mouth, he'll start eating.")

The former Jordan house stands on a street now named "Ulitsa Annuszka." Both you and Lutz like the name. You wonder if Annuszka, possibly with the stress on the first syllable, might be a girl's name.

You climb back into the car after leaving the ravine. The car is like an oven. With all the windows rolled down, you drive in the direction of the stadium and the Walter Flex Barracks. "Wild geese are rushing through the night," Lutz remembers. A barracks named after a poet. H. knows the whole long poem about Hermann Löns by heart and recites, indicating aloofness by declamatory exaggeration: "When Löns left for France from his heath back here, / Flying by his side chattered Markwart, the jay. / Löns—! Whither? To war and well-nigh fifty years? / Under your helmet your hair is turning gray!"

Come off it, Lenka said. She hates it when her elders recite this kind of stuff. Look here. Just look at this and tell me what sort of a person takes these photos.

Lenka has found a photo in the paper. It shows an old Vietnamese woman with a gun barrel at her temple, a G.I.'s right index finger on the trigger.

People take this kind of picture to make money. Lutz asks, Why don't you save your anger for that soldier?

Lenka is a child of this century. She knows about murderers and isn't interested in what makes them tick. What does a person feel who photographs murderers in the course of their assignments, instead of trying to prevent the murders: that's what she'd like to know. Nothing, you say. Probably nothing.

What beasts, says Lenka. She can't look for long at pictures or documentaries showing torture or death scenes, or would-be suicides on the edges of skyscraper roofs. She always thinks of the man behind the camera who is taking pictures instead of helping. She rejects the common division of roles: the one who must die, the one who will be the cause of the death, but the third person stands by and records what the second does to the first.

She demands unconditional involvement.

Nobody notices that you've fallen silent. *Thema cum variationes.* Stepping out of the line of murderers—where to? Into the platoon of spectators who supply the appropriate comments, admonitions, and battle descriptions?

One can either write or be happy.

During the night before the scorcher, before the short sleep in the morning, when everything had become clear, you also realized that you would have to proceed fearlessly and yet gently in order to excavate the geological layers (up to the tertiary). With a "skillful hand," you thought, full of irony, a hand which mustn't be afraid to cause pain, but must beware of causing it unnecessarily. And not only the hand, but also the person to whom it belongs, would have to shed any protective coloration and become visible. Because one acquires the rights to material of this kind by personally involving oneself in the game and by keeping the stakes sufficiently high.

But you knew at the same time that it would have to be nothing but a game. That there was to be no witches' trial—ordeal by fire and poison—no confessions extorted by the threat of violence; you even knew for a short while, and admitted it to yourself, what it really was that got this little game going: curiosity.

One can, after all, play a game with oneself about oneself.

A game in and with the second person and the third person, for the purpose of their fusion.

Two fires form the closing of this chapter, as dissimilar as fires can be, yet inseparably tied to each other in Nelly's memory: these things are beyond our control.

The Kristallnacht—the name was coined later—was carried out between November 8 and November 9: 177 synagogues, 7,500 Jewish businesses within the confines of the Reich were destroyed. In the course of governmental action, all Jews were expropriated after this spontaneous outbreak of public indignation; their sons and daughters were expelled from schools and universities. No Jewish girl is in Nelly's class. Years later, a girl from her class will refuse to sing the carol "Noel, Noel, Born is the King of Israel!" because of its glorification of Judaism. The music teacher, Johannes Freidank, whose son was killed in Poland during the first days of the war, flies into a rage and tells his favorite class—they made an excellent choir—that Jewish girls never used to refuse to sing Christian songs. Nelly's classmate won't tolerate being compared to a Jewish girl. The music teacher, fuming with anger, challenges his pupil to report him.

She didn't do it.

A speech that Dr. Joseph Goebbels gave in 1937, a speech that Nelly, too, may have heard over the radio, contained the following sentences: "Without fear we may point to the Jew as the motivator, the originator, and the beneficiary of this horrible catastrophe. Behold the enemy of the world, the annihilator of cultures, the parasite among nations, the son of chaos, the incarnation of evil, the ferment of decay, the formative demon of mankind's downfall."

Somebody must have said to Nelly: The synagogue is on fire. She doesn't know who said it. Although it is Charlotte's face, "perplexed-shocked," which appears at the cue of "burning of the synagogue." Nobody said: Go take a look!, least of all her mother. More likely the unequivocal order: Don't you dare . . .

It's unbelievable and inexplicable that she went there, but she did go, you can swear to that. How on earth did she find the little square in the old part of town? Had she known where the synagogue was, in her town? And she didn't ask anybody, that much is sure.

What was it that attracted her, since it wasn't the wish to gloat over other people's misfortune?

She wanted to see it.

November 9, 1938, doesn't seem to have been a cold day. A pale sun lit the cobblestones and the grass that grew in the cracks between them. The small, lopsided houses began where the cobblestones ended. Nelly knew that the little square and its surrounding houses would have appealed to her, if it hadn't been for the still-smoldering ruin in the center. It was the first ruin Nelly had seen in her life. Maybe she'd never heard the word before, certainly not in its later context: ruined city. Ruined landscape. For the first time she saw that the walls of a stone building don't burn down evenly, that they end up in a bizarre silhouette.

One of the small houses must have had a dark doorway where Nelly could hide. She may have leaned against a wall or one of the wings of the door. She probably wore her navy-blue sweatsuit. The square was empty, and so were the windows of the small houses around it. Nelly couldn't help it: the charred building made her sad. But she didn't know she was feeling sad, because she wasn't supposed to feel sad. She had long ago begun to cheat herself out of her true feelings. It's a bad habit, harder than any other to reverse. It stays with you and can only be caught, and be forced to retreat, step by step. Gone, forever gone, is the beautiful free association between emotions and events. That, too, if you think of it, is a reason for sadness.

To Nelly's great amazement and alarm, people were coming out of the door of the burned-down synagogue. This meant that the lower floor, where the Jews most probably had some kind of altar —as is customary in other churches—wasn't completely burned out, or destroyed and buried by fallen debris. It's sometimes possible, then, to enter still-smoldering ruins—All of this was entirely new to Nelly.

If it weren't for these people—an inner image whose authenticity is undeniable—you wouldn't be able to claim with such certainty that Nelly, a child with imagination, was near the synagogue on that afternoon. But the human figures who were running fast, yet without haste, from the door of the synagogue to the small frame house straight across, no more than twenty steps—four or five men with black beanies on their heads, and in long black coats—these were men whom Nelly had never seen, either in pictures or in real life. She didn't know what a rabbi was, either. The sun had jobs to do. It shone on the objects those men were holding in their hands (were "rescuing," Nelly thought intuitively). A kind of chalice must have been among them—is it possible? Gold!

The Jews, legless in Nelly's memory because of their long caftans, went into their destroyed synagogue at the risk of their lives and rescued their holy, golden treasures. The Jews, old men with gray beards, lived in the miserable little houses on Synagogue Square. Their wives and children were perhaps sitting behind the tiny windows, crying. (Blood, blood, blooood, blood must be flowing thick as thick can be . . .) The Jews are different from us. They're weird. Jews must be feared, even if one can't hate them. If the Jews were strong now, they'd do away with us all.

It wouldn't have taken much for Nelly to have succumbed to an improper emotion: compassion. But healthy German common sense built a barrier against it: fear. (Perhaps there should be at least an intimation of the difficulties in matters of "compassion," also regarding compassion toward one's own person, the difficulties experienced by a person who was forced as a child to turn compassion for the weak and the losers into hate and fear. This only to point out the later consequences of previous events, which are often wrongly summarized merely by the correct but not exhaustive account: 177 burning synagogues in 1938 make for ruined cities beyond number in 1945.)

Nelly was too embarrassed to stay where she was standing. Charlotte had taught her tact: mostly things one didn't do. One didn't stare at the mouth of the hungry while he was eating. One didn't talk to the hairless about his bald pate. One didn't tell Aunt Liesbeth that she didn't know how to bake. One didn't stand there gloating at others' misfortunes.

Nelly counted the strange, bearded Jews among the unfortunates.

But now to the fire in the wicker chair. It can't be ascertained whether the fire took place before or after November 9. Nelly's brother has completely forgotten the time in his life when he was considered an intractable child because of his violent fits of temper. One word, the word "charred," perhaps justifies at least superficially the leap from the synagogue to the Jordan children's room. The maid Annemarie is alerted by the smoke billowing from under the door. She fetches her mistress, Charlotte, who races upstairs. Whiskers Grandma on her bow legs comes downstairs anyway at the least sign of a disturbance. Wet towels beat out the fire. When Nelly comes home from school, she finds the charred wicker chair, an obstinate, already punished brother who has just begun a career as an arsonist and must be regarded as a different person from now on, and a mother shaken to the bone, suddenly faced with the possibility of one of her children being no good.

The next day, Lutz puts his right hand on the hot coils of the electric stove. He has blisters on all the fingertips of the hand that set the fire. Again the mother has to be called. The house echoes with sounds of lament and pity, an oil bath is prepared for the poor, sick hand, the little boy sits on his mother's lap and lets himself be comforted. There there, don't be upset. It'll soon be all better.

Nelly squats on the sand mountain. She's caught a matchbox

full of ladybugs, her favorite creatures. Built a sand town for them, streets, squares, trees of green weeds. The ladybugs have to prove their gratitude by strictly following the prescribed streets and paths. They won't do it. They're running on the ground every which way and have to be punished. Nelly builds underground sand caves: prisons for the ladybugs. Serves you right, Nelly says in righteous wrath, after shoving the ladybugs underground, it serves you right, it serves you right. You're bad, wicked, disobedient. Single ladybugs work themselves free; violently and hastily she covers them with loose sand, again and again, as soon as they try to escape. I'll show you. Why should she cry, she's actually quite delighted.

Lenka, you say in the car—the tips of the poplars around the stadium are coming into view—Lenka, how about it? Lenka groans. But she does begin to massage your shoulders. Like iron, she complains. Stiff, stiff. Don't make yourself so stiff all the time.

When did it start?

8

"With my burned hand I write about the nature of fire." (Ingeborg Bachmann)

The craving for authenticity is growing.

Artificial light as early as 4 p.m., goddamned fall. Fall is the season when wars start. When the U.S. Air Force dropped its first bombs on Vietnam in August 1964, our well-trained nerves sounded the alarm: War! (We were thinking: War here at home.) The years 1956, 1961, 1968, and 1973 bear out the theory of autumnal crises, while other years refute it . . .

Chile. The recorded voice of a murdered president. The picture of the poet, lying in state in the ruins of his devastated house.

When it's 4:30 p.m. Central European time, it's 11:30 p.m. in Chile. Whoever reads these lines three years from now, at the earliest, will have to make an effort to recall: Who was Corvalán? One of the many for whom we could do nothing.

He was, at any rate, a person who would not be reaching for a book, for pages of writing, during these weeks, but for a rifle, if he could.

This—and the increasing fear—explains the delay between chapters. The past—whatever the continuously accumulating stack of memories may be—cannot be described objectively. The two-fold meaning of the word "to mediate." To be the mediator between past and present—the medium of a communication between the two. In the sense of reconciliation? appeasement? smoothing out? Or a rapprochement of the two? To permit today's person to meet yesterday's person through the medium of writing?

From the beginning this chapter had been earmarked to deal with the war; like all the other chapters, it has been prepared on sheets with headings such as Past, Present, Trip to Poland, Manuscript. Auxiliary structures, devised to organize the material and to detach it from yourself by this system of overlapping layers, if not by the simple mechanism of cause and effect. Form as a possibility of gaining distance. Forms of gaining distance, which are never accidental, never arbitrary. The blunt capriciousness that exists in life has no place here.

(A news item of September 20, 1973: The peaked cap which Hitler used to wear before 1933, authenticated by persons close to the Führer, is being auctioned off in Cologne. Its starting price: 75,000 marks.)

An authentic declaration by Dr. Goebbels, with reference to the so-called Anschluss, the incorporation of Austria into the German Reich: "At last the Teutonic Empire of the German Nation has come into being." Nelly had sat by the loudspeaker listening to the delirium of joy bursting forth in a city named Vienna, a jubilation that could no longer be distinguished from a howl, which rose as though a force of nature were exploding, but which moved Nelly's inner depths in a way no force of nature had ever moved her before; she was trembling, and her father's brown writing desk bore the sweat marks of her sopping-wet hands.

Charlotte Jordan, who wasn't able to take proper care of her children because of the damned store, promised to smash the radio to bits; the girl is going off her rocker.

Now let's not throw out the baby with the bath water.

Always expecting the worst.

Cassandra, behind the counter in her store; Cassandra aligning loaves of bread; Cassandra weighing potatoes, looking up every once in a while, with an expression in her eyes which her husband prefers not to see. Everything we do is an accident. An accident, this husband of hers. These two children about whom she has to worry so much. This house, and the poplar in front of it, completely alien.

Charlotte, who was born at the turn of the century, is now thirty-nine. She has put on weight. She's wearing her hair in a twist; last Christmas her husband gave her a silver fox, a sheer waste of money, where is she supposed to show it off? She has begun to dye her hair, a toothbrush with blackened bristles lies on the glass shelf in the bathroom, next to a tube of hair coloring. German chemistry was highly developed even then, but the hair colors of those days can't compare with what we have today. Charlotte's hairline was a reddish brown. Nelly inspects the blackened toothbrush as though it might betray a secret of her mother. She stands in front of the bathroom mirror, undoes her braids, tries out different hairdos, and makes faces. Then she stares into her own eyes, and says slowly and clearly: Nobody loves me. (An authentic sentence, although there obviously exists no printed proof of it, unlike Dr. Goebbels's statement about the Teutonic empire. How can anyone be made to understand that these two completely unrelated sentences are, in your opinion, somehow connected? That, precisely, would be the kind of authenticity you're aiming for, and this trifling example shows you where an actual acceptance of your goal would lead: into the unfathomable, to say the least.)

Four, five years later, pessimism may become punishable by death, since the more desperate the situation, the more drastic the measures against those who call it "desperate." In 1944, Charlotte Jordan declared in public—that is, in her store, in the presence of three customers whom she thought she knew well, one of whom did, however, hold a leading position in the National Socialist Women's Organization: We've lost this war, even a blind man can see that.

Three days later, on a summer evening, Charlotte was sitting with her daughter, Nelly, and her mother on the lawn behind the porch, wrapping sugar candies for Uncle Emil Dunst's candy factory, when two gentlemen appeared, in trench coats despite the summer temperature, and demanded to speak with her, preferably inside the house. Bruno Jordan, who walked in on the situation, placed a blanket over his wife's legs to conceal the sight of her shaking knees from the two gentlemen: His wife was sickly, she easily caught a chill.

To the children: Those two? Good Lord, two gentlemen from the Tax Bureau. An acceptable explanation: such things readily occur in the business world.

To the gentlemen: Never! said Charlotte. Never did I say a thing like that. The war lost! Somebody must have misheard, and I mean mis-heard!

How come Nelly didn't notice how her mother was inwardly shaking with fear—every time the doorbell rang, for instance, especially in the evening—that she didn't sleep much for five, six weeks, until the conclusive interview in the Gestapo building, where she was told the matter would be dropped, since the other two witnesses hadn't heard her make any such remark, and so far Frau Jordan's reputation had been above reproach— Leo Siegmann, her husband's old friend with the gold party button, had "pulled every string possible."

An assumed dialogue between Bruno and Charlotte Jordan on the evening of that day. Bruno: For God's sake, be careful from now on. You were lucky.

Charlotte: Lucky? She had a provocative way of repeating words with which she disagreed. Thanks a million. But one thing's sure: from now on, I'd rather bite off my tongue.

Well, then that settles that.

Yet the remark that had caused the trouble was extremely moderate compared to what she had said at the beginning of the war. Namely: The hell with your Führer.

Imagine the scene as follows: Time: Late evening of August 25, 1939; Place: The dimly lit stairway of the Jordan house. Characters: A mailman; Bruno Jordan standing across from mailman; Nelly, mute as always on such occasions, in the door of the apartment; halfway up the stairs Charlotte Jordan; and higher up, leaning over the banister, Whiskers Grandma.

Why does she say: your, Nelly thought, your Führer?

While Bruno Jordan grabbed his wife by the arm, in one of his "iron grips," probably, and uttered two sentences: one to Charlotte: For God's sake, woman! Your talk could cost us our heads. And the other to the mailman: Don't take her seriously. My wife's nerves aren't the best.

Whereupon the mailman made a gesture that meant: Never mind, and walked off. An authentic occurrence which requires interpretation.

Charlotte strictly avoided and forbade her children the use of vulgar words. She'd say: "darn" but not "damn." She'd say "dumdum" but never "ass." There is no record of her ever calling the Führer stronger and riskier names, either to herself or half aloud to her husband in the evening, when the children were asleep in bed and the Jordan couple sat reading under the living-room lamp; it is possible that she had reached the height of abuse on that first evening, which was, however, topped later, after the end of the war, when she gave him the title "that goddamned lousy criminal."

That particular first evening was composed of all possible levels. It was Lutz's seventh birthday, which had been gaily celebrated within the family circle; in the evening the uncles had come to pick up their wives and children, who had spent the afternoon at the coffee table, praising Whiskers Grandma's crumb cake, exchanging pleasantries. After a period of unpleasant misunderstandings among relatives, everyone seemed to wish for a reconciliation. Aunt Liesbeth praises Aunt Lucie's elaborate hairdo, Aunt Lucie can't express enough surprise about how beautifully little Manfred (Cousin Manni, the premature baby) has developed lately. And after supper, all three brothers-in-law—Bruno Jordan, Walter Menzel, and Alfons Radde—stand up to drink a toast to the prosperity of their families, as seems fitting. Nelly is silent, but she is sensitive to the vibrations; she has a feeling of relief, of "bliss" perhaps. Whiskers Grandma is wiping her eyes with a corner of her apron. Everybody feels that the reason for being alive is to live in peace and harmony with each other. Shyly someone says: Now, isn't that much better. You can say that again, says Bruno Jordan.

Everybody says goodbye. The Jordans lay pillows on their windowsills, and look out, to let the evening come to a peaceful end. No big words now. No words at all. Just the peace and quiet of the evening.

Somebody's coming, said Charlotte. A black figure, walking in the dark along the deserted street. Funny, he's going into all the houses. (Not into all of them, but into many, because several different age groups were being drafted at once.) What's he doing, knocking at every door? Looks almost like a mailman. You know, that is a mailman. What does he want, at this hour of the night? You know what I think he's bringing?

The worst, always the worst. Instead of staying calm. Instead of waiting to see if he's coming to our house, too. When there'd still be time to pronounce a phrase like "draft notices." And even then it may be premature to speak of war. But no. Charlotte has to get it out all at once. You know what? He's handing out draft notices. I'm telling you, there'll be a war!

As though hypnotized, she follows the man with her eyes as he goes from door to door in the Bahr houses, as lights go on in a number of apartments, as he finally crosses Soldinerstrasse, at a neat right angle, heading straight for her stairs, without a moment's hesitation. At that point, Charlotte detaches herself from the window and runs upstairs to Whiskers Grandma, to inform her of the impending event—while the man climbs the stairs, one step at a time, since he's tired; he needn't ring the bell, Bruno Jordan has already opened the door, the man hands him the dirty yellow envelope: I've got something for you.

Bruno, collected: Here we go again . . .

The mailman, tired: Yep; seems that way.

And after that, from halfway up the stairs, Charlotte's exclamation: The hell with your Führer.

In other words: Nelly's mother was deserting the Führer. Her father must go to war. War is the worst of all things. Her father may be killed in action. The Führer knows what he is doing. Now every German must be brave.

The draft notice is for the following morning, at nine o'clock. Meeting place: the Adler Garden. On a day like this, children may be "absent" from school. "Please excuse the absence of my daughter; her father was drafted and she had to accompany him to the station." Slightly modified, it might be the text of an obituary notice, one need only change "was drafted" to "passed away" and "to the station" to "on his last journey." Nelly couldn't help feeling that she was on a last journey—she had inherited her mother's pessimistic streak—Oh, may he re-est, may it all come to an e-end . . .

No tears, oh no.

Heinersdorf Grandpa arrived on his bicycle to say goodbye to his son. Are those people calling in the veterans? Bruno Jordan was forty-two. First, everybody stands around waiting in the Adler Garden. Almost half of every day, the soldier waits his life away. Garden chairs and garden tables are at their disposal. The dispensing of beer is of course forbidden. There are more civilians than future soldiers, who can be recognized by the tied-up cartons they're carrying around with them, or placing at their feet. The order: "Fall in!" familiar to all, gives them quite a jolt this time. Her father stands impeccably aligned in the second formation. A list of names is being read. Orders are given which set the column in motion in the direction of the station, a short distance away.

A song. "The birds in the forest / they sing so loud and clear / in my country, my country . . ." Her father never could sing.

The families, the wives and children, on the sidewalks on both sides of the marching column. At the corner of Bahnhofstrasse Bruno Jordan turns around. He waves; a gesture which means: Don't come any farther. Contrary to expectation, Charlotte obeys. She stops and bursts into sobs. Nelly's father has the face of a man who must hold back his tears. On the walk back—Charlotte always cried loudly in public when a catastrophe hit her family, therefore Nelly must control herself, she is pulling her brother after her—right in front of the dairy store, Heinersdorf Grandpa makes an astounding declaration: Little girl, you won't see your father again. Mark my words.

Usually, prophecies aren't Heinersdorf Grandpa's thing. Nelly still hears her father's parting sentence: Stand by your mother! Now she must also lock her grandfather's sentence away inside herself, for safekeeping. There were times when sentences like that seemed to pile up. Where would she be if she dealt with them carelessly?

But her mother, Cassandra, tears into her husband's father. How can you say such a thing!

To think that on that Monday, thirty-four years ago, someone may have sat at his typewriter—someone who may be dead by now, whose name you don't know—somewhere in the world, someone who shakes his head at the news of the German mobilization, absorbed as he is in his work. Without a thought for a ten-year-old child or a desperate old man. And to think that you are now that someone, while the children in Israel and in Egypt accompanied their fathers to the rallies yesterday (today is Sunday, October 7, 1973), where an old man—perhaps the survivor of a Nazi concentration camp; perhaps a man who can neither read nor write—says in Hebrew or in Arabic that they should be prepared never to see their father again. You remain seated at your typewriter, absorbed in your own affairs, while "the fighting continues with unabated violence" at the Suez Canal.

History's accursed tendency to repeat itself: we must brace ourselves against this.

During the night you woke up abruptly, between two and three in the morning. You felt your daily habit of writing somehow challenged.

In your dream you found yourself in a rambling country house, a kind of hotel, that was teeming with people; bearded, white-faced men in wild getups, none of whom you knew, but who spoke to you as though you had all come together for a common purpose that needed no further explanation. In a whitewashed, incidentally rather primitive, room to which you withdrew, you were surprised to come upon a small, deformed man—the top of his head was egg-shaped—who left immediately, at your request. But minutes later he was hurled back into the room in a most horrible way, through the splintering door, hanging upside down on a swinglike rope contraption which torturers were pushing back and forth, while they beat the little man and yelled at him to disclose certain information. To your indescribable horror you realized that the little man was unable to speak, he had no mouth. The lower half of his face, which rose up close in front of you at every second push of the swing, was smooth and white and mute. He could not obey his torturers' commands even if he had wanted to. In desperation you thought—a thought you immediately canceled in your mind— they ought to let him write if they want to find out something from him. At that instant, the torturers untied him, set him down on your bed, handed him a pencil and narrow strips of white paper, on which he was to write down his answers. The poor creature uttered sounds that made the blood freeze in your veins. But the worst of it was that you understood him: he didn't know anything. They continued to torture him on your bed.

Your horror continued for hours after your reluctant awakening. It was focused on the moment when you had thought of what the torturers ought to do in order to attain their end: make the mute man write. And you had stood by, paralyzed, tied to the role of spectator; and couldn't step forward to come to the aid of the victim. You'd give a great deal to be able to forget your dream.

There was an SS man named Boger, in a German concentration camp, who invented an instrument of torture, later called the Boger swing. You thought your writing would make the bottom layer rise to the surface, but it may be impossible to be alive today without becoming implicated in the crime. A famous Italian has said that twentieth-century men resent themselves and each other for having shown their capacity to live under dictatorships. But where does the reporter's accursed duty begin—for the reporter is an observer, whether he wants to be or not, or else he wouldn't be writing, he'd be fighting or dying—and where does his accursed right end?

Where are the days when the murmuring conjurors of the past tense were able to persuade themselves and others that they were dispensers of justice? Woe to our time, which forces the writer to exhibit the wound of his own crime before he is allowed to describe other people's wounds.

If Pablo Neruda's last manuscript had been stolen, the loss would have been irreparable. Thus, writing, even on a day such as this, suddenly becomes a duty which surpasses all others, even if it means reopening questions about which everything seems to have been said, and about which the rows of book spines in the libraries are no longer measured in yards, but in miles. In spite of everything, the war is still unexplained, insufficiently discussed. We have agreed to write about a certain aspect of the war, or to adopt a certain style when speaking of it, or to condemn it, but one feels a sort of omission in the writing, an avoidance of certain things which shake up the soul anew. The Pole Kazimierz Brandys, whom you quote without quotation marks, also speaks of an insane transformation of circumstances due to the war.

Of a laying bare of the innards.

But the absence of insane transformations may also be a disappointment. Exclamations, repeating themselves ever faster, ever louder, as if in a maelstrom: Danzig! Polish Corridor! Germans! Murder! For Nelly, Lebensraum culminated in the logical cry: "Gleiwitz transmitter! Western Plateau!" And in the sentence "As of this morning we're going to return the fire." A sentence that lifted the heart and let it drop as though it were a tennis ball, and a sentence of the Führer could make it bounce.

Herr Gassmann, Nelly's history teacher (Nelly was by now in the first year of secondary school), appeared in his brown unit leader's uniform and announced: It is as if these sentences were spoken by the venerable mouth of history itself. Professor Gassmann expressed what Nelly felt, but he didn't say whether he, too, was secretly disappointed by the uniformly beautiful fall weather that lasted all through the Polish campaign. Did he, too, not wish for a life that would be like a continual special news bulletin, did he not regret at least a little bit the unchanging daily routine?

Nelly has become addicted.

The jubilation that accompanied the marching of the garrison troops from the Walter Flex Barracks along Soldinerstrasse might have been louder, but it had to be taken into account that the street had few houses. Nelly and Charlotte Jordan, who threw packs of cigarettes into the military vehicles, in which soldiers sat in rows, holding the barrels of their rifles straight at nose height, were not the only ones in the street; other residents had also come out, most of them people who clung to the August 1914 notion of a war starting with the distribution of small bunches of fall flowers to the troops marching to battle. What did it say on the truck? "We'll be home for Christmas!" That's what it said. A hopeful message.

We are dealing with an underdeveloped era, as far as communication is concerned. Nowadays, the first live pictures are instantly transmitted from any war—even from Chile, where the junta naturally imposed its censorship, immediately after imposing martial law. Secretly shot films lose their professional quality, they're unsharp, erratic, violently shaky. The cameraman films his own murderer, the man who is aiming his rifle at him. The camera shoots as he sways, falls, the picture stops. And then: contorted corpses along a dusty highway, on which people walk, past the corpses, without looking.

The correspondents of Western news agencies were not able to supply their readers with similar photos from Germany, at any time between 1933 and 1945. The corpses weren't lying around outside. They died in cellars and in barracks. It was a concession of the killers to the European mentality, which did not remain totally unrewarded. The reward was called non-intervention.

Historians rejoice in the wealth of documented material from the times in question. One reads that for the thirteen Nuremberg trials alone, sixty thousand documents were accumulated, whose complete evaluation, let alone publication, would swallow untold sums of money. There seems to be no lack of documents, either today or during the years the Jordans, the Menzels, the Raddes lived through. Assuming the residents of Soldinerstrasse had had access—by accident, or by listening to enemy transmitters (which were possibly keeping silent on the subject as long as their governments were engaged in negotiations with the government of the German Reich)—to certain communications, promises, claims, rejections, ultimatums, guarantees, protocols of secret discussions. ("Danzig is not the issue that is at stake": Adolf Hitler to the high command of the German armed forces.) Assuming that they had gained insight into the wording of last-minute nonaggression pacts and had known not only the conditions of the sixteen-point program to the Polish people—it was transmitted by all German radio stations—but had also been informed about this program's role as an alibi. Late in the evening of August 31, when the sixteen points were being broadcast, the beginning of the assault on Poland was scheduled for September 1, 4:45 a.m., and the special commandos who were to feign Polish attacks on the Gleiwitz transmitter, the customs house in Hochlinden, District of Ratibor, and the forester's cottage in Pitschen, District of Kreuzburg, were already dressed in Polish uniforms. Assuming that they had actually been informed of Mussolini's letter, which delayed the start of the war, initially scheduled for August 26, by six days, because the Italians declared that they were not sufficiently prepared to fulfill their obligations toward their German Axis partner; assuming that these and other secret orders had been accessible to every household, what would have been changed?

The question implies the answer.

The Jordans have a family photo, taken by the noncommissioned officer Richard Andrack, who was sharing a desk in the Armed Forces District Command with Bruno Jordan after the Polish campaign, after the older soldiers had been transferred to home duty. Richard Andrack was a photographer by profession and a hypnotist on the side. The photo was taken with a flashbulb in the parlor, in such a fashion that the camera stood on a tripod in the door that led to the living room and caught exactly the group of persons seated around the tiled coffee table. Parents and children sit on two armchairs and on the couch, next to each other and across from each other. A certain stiffness is due to their lack of experience in posing. Nonetheless, sitting stiffly erect, they look smilingly past each other into the four corners of the room.

One will never be able to prove that millions of similar family photos stacked one on top of the other had anything to do with the outbreak of the war.

It really is the way Emil Dunst told his sister-in-law Charlotte, after running Jew Geminder's candy factory until every essential ingredient for the manufacture of candy had become "scarce": We Germans work our asses off, we sure do. I'd like to see anybody else work as hard. And don't talk to me about all the other bullshit!

At the same time, great satisfaction at the news that German units had "made contact" with the enemy. Nelly asked herself how one could keep the enemy away and make contact at the same time. The answer was simple: one made contact with the enemy in order to destroy him. One dealt him fatal blows with an iron fist.

It took Nelly twenty-five minutes to run to the Kyffhauser Cinema to see the latest edition of the afternoon newsreels amid an audience of children and old people who uttered sounds of rapture and ducked their heads when German air squadrons thundered across the newsreel sky, and broke into derogatory murmurs when the camera swept across the faces of Polish subhumans, who were being driven into captivity. The feature showed "Robert Koch, the warrior against death," *An Ideal Husband*, with Heinz Rühmann, also *Charley's Aunt*, and *Once Upon a Gorgeous Ballroom Night*. The municipal theater opened its season with *Viennese Blood*.

The newspapers which lay in the car, next to the ancient yellow oilcloth lion, your little mascot, during your two-day trip to Poland on July 10 and 11, 1971, happened to publish excerpts from the Pentagon papers, which a man named Ellsberg had been able to steal and make accessible to the general American public. Lenka, who must have glanced at the papers at one point or another, suddenly mentioned it, initially by asking the following question: Do you know an adult who is actually happy?

That may have been the time you all began listening to sentences Lenka said in which the words "actually" or "incidentally" appeared. For whatever reason, it mattered to you that Lenka considered you a happy adult, while her Uncle Lutz thought that the time had come to enlighten his niece about young people's demands for happiness, and real life.

You had just stopped at the stadium entrance and were about to get out of the car. You had asked to stop, ostensibly to get the circulation back into your foot, which had fallen asleep, but in reality because you wanted to feel the wood of the turnstile next to the cashier's booth once again, and to hang once more from the banister that runs along the poplar-lined main path on both sides; its rough iron instantly burns the hands.

Do you remember the heat that day? It was almost 1 p.m., and you were hoping it wouldn't get any hotter. You were holding the turnstile in your hands, turning it unconsciously, playfully, back and forth, at first not in the least surprised, and then extremely surprised, that it was still creaking at the same spot and in the same manner as twenty-seven years ago (did that not have to be an illusion? Illusion now, or illusion then?); you leaned against it, finally, blocking the turnstile; hesitantly and of course jokingly you said to Lenka that H. and you were "happy adults."

Lenka, who had heard this expression often, accepted your joke, concealed what she thought or saw underneath, raised exaggerated eyebrows, and said: You two?

Why must it be a fault if your children don't think that you're "happy"? An argument ensued about the old-fashioned word. You were aware that you wanted to see Lenka's eyes free of doubt— that is, childlike—at least once more, at least for the remainder of the day. By devious means you pushed her to admit that she really and truly didn't consider you "unhappy"—quite the contrary, even. However, she didn't say what the contrary of unhappy was. (Lenka doesn't say what she doesn't want to say, unlike you; at Lenka's age, Nelly didn't say what she didn't want to say, either. It might be worth thinking about the point when one starts saying words which one doesn't want to say.)

Every fall, the Hitler Youth contests in running, broad jumping, and volleyball took place in the stadium. Nelly's achievements were considerable, and were acknowledged with a victory pin and a scroll. Nelly was at the top of her athletic potential and belonged to the ten best of the local Jungmädel team, who were allowed to participate in the district contests, which also took place in the stadium. Every patch of grass, every dirt track, was teeming with girls and boys in black athlete's trunks and white shirts, with the swastika in a rhomboid sewn on in the center; and the stands and locker rooms were teeming with brown skirts and white blouses, blue skirts and short black pants, black triangular kerchiefs and braided leather knots, Hitler Youth daggers and shoulder straps; yelling, eager, sweating crowds being organized into troops and sent into the competitions, tamed and controlled by fractions of seconds and millimeters of difference.

Steeling the body. Steeling body and mind with athletics.

The Pentagon papers, for whose theft and publication Daniel Ellsberg has meanwhile stood trial and been acquitted. Lenka wanted to know if it was humanly possible that a series of Secret Service manipulations and a chain of abominable negligences and the incredible incompetence of those at the top, such as the President of the United States, John F. Kennedy, could unleash a sequence of revolutions, counter-revolutions, assassinations of recent allies, which had to be called "war" from a specific moment on, the Vietnam War.

Humanly possible, yes. Under certain conditions, you said. And you named a number of them. The white President of a large powerful country must, among other things, deem the way of life of his class and his race the only human way of life, and thus might carelessly sign a telegram whose importance for a population of a different skin color and another way of life he may realize only later.

Lenka uses words like "crazy," "disgusting," "shitty"; the choice of words you used when you were young has faded with the war and other annihilation campaigns. "Horrible," "awful," "obnoxious," "dreadful" have been used too often. Only people like Aunt Trudy—Trudy Fenske, who was divorced during the first years of the war, which was of course a dreadful thing—continue to use these words, even though the reasons for using them have been diminishing.

Suddenly you understand why Lenka didn't want to call you two happy (the two of you together maybe, but each of you separately? Hardly . . .), and why she was determined to find her own kind of happiness. The way both of you walk, your cramped posture, the mechanical plodding of unexercised legs, your anchored purposefulness, must tell her enough about you.

Could you possibly have a feeling of envy as you watch her swing herself over the iron guard, sideways, lightly supported by one hand? (A talent for high jumping, her gym teacher had said, unused, unfortunately, like all her other talents; it might have amounted to something. A bored wave of her hand: Competitive sports? Forget it!) The way she suddenly falls into a dance rhythm that seems to be inborn, the way she is dancing ahead of you all, making the wooden turnstile swing; your fleeting regret about your own prematurely imposed inactivity and now progressive rigidity, calcium deposits in the joints.

Furloughs were granted when the general situation permitted it—as in October 1939, when Poland was "written off"—10,572 dead, 30,322 wounded, 3,402 missing, on the German side. Two new Reich districts, Danzig and Posen, had been "forged in the fire of battle." It was November. A foggy afternoon. Nelly was coming home from "service." An unknown, heavy, battle-gray overcoat was hanging on the coat rack in the vestibule, together with a soldier's cap and a brown leather belt with a silvery glistening buckle with the eagle and the inscription: *God with Us* engraved upon it. The odor of the coat, into which Nelly buried her face before she was able to go into the dining room; cigarette smoke was floating in the air once again, at long last, after so many weeks; her father was sitting at the table, her brother Lutz in his lap, her mother across from him, at the busiest of business hours, on a Saturday afternoon. She was pouring coffee for Nelly's father, with a look in her eyes . . . Nelly immediately burst into tears. As almost always, her tears were misunderstood, and interpreted as boundless joy at her father's homecoming; as almost always, she was showered with the wrong consolations and undeserved kisses. However, the thought that had flashed through her head: Now we're in for the drama of homecoming, that thought was certainly worthy of tears.

One must eventually break the silence about difficult things. We're coming to her father's ashen face.

Eventually there comes the time to stop describing the weather. That particular November wasn't foggy throughout, it had its sunny days. The day you must describe was sunny. It was a Sunday, a Sunday morning, between noon and 12:30, because the Jordans ate at 12:30, and the telephone call occurred shortly before. In the evening and on Sundays the telephone was transferred from the store to the vestibule of the apartment, where it stood on the white table in front of the coat rack. Nelly was in her room, absorbed in her books, as usual; she heard her father's voice cry out: "Leo!" happy to hear the voice of his friend Leo Siegmann, with whom he shared a desk in the office of their infantry unit in a "godforsaken dump" on the western bank of the Bug River, and who had the switchboard connect him—because he felt bored— with his friend Corporal Bruno Jordan, currently on furlough. (Yes, it's sunny here, too . . .)

More.

They talked for a good five minutes. Charlotte Jordan was getting slightly annoyed about this disturbance right at mealtime and called the children to the table. Nelly stood in the door of her room, directly behind her father; she could see her father's face in the vestibule mirror; she heard him say a couple of words in a totally changed tone, questioning words mostly, which were being answered at greater length at the other end of the line.

You did what?

I see, when?

The day before yesterday. I see.

How many did you say?

He then repeated a figure which must have been the figure Leo Siegmann had given him. You couldn't swear to it, but you think it was five. (The figure 5 as a meat hook.)

More.

At this point, her father's ashen face appears. Nelly is sure she saw it in the mirror. A gray, sunken face. She insists: Her father reached for a sleeve of his battle-gray overcoat, to steady himself. He hurriedly ended the conversation with Leo Siegmann. Without paying attention to her, he walked into the dining room with buckling knees and dropped into a chair. From then on, words fail her.

There is no memory of the rest, and the words in which Bruno Jordan informed his wife of his conversation with Leo Siegmann shall not be invented.

The gist of it was as follows: the day before yesterday his unit executed Polish hostages.

Meaning—but not with certainty—hanged. The number: five. And Leo Siegmann's sentence: Too bad you weren't there.

You could vouch for this verbatim quotation: Too bad you weren't there. That's what he said.

And for the fact that Charlotte stopped eating.

And for him saying, later, without being prodded: That kind of thing is not for me.

And for an exchange of looks between her parents, not meant for the children, barely meant for each other. Two married people, hiding their eyes from each other.

The word "ghastly," it does seem to be usable still. Let's sum up then, not only this scene, but also Nelly's sensations, with a word that was unknown to her: "ghastly."

She cast down her eyes and didn't give herself away.

To be able to reply truthfully to Lenka's questions. She is reading—toward the end of October 1973—a detailed description of the persecution of Jews in a small German town. For quite some time Lenka has dropped the word "German" from her vocabulary. She has no need for the word; it means nothing to her; she has absolutely no use for it; she thinks it's simply an overstatement; it strikes her as repulsive, actually. She is sick in bed, as almost always during fall vacations, coughing, but refusing tea, mufflers, and ointments, books lie piled around her; how can one go on living "after that?" she wants to know.

It's in the form of a question. And a statement: You're actually asking quite a lot of us.

Two years ago, she wasn't saying things like that, but how is one to know at what point she started thinking them? Perhaps the very second she began twirling the wooden turnstile in the stadium in L., today G., the wooden entrance cross, before your eyes?

For a long time, she has been in the habit of keeping recent conclusions to herself and letting them go suddenly, ruthlessly, as a surprise, without explanation, the way one lets go of a wild dog that has been held captive for a long time.

And we're supposed to understand all of that. I, at any rate, don't understand it, Lenka said.

And do you think that you . . . I mean your generation . . . could not let similar things . . .

That sort of thing?

Lenka didn't repeat her question of two years ago: Why are there no happy adults? She still hasn't been told about the scene that centers on Bruno Jordan's sentence: That kind of thing is not for me! Do you envy her for never seeing her father's face turn ashen? Yes, you do.

You tell her about Nelly's walk to the burned-down synagogue, while the radio, which Lenka always keeps on in the background, softly announces that the U.S.A. has placed its troops in a low state of alert in the States, the Pacific, and Europe, in order to be prepared to deal with the dispatch of Soviet troops to the Middle East war zone at any time. Four more followers of Allende have been condemned to death in Chile, and shot by a firing squad. (We also heard the sound of women screaming and weeping in the Santiago morgue. That is progress. There is no sound track from German Gestapo cellars. The number of Chilean victims during seven weeks is larger than the number of German victims during the first six years. There was armed resistance, in Chile.)

While you tell her, you feel that things are not getting any clearer, but rather more confused. You feel the emphasis shifting continuously to issues which are being formed as you speak . . .

How can you make Lenka understand that Nelly's childhood continued colorfully, beyond these issues. She hardly noticed them. The collecting manias, for instance, to which Nelly became addicted, just like everybody else: the collecting of pictures printed on glossy paper and cellophane, the manufacture of albums from old notebooks, the pages folded down the middle; during every recess, even during class, the notebooks were passed around to exchange the pictures, under the benches, at the risk of having the valuable book confiscated. Flowers for animals, decals for cigarette pictures.

But the things we wrote in autograph albums were the same as yours, Lenka: "Steel and iron will rust and bend, but our friendship will never end!" (Meanwhile, as the war continued, and certain unbelievable information reached a world which had remained incredulous for a long time, considerations were being weighed: whether it might not be expedient, not to say necessary, to exterminate all German children after the war. The Pole Brandys tells how an older relative expresses this thought and how his mother gazes at him pensively before she says: But you're not normal . . .) But we also put quotations by the Führer in our books. Nelly's girlfriend Hella Teichmann preferred the following: "Whoever wants to live must fight. Anyone who refuses to fight in this world of never-ending struggle does not deserve to live!"

What does it all prove? Nothing. There isn't a single hint in any of the books piled up on your night table about how similar scenes in German living rooms were concluded. The Jordans didn't say grace; occasionally they'd say the habitual "Enjoy." Meals were eaten without formality, and ended without formality. You got up and pushed your high-backed black chair under the table. The children cleared the table. The maid Annemarie eats in the kitchen, she'll wash the dishes—Nelly dries them—before she can finally have her Sunday afternoon off. Nelly's parents have retired to take a nap. Nelly was duly reprimanded for the gravy stain she had made on the clean tablecloth: You're all thumbs. It was unthinkable that any gesture might have been changed or omitted, just because of the news that her father had missed becoming a murderer by a hair's breadth. Order must be maintained.

Lutz, who can rightfully say that he is opposed to any hypersensitivity, warned you about going too far. He stayed close to you, while H. and Lenka picked mugwort stems along the edge of the stadium to take home and dry as meat seasoning. (You remembered the unpopular medicinal-herb-gathering drives. Right here at the stadium huge patches of yarrow, St. John's bread, and camomile used to grow—and still grow. Bulging bags on the handlebars of your bicycle, the attic laid out with newspaper, the sticky heat, permeated with the pungent aroma of drying herbs; the view of the town from the small attic window, the river and the meadows beyond, a panorama of sunshine and large rapid cloud shadows, an extremely sharp and beautiful picture.) A quick exchange of half-whispered words about the danger of going too far. He thinks he's detecting certain intentions in some of your remarks, more so in your silences, more so in the expressions on your face, which he must still be watching: since the time he changed from your younger to your big brother and developed a kind of concerned attention for his sister, without having been asked to by anybody. He has no intention of meddling, of prying for confessions, still less of dispensing advice. He merely wishes and feels compelled to warn you. To remind you that there are certain limits. He speaks cautiously, in a way he never speaks when he is called upon to explain a technical problem to you, the inner workings of a generator, for instance, which hold no secrets for him. Don't misunderstand me, he says, and you understand him perfectly: he is worried, because he is forced to love something which he can't completely approve of; he doesn't want things any other way, but he doesn't want to see the object of his love endangered, vulnerable, exposed, he wants it to be able to defend itself. He realizes more or less why you're smiling when he starts talking to you in this way. He realizes more or less that he cannot have his wish, and this makes him a little helpless, sometimes, at other times a little cross.

What kind of limits? Half whispered: For instance, limits on what you discuss with Lenka. In what way? Kids shouldn't be overtaxed. One can ask too much of them. You ask: What about us? When we were kids? When we were fed on half sentences all the time? Incomprehensible glances that went past us? Locked doors? And those horrendous scenes?

So.

Lutz knows nothing of horrendous scenes. He was seven in November 1939, when Nelly was ten; it's not the first time that age makes a significant difference. You fill him in with a couple of half-whispered words—after all these years. He doesn't need many. In a certain respect he was present after all, he doesn't seem totally surprised. Still, he finally says: I believe that there are limits to everything. That they—our parents—must remain off limits, that they must be taboo.

A request you understand, to say the least.

While Lenka and H. stow their herb stems in the trunk, your four hands lie side by side on the top of the trunk for a few seconds. Look at that, Lenka says. How different they are . . . She's always hated the shape of her fingertips: Square, she says, and to you: Why didn't you let me inherit yours? H. discovers that her fingers look like Lutz's. How perverse! says Lenka, an expression she was particularly fond of at that time. But she was pacified.

She has nothing against Lutz, though it would never occur to her to call him "Uncle." It happens that each describes the other as "decent," although the word doesn't hold the exact same meaning for both. To Lenka it means "fair." Two years ago, fairness was the quality she valued most highly in a person. When Lutz calls women and girls "decent," he means more or less that they don't play around. In the case of men he says they're "okay." Lenka, for her part, appreciates it when he glances approvingly at her hair and asks how much longer she is planning to let it grow; or when he tells her that her parents in their youth—when you were only a gleam in their eyes—always had to kiss right under the street lights, after the three of them came out of a movie.

But she had absolutely no appreciation of the story he began to tell at that point, she even tried to stop him from pursuing it. Lutz, though, was determined to tell this particular story at this particular moment, if only to prove that he, too, had seen all kinds of things when he was ten years old. Moreover, he insisted that you also knew the story, but you didn't, and Lenka tried to use your disagreement to distract him from telling what she definitely didn't want to hear. Lutz must have been in the first year of secondary school when a classmate, Kalle Peters, shot another classmate, Dieter Binger, called "Dingo," in the stomach, during an afternoon of war games, with an old army revolver he claimed he had found on the troops' exercise field behind the stadium. At that point you recognized the story and broke out in a sweat.

Lutz told how the teacher had beaten Kalle Peters in front of the class, before Kalle was dragged to the principal, where he was beaten until he could neither walk nor stand. Meanwhile, Dingo lay in the hospital, in critical condition, but he pulled through, you now remembered. You even remembered why he was called Dingo, and also why you had had to forget the story: because nothing is more repulsive to you than the thought of a person being beaten, and unable to defend himself, while others look on—there are almost always those who look on—and do nothing about it.

One look at Lenka convinced you that although she might not have inherited your fingertips, she did inherit this almost pathological repulsion, one that she now accepted, for the days when she used to ask you to reverse a horrible event—to revive a dead bird, or to turn the wicked sorcerer into a good one—were long gone.

At one point during the day she will have an inexplicable, exaggerated fit of rage. It occurs at noon, as one of the many cars from the West inconsiderately takes the shady parking spot you'd been waiting for. She rolls down her window and screams at the grinning driver: You goddamn stupid Kraut! But she'll never say another word about this story. Meanwhile, you realize how rarely you are present when something happens to her. She answers this only with silence. You'd be "a show-off"—to use her kind of language—if you claimed that you knew her inside out.

Lutz also said, during your verbal exchange at the stadium, that it made no sense to take world history too personally. It might even be a roundabout way of overestimating oneself, to pretend to be personally involved, and to find the proper word for that involvement. You, in turn—familiar as you are with the temptation to defer to his interpretation—tell him, although less and less frequently, that he is not being modest, merely uninvolved. Sober, he says, just sober, and therefore less prone to succumb to political intoxications.

Incidentally, most of the predictions he allowed himself to make as far as your affairs were concerned turned out to be accurate, and contrary to your wishful thinking. He has that sober view which he doesn't expect you to have or wish to impose on you, as though a sober outlook could do you harm. Maybe he's also suspicious because your soberness is naturally directed toward different things than his, and because each of you is romantic, even sentimental, about different things: in this case it's his childhood. He doesn't want to see it damaged.

Actually, who would be harmed if you dropped the matter? Who would be the poorer?

Because the sober present-day view with which you examine the past, and which would have been blurred with antipathy, not to say hate, a short time ago, contains its ample dose of unfairness. At least equal to its dose of fairness. Objects, helplessly imprisoned under glass, without any contact with us know-it-alls who were born later. And when you ask yourself if you could stand the same stern look scrutinizing yourself . . .

Bruno Jordan's declaration: That kind of thing is not for me! is significant. Only now are you able to see that the face Nelly saw for a few fleeting seconds in the vestibule mirror on that November day reappeared seven years later when he came back from captivity. It was the unrecognizable face of her own father that had devastated Nelly. It took her years to understand that he was recognizable even during those brief periods.

"That's not for me" is easily said, but not in this—how to describe it—this tone of desperation.

It should be said that certain words were beyond Bruno Jordan. Of course he was able to name exact figures—with a precision in which he did not usually excel—to the salesmen of large companies who walked modestly into his store and waited for him to finish serving a customer, and who treated him as though he were their intimate friend (which he seemed to believe, sometimes): of course he was able to give them the exact figures as far as orders of sugar, noodles, and Maggi bouillon cubes were concerned; naturally, he knowledgeably discussed the week's "take" with his wife on Saturdays; incidentally, the receipts maintained a satisfactory, though in no way overly high, level, if one discounts the decrease in profit following the controlled economy of foodstuffs during the last years of the war. Naturally, his customers' affairs were a frequent subject of conversation. To his children he spoke in a childish tone, and not about any serious subjects—the way adults who can't imagine that children will ever become adults usually speak to children. As though only the adult were a valid human being.

For instance, he deemed it inappropriate to inform the children —and in particular his daughter, Nelly, who he knew worried about her mother terribly—that Charlotte Jordan had finally agreed to have her goiter surgically removed. It would be done in the city hospital, with local anesthesia, under the expert supervision of the head surgeon, a Dr. Leisekamp. During the operation, the patient would be forced to speak continuously for two hours, to avoid injury to the vocal chords. (At the crucial point of the surgery, when the doctor had to concentrate, he asked her to count, or else to recite poetry, which she bravely did. "Great-grandmother, grandmother, mother and child / all huddled against the storm so wild," a poem which the doctor didn't know, and which he asked her to repeat. "One bolt has taken four lives away / And tomorrow is a holy day.") A conversation which prompted the head surgeon to remark: This woman can do more than bake bread (the very thing Charlotte wasn't allowed to have; for three weeks she was fed on soups from an invalid's cup with a pointed snout). In some crazy fashion, this sentence linked Nelly's mother to Queen Louisa of Prussia, whom she had just studied in her history class: every inch a queen!

The children had been told that their mother had gone to spend some time with Aunt Trudy Fenske in Plau am See. A plausible explanation. It tied in with rumors of Aunt Trudy's crumbling marriage, which, though not directly mentioned, must have reached the ears of the children. Charlotte was the best possible rescuer in all family troubles; even Nelly thought so.

But unfortunately the apprentice, Erwin, was clumsy enough to inform his boss, in Nelly's presence—at Whiskers Grandma's birthday coffee table: which means it was October, that is October 1940—that he should go back to the hospital immediately to take the Missus fresh towels and a fresh nightgown, which she urgently needed.

Where was her mother?

Nelly made a huge scene. Her mother was in the hospital. Her mother had had an operation. They had lied to her. Her mother could have died and she wouldn't even have had the slightest notion that she was in danger. She screamed and cried until she was exhausted.

This was one of her last outbursts in the presence of other people, helpless relatives who stood around her and told her to be reasonable. To calm down. Who finally let her be, shaking their heads and exchanging looks, the last of them her father, Bruno Jordan, who kept stroking her hair, assuring her over and over that he had only wanted what was best for her.

Nelly continued to cry. She didn't even want to think that her father had wanted what was best for himself, not for her: because he hadn't known how to tell her the truth, and because he wouldn't have known how to conduct himself in front of her on the day of her mother's operation.

This kind of verbal impotence. Which imprisons a person within himself, without giving him a clear understanding of this self. All these lives, which you're not entitled to judge. Had they not been particularly dependent upon the murderous coincidences of this era, one wouldn't need to speak of them.

(Futile conversations with Lenka about her grandfather.)

You figured out that the year you drove to Poland, you were the same age your parents had been at the beginning of the war. Is it possible that Lenka considers your lives basically concluded, the way you considered your parents' lives finished at the time? Does she consider you elderly?

All three of you realize, suddenly, that "it doesn't say in any book" (as Charlotte would have expressed it) that most of your lives, or the "best part," is behind you. You experience a brief, unmotivated flicker of *joie de vivre*, an intensification of colors, lasting for several minutes. It's nothing, absolutely nothing, that could be expressed in words. It's a deep breath, an exchange of glances back and forth. (H.'s eyes in the rearview mirror.) It is something that makes you able to place your hand on his neck, that makes him rub his head against your hand. That makes Lutz, who always feels compelled to sing, burst forth in his mighty basso profundo: "With my bow, my arrow . . ." Something that Lenka does or does not understand, that makes her shake her head.

The most beautiful thing under the sun is being under the sun.

9

In April 1973, you were driving home alone, not on the highway because of a detour, but over side roads through a number of villages. You were tired, therefore tensely alert, and you ran over a cat. It happened on a village street paved with cobblestones. The cat was coming slowly from the left, but strangely enough didn't react at all to the approaching car; you couldn't brake sharply, the street was wet. You saw how the cat cowered in terror. All you could do was to get it between the wheels. There was a thud, not loud, but horrible. You had to go on. You stopped and looked back. It was lying in the road, then painfully it got up. Limping on both hind paws, it dragged itself to the other side of the street and disappeared in a hedge, almost walking normally again.

Nothing was in sight on the sparsely lit village street; no traffic, no people. The cat had set out five seconds too early, or you, five seconds too late. You can't believe that this has happened to you, at least you aren't ready to accept it; you have to stop again to calm down. Home at a snail's pace, not a word about the incident. In a short English text that you're trying to read before going to sleep, one of the characters, drunk, disconsolate, repeats the same words over and over: "I was a nice girl, wasn't I?"

To wake up in the middle of the night. The helpless crying. *But I was . . .* All your chances, lost forever, crowded around you that night.

Nelly must have pushed her way into "serving" with the Hitler Youth. She stands in a long line outside the door to the gym, where the important process of registration is taking place. Soon after, she is sitting in a classroom. On the first evening she sings with all the others: "In the forest stands a house," a children's song with very simple words accompanied by hand motions. It was an embarrassing performance, and Nelly felt awkward, but she got over her discomfort by laughing out loud—maybe too loud—when the leader broke into gay laughter. It was a satisfying relief to laugh for the leader's sake, and to disregard her own inappropriate state of mind: embarrassment. What a pleasure it was to enjoy the joviality of the leader, a merry young woman by the name of Marianne, called Micky. Just call me Micky, I look like Mickey Mouse, anyway. Another kind of pleasure was to crowd around the leader, together with all the others, at the end of the evening, forgetting one's own shyness, to grasp her hand, to enjoy the extraordinary familiarity. And on the ride home, to become familiar with a new word by repeating it to herself: "comradeship."

It meant the promise of a loftier kind of life, far removed from the small area of the store, filled with cans of fish, bags of sugar, loaves of bread, barrels of vinegar, sausages hanging from the ceiling; far removed from the bright squares of light reflected from the store on the close-cropped stretch of lawn; far removed also from the white figure in the store smock who was standing outside waiting for Nelly: her mother had probably been waiting for a long time. Where had she been this late? She should wipe her feet well, she had probably waded through every puddle in town. What had she been doing? Singing? You can sing at home just as well.

Not a word about "comradeship." She wiped her feet. Where

Micky sang and played and marched with them and taught them games, there was something her mother couldn't give her, something she didn't want to miss, although, or rather because, she always felt like a stranger among others. Because she continued to be plagued by the same kind of embarrassment on all sorts of occasions which the others didn't seem to mind at all, and because this embarrassment and the self-control she constantly needed to overcome it were showing up her weakness, and were indicating the long road that was still ahead of her before she'd become the person that Micky wanted to make of her.

It meant being tough. A cross-country hike was planned; it fell on the day her mother was to be discharged from the hospital. Nelly had been looking forward to her mother's return more eagerly than anything else. Her father offered to ask Micky to excuse Nelly because her sick mother was coming home after a dangerous operation. Nelly hated cross-country hikes, but naturally she insisted on going, regardless of the resentment she was causing. She also refused Whiskers Grandma's offer to bandage her heels (her feet always developed blisters on those marches). When she came home, her mother was lying on the couch, and Nelly had to limp across the room to greet her. Her mother's worried questions and Whiskers Grandma's irritated explanation. Nelly argued, she went so far as to claim that the blisters on her feet were from the day before. She saw her mother get upset, she couldn't stop, couldn't give in, she tolerated no criticism of the awful cross-country hike. Until she finally burst into tears, and so did Charlotte, who should have been spared any kind of upset. Whiskers Grandma, who rarely disapproved of her favorite granddaughter, followed Nelly to her room to tell her that if she upset her mother that badly, the newly healed wound might break open again.

Nelly was keenly aware of the dilemma, but there was no way out. Whatever she did would be bad. A kind of dead-end street. (Only much later, only today, do you know what those "unsolvable" conflicts mean: that one has to make a choice between two mutually exclusive kinds of morality—both of them applicable to oneself—in order not to be crushed.) Nelly, distraught, stopped sobbing; she gave up crying almost for good. She grew brave and self-disciplined. This was much appreciated.

In the autumn Nelly fell ill. She must have caught a cold during a long open-air exercise on the playing field in the Zanzine Woods, which you plan to visit in the afternoon of the first day of your trip. This time even Charlotte didn't understand. The afternoon had been warm, even she wouldn't have objected to a longish stay in the open air. But Nelly was feverish when she got home; she displayed a strange aversion to talking and didn't feel like moving at all. The doctor said that bronchitis was not serious but should be watched. Or was there maybe something else, besides the illness? Nothing that Charlotte knew of.

The assembly in the open air had been a tribunal. A comrade by the name of Gerda Link had brought disgrace upon the honor of the Hitler Youth: she had stolen five marks and thirty-nine pfennigs from a comrade's coat pocket in the locker room of the athletic field, and had denied the theft to Group Leader Christel when the latter had questioned her. But there was proof of her guilt. Now she was standing alone next to the group leader at the short side of a rectangle whose three other sides were formed by the three lined-up squads of the Jungmädel unit.

First they sang: "To freedom only have we pledged our lives." ("Freedom is the fire, it's the radiant light, as long as it stays burning, our world will keep its might.") After that, Squad Leader Micky, with her frizzy, reddish-blond hair, her thick glasses, her turned-up nose, and her braid, stood in the center and shouted:

FROM THE ME TO THE WE. *By Heinrich Annacker.*

The me once seemed to be the central pole,
and all revolved around its woe and weal.
But growing humbleness helped to reveal
that you must aim your eyes upon the whole.

And now the me is part of the great We,
becomes the great machine's subservient wheel.
Not if it lives—but if it serves with zeal,
decides the worth of its own destiny.

(You copied this verse. Other songs come to your mind, although not without difficulty, not always with all the lines intact, or sometimes with, of all things, the beginnings missing. You can't count on H.: in his memory the unloved verses have withered away, except for a few mostly botched-up lines which he had never understood and which he had sung without knowing their meaning. Lenka can't stand these songs, not even as historical documents. She played deaf during the ride from L., now G., as the three of you tried to recollect the words that glorified or demanded the eastward advance, the ride, the march of the Teutons, the Germans: "We'll ride toward the eastern lands." "Do you see dawn in eastern skies?" "Raise your flags to easterly winds." And so forth. Lenka said: They must have had terrible complexes, those people. You're thankful for her tact in saying "they" and not "you." And the Poles? How many songs did they have, summoning them to raise their flags to the westerly winds?)

But the Jungmädel Unit Northwest is still lined up at attention in the Zanzine Woods, and Gerda Link is still waiting for the sentence to be pronounced in person by Christel. When Christel takes a step forward and begins to speak, Nelly feels the sweat streaming down her back (something Charlotte Jordan hadn't counted on: Nelly perspiring while being exposed to a slight wind). Christel has colorless hair that curls under, and magnetic eyes. When in a state of rapture, she speaks in a high, ringing voice and dramatically draws out the vowels, but she is impeded by braces on her teeth. She lisps. Next to Christel, Micky is a subordinate deity. To attract Christel's attention is the highest, or, if it's in anger, the worst distinction for anyone.

Now Christel is checking her anger; she shows grief and disappointment, which are far more terrible. Her voice is muted; the personal pain that Gerda Link has inflicted on her, the disgrace she has brought upon every single member of her unit, the dishonor heaped upon all of them, but most of all upon her leader, is almost unendurable. Far be it from her to expel a Jungmädel forever from the group, no matter what she has done. But she thinks it necessary and appropriate to relieve the offender for three months of the badge of membership in the Jungmädel League: the black kerchief and the leather knot.

Gerda Link's squad leader steps forward, a short buxom girl with bowlegs. She stands before Gerda Link, who can be called beautiful in comparison: she has an elongated face, darkish skin, a narrow, finely chiseled nose, and long, dark hair. The squad leader relieves the offender of her kerchief and knot, while Micky shouts across the playing field in a loud, strained voice: To be German means to be true! A song follows, the song of the Hitler Youth: "Onward, onward, fanfares are joyfully blaring. Onward, onward, youth must be fearless and daring. Germany, your light shines true, even if we die for you . . ." (These songs proved to be right, at least in part: many of those who sang them are dead. "Our flag will lead us to eternity, our flag means more to us than death.")

Nelly's emotions as she rode home on her rickety bicycle, down Adolf-Hitlerstrasse, then up Anckerstrasse, a considerable upgrade that she took without having to dismount, perspiring of course, with her sweater unbuttoned, panting and taking in great gulps of raw night air: no need to describe her condition. The words "shock," "despair" would be too strong, and she's not permitted to admit to herself that she's afraid. According to her own convictions, she should have felt disgust for Gerda Link instead of this spineless pity; she should have felt enthusiasm for the leader's straightforwardness, instead of, well, fear. As so often before, it was the impossibility of seeing clearly. Then came the fever, she could retreat to her bed.

In her feverish state, Nelly saw Gerda Link's dark face, her curly hair billowing from bright-green barrettes, her deep-red lips. She admitted to herself, to her own bewilderment, that she didn't want to go on serving in the unit until kerchief and knot had been returned to Gerda Link. In devious ways she managed to have the doctor—with whom her mother had had a whispered conversation in the hallway—give her a written excuse that exempted her for the entire winter from serving, for reasons of "chronic weakness of the upper respiratory tract." She avoided meeting anybody. Once she ran into Micky, to whom she explained at length that she had been seriously ill, the doctor had feared a case of "double pneumonia." Immediately after, she was furious with herself for having said "double," for having jeopardized the veracity of her statement by exaggeration. For a long time she was bothered by the thought that Micky could call her bluff. She realized perfectly well that she'd been a failure. In March, on one of the last cold days, Micky caught up with her and divulged the news that she was being considered for a leadership position.

The Pole Brandys postulates that sin in our time consists of not wanting to know the truth about oneself. Statements of this kind, which reveal as much about their author as about their subject, can be neither proved nor disproved. You agree with them; which doesn't mean that "salvation by self-knowledge"—Brandys's aspiration—is attainable, and that the unmasking by reality will be bearable.

Gradually the notebooks, diaries, notes—overlapping and superimposing on each other—are piling up on your desk; your limited time is being used up by a work whose outcome remains doubtful; a growing stack of paper is putting you under increasing pressure. Meanwhile, you're becoming more and more aware of your inability to manage, in the sense of "to interpret," the steadily proliferating material (the water, called forth by the sorcerer's apprentice, carried by the broom, threatens to inundate everything).

Yet, at the moment, nothing is needed but a direct explanation of the fact that Nelly accepted Micky's offer, against the explicit objection of her mother.

It is significant that this explanation still isn't entirely clear. "Ambition," "self-importance"—those are tried-and-true catchwords with a ring of sincerity, and it isn't being claimed that they do not apply, at least in part. But that's just it: only in part. And it's the remainder, not covered by ambition or self-importance, that is interesting. (It would be nice if you knew whether or not there was ever a moment in the child's life when she first had the impulse to step before others, on her own initiative, when the fact that others had to follow her orders gave her a sense of satisfaction. It would be nice—in an aesthetic, not in a moral, sense—if a pertinent image, or a series of images, could be inserted here. Nothing of the kind. You see nothing.)

The third catchword might be: "compensation" ("adjustment," "restitution," "reward"). In this case, the images are vivid. Nelly was involved in a compensation deal, and it could almost be assumed that she knew it, because she was crying as she defiantly railroaded her mother into giving her permission. Recognition, and comparative security from fear and from overwhelming guilt feelings are guaranteed, and she in turn contributes submission and strict performance of duty. There had been moments when she wasn't able to cope with her doubts. She rids herself of any possibility of doubt; above all, of self-doubt. ("The weak must be hammered into oblivion." Adolf Hitler.) To her, the goods were worth the price: not a word about it, not even from an inner voice. Only the inexplicable tears, and Charlotte's frightened look, the hastily given permission. To think that it means that much to you!

At about that time, Nelly was once again spending a few days with her Aunt Lucie on Hindenburgplatz. She liked to go there, because Aunt Lucie was great fun, sometimes—as mentioned—a bit "free," and she was apt to use certain suggestive words in the presence of the children, words such as "green apples" for the tiny budding breasts of very young girls. Nelly played with Astrid at Aunt Lucie's. Astrid, the same age as she, whom she called, not quite correctly, her cousin, who apparently had no father, and whose mother was never around. But Nelly had heard whispers about Astrid's mother: that she was the "unfortunate" twin sister of the fortunate Aunt Lucie. Astrid, who attracted and repelled Nelly, because she always insisted on games that had something dirty about them. For instance, going to the toilet together and taking a look at each other. Or at dusk, when the street lights were lit around Hindenburgplatz, and lovers were necking in the shade of the trees, to go out on the balcony and loudly shout "Shame!"

But one evening a strange woman was sitting at the supper table across from Nelly, staring at her with fixed, even piercing eyes. This woman had Aunt Lucie's face, but something had made her face collapse. She was Aunt Dottie, Astrid's mother, Aunt Lucie's twin sister, who was here "on leave." Nelly knew only about soldiers on leave, and it took her some time before the word "institution" emerged from the confusion of her mind: Aunt Dottie was on leave from the institution. (It was the Brandenburg Mental and Nursing Institution on Friedeberger Chaussee; you saw the buildings on Sunday, July 11, 1971, on your left as you were driving toward the former town of Friedeberg.)

Aunt Dottie had a slowing-down mechanism inside her. Or else she lived in a different, more viscous air, which didn't permit her to make fast movements. Nelly was reminded of slow-motion pictures. She wondered if Aunt Dottie could manage to fall off a horse with infinite slowness, without hurting herself, and if in this manner she might possibly profit by her odd condition.

(For several days now, Lenka has been singing a dark melody

day and night, and it made Aunt Dottie surface in your memory
with more clarity. Aunt Dottie, whose real name was Dorothea,
you later learned, and who had earned the demeaning name of
Dottie in her childhood by her conspicuous clumsiness. Lenka
sings: "Sometimes it seems to me things move too slowly. Is there
no answer or can I not hear? Sometimes it seems to me things
move too slowly, nothing is near . . .")

It startled Nelly when Aunt Dottie broke her silence and addressed her, Nelly of all people, with her brittle voice: Would it be
all right if she buttered a slice of bread for her? Nelly nodded
before the others could protest. She had to wait quite a while for
her bread, which caused her and the others to lose interest. Aunt
Dottie handed her the carefully prepared slice, having spread it
with butter and bacon fat, one on top of the other: two layers,
clearly visible at the spot where Nelly had taken a bite. All hell
broke loose. Everybody tore into Aunt Dottie: Astrid, her daughter, the loudest: You see, it's hopeless, she just can't pull herself
together. Aunt Dottie made confused, defensive gestures. They
tried to grab the bread from Nelly's plate. Of course she didn't
have to eat what that crazy woman had concocted. Aunt Dottie
looked at Nelly. Nelly held on to the bread, took a big bite,
chewed, and said: But I like it. To top it off, she claimed that
bread with bacon fat and butter was one of her favorite treats.

In the ensuing hush, she ate alone and had to take care not to
smack her lips, and not to look up again so as to avoid meeting the
crazy woman's eyes. But she did look up, directly at Aunt Dottie.
Then she looked down and felt herself blush. Was it conceivable
that crazy people could show gratitude in their eyes?

She must have been mistaken. It was typical of her to feel
ashamed in the face of a crazy woman. Nelly was familiar with the
"unfit-for-life" concept, everybody was familiar with it: One
learned it in school, one read about it in the papers. In Nelly's
biology textbook, certain pictures created a horror of those people
(as well as of members of the Eastern race or, above all, of the
Semitic race), and Fräulein Blümel, her blond biology teacher,
with a large, soft mouth painted bright red (she was from Berlin!)
and skin with large pores, compared the lives of birds, mammals,
fishes, and plants—where nature in her great wisdom sees to it
that the unfit are eliminated in order not to weaken the species—

with the life of human beings who were made effete by false humanitarianism, and who corrupted their once pure, healthy blood by adulterating it with inferior and sick strains such as the Negro in the French culture, the Jews in America.

The euthanasia program was carried out between February 1940—the time when Nelly met Aunt Dottie—and the fall of 1941. It claimed 60,000 victims. Nelly didn't know anything about the program; neither, of course, did she know the names of the three cover-up organizations in charge of its smooth execution; the program had been ordered by the Führer but had not been given legal status "for political reasons": the Reich Study Group on Mental and Nursing Institutions, with the function of detecting the sick by sending out questionnaires and evaluating them; the Public Welfare Foundation for Institutional Care, charged with financing the undertaking: the apparatus for detecting and transporting the sick cost money; salaries had to be paid to physicians and other medical personnel; and industry, after all, didn't furnish the monoxide gas free of charge, either. Finally: the Public Welfare Company for the Transportation of the Sick, Ltd., which was entrusted with the "transfer" of the victims; its omnibuses, with cloth-shrouded windows, were the targets, for instance, of the children of Hadamar in Hessen—a town in whose vicinity a "nursing institution" with facilities for the gassing of the sick was located —who called after them: There goes another load about to be gassed!

What Nelly did know, or sensed—for in times like these there are many gradations between knowing and not knowing—was that there was more to Aunt Dottie's death than met the eye.

It was normal for Aunt Lucie to cry. Aunt Lucie, clever at everything, had been helping Charlotte in the store since Bruno was drafted; but it was strange that Aunt Lucie talked to Nelly's mother in a whisper whenever they spoke about her twin sister's death. Still, the family had been duly notified by the mental institution in Brandenburg (Havel), the institution to which Lucie's sister had been transferred in July 1940 "in the course of measures by the Reich Defense Commissioner," and where she had suddenly and unexpectedly succumbed to pneumonia.

(This time the authorities had not been guilty of one of those ghastly slips which caused the district leader of Ansbach to complain in writing that a family had received not one but two urns with the ashes of the deceased; that appendicitis had been given as the cause of death in the case of a patient whose appendix had been removed ten years earlier; that an announcement of death had been sent while the supposedly deceased person was still alive at the institution in good physical health.)

More suspicious than anything, however, was the fact that Charlotte—who was fond of saying about herself that she would always call a spade a spade—that Charlotte clammed up completely as far as Aunt Dottie's death was concerned.

For fractions of a second, Nelly had seen an unfamiliar expression of shock, disbelief, and fear on her mother's face.

"Give me an answer I want to hear," Lenka sings.

But Aunt Lucie had a violent attack of migraine; for days she lay prostrate in a darkened room, kept vomiting, and didn't eat or drink. When she recovered and appeared among people again, her face had taken on a greater likeness to her dead twin sister.

It's hard to determine which has to come first: the readiness of people to have their hearts prepared to sanction murder or the coffins that are being wheeled past them. Supposedly not all the sixty thousand mentally defective persons—among them also "idiot children"—were killed by gas. (The Bishop of Limburg writes in 1941: "After the arrival of those transports, the citizens of Hadamar observe the smoke rising from the chimney and are unnerved by the lingering thought of the poor victims, particularly when shifting winds cause discomfort by the nauseating odors they carry.") No: even later, when the gassing program had been discontinued, there was death by Veronal, Luminal, morphine-scopolamine.

But the truly original invention of the gentlemen in charge of the execution of the Führer's order was the gas chamber, "rooms of normal size and type adjacent to other rooms of the institution." Later they were sent east for further use, in the Polish town of Lublin, for instance. Only a year later, Rudolf Hoess, the commandant of Auschwitz, expresses thanks to the inventors of these facilities, and especially to the testers of the gas. All of this—pertinent to the subject matter but not to any individual—is again noted here for the children of the former children of Hadamar in Hessen, Hartheim near Linz, Grafeneck in Württemberg, Brandenburg (Havel), and Sonnenstein near Pirna.

The thought that everybody in Germany should have had the urgent wish to empty out, to tear down his dwelling—rooms of normal size and type—to change its very foundations so as not to have it resemble a gas chamber is, of course, unrealistic and will cause resentment, because we'd rather open our hearts to murder than open our four comfortable walls to chaos. It seems easier to change a few hundred, or thousand, or million human beings into nonhumans or subhumans than to change our ideas about cleanliness and order and comfort.

Nelly was slovenly and untidy. Charlotte Jordan often was at her wits' end about how to teach her daughter to behave like a "civilized Middle European." To wash herself thoroughly every day. To shine her shoes every night. To put her clothes away neatly. To scrape the dirt off her shoes carefully before entering the house. To pack her school bag the night before. To unwrap uneaten school sandwiches and eat them at night. To brush her teeth mornings and evenings. To darn or mend torn clothes immediately. A stitch in time saves nine. Never put off till tomorrow what you can do today. As the twig is bent, so grows the tree. If at first you don't succeed, try, try again. I really and truly expect only the bare minimum, so help me God.

In the Jungmädel camp, the leader or her deputies inspect the dormitory, the chests of drawers, the washrooms, every morning. One time the hairbrush of a squad leader was publicly displayed because it was full of long hairs. That was no way for a hairbrush to look if it belonged to a Jungmädel leader, the camp leader said at the evening roll call. From that moment on, Nelly hid her hairbrush in the soap compartment of her trunk, because she couldn't manage to pick every last hair from her brush, and because she didn't want the camp leader, of all people, to dislike her. When she herself was on inspection duty, she reported three pairs of unshined shoes and an apple rotting in her friend Hella Teichmann's drawer. That's how she did her duty, without favoritism. By the end of the day, even Hella had understood that Nelly had only done her duty. At bedtime, the camp leader shook Nelly's hand firmly. Two Jungmädel in the hallway played the good-night song, "No fairer land in our time," on their recorders. At the next morning's flag salute, Nelly was to recite the motto of the day, which she repeated to herself at least a dozen times before falling asleep: "You must practice the virtues today which nations need if they want to become great. You must be true, you must be brave, you must form a single, great, noble comradeship with each other" (Adolf Hitler). The camp leader said, and Nelly was glad to hear it: They, all of them, the future leaders, would be part of the nation's elite.

Self-accusations and excuses balance each other out.

Statistics—for instance, the suicide rate—show that the war brought with it a considerable improvement in the civilians' public health. It may have been a kind of uplift by autosuggestion, an order to oneself not to conk out just now, when every individual could tell himself that he was needed. Charlotte quit complaining almost entirely and ran the store with a vengeance; the state was obviously saddling her with more than she could be expected to handle, and oddly enough, this made it lose some of its power. Once, when a policeman entered her store on a winter evening shortly after seven, in order to remind her of closing time—a relic of the era of so-called free competition—she hurled her enormous bunch of keys at his feet with a grandiose flourish: There, why didn't he lock up the store himself. Why didn't he take it over right now, lock, stock, and barrel, that would be fine with her, in fact she'd be delighted! Why didn't he report her. Why didn't he close the store and look for a different manager. She, Charlotte Jordan, would love to take it easy for once and sit on her ass and live off her allowance as a soldier's wife . . .

Nelly saw the policeman step back toward the door, motioning to Charlotte to calm down, and she saw the triumph in her mother's face after he had gone.

Why are you more and more disturbed by the fact that all of these people are at your mercy? Take Charlotte. She can't protest, can't rectify or amend anything, can't correct the word "triumph" if she finds it wrong. You can say what you want about her, whatever comes to your mind. You can voice opinions which won't become any truer by spreading them. You can puzzle over one of the last sentences that Charlotte spoke before her mind dimmed, after she turned off, with a gesture of finality, the excited radio newscaster in 1968, the year of her death: There are more important things.

Mockery. Yes. It was mockery that Nelly saw in Charlotte's face after she'd sent the policeman on his way. Nelly remembered the expression because it was a rare one for her mother.

Late in the afternoon, when you open your suitcases in the hotel, it turns out that Lenka has taken a book along, even though she knew that she'd hardly have time to read. She never travels without a book. She doesn't open the book that night because you talk until late. But *Job* by Joseph Roth lies on her bedside table, and it occurs to you later that both book and author would have fit into your conversation. When Nelly was fourteen years old, this author had been dead for four years, but she had never even heard his name, let alone read his tale of Mendel Singer, the Jew, which makes Lenka cry every time she reads it. How many endless years did it take for Nelly to find out that Joseph Roth, a writer in the German language, an exile because of his Jewish descent, died at age forty-five in a charity hospital in Paris. You know it would be wrong to burden Lenka with sadness over these lost years. You are silent. But the realization that wasted time can never be regained becomes more and more irrefutable.

Around noon you circle St. Mary's Church for the first time. The space it stands in is less crowded than it used to be; the houses around the market square were destroyed at the end of the war and were replaced by new rows of houses at a greater distance from the church, which now looks more handsome. You're happy that H. and Lenka admire the church, an example of pure Romanesque architecture down to the last detail. Weren't you confirmed here? asks Lutz. Of course.

Across from the west portal of the church is the new restaurant on the market square. Lutz has a Polish-language guide with him, but it is of no help in interpreting the almost illegible menu. The waitress in her black beehive hairdo tries her best, you try your best; finally you fake agreement with suggestions whose meanings are a mystery to you.

You have a good, cold yogurt soup, stuffed roast beef, and excellent raisin ice cream. Lutz knew right away that you'd get decent food here. From where you're sitting, near the large windows, you look out on the construction fence surrounding the entire square: the fountain, and the old cobblestone pavement on which the market stalls used to be set up on Saturdays, and the ancient chestnut trees with their crowns towering high above the fence, of course. Does Lutz remember the old Italian ice cream parlor on the square? Lutz remembers. He liked their lemon ice best, and you can't believe that he doesn't remember the Malaga-grape ice cream that you could get only there and nowhere else in the world. The Malaga ice cream, to which Horst Binder—what made that name enter your head all of a sudden?—treated the accordion student Nelly Jordan one afternoon, after he had lain in ambush for her at the door of her accordion teacher's house in the old part of town.

On this occasion it turns out, incredible as it is, that Lutz has no picture of Horst Binder. He tastes the name on his tongue: Binder, Binder . . . He must have lived close to our place? In the middle one of the Bahr houses, ground floor left. It's only, says Lutz, because he never went outside, I think. Or did he take part in any of those games—kickball, cops and robbers, cowboys and Indians? Because that's something I would know.

No, Horst Binder never went outside. Horst Binder didn't play any games. He set foot outside only to go to school, or to Jungvolk duty, and—disconcertingly—in the spring of 1943, in order to follow Nelly, at a distance of ten to twenty yards, to her accordion lessons on Tuesday afternoons at four. To the pug-faced Fräulein Miess, who unsuccessfully tried to wring a semblance of accomplishment from her pupil Nelly. While Nelly, in the dusty plush-upholstered chamber of her music teacher, had to play "A Gypsy's life is a merry life" (a song that wasn't forbidden in spite of the authorities' persecution of the Gypsies), Horst Binder was slinking around the entrance door, and when Nelly finally came out, her sheet music under her arm, he stepped forward and stared at her soulfully.

Does Lutz at least remember the soulful look? No. When he racks his brains, he remembers at best a tuft of hair, a dark, straight string of hair falling from a perfectly straight part, down his forehead almost to his left eye. Well? Does he remember right?

Exactly right. Because Horst Binder aped the Führer's hairstyle in an almost sacrilegious way. Everybody grinned when he walked down Soldinerstrasse with long, somewhat dragging steps, his back slightly rounded, and lifted his arm for the Hitler salute, in a measured, deliberate gesture. But nobody ever laughed in his face. Nobody had ever seen him laugh, either.

Lenka doesn't want to hurt anybody's feelings, least of all those of the present company, but she must say that the attentions of a young man of that ilk don't exactly throw the most flattering light on the girl he pursues. Am I right to think that he should have been sent packing, the quicker the better?

That's easily said. You aren't claiming that Nelly was exactly thrilled when Horst Binder stepped in her way and stared at her urgently with his soulful brown dog's eyes. That boy, said Charlotte, is just plain touched in the head. Had she known the extent of his pursuit of her daughter, she would have been able to stop it short by a brief, pointed conversation with her customer Frau Binder. Although there was talk that Horst Binder wouldn't listen to his mother, a mousy, obviously unhappy woman, and that even his father, the railroad secretary Eberhard Binder, was gradually losing all control over him. Nelly, then, wasn't all that keen for an abrupt end to this strange relationship? (Because strange it was, God only knows!) The answer has to be no. Not necessarily.

But for heaven's sake, why not?

Who can tell. Not that Nelly was blind. Not that she wasn't able to see her pushy escort for what he was: ridiculous, a pain in the neck. But she was also flattered by his sticky devotion, and his darkly glowing eye behind the dark string of hair seemed to indicate mysterious entanglements, and it was, after all, a terribly tempting, although reprehensible, thrill to string someone along, someone who himself had so many people on a string (these were Charlotte's words: He has them all on a string!).

These things never work out, Lenka said quite correctly, and she resents your grins. Because she knows what she's talking about.

You have no idea how well I know you! That's what Charlotte Jordan said to her grown-up daughter, who couldn't have cared less whether her mother knew her well or not; but fourteen-year-old Nelly had to be on her guard. She denied that Horst Binder ever bothered her after the accordion lessons. Has he bothered you again? It's simply incredible. Just don't have anything to do with him.

For a short time, Nelly practiced the pieces for Fräulein Miess with determination, and she actually attained a certain virtuosity. Fräulein Miess opened the little window of her attic room to let spring come in, and she sang in her reedy voice, inspired by her pupil's unexpected progress, the suggestive words: "He should ride into the ha-ha-ha, ha-ha-ha, hay, yoohoo, in the hay, yoohoo, he should ride into the hay." Nelly played with gusto and leaned on the bass keys for all she was worth. Was Horst Binder standing in the doorway across the street, keeping an eye on the window with the white curtains and the two impatiens plants? Was he listening to her dashing performance and the ridiculous singing of Fräulein Miess? Did he ever find anything ridiculous in this world? Did he ever laugh?

But did the Führer laugh?

Horst Binder talked about nothing except the Führer. With his life he demonstrated to Nelly the life of the Führer, and she'd have to crawl into a mouse hole if she were to compare herself with him. Horst Binder believed—no, and this was the fascinating part—he *knew* that the Führer had Germany on his mind day and night, and that he needed human beings like him, Horst Binder, as he needed the air he was breathing, so they would be the vessels of his thoughts. Horst Binder spoke and Nelly listened. She had to ask herself if she could be a "vessel." In her mind's eye she saw an Old Germanic pottery urn, because naturally it had to be a worthy vessel; no modern, mass-produced item would do.

She asked Horst Binder shyly if they could perhaps walk by way of the market square. A fleeting, astonished raising of the eyebrows, then, wordless, he turned into Richtstrasse. He didn't care where they walked, as long as he could talk about the Führer's daily routine, which he had pieced together in its entirety out of hundreds of single items of information. Nelly gathered from his hints that Horst Binder tried to do what the Führer was doing at every hour of the day, and she was ashamed that her thoughts were straying to the question: Would somebody from her class be at the Italian ice cream parlor to which she was determined, at all cost, to drag Horst Binder in his Jungvolk uniform with the green braid of the Youth Platoon commander.

It was easier than she thought. Oh, she said, since we're here, I'll just have a quick Malaga-grape ice cream! and she went straight into the parlor, where a genuine Italian worked the shiny ice cream machine, and his wife, also a genuine Italian, did the selling. In the background Nelly had seen three girls from her class, who were now staring at them. Nelly had to act, since one couldn't depend on Horst Binder in practical matters. She ordered two Malagas "to eat here," since a Youth Platoon commander in uniform was not permitted to lick ice cream on the street. By a clever maneuver she made Horst Binder pay, squeezed through to one of the tables in the back, waved nonchalantly to her class-mates, sat down, and directed Horst Binder to his chair. Now he could go on talking, and talk he did, because he had just thought of the word that fit his attitude toward the Führer: he was infatu-ated with him, and this was his honor and his pride.

You reassure Lenka: Yes, Nelly gave him the cold shoulder after a while. It isn't the whole truth, which Lenka, as you hope, wouldn't understand. Eating ice cream couldn't have been all there was to it. It was inevitable that Horst Binder tried to grab Nelly's hand—it was in Wollstrasse, which has completely disappeared—and that Nelly withdrew her hand, because his was damp and slithery; that Nelly turned her head when he breathed on her face, because he had bad breath. By that time they were in a doorway on Richtstrasse, which is still standing. It was unavoidable that Horst Binder, with a pained look of renunciation, and in a pained, disappointed voice, would declare their relationship to be "purely spiritual," whereupon both were silent for a long time, he re-proachful, she feeling guilty. This went on during the whole long way from the slaughterhouse to her home. After that, Horst Binder talked to her frequently about the beautiful meaning of self-sacrifice to a higher endeavor or a higher human being, and Nelly, who wanted to punish herself, suffered his company with even greater friendliness than before.

What was still needed: that she was sent to the house where Horst Binder lived—the same house where old Lisicky lived, from whom she was supposed to get asparagus—and that she went to the cellar, where she thought she'd find the old man, and that she saw Horst Binder there, leaning with his head against a ledge of the wall, having himself whipped with a switch by Bucker, the feared, brutish street-gang leader; that their eyes met, which had never happened before, and that she saw an expression in Horst Binder's eyes (it wasn't pain or fear or rage—something entirely different, something unknown to her) that made her run away.

Horst Binder never bothered her again. Occasionally she would see him at a distance, without feeling any particular emotion. Only when she learned—it was in spring 1945, as they were meeting stragglers from their hometown, fellow refugees—that Horst

Binder had shot his parents, then himself, with his father's service pistol, before the takeover of the town by the Russians, only then did a memory come back, to which you can now give a name, now that the memory is being refreshed. You tell Lenka about Horst Binder's end while you're walking back to your car across the boiling hot market square. Insane, says Lenka. She isn't keen on hearing details. It then occurs to you that you don't know the details, because you hadn't felt the urge to imagine them. Now, in the sweltering car which slowly circles the market square (while you're exchanging a few observations with your brother, Lutz: The railroad viaducts, they used to be warehouses; the approach to the Gerloff Bridge; to the right of here was a hardware store, that's where I bought you your first jackknife, for Christmas; I remember it, do you?)—now the death of the Binder family is taking place before your inner eye.

Scene: the bedroom. Dramatis personae, out of the past: Frau Binder, a gray, frightened little mouse. Herr Binder, an impotent, everyday face above the railroader's uniform. Horst, the son, now sixteen years old, darkly determined to do his last deed. German families kill each other in the bedroom. Has there been an exchange of words? Nowhere is the silence as abysmal as in German families. Wouldn't Horst Binder at least have said something, anything, such as: Well, I'm going to put an end to it now. Or: Well, I'm going to do away with us. (His pasty-white face with the eternal strand of hair over his eye, the eye which perhaps now, in those last minutes, finally glows in boundless self-hatred.) Horst Binder, the troop leader, had been taught the use of weapons, only it hadn't been calculated that German parents and a Hitler Youth leader might be targets of his shots. Wasn't there a rumor that he had surprised his parents in their beds in the morning? In that case, had there been time left for him to enjoy the spread of deep red stains on snowy-white bed linen? Or did he stretch out immediately on the flowered bedside rug and push the pistol barrel into his mouth?

Old Lisicky, who was the air-raid warden, had a passkey to all the apartments in the house. He entered the Binders' apartment in the evening, and what he saw made him call together all the neighbors who hadn't fled yet. The difficulties of disposing of three bodies, unnoticed, during a brittle frost. Bloodstained bed sheets, too, present the most unpleasant problems; maybe they were disposed of in the garbage dump at the bottom of the ravine.

What counts now is accuracy. What did Nelly feel when she heard the news of the Binder family's death, in April 1945, in the village of Grünheide near Nauen? Loathing? Horror? Dread? Nothing of the kind. Much later, in the midst of other activities which seemed to be demanding her full attention, the neglected feelings caught up with her.

The key word "infatuated" remained unresolved. Was Nelly supposed to have known it? Sure. Her mother had used it twice in connection with the family, both times with appropriate contempt, and both times directed at her husband's family: at his sisters' husbands.

Bruno Jordan's sisters had bad luck with their husbands. Terrible to say, especially in front of the children, but they were unfaithful to their wives. Whose fault it may really have been— don't let's get into that here and now, down to the last gory detail. But one thing is sure: that girl must get out of there, no ifs, buts, or maybes. Thus spoke Charlotte—during coffee at an outdoor table in Heinersdorf—meaning, in this case, her sister-in-law Trudy Fenske, née Jordan, who has lately—it is summer 1940— been writing unhappy, even desperate letters from beautiful Plau am See: The red-haired secretary of her husband, automobile repair-shop owner Harry Fenske, seems to have set her mind on taking this man away from his rightful spouse. She said it herself to Aunt Trudy, right to her face, and recently she has even claimed that she's expecting a child by Harry (Bruno! The children!), and he, when confronted with it, had nothing but lame excuses.

Well, for Charlotte this whole thing was as obvious as a turd in a punch bowl. If that's the way it is, there's only one thing to do: Get out of it, but fast, and good riddance.

Trudy won't want to.

What? Not want to? But what on earth is she waiting for? To be kicked out bodily?

She thinks he'll change his mind and come back to her.

He? But he's infatuated with that redhead!

In Heinersdorf Grandma's garden, strawberries and black cherries grew in rows strictly aligned with the rectangular wire fence, the rain barrel had a round, wooden cover, and geometrically laid-out flower beds adorned the front of the house. If Heinersdorf Grandma were a different sort—spendthrift, for instance, but this word can't even be tentatively applied to her—the old Jordans wouldn't be where they now are, thank God. Sure, she turns every penny over twice. But didn't she have to do it to get out of their basement flat on Schönhofstrasse, to buy her little house (the price: 16,000 reichsmarks), to have at last some greenery around her and be her own boss?

The dog Laddie, a short-haired brown mutt, runs between the children's legs. The chickens are in their coop, the rabbits in their hutches. Everything in its place. Except Heinersdorf Grandpa, who's full of it, as usual; who takes the children to the door of the laundry room, makes them expect something special, and yells into the empty room: Turn round, Dobbin, turn!, until Nelly's brother, Lutz, remarks that there is no horse. Then Heinersdorf Grandpa says: Nope, there sure isn't. I only mean, in case there is, so's he doesn't kick.

Always this tomfoolery.

Don't you ever come home with a fatherless brat! Heinersdorf Grandma had warned her growing daughters time and again. Aunt Trudy has always had a good but foolish heart, and she lost it to Karl the sailor at a New Year's celebration, when he told her a little about loneliness at sea, and a little about his woes with women. And that's how it happened: Aunt Trudy told it to her sixteen-year-old niece, Nelly, one night, as they were lying side by side on straw in an emptied-out classroom in an unfamiliar town during their flight, and she was talking about the tragic accidents and events in her life.

And so it happened. The sailor disappeared. Aunt Trudy was forced to have an abortion, performed by a midwife (I wouldn't wish that on my worst enemy!), and to keep it a secret from her mother. The night in the same room with her sister. The pain. The blood. The teeth marks on her pillow. Greater fear of her mother than of death. The Jordans always were a decent family.

After that, Aunt Trudy was no longer able to have children. But Harry Fenske was a noble human being. When his intended made a clean breast of it one day, he forgave her and never spoke of it again. Only, later, this unfortunate thing with the redhead, and the fact that at the time the government was so keen on children. A

German man, the judge of the divorce court said, should live with the woman who can bear him children.

When Aunt Trudy's brother, Bruno Jordan, and Heinersdorf Grandpa, her father, had rescued her from the den of iniquity (still more or less against her will); when the divorce had become final; when the living-room set, in stylish matte finish, and Aunt Trudy's favorite rug had arrived from Plau am See, she moved with her adopted son, Achim—who was just then entering school and didn't seem to display great learning ability—into a two-room apartment on the third floor of a house on the main street. She took a job as a saleswoman in Bangemann's department store, and soon she knew everybody and his neighbor. When her niece Nelly came to see her, she talked to her as to an adult. In the fourth year of the war, she got Nelly a set of underwear, belonging to a customer, in exchange for butter supplied by Charlotte. "Sexy underwear," she said with a rueful little smile, as she handed it to Nelly.

Three years later Charlotte Jordan had the opportunity to apply the word "infatuation" to her other brother-in-law, Uncle Emil Dunst.

There's a documentary on TV about the control of drug abuse in America. A group of youthful former drug addicts bring a girl named Barbara to the point where she cries out, weeping and screaming: *I need help!*, because total capitulation is the necessary prerequisite for a possible cure.

How did we become what we are today?

10

You expect the child Nelly to walk the plank for you. To prostitute herself. Aren't you fooling yourself by thinking that this child is moving on her own, according to her own inner laws? Living within preconceived patterns—that's the problem.

It's humming, Bruno Jordan used to say when things ran smoothly. On Saturdays, the store hummed. And so did the sale of bananas at reduced prices. Erwin, the apprentice, had to oil the store's delivery bicycle until it hummed.

Man is the product of his environment, says your brother, Lutz. Don't worry, it'll hum.

The child is your vehicle the moment she starts humming. To what purpose? You hope that it was sheer coincidence that you dreamed of your own death a couple of nights ago, clearly and in great detail: to be more exact, you dreamed of your gradual irreversible dying, and the indifference of the others, of one doctor in particular, who lavished routine assistance and heartbreaking factual comments on you; but most of all, your own acceptance of the verdict: one more hour. And your helpless outrage at your inability to revolt against the understanding that one shouldn't take excessive interest in oneself, because in so doing one might offend others, and perhaps be a burden to them—a fate that seems to be worse than dying. .

That's the last thing, to be a burden to someone. Charlotte Jordan, at any rate, preferred to be indebted to no one. Rather go down with flying colors than expect help from others.

The child Nelly strikes you as being helpless, and it is you who put her in that position: intentionally, one might say. Now you can no longer call her by any other name, and yet it had been your wish and your intention to call her by that and no other name. The closer she gets to you in time, the less familiar she becomes. And you call that strange? (And you call that straightened? Charlotte Jordan would say, when she walked into Nelly's room. And you call that clean? And you call that eating?)

Nelly is nothing but the product of your hypocrisy. It stands to reason that anyone who attempts to change a person into an object in order to use that person for a confrontation with the self has to be hypocritical if he later complains that he can no longer expose himself to this object; that it's becoming more and more incomprehensible to him.

Or do you imagine that you can understand someone of whom you're ashamed? Whom you defend, whom you misuse in order to defend yourself?

Frankly, do you love her?

Good God, no, would be the truthful answer, but at this point doubts crop up, because the way you've been treating her is what is usually defined as love: a net over her head, tied the way you want it, and if she gets tangled up in it, too bad for her. Let her find out how it feels to be trapped. (To be wedged between two unacceptable alternatives: that is to say, without an alternative.) Let her learn early what her face expresses. Let her have a full taste of the fear of acting out of character.

The dictionary defines the word "sympathy" as "compassion, a feeling of affection and concern." But, you have to ask yourself, how can one hope to arouse a feeling of sympathy for a child who has begun to steal? And who will go on stealing over the years, with fewer and fewer scruples? She's stealing only trifles, but Charlotte Jordan, who was adamant about crime, would have called it stealing had she ever found out (but even Charlotte can see only what she's prepared to see) that her daughter had begun to swipe candy from the glass jars on the store counter, furtively, in passing; at first only the cheap kind, but later nothing but the most expensive. Theft, in other words. A double infraction of prohibitions: to sit at the living-room window—on one end of the sofa—and devour stolen sweets while reading the SS newspaper, *Schwarze Korps.*

Because *Schwarze Korps* is one of the things strictly forbidden by Charlotte Jordan, though never by Bruno Jordan, who is less concerned with his daughter's spiritual welfare. However, no special interdiction is required for the two volumes, *The Man* and *The Woman.* The fact that they are kept in her father's chest of drawers, beneath a neat pile of boxer shorts, relegates them to the realm of nonexistence. The thought of pulling them out and reading them openly cannot arise. The volumes contain large-format plates of a naked woman and a naked man; their inner organs can be laid bare by folding back covering layers of paper. A risky business (Charlotte's expression), because the coloring of certain inner organs, which successfully aims to surpass nature's colors, might easily instill a lasting disgust in someone's overheated imagination.

Nelly pretends to herself that she knows, knowing full well that she doesn't know. She emphatically reprimands her brother—although without telling their mother on him—when she surprises him with red-haired Elli at the wire fence of engineer Julich's place. In indignation she calls Elli, who is the older, "dirty" (she immediately concludes that her brother has been seduced), and is called an old slut in return.

At night, her brother, Lutz, plays innocent, and hypocritically demands information so he won't have to depend on strangers. He wants to know exactly how children are made. Nelly, equally hypocritical (the word keeps coming up), plays along, hedges, pretends to be morally concerned, but she also feels flattered and insists upon vows. Her brother Lutz complies: he insists that his memory is totally unreliable. Whatever is told him at night will disappear completely by morning, cross my heart and hope to die. Does he swear to that? He does, with a clear conscience. Whereupon an old tradition from earlier childhood has to be revived: whoever has anything more to say "afterward"—although that might be totally undesirable—must ask the other's permission by three knocks on the wall. Her brother agrees to that, also. Finally, the longed-for information, revealed in three or four sentences— the extent of her knowledge. Sentences which have, unfortunately, been lost, but the inimitable tone of Lutz's concluding remark has remained: Oh, so that's how they do it . . .

A tone between disappointment and satisfaction. An even balance of the two. If you remember correctly, there was, above all, a trace of male supremacy mixed into that tone. And then no more about the subject.

It probably wasn't long after this incident that Charlotte and Bruno Jordan agreed that their children should no longer sleep in the same room. The event Nelly had been waiting months for had come about, which she then (hypocritically!) reported to her mother, as if she didn't know what to make of it, whereupon her mother put an arm around her shoulders and called her "my big girl"; now she had to take even greater care of herself and always keep especially clean. Nelly was barely thirteen, and Charlotte thought it was "all too soon"; this is what she told the maid Annemarie, who repeated it to Nelly and to Aunt Lucy. The next day, Nelly was not allowed to climb the ladder in the store, to arrange loaves of bread on the uppermost shelf. It gave her a feeling of satisfaction: everything was following its proper course.

As a result, Frau Kruse—who lived in a second, smaller apartment, next to Hermann and Auguste Menzel in the upper story of the Jordan house for 25 marks a month, one room and a kitchen— had to be given notice; the landlord, Bruno Jordan, had other plans for his living space. Frau Kruse considered his request unacceptable in times of war, and cited the dreadful living conditions our soldiers encountered in the East (seven children in one room), in a letter obviously drafted by her son, who was deferred because of war-essential work (and, incidentally, enjoyed ample living space himself), whereupon Bruno Jordan objected to a comparison between his children and Russian or Polish children. Frau

Kruse moved. Nelly had a room of her own, with a table covered with black oilcloth, on which she was able to do her homework while from her window she looked out over the whole town, the river, and the plains. The former Kruse kitchen became a storage room for scarce food items, chocolate among others.

Normally, this room was locked, but Nelly was able to get hold of the key; her specialty was milk chocolate, and she grew more and more brazen about swiping it. Lying in bed, reading, eating chocolate. Calling down: Yes yes! When her mother called up from the stairwell: Lights out! She'd turn her light off for a few minutes, then veil it with a scarf and go on reading until one, two o'clock in the morning sometimes, which prompted customers who'd occasionally walk past the house late at night to question the light in her window. That just happened that once, last night, Nelly said when questioned. An exception, really. It won't happen again.

Did her brother, Lutz, remember who it was who briefed him about the facts of life, or had his memory acted in keeping with his boast: that he had none?

You were all tired around noon. Lutz proposed to drive over to "the other side," since, according to experience, the heat worsened in a city, due to its absorption by stone, until around 3 p.m. Across the bridge, into the outskirts. Both of you had to admit: no other part of the former town of L. was as unknown to you as this one. In the past, the expression "across the bridge" made you think of people who worked in rope or burlap factories. The poor lived "across the bridge," in little old houses which leaned against each other, or else in badly constructed tenements. In the spring, the cellars were flooded. Their children didn't go to the same schools as you, they didn't bathe at the same spots in the river, but outside the supervised bathing area, where there were sand bars and eddies, and where they established intimate friendships with raftsmen and barge captains. STRAUCH & SONS read a faded sign on the brick wall of a factory building. Strauch, Lutz said pensively, Strauch, wasn't that . . .

Yes, Strauch was Dr. Juliane Strauch's father or grandfather—one of the richest businessmen in town, who had donated the statue for the fountain in the marketplace that the people used to call "Strauch-Marie," after him. But nothing more about Fräulein

Strauch, Ph.D., at least not yet. Meanwhile—as you slowly drive
through the narrow streets on the other bank of the Warta, which
you're seeing again for the first time—you remind your brother
who taught him the facts of life. Vaguely, he says, now that you
mention it, I seem to remember something. Lenka thought such
valiant sisterly efforts deserved a little more gratitude.

At an unexpected spot you suddenly came out on the riverbank,
a gently sloping shady grass incline. Let's stop here for a while,
Lenka said.

Even you were surprised by the view. The river starts in on its
broad sweep at this spot, widens toward the east, and disappears in
the underbrush of its embankments. And beyond the river, the
skyline of the town—curving railroad tracks, warehouses, the
church, residential buildings, the way it's shown on the postcards
at the newsstand. In the foreground, the modern concrete overpass, built high into the air, that leads to the bathing area.

And it is now, in front of this view which you yourself hardly
expected, which surprised even you, it is now of all times, that
they, Lenka and H., think they understand. Yes, they said, it made
sense. There really was something to it. A town on a river, one
could remember this. They remembered poetry, they quoted lines:
"Behind the fields, far / behind the meadows / the stream . . ."

The two of you, Lutz and yourself, are silent.

H. and Lenka spread their old windbreakers on the grass. It's
worth mentioning that you felt good, laying your head down on the
earth. That you blinked your eyes shut and open again, until the
image—the town on the river—became firmly rooted behind your
closed lids. There was also the smell of the water, and a soft
gurgling sound. And of course there was the shimmer of the
water's surface, the glistening of each individual wave. Except that
no description in the world—even if you were able to name each
gray-silvery willow leaf—can reproduce the absolute contentment
of one of those rare moments in life when everything is in harmony
and in its proper place.

Of course the picture didn't meet an unprepared eye, although
you realize this only now. The priming which had been applied
decades earlier resurfaced, and added depth to your perception.
Nelly had watched the sun rise over the town and the river once,
on an early Sunday morning, from the window of her room,

wrapped in a blanket. (Charlotte, whose bedroom was right under Nelly's room, caught her daughter, forbade her to get up that early, predicted a cold, and finally insisted that she at least put on socks—exactly the thing you'd insist on if you came upon Lenka in a similar situation.) But this unforgettable morning, together with thousands of glances out her window, or out Whiskers Grandma's window, some five yards to the right, at which Nelly often stood in the afternoon, in tears once, because her mother had forbidden her to see the film *The Great King* with Otto Gebühr: All these impressions combined to form the background that made the colors of that afternoon, so many years later, stand out freely—you almost said: boldly.

Lenka, with the infallible sense all children have of their parents' moods, lay on her old windbreaker, her head close to your shoulder; she fell asleep instantly. You watched two children, a boy and a girl, climb the high steps of the new overpass to the bathing area, hand in hand, counting the steps in Polish. You counted along with them, in German, up to a figure you don't remember. Then, suddenly—quite some time had probably passed —three figures came walking toward you in an uncertain kind of weather, on an unknown gray street, three people who had absolutely no relation to each other, as you keenly felt: Vera Pryzbilla and Walpurga Dorting, two girls of your former class, with whom you had never been friendly, and between them your old friend Jossel. Absorbed in calm conversation, they came toward you, they saw you, but seemed to have no desire to explain to you why and how they, of all people, who couldn't possibly know each other, had come together at this point.

The officer awakened you with a soft call. With polite but determined gestures he made you understand that it was forbidden to camp on the embankment. You, in turn, gestured that you hadn't seen the sign—you couldn't have read it, but you would have understood its meaning—and that you were ready to obey by rapidly departing.

A few passersby and residents of nearby houses watched the incident with dispassionate interest. The two children—a boy and a girl—were still, or perhaps again, climbing the stairs. Barely half an hour had gone by. The officer saluted and started his motorcycle, which had a sidecar. *Bye bye*, Lenka said, nice of you not to have come sooner.

What next? The school, you said. Böhmstrasse. Do you know the way? In my sleep.

It was in your sleep that the two girls, Vera and Walpurga—who had been friends since Walpurga's belated arrival in Nelly's class —had ferreted out your friend Jossel, whom they couldn't have known during their lifetime. What could this mean? Not to mention other incongruities: the two girls still looked like sixteen-year-olds —Vera was wearing her pony tail, Walpurga her long loose hair— but Jossel had been the age he would be today. And the intimacy of the three, which distorted the true situation, Jossel having been your friend for years, whereas the other two—God only knew where they might be!—had never been close to Nelly, and hadn't the faintest knowledge of Jossel's existence. However, had he met you at that time, when you three were sixteen (in this respect your dream was correct) and he was a young man, without his beard, without the expression in his eyes, an expression that isn't easily definable: "lost" seems to come closest; back then, when he, the Viennese Jew, had been caught in France and shipped off to Buchenwald. Had Jossel come to your town at that time—which would, of course, have been unthinkable—he might possibly have walked down a random street with Vera Pryzbilla, the Baptist, and her girlfriend Walpurga, the daughter of a Christian missionary (who had lived in Korea for years and spoke fluent but incomprehensible English that even their English teacher couldn't understand), rather than with Nelly. If it had been the dream's intention to point out this upsetting fact, it had fulfilled its purpose. Recall the guards from the gates of consciousness.

Especially at this particular point, when truthfulness would be most rewarding, which isn't always, perhaps only seldom the case, you come across a new type of amnesia. It doesn't compare to the gaps concerning your early childhood, which seem to be self-explanatory, those blurred or white spots above a strange, sunny landscape, where awareness floats like a balloon in the changing wind, obviously casting its own shadow. But now your awareness itself seems to fall victim to a partial brown-out, entangled as it is in the events it should rise above through remembering. The task becomes unsolvable. However, you are determined to eliminate inventions, to use the memory of memories, the memory of fantasies, only as secondhand information, as reflections, not as reality.

(You read that Adolf Eichmann is supposed to have had an extremely bad memory.)

It simply can't be true that fewer things began to happen all of a sudden. It is like shoveling desert sand against the wind to keep a particular track from being completely obliterated.

Nelly must have been barely twelve when she joined the candidates for leadership who served not in the school classrooms but in a special "home": three, four bare rooms under the roof of the former welfare building, which is still standing. There had to be initiation ceremonies, stricter rules, in order to learn the duties of a model for others. They certainly must have had an impact on Nelly. But not one of these assumptions—which are almost certainties—evokes an image, a quotable sentence. Only one image and one sentence have been preserved about this time in her life, both, however, with the utmost precision: in front of the door of her school library, Nelly runs into Dr. Juliane Strauch, who is in charge of the library; Nelly is startled, as she always is when she runs into Fräulein Strauch (although she secretly hopes for these encounters); she gives the Hitler salute, which is, however, not returned; instead, the teacher places an arm on Nelly's shoulder and honors her with a sentence: Well done, girl! Of course I hadn't expected anything less of you.

If somebody were to say that Nelly could have gone through much less trouble than playing a role in the Hitler Youth, in order to hear this sentence, that somebody would be right. As for Juliane Strauch, her German and history teacher, called Julia, your memory couldn't be more exact. Her face, her figure, her walk and behavior have been preserved within you for twenty-nine years, whereas the memory of the period during which she was so important has become rather shredded. As though she had attracted Nelly's concentrated attention to herself alone. (Perhaps one shouldn't draw any hasty conclusions from these observations, least of all analogies. But might it not be true that, except for the particular laws of memory formation during childhood, a slower, perhaps more thorough rhythm of living furnishes a better condition for the development of those sections of the brain which store events than the continuously increasing haste with which persons, objects, and events drift past us, which we're almost embarrassed to call "life"?)

Well, whatever. You don't exactly want to claim that you're able to describe Nelly's first meeting with Julia Strauch—it probably was a brief passing on the school stairs—but you can vouch for the truthful description of their last meeting. After that, there were only brief encounters in the Hermann Göring gymnasium, and in the large dance hall of the Weinberg Inn, places which served to accommodate refugees from the East in January 1945. As the leader of the National Socialist Women's Organization, Dr. Juliane Strauch played an important role in the care of those refugees, while Nelly was charged with auxiliary tasks, which will be described in due course.

The winter of 1944–45 was cold from the start, and it was coldest in the pale, bare streets around Schlageterplatz, swept by the wind that blew unimpeded through two rows of symmetrically aligned houses. Nelly felt cold in her confirmation coat, while she paced up and down in front of Julia's house, counting the minutes until the clock struck four. She was angry with herself for feeling so disconsolate. But she knew herself: shortly before the fulfillment of something she had wished for long and hard, her happy anticipation collapsed—an inherent weakness of hers, which forced her to develop and refine her talents at pretending.

Nelly felt embarrassed as she rang Julia's bell, but fortunately the instant the steps approached the other side of the door, the old excitement sprang up again inside Nelly, stimulated by a simple method: she rehearsed her glowing fantasies about an invitation to Julia's house. Because one obviously didn't go to Julia's house without having been invited.

Of course Julia wouldn't think of embarrassing Nelly with an apologetic remark about the dry oatmeal cookies, the thin tea, or the barely heated room. Julia was able to radiate relaxation in any situation, an ability which made her inviolable and not only superior—the word would be too weak—but sublime. It cost her nothing to counter the unavoidable fits of laughter of her fourteen- and fifteen-year-old students with the seemingly amused remark: I don't see what's so funny, unless it's me.

Her greatest achievement must have been the considerable, though undetectable, effort with which she probably tried to bridge the wide gap that separated her outward appearance from that of the ideal German woman, a phenomenon she never tired of extolling. Not only was she short, but she had black hair and markedly Slavic features, which the biology books defined as "flat." She was, moreover, the only female intellectual Nelly knew in her youth (disregarding Professor Lehmann, the wife of a man who was probably Jewish) and she had not felt it necessary to get married and contribute children to the German nation. She did, however, insist that she be addressed as "Frau Doktor," rather than as Fräulein. After a certain age a woman had earned the right to be addressed with the honorable title "Frau." In history class she occasionally remarked that a consequence of European history— the result of an unfortunate godforsaken mixture of the noblest blood with the vilest—was that pure Germanic thinking and feeling could often be found in persons whose exterior appearance didn't permit such an assumption; in short, that a Germanic soul was hidden inside such persons.

Such sentences, which you hesitate to commit to paper because they might easily sound invented, were quite natural to Julia. As a matter of course, she also said in confidential conversations that Germany had to make use of all her assets now, including her youth, to win the decisive battle against her enemies. Lately, however, she had been noticing signs of unruly behavior in her class—which was precisely what she'd wanted to discuss with Nelly—transgressions against the basic rules of discipline: the formation of small cliques.

Nelly had to agree with Julia, unreservedly, on every point, the way she always agreed with Julia. But can the colorless word "agree" do justice to something that was more of an alliance, a deep affinity, although also a form of captivity, as far as Nelly was concerned? Nelly's first experience of love was that of captivity.

After classes she'd stand outside the school. On Böhmstrasse. You had no trouble finding it, as you had predicted, even though the street that led to it from the Warta embankment, straight through the center of town, has been changed radically, or rather, modernized. Straightened. Widened. It was 3 p.m. Fortunately, the stretch of street in front of the school lay in the shade of the houses across the street. The trees gave depth to the shade. (You could have sworn that they were pink hawthorn, but they became linden trees when you studied the photos later with a magnifying glass; of course they may have been newly planted—twenty years ago, that is.) You were able to deduce from the sign next to the entrance that the school had become a teachers college.

Unlike most of the other teachers, Julia used the exit that was reserved for students of the lower grades. She mostly stayed in her library, rather than in the teachers' room, and kept her distance from the other teachers, who certainly respected her but were hardly fond of her. People who can't conceal the fact that they consider themselves more perfect than others are rarely popular. But Nelly, devastated like everyone else by the unbridgeable gap between Julia's perfection and her own shortcomings, Nelly would stand outside the school (ostensibly waiting for a girlfriend, her school bag on the low wall that ran along the grass), hoping to be singled out by a glance or a greeting from Julia.

"Devotion" was one of Julia's favorite words. In that respect, at least, Nelly felt able to meet Julia's demands. Among the women she knew, not one led a life Nelly would have wished or might have imagined for herself: except Julia. (Julia! Julia! Charlotte would say. If Julia asked you to jump out the window, you'd jump, right?) Nelly listened for the sounds that came from Julia's kitchen, sounds of somebody being busy in there. Was it true that Julia had an older sister who kept house for her? Julia made no attempt to explain the sounds.

The question was not whether she demanded more of Nelly than of the others: that went without saying, since Nelly had no trouble excelling in German composition or in history reports, which Julia graded more severely than those of the others: that was perfectly all right. Minor extra tasks could be interpreted as proofs of confidence and marks of distinction: she often let Nelly arrange a class outing, or asked her to tutor a boy who had every reason to fear that he might flunk his secondary-school entrance exam.

It was, of course, a high point of confidence when Julia, who was responsible for the celebration of Hitler's birthday in the auditorium, entrusted Nelly with the recitation of the main poem: "When need rises / like a flood up to a nation's chin, / the Lord / picks the ablest / from among the wealth of men at his disposal. / With his own hand / pushes him / mercilessly, it seems / into the lightless abyss, / deals him / fatal wounds / and burdens his heart / with a pain more bitter than that of all his brothers."

Lenka said: What a memory. I can't remember a poem for

longer than a year. A test shows that she's right. Only fragments, even of the most popular Goethe poems. However, an indestructible store of scullery-maid ditties and horror ballads from early childhood, also Spanish songs from old records, which can't be played on the new turntable; also Morgenstern and Ringelnatz.

(She can lie around for days, listening to music. Is that how you want to finish off the year? you ask her. Leave me alone, she says. The last year hasn't been good. You mean your laziness? I mean that I'm beginning to get accustomed. To what? To everything being pseudo, me too, in the end. Pseudo-people, a pseudo-life. Or haven't you noticed? Or maybe I'm not normal? Or are the people who don't even think about it right? I sometimes feel that another piece of me is dying off. And who's to blame? Nobody but me?

A fear for her surges up inside you, a new kind of fear. Writing should be different, you think, totally different.)

Like every lover, Nelly pines for irrefutable proof of requited love, a proof that shouldn't be linked to merit. It happened that Julia held a class for Nelly all by herself, and it was one of the most extraordinary events of her school years: they discussed the Nordic hero legends, whose spotlighted figures are steeped in blood but never guided by base motivation, and unrepenting Hagen, the darkly tragic knight, the truest of the true, who dips his sword into the blood of his master's enemies, whose dying song Julia knows by heart and recites: "Accursed be the female race / all treachery and lying / 'tis for two wenches' smooth white faces / that Burgundy lies dying! / And should the world's great treasure / Siegfried once more appear, / into his back with pleasure / I'd plant once more my spear."

Finally, at the end of the class, Julia looked Nelly full in the face, and Nelly concealed what she had understood: Julia hated being a woman. And Nelly had to admit that that was not at all the way she felt herself.

At the end of a chain of thoughts that had too many links to enumerate them, you see a picture: Nelly in the so-called parlor, at one end of the sofa, absorbed in forbidden *Schwarze Korps*, which she could read around 4 p.m. without the risk of getting caught. In it she reads a report about institutions called "Wells of Life" (you learn many years later that one of its branches was in Thomas Mann's former house in Munich): houses in which tall blond blue-eyed SS men are brought together with brides of similar background for the purpose of producing a racially pure child, whom the mother then offers to the Führer as a gift, as the *Schwarze Korps* approvingly stressed. (Not a word that the same organization was engaged in large-scale child theft in the countries occupied by the German Army.) You clearly remember that the author of the report sharply or mockingly attacked the outmoded prejudices that found fault with the above conduct, conduct worthy of idealistic German men and women.

It shall be truthfully said that, after reading the article, Nelly sat with the paper across her knees, clearly thinking: No, not that.

It was one of those rare, precious, and inexplicable instances when Nelly found herself in conscious opposition to the required convictions she would have liked to share. As so often, it was a feeling of guilt that engraved the incident in her memory. How could she have known that bearing guilt was, under the prevailing conditions, a necessary requirement for inner freedom? There she sat, a thirteen-year-old girl wedged between her mother's warnings not to "throw herself away" and the *Schwarze Korps'* request for unconditional submission for the sake of the Führer. Anything connected with her sex was complicated to the point of being unbearable. She had read a novel about the Thirty Years' War in which a girl, Christine Torstenson, intentionally infected herself with the plague, in order to enter and infect the enemy camp by "giving herself." Not that, Nelly had thought at the end of the novel, filled with admiration and fear. She ran into the kitchen, to stir oats, sugar, milk, and cocoa into a sweet pap which she spooned into herself while staring out the window with unfocused eyes, the paper on her knees.

In the schoolyard (which you entered on July 10, 1971, walking past the red brick school building on the right, through the wrought-iron gate, which was unlocked, as it had always been) Julia used to follow a habitual track when it was her turn to supervise recess. She'd march with long strides, her hands behind her back, in her flat shoes with the worn-down heels, her stockings darned way up her calves. Her attentive eyes were everywhere. There were no fights during her recesses, nor did she have to reprimand anyone for forbidden ball playing, snowball throwing, or improper conduct. Sometimes she'd motion a student to step up to her, and ask her about her private life: had her mother returned from the hospital, had her father written from the war, how was the room and the landlady, in the case of girls who came from out of town. It was evident: the most brazen, who secretly made fun of her, were meek after she dismissed them. If you didn't run with the pack, but stood with your back against the red brick wall of the gymnasium (at a spot where a bench has now been placed, on which a stocky man in a blue work shirt was sitting, taking a rest, on that Saturday afternoon, when you walked into the schoolyard after so many years: the superintendent of the teachers college), if you didn't run with the pack, you could discern individual students or whole groups coordinating their rounds with Julia's, so that their paths crossed at certain points, or ran parallel with hers for a time. Or else, so that they didn't touch. Nelly didn't want to be one of the many who were never given the honor of being addressed. She therefore stood by herslf, so that, when the bell rang for class, and the courtyard emptied out, Julia would take up her position at the school door and catch Nelly, who'd be going in among the last; she'd lightly lay a hand on Nelly's upper arm, and climb the ten steps to the schoolhouse with her; she'd even stop outside the door to the library and talk with her about the class's failure in the most recent composition.

Not that that failure had been Nelly's: that wasn't to be expected in German composition, Julia didn't even hint at that. But why was it that so many wrote fluently about "a nation hemmed in" or about "the Nordic spirit in the poetry of antiquity," but were totally unable to deal with a subject as easy as "the first snow"? Nelly couldn't say, and she wouldn't have expressed her assumption: that it was a lot more difficult to write about personal matters than about general familiar everyday notions. She remembered clearly: while describing the particular Sunday on which the first snow had fallen that year, she never forgot for a second for whom she was writing. A touch of deceit permeated every line; she had described her family as just a trifle too idyllic and herself as just a trifle too virtuous: exactly the way she thought Julia wished to see her. (The deceit, and the fact that she remained conscious of it, as much as her longing for truthfulness, was this perhaps some form of salvation? A vestige of independence, which she was able to resume later?)

In order to win Julia over—or to deceive her, which seemed to amount to the same thing—she had to refrain from blunt maneuvers and ensnare the demanding teacher, who was not easily flattered, in a web of the subtlest weave: looks, gestures, words, lines that lay within a hair's breadth of her true emotions, without ever fully blending with them.

That probably was the reason why Nelly—after the highpoints of exaltation, when Julia had placed a hand on her shoulder in parting, and nodded in her famous fashion—why Nelly collapsed on the stairs to her classroom and felt overcome by a sadness which frightened her and which she refused to acknowledge. It wasn't right that moments of the greatest bliss always ended in emptiness —not to say in disappointment: a word that didn't come to her mind. She'd drop into her seat, show no interest in Fräulein Woyssmann's English exercises, and didn't care what grades she'd be given for her translation; she'd huddle with her friend Hella over a sheet of paper and play Hangman.

It was about this time that Charlotte Jordan noticed that her daughter was tearing her cuticles to shreds, which she naturally, although unsuccessfully, forbade.

You didn't enter the schoolyard proper. You went no farther than the corner of the house, that's when you spotted the superintendent. No one entered the schoolyard during vacation time— unless there was a war on, when students of the upper grades were appointed air-raid wardens for a week, when four of you slept on cots in a classroom and cooked your meals in the school kitchen. Dora, the only girl who knew how to cook, had taught them how to make dumplings, which they had eaten over there, behind the linden trees. Julia, the chief warden, had sat at the head of the crude plank table and praised the dumplings. It must have been a hot summer. They had made a mistake about the quantity of dough, the remaining dumplings were surreptitiously drowned in the Cladow, during the night, despite the huge poster in the kitchen: "Fight Waste!"

In the daytime, air raids were still few and far between. In the evenings they'd sit in the dark, under the linden trees, and sing whatever Julia asked for: "High fir trees point to the stars," "No finer land than our land." Julia asked what they all wanted to be. Dora thought she'd like to be a nurse; Hella wanted to take over her father's bookstore; Marga, who had been evacuated from Berlin, hoped to use her talent for drawing. Nelly said: Teacher. Julia nodded. For a long time Nelly had waited for an opportunity to show her teacher her desire to emulate her. Now she had done so, but at the same time she feared that Julia might think her pushy.

Music was coming from the open window of a neighboring house beyond the small lush green ravine, at the bottom of which ran the Cladow. Somebody had his radio on loud, there was the sound of a flute, followed by a rapid crescendo on a piano. The melody touched you deeply, unexpectedly—if that's how you can still describe a welling up of tears. It seemed unbearable to you that you'd never be able to meet the woman—you imagined a young woman—who was listening to the music in that room up there, that you'd never even be able to see her. You only wanted to crouch in the cool green embankment of the Cladow, still as completely overgrown with ferns and ivy as in the past; you wanted to close your eyes, listen to the music, and forget yourself at last. Because it's only when one forgets oneself that the gap between that which one forces oneself to be and that which one is briefly closes.

Nelly kept a diary in those days; fortunately or unfortunately, it was burned at the end of the war, in the pot-bellied stove of the village tavern in Grünheide near Nauen, where the Jordan family, without Bruno Jordan, who was in Russian captivity, had found lodgings after the first three weeks of flight. That thing has to go, Charlotte Jordan decreed—she had, of course, been a secret reader of her daughter's diary—before the family took to the road once more, since the Red Army was preparing to march on Berlin. She lifted the three iron center rings off the stove top and watched the immolation of the dangerous notebook: If the Russians find that among our stuff, we've had it, dumb naïve thing that you are! "The Russians" never suspected or searched for papers of the Jordan family, but you didn't have the strength to express genuine regret over the destruction of this irreplaceable, though doubtless incriminating, document.

Has it been mentioned that Julia had blue eyes? Light-blue according to some, cornflower-blue according to others. On that January afternoon, she fixed these eyes on Nelly, with their habitual intensity, when she came to the point in her conversation with

her student when she wanted to talk seriously. She didn't reprimand, but remained encouraging and understanding. Exactly the
tone which—as Julia knew only too well, as Nelly knew that Julia
knew—had direct access to Nelly's "innermost being."

Her friend Hella and herself: there had been several causes for
reprimand during the past six months Julia was discussing. Not
during her own classes, that went without saying. They both
laughed. But Fräulein März, for instance, had bitterly complained
about Nelly's lack of interest in mathematics, which Nelly made no
attempt to hide. Really? Old März? Nelly said with her eyes.
Everyone at school knew that she was Julia's only serious rival, a
cool, scientific type, short-cropped hair, glasses, unbribable. Nelly
was afraid of her. Her look was acknowledged, and to a lesser
degree returned. But Professor Gassmann had been deeply upset
that Nelly had taken the liberty of eating during his class. Really,
Professor Gassmann! As soon as he turned his back, all hell broke
loose, anyway. Julia knew about that, and dropped the matter.
Fine, fine, let's speak about what's really important: Julia wanted
Nelly to think about her relationship with her friend Hella, and to
draw the conclusions herself.

As always, Julia had put her finger on the sore spot. At fifteen,
Nelly's main concern was not the outcome of the war—Germany
couldn't lose, that lay beyond the realm of human possibilities—
but the worry that she might lose her friend. Hella tended to be
fickle. Just now she'd become intimate with a girl named Isa, who,
in Julia's words, showed "little mind, but an abundance of other
advantages," and Nelly had been forced into making concessions
that went against her grain in order not to lose Hella. Julia had no
need to go into details. Nelly understood: traces of insubordina-
tion. She fleetingly thought that Julia was overlooking the real
danger: it wasn't Hella and Isa, with their love of impudent
pranks, with their exchange of notes during class and their secret
conferences during recess, that always involved the names of boys,
but Christa T., the new girl from the Friedeberg area, who didn't
show off and had no need for Julia, and from whom Nelly had just
extorted the halfhearted promise that she would write to her during
the Christmas vacation.

Not a word about that to Julia. Instead, the appearance of being
reasonable, as always, and yet, although unintentionally, a touch

of distance. Which was enough to make Julia pronounce the sentence Nelly had vainly waited for for so long: Well, you and I know what we mean to each other, don't we?

The sentence came too late, no doubt, and had almost lost its magic effect. Nelly wouldn't have admitted it to herself, but she felt a sneaking suspicion that Julia might be calculating.

(Strangely enough, Julia's last words, before she died of typhoid fever on a transport to Siberia, are supposed to have been: As God wills. This is surprising, because she never showed any trace of religious feeling when Nelly knew her. Incidentally, her conduct is said to have been exemplary, helpful to the point of self-sacrifice, during the transport: information that answered, at least in part, a question Nelly frequently asked herself after the war: If a so-called honest idealism had been decisive in Julia's behavior, or if she'd immediately betrayed the past, as did almost all those whom Nelly saw at the time, or if she had remained "true" to herself, whatever that meant?)

Back out in the wind-swept street. It was pitch dark now. Her visit with Julia hadn't fulfilled all that Nelly had hoped for. As usual. Thus, one side of Nelly spoke to the other side, because she had developed the habit of watching herself walk and talk and act, which meant that she had to judge herself incessantly. It often kept her from talking freely, from taking action when it was necessary. Once, on Ludendorffstrasse, she ran into a girl from her Jungmädel unit who rarely showed up for "Duty," and to whom Nelly had therefore sent a written admonition. The girl's mother took issue with Nelly, publicly, in the street, making it quite clear that a young thing such as Nelly had no right to give her daughter orders. And Nelly just stood by, instead of insisting on her rights, hastily agreeing with the mother, because the side of her that was not standing in the street, but was looking down on the incident, was telling her that she ought to be ashamed of herself.

Let's walk a couple of blocks. Let's get out of the car. In this heat? Lenka said. Isn't there anyplace here where you can swim?

Not here, not on Hindenburgplatz, which is around the corner, changed to its advantage—as must have been mentioned—by its wild abundance of grass, the Saturday-afternoon card players, and the benches between the trees which surround the square. A picture into which one would like to fit. The schnapps bottles under the benches, kids on the knees and at the feet of their fathers. Wide-hipped, full-breasted young women, four on a bench, with infants in their arms.

Nelly's Jungmädel unit used to meet Wednesdays and Saturdays on the southeast side of the square that led into the former Böhmstrasse; that's where they used to line up. Nelly, too, made her team line up, according to size, in rows; she'd hold a roll call, always worried about the result, because her ability as a leader was measured by her unit's attendance. She'd order: "Right face!" and a formation by threes, for the report to her group leader, who had only just arrived. After that, they'd march off to the compulsory exercises. Nelly didn't march in the column, but, like the other leaders, outside, to the left of the column. Left, left, left, two, three, four. A song: "Let's try out something new today / to march a march in a different way / into the western woods so dark / where the wi-inds howl and the do-ogs bark . . ."

The backs of the column. The pavement of the streets. The house fronts. But not a single face. Memory fails you in the most incredible, downright embarrassing way. No names either, neither of the leaders nor of those under them.

Language won't allow you to call this fact remarkable. Only group or crowd images seem to have been remarkable. Marching columns. Rhythmic mass exercises in the stadium. Halls filled with people singing: "Sacred fatherland, / when dangers abound / your sons surround / you, sacred fatherland . . ." A circle around a campfire. Another song: "Rise, O flames"; again no faces. A giant rectangle in the market square, made up of Hitler Youth, boys and girls; they stand in formation, an assassination attempt has been made on the Führer. Not a single face.

You weren't prepared for this. The school, the street, the playground offer up bodies and faces which you could paint to this day. Where Nelly's participation was deepest, where she showed devotion, where she gave of herself, all relevant details have been obliterated. Gradually, one might assume. And it isn't difficult to guess the reason: the forgetting must have gratified a deeply insecure awareness which, as we all know, can instruct our memory behind our own backs, such as: Stop thinking about it. Instructions that are faithfully followed through the years. Avoid certain memories. Don't speak about them. Suppress words, sentences, whole chains of thought, that might give rise to remembering. Don't ask your contemporaries certain questions. Because it is unbearable to think the tiny word "I" in connection with the word "Auschwitz." "I" in the past conditional: I would have. I might have. I could have. Done it. Obeyed orders.

In that case, no faces. The ability to remember lies dormant. Still to this day: a feeling of relief, if you're honest. And the realization that language acts as a filter in the process of minting expressions. It filters: in the sense of what is desired. In the sense of what is mentionable. In the sense of what has been established. How can established behavior be forced to yield spontaneous expression?

AMT, Lenka says.

What's that supposed to mean?

You're heading for the small corner café; it's new. It's almost empty, a man is sitting behind the piano, a cup of coffee costs 10 zloty. It is Turkish coffee, good and strong, served in large cups. With strawberry tarts. A couple of drunken teenagers walk in. One of them bothers two girls at the table next to yours. The waitress, a buxom, good-looking middle-aged woman, speaks to them sharply, with determination, and shows them the door. They stumble out without much protest; outside, one of them falls heavily against the large windowpane. That certain expression, a mixture of disgust and superiority for irresponsible men, appears on the faces of all three women, an expression you've been seeing on many women's faces lately.

AMT is a new technical definition from Lenka's biology class; it stands for: Animal-Man-Transition period. We're in the middle of it, Lenka says, aren't we? Some are more animal, others almost human.

During those days she was painting men crouched inside capsules, each by himself. Every once in a while an encapsulated couple. And sad self-portraits. The other day she told you about a dream, or a nightmare, in which she'd kept walking for the longest time. A movie camera was watching every one of her gestures day and night, and a huge movie house, filled with unsuspecting spectators who had come in off the street to see a random two-hour feature and were obliged to stay in their seats and watch Lenka's life unfold on a giant screen. For days, for weeks. "A drag" is an understatement for what these people thought of it, she said, and me too, as you can imagine. At such moments it would probably be beyond human strength to suppress the exclamation: But how well I know all that! She raised her eyebrows. What do you mean? Did you ever have the feeling that you were being filmed? No, I didn't think along those technical lines: in my case, the camera was the eye of God, and the permanent audience was God himself. You believed in God that long? Believed sounds as though not believing might have been a choice, but that wasn't so. Incidentally, what's the difference between the eye of God and the eye of your camera?

Lenka wanted to think that over.

Perhaps all we can do is point out our difficulties to those who come after us. To talk about what happens when the roads that are open all lead in the wrong direction. Perhaps you should grieve over losses which Nelly suffered—which she suffered irrevocably, as you now realize. Perhaps you should grieve for the child who took her leave at that time: unknown to all and loved as the person she might have been. Who took her secret with her: the secret of the walls which caged her, that she'd grope along hoping to find the gap that would make her feel less afraid than the rest. But fear it was, nonetheless.

In those days her fear expressed itself as a continuous penetrating feeling of inner alienation, whose very track consisted in the effacement of tracks. A person who wants to pass unnoticed soon stops noticing anything. The horrible wish for self-surrender doesn't allow the self to emerge.

Lutz and Lenka were quarreling, you didn't know about what. Lutz was saying that rebellion against the established order could of course be heroic, but that it always had a comic side effect. The established order proved its right to be simply by being.

How did you get onto that subject? you asked.

Because of AMT, Lenka said. Lutz is conservative. Realistic, said Lutz, whereas you're all romantics.

You left the café and suddenly felt miserable. Not far from the spot where you climbed back into your car, not more than three minutes away, must have been the former district headquarters of the Hitler Youth organization, in the former Franz-Seldtestrasse, a two-story house which you would probably have recognized. Nelly never walked into that house without being overcome with fear, and never walked out without a feeling of relief. You would have had the time, even though it was past 4 p.m., and you finally wanted to check in at the hotel. Nobody would have objected if you had proposed the small detour. But it didn't occur to you.

It is only today that you think of it.

11

The final solution.

You've forgotten when you first heard those words. When you gave them their proper meaning; it must have been years after the war. But way after that—to this day—every tall, thickly smoking smokestack forces you to think "Auschwitz." The name cast a shadow which grew and grew. To this day, you can't bring yourself to stand in this shadow, because your otherwise lively imagination balks at the suggestion that you might take on the role of the victims.

For all eternity, an insurmountable barrier separates the sufferers from those who went free.

On July 31, 1941—a vacation day, and probably hot—Nelly may have been lying in her favorite potato furrow under the cherry trees in the garden, reading, while a lizard sunned itself on her stomach. In summertime, the radio was on the porch; perhaps Nelly jumped to her feet at the sound of the fanfares which preceded special news bulletins; perhaps she ran to the porch to hear the news of the continued German advance into Russia. Her father was no longer in the war. After the Polish campaign, his age group had been demobilized, and he, who had been deemed "fit for garrison duty at home," had been assigned a desk job as a noncommissioned officer in the orderly room of the District Command Post in L.

This was, more or less, the way Nelly spent the day on which Reichsmarshal Hermann Göring, by order of the Führer, entrusted Reinhard Heydrich, chief of security police and head of national security, with the "final solution of the Jewish problem in the zones of German influence inside Europe"—the same Heydrich who had received orders to carry out the final solution within German territory on January 24, 1939, when Nelly was not quite ten years old.

Both dates deserve to be remembered more than a number of others. This Eichmann, Lenka asked the other day, who is this man? You all fell silent. Then you asked to be shown her history book. Ninth grade, she said, sullenly going to look for it among her discarded schoolbooks in a box in the basement.

Almost one hundred pages dealt with the Fascist dictatorship in Germany. You checked and discovered that the name Adolf Eichmann was not mentioned. Heinrich Himmler occurred twice, once quoted as saying: "Whether other nations live in prosperity or die of starvation concerns me only insofar as we may need them as slaves for our culture. Otherwise I'm not interested."

Posen—today Poznan—where this speech was delivered before the leaders of SS units on October 4, 1943, lay a mere fifty-five miles from Nelly's hometown. As a child, she never went that far east. You quote a few more sentences from the same speech, for Lenka's benefit: "It is radically wrong for us to take all of our guileless soul, our kind hearts, our generosity and our liberalism into foreign nations." Lenka is looking over your shoulder, together you're reading what cannot be read out loud: "Most of you must be familiar with the sight of corpses piled up by the hundreds, the five hundreds, the thousands. Having had to go through that kind of experience, and to have remained decent human

beings—not counting a few exceptions, due to human weakness—
has toughened all of us. It is an unwritten, never to be written,
page of glory in our history . . ."
Lenka says nothing.
Page 206 of her history book shows a picture of the camp gates
of Auschwitz-Birkenau. (Lenka's association is: Franci. Franci
from Prague, whom she has loved since early childhood, and who
walked through these gates.) Under the picture are four quotations
from an exchange of letters between I. G. Farben and the Auschwitz concentration camp, with reference to a shipment of
women from the camp to the factory, for experimental purposes;
at the price of 170 marks a head; 150 women die of the experiments, the information is given with precision. "We shall be con-
tacting you before long about another shipment." Lenka has no
association.
What does I. G. Farben mean to her?
To you, I. G. Farben is the vast complex of red-brick buildings
that had been built to the right of Friedeberger Chaussee in the
middle thirties, a rambling terrain with factories, in which the
city's last remaining unemployed found work and pay (want ads in
the *General-Anzeiger*). During the war, the barracks which housed
the Volga and the Volhynia Germans also stood on the terrain; the
Führer had led them back home into the Reich, so that they could
work at I. G. Farben and receive hand-knitted mufflers and mittens
and homemade spice cookies as Christmas gifts from the Jungmädel—Nelly among them. The Volhynia German women wept
when the Jungmädel sang "Heitschibumbeitschi," they wiped their
eyes with the corners of their black kerchiefs, which they kept on
their heads even inside the room (room was hardly the word for it:
the insides of barracks, with plank tables and bunk beds, and a
bad smell), and they expressed tearful gratitude for the beautiful
presents, and some of them tried to kiss the young ladies' hands.
Nelly didn't like going to the barracks, but she knew there was
no getting out of it.
On page 207 of Lenka's schoolbook is a map—6″ x 4″—of
"Fascist concentration camps throughout Europe during World
War II." The towns aren't marked on this map. The North Sea and
the Baltic Sea are indicated, as are the main rivers: sixteen larger
black dots mark the major concentration camps. Five of these are

underlined, to indicate that they were extermination camps. The map is studded with small dots ("secondary camps") and small crosses ("ghettos"). You can physically sense Lenka's understanding, her first, of what kind of landscape her mother spent her childhood in. From the geographical location of the extermination camps Chelmno, Treblinka, and maybe also Maidanek, one can assume that transports of human beings destined for these camps passed also through L., on the eastern railroad. Trains destined for Auschwitz and Belzec probably used the southern route. Never did Nelly hear anyone around her mention any such transport, neither during nor after the war. No one in her family worked for the German railroad in those days.

Lenka said, so far as she knew, most students in her class—including herself—hadn't examined the map very thoroughly. She said they hadn't felt (hadn't been *made* to feel, you think) that this map concerned them more than other documents in the book. Your shocked surprise, mixed with a touch of irritation, collapses as you ask yourself if it was not desirable rather than objectionable that these children no longer suffered from a guilt feeling which might have compelled them to examine the map more closely. Unto the third and fourth generation: the horrible dictum of the vengeful God. But that is not the point.

You've watched droves of people happily eating their apples and their sandwiches while tramping across the onetime drill field of Ettersberg, a sight that filled you with amazement and fear rather than with indignation. Moreover, someone tried to explain to you that the remodeling of the former SS barracks in the Buchenwald camp into a kind of tourist hotel had been an efficient way of saving material and expense. He didn't use the word "hospitality," but that was the gist of what he was saying, and he didn't understand your question: Did he really think anyone—a foreign tourist, for instance—would be able to go to sleep in that house? Frankly, he said, I don't know what you mean. Your proposition, that current visitors to the former concentration camp abstain from eating, drinking, singing, and piped-in music for the brief duration of their visit, struck him as unreasonable. Frankly, he said, that's not being realistic. You've got to take people the way they are.

When did the tutoring at Professor Lehmann's take place? After

July 31, 1941, at any rate. Probably even after January 20, 1942, date of the so-called Wannsee conference, in which Adolf Eichmann was finally permitted to participate (although as the lowest in rank). In the course of this conference—to his boundless delight—a plan was approved with almost euphoric unanimity by all Secretaries of State and other high officials, a plan whose execution would give him the opportunity to deploy all his ability and talent: "to comb" Europe "from east to west" for Jews.

You should know about Adolf Eichmann, Lenka. A man who couldn't bear to be unsuccessful; who spoke in slogans until the very end, even about his own death: a master and a victim of that lethal use of language which brings yearned-for absolute political equality to some and annihilation to others—annihilation at the hands of persons who are permitted to commit murder without remorse by a language stripped of conscience. Because they can feel only that which has been decreed. Adolf Eichmann is the most dangerous, he is the man who comes closest to his contemporaries' concept of "normal" behavior. A man who completely subordinates himself to the reevaluation of all values, as decreed by the state, and who, till his death, saw his crime only in his obedience —and he had been taught to consider obedience a virtue.

If you remember correctly, it was in the fall that the Professors Lehmann, long-standing customers of the Jordans, sat in the parlor with Charlotte one afternoon and began speaking about their origins, with increasing nervousness. It's strange and inexplicable that Nelly was present throughout, probably at her mother's request; Charlotte had wanted to offer her daughter as a student to the professorial couple, and hadn't anticipated the course the conversation was going to take. But Professor Lehmann had to assure them over and over that his dismissal by the Board of Education because of racial unreliability was based on a fatal error, which he, Lehmann, was trying to clear up by means of copious petitions to the competent authorities, and ultimately to Herr Himmler in person.

Professor Lehmann had copies of the documents with him, and asked Charlotte Jordan to look at them, against her will. They proved beyond a doubt that, though raised by Jewish parents, said parents had not been his natural parents; that he had an almost unbroken chain of proof of his assertion: that he was the son of a simple girl of pure Aryan blood, now deceased, unfortunately, his illegitimate mother. A girl who had had absolutely no opportunity to engage in intimate relations with non-Aryan men. As far as he, Lehmann, was concerned, he was calmly, most calmly, awaiting the outcome of the investigation.

Nelly never forgot the white fluttering hands fussing with the papers, nor the spooky laugh, as Professor Lehmann asked if he looked in any way like a Jew. Professor Lehmann had a light, round, slightly doughy face and sparse reddish hair; Charlotte Jordan hastily assured him that no Jew looked like that. Then she hurriedly switched the conversation to the fuel-less cooker the Lehmanns had constructed, in keeping with the electricity-saving recommendations of the newspapers (under the heading: "Fight the Coal Thief!"). Frau Lehmann, a language professor like her husband, had also been dismissed in the course of the racial purge, and had attained remarkable results with the fuel-less cooker; she was willing to share her secrets with anyone who might be interested.

Nelly had no objection to Herr Lehmann's teaching her how to pronounce the English *r*, which she simply couldn't do. She'd sit at the Lehmanns' oval living-room table covered with crocheted lace, and patiently go through the tongue exercises which, though the tongue-tip *r* remained inaccessible, did lead to a satisfactory result. It would be an exaggeration to say that she had never for a moment been able to forget that her teacher was suspected of being Jewish. But he himself, with his boundless friendliness that almost touched upon obsequiousness, did not allow her to feel at ease. Her hands were sweaty as she sat across from Herr Lehmann, sweat seeped into her English book. She couldn't get over the feeling that her teacher was afraid of her, and she realized that she couldn't free him of this fear by exaggerated friendliness. Every word they exchanged sounded false to her. But it was unthinkable to put a stop to the torture of these lessons, since the Lehmanns were now trying to keep alive with private tutoring.

Nelly envied her brother, Lutz, who was not burdened by ambiguous feelings and let Herr Lehmann cure him of his lisp by placing a single poppy seed on the tip of his tongue, so that he could move it around his mouth until the tongue found the proper position for pronouncing a sharp *s*.

It never occurred to Nelly to think that her mother might be courageous, sending her children to the Lehmanns. Charlotte later said that she thought it was a disgrace how these two venerable teachers were thanked for their many long years of service. And she had felt sorry for them. At that point, she was no longer sure whether or not she believed what the professor had tried to prove with his papers. At any rate, these people constituted no danger for her children, that much she knew for sure. In the case of an interrogation, she would have maintained that Professor Lehmann's documents had convinced her of his Aryan origins.

Nelly felt no aversion to this possibly Jewish man. She didn't admit to herself that she felt sorry for him. A pervasive embarrassment poisoned their meetings, all the more so when Professor Lehmann felt that he had to comment approvingly on reports by the German High Command. Never will the Russians subjugate the Germans, he would say, and Nelly, who wholeheartedly agreed with him, had to ask herself if it was perhaps fear that drove him to make these exaggerated statements.

A young woman, born after those times, quite casually told you the other day that, after taking a sauna in a particularly narrow room, she had dreamed for the first time that she was being gassed. Strangely enough, she had been carrying a child in her arms while she was being gassed, her own child, although she was childless. She hadn't been able to return to the sauna after the dream. Silly of her, to be sure, but the dream experience had been horrible beyond description.

It's a well-known fact that Heinrich Himmler was a strict, exacting, pious man. The same adjectives would accurately describe the father of Rudolf Hoess, the first commandant of Auschwitz, whose notes you read for the first time exactly one year ago (it's March 1974) while you were taking a cure, following a strict diet, with long walks and saunas (the latter being the association) and massages and exercises. (There first have to be the parents of mass murderers, before there can be mass murderers.) The book could be taken out of the library by special permission only. It was lying on the small white table in your room. The reading dragged; you were reading other books in between. The doctors, who also check on their patients' reading matter, weighed it in their hands, and put it down again; they had no objection. By that time, most of them were younger than you; names that were engraved in the memory of your generation no longer had any meaning for them.

It would probably be saying too much to suggest that, while reading the book, you were subconsciously looking for a reason to make you stop your own work, the writing of this very book. Unfortunately, there were no copy facilities and you were forced to copy excerpts by hand; the author of these notes, the aforementioned commandant of Auschwitz, had jotted them down in a Polish prison during the months preceding his execution. Nothing unusual happened: the copying hand didn't give out. The sane inner control system continued to function, a part of its function being to keep separate that which must not be merged, under punishment of insanity. It separated the process of copying from the process of writing; the notion of what might have been from the memory of what actually happened; the past—insofar as this is possible—from the present. In other words, it maintained those controls which keep us sane. However, it had no power over the secret disintegration caused by the insidious poison of despair. It could not prevent minor misfirings which did not endanger the overall structure; such as: certain dreams which make it impossible to go back to sleep; the sudden unexpected transformation of a harmless scene into sheer horror; for instance, while waiting in line at a service station someone remarks: "Gas her up, please"; the ongoing obsession to classify the hospital staff and the patients as participants in mass crimes: a term that describes not only crimes committed against masses of people but also a massive surge of perpetrators and accomplices. Certain discoveries, especially the possibility of using Cyclon B gas as a means of mass extermination of human beings—first tested on nine hundred Soviet war prisoners in the old Auschwitz crematorium—had a "reassuring effect" on Commandant Hoess, "since the mass extermination of Jews had to be dealt with sooner or later, and neither Eichmann nor I had a clear concept of how to annihilate the masses of people that had to be expected. Now we had discovered the gas, and with it the procedure."

What do you expect of Lenka's history book? That it stop the course of time? That it relegate the unhappy awareness to future generations? That it prevent the fading of everything, including the horror?

The other day, exactly two weeks ago, at the beginning of March 1974, during a birthday celebration in the family (old photo albums, memories), your brother, Lutz, said: I could have killed that Emil Dunst in those days. I used to hate his guts.

The children had no idea who Emil Dunst was. Your grand-uncle who had the candy factory. There was a photograph of his grave: Aunt Trudy had a passion for taking photos of richly decorated graves of close relatives. "Here lies my beloved husband, far from home . . ." (Typical of Aunt Olga.) Jesus, your brother, Lutz, said, Emil Dunst, what a son of a bitch. Do you remember how he suddenly appeared in the summer of 1945—we were still asleep in the Bardikow barn—calling out to us, still from a good distance away: I hope you know that your father is dead! You can be sure the Russians did away with him. I could have strangled that bastard. Emil Dunst had once tried gas on himself. The happy little flames all around the candy tables, which kept the mass warm and pliable, were, after all, gas flames. If you opened the gas and didn't light the flames, and hung blankets all around the table, the gas under the table reached a concentration capable of doing away with two people—Uncle Emil Dunst and the aforementioned Frau Lude. As Gottlieb Jordan, Heinersdorf Grandpa, expressed it: they tried to do away with themselves. What a jellyfish! He keenly felt the difference between a man struck by tragedy and one wallowing in self-pity.

It was Heinersdorf Grandpa who found the two, a sight he didn't wish upon his worst enemy. Yes, sir, he himself pulled them out from under the table, and he often said later: I should have left them lying there, it would have saved the girl a lot of heartache.

The girl was Aunt Olga, who couldn't bring herself to show her husband the door, which Charlotte Jordan would have done without another word, according to her own statement, that summer of 1945, if only she'd had a door to show him. She merely tore into him when he announced that her husband was dead. You just keep your filthy trap shut! To which he, who didn't easily take offense, simply replied: Okay with me. Find out for yourself.

Manners quickly deteriorate out in the open. Still, Charlotte did possess the information, vague though it was, that her husband had been seen alive in a distant place long after the day on which Emil Dunst claimed that he had been shot.

Emil Dunst's long-forgotten face kept appearing behind the Auschwitz commander's book, in answer to your question if you knew anyone who could have played a role in this book. Emil Dunst! He would have qualified. You remember how he used to pronounce certain words. Dirty Polacks! Jew bastards! Russian swine! He fitted every aspect of the extermination machine which Hoess was describing. He would have stood watch at the ramparts. Among the escorting crew. Among the selectors. Among those who opened the gas jets. The custodians of the ovens. He fitted in with the crew that would sit together in their quarters at night and drown their self-pity in schnapps. And lest you forget, he, too, used to speak of "the swine within," which Rudolf Hoess overcame so successfully within himself.

However, the man did lack one thing: efficiency. Sad to say, but Emil Dunst was lazy. Eichmann and Hoess were extremely hardworking German men, obsessed by their task, and nothing drove them to greater despair than the lack of understanding and the negligence of those around them, which kept them from doing an exemplary job.

The Allied Forces did not publish the first news they received of the extermination camps. The reason: they couldn't believe it. They didn't want to become guilty of spreading horror propaganda. We, the people of today, don't put anything past anybody. We think that anything is possible. This may be the most important difference between our era and the preceding ones.

Perhaps this awareness must unavoidably be lost again.

At this point, let's mention the performances Nelly carried out, apparently with the greatest of ease.

Let's start with the more harmless ones: singing in the military hospital. The former mental institution on Friedeberger Chaussee had been turned into a military hospital. Nobody wondered what had become of the insane, whose beds had been given to the wounded. Under the guidance of the group leader, Christel, Nelly had rehearsed her own beautiful program, taking into account the tacit understanding that wounded soldiers require a light diet. The *General-Anzeiger*, whose reporter describes such a musical event in the hospital, records that not a single battle song was sung, no song of the movement, nothing that smacked of war, instead: "A music man am I by trade" and "I'm so happy-go-lucky / I laugh and I sing. / I'm so very lighthearted, / I'm like a bird on the wing."

Calls of ho-ho and applause from the ranks of the lighter casualties. The severe cases, whose ward was filled with a sweetish odor in spite of the open windows, and who were allowed to hear only one song, asked for: "Rosemarie, oh, Rosemarie / my heart is crying out to thee." By the indentations in the covers Nelly could tell that many had lost limbs: legs, arms.

As a finale, the Jungmädel sang "Lilli Marlene" for everybody, outside in the hall, until they were all choked up with emotion. And at the very end, the wounded soldiers in their beds sang a thank-you song for the Jungmädel. They sang and sang and wouldn't stop. They lay looking up at the ceiling, it had grown dark, the Jungmädel had to sneak away, while the singing continued.

It's always worst at night, said the young blond nurse who was showing the Jungmädel to the exit. Charlotte, who was waiting for her daughter in the open window, merely said: Who's going to put those poor men's bodies back together again?

By now it was long past 4 p.m. on that Saturday, July 10, 1971, in G., the former L. (It was an hour after your rest in the new café.) The time had finally come to check in at your hotel.

As a child, Nelly had never entered this or any other hotel. Lenka receives the key with the attitude of a world traveler. Your rooms are on the ground floor. The day's heat is hanging inside them. By way of Russian you're fortunately able to decipher that there's a shower on the second floor. The key is at the desk.

Let's go take a shower, okay?

Okay.

Lenka thinks showers like these are fabulous. Nothing fancy, just a glossy bluish-gray paint, and the drain on the floor. She opens the faucets full force, permits you to soap her back, you call her Fräulein Fish. You just wait, she says, and sings out loud: "Everybody's singing ochen kharasho." You object, since the booth may not be soundproof, whereupon Lenka says in English: *I like you . . .*

Then she sees herself in the rapidly fogging mirror, the shower cap on her head. Without hair she could get a part in any horror movie, she tells you. Later, she hands the key to the shower to her uncle, announces that she's going to take a nap, and lies down on the bed next to the window, separated from yours by the two night tables. You've almost fallen asleep when she says, in a wide-awake voice: Come to think of it, it's enough to make you want to cry your eyes out.

You knew instantly what she was talking about.

You needn't say anything, she says, I know I'm being silly, but it's even sillier to sleep peacefully while things like that are going on. Perhaps the worst of it is how anybody seems to be able to get used to anything.

You suppress the soothing words which first come to your mind. You don't want her to start doubting so soon. You don't want her face to take on that certain knowing expression which you can no longer wipe off your own face: Don't tell me: I can see through it all!

The ability to adapt is one of the reasons for the survival of the human species, you tell her.

That's clear, says Lenka. But what if humanity adapts to those very things which will destroy the species? Huh? Then what? Say something.

Yes, you say. Perhaps we shouldn't let ourselves be contaminated by general insanity.

Beg your pardon?

I mean all those people who really believe that most people's thoughts and actions are normal.

Sure, says Lenka, I know what kind of people you mean.

And?

No "and." They really get on my nerves. But I feel sorry for them, too.

And doesn't it frighten you to find yourself thinking completely differently from the way they think?

Frighten me? says Lenka. When I see what's wrong with them?

But what if they threaten you, seriously?

Then I start screaming.

But doesn't it ever occur to you that they must be right, since they're in the majority?

Nope, says Lenka. I'm not suicidal. Or do you mean to say that that occurs to you?

Never mind me, what about our nap?

You're avoiding the issue, says Lenka.

The room overlooked the courtyard. A driver was parking his car in a shady corner; then all was quiet.

By the way, Lenka said, her voice already trailing, I had a terrible fight with Ulli the other day.

What about?

We'd been reading *Mario and the Magician*. Incidentally, I think that's an incredible book. I said nobody in our class would resist the magician.

And Ulli?

He yelled at me: What made me think that I was any different? Did I think I was so much smarter than the rest of them? I know I'm not, but I think I would have seen through him.

And would you have? you ask, almost asleep, and strangely satisfied. You know what's going to be next: the funeral procession again. This time it's moving along a white gravel path close to the edge of the Baltic Sea; to the right you can see little whitecaps all along the beach. At the head of the procession, a band is playing "Immortal Victims." The people around you are all dressed in black, but your gray everyday overcoat does not offend them. They're telling you the names of the most prominent among the participants. But you know them, anyway. From a loudspeaker along the road you hear the voice of a well-known announcer, who says, almost in tears: He is now stepping into the hall that holds so many dear memories for him. What hall? you think, since you know what's going to come next: the procession hesitates before a huge unhewn boulder at the edge of the cemetery, on which nothing but a name has been chiseled: Stalin. Each time, the people in the procession become confused. Has he died, then? Has he already been buried? Whom are we burying now?

After you dreamed the dream for the first time, you asked H.: When will we start speaking about that, too? To get rid of the feeling that, until we do, everything we say is temporary, that only then would we really begin to speak.

H. thinks that one must live with one's layers of dreams from various periods in time. That you must beware of living in dreams: otherwise those periods would get the better of you. He, who has a quotation for everything, quotes Meister Eckhart: The decisive moment is always the present. You, he says, live toward the future. I don't. I live today, I live now. Moment by moment.

The greatest damage that has been done to all of you will not be mentioned. The lifelong consequences of the childhood belief that, one day, the world will be perfect. In April 1940, Nelly reads in the *General-Anzeiger* that the wooden sandal has been invented: "We walk without ration cards." Recipes for meatless stews and ersatz liverwurst spread. The Hitler Youth paper drive (in which she participates with flour sacks and a wagon). Radio criminals who listen to foreign news stations are sentenced to hard labor. A photo: women team members: mothers behind the plow. The world's most advanced close-range reconnaissance plane, Focke-Wulf 189, is being put into service. The killed-in-action notices fill more than one whole page of the paper: "Beloved, mourned, and unforgotten." The V sign becomes the victory symbol on all fronts. Fall 1941. "The fate of the Soviets will be decided during these fall days." The municipal theater presents *Tom Thumb* as its Christmas performance for small and tall audiences. Nelly sees Hans Albers in *Trenck, the Pandur*, Heinz Rühmann in *The Main Thing Is Happiness*, Willy Birgel in . . . *Rider for Germany*, Luise Ullrich in *A Mother's Love*, Ilse Werner in *U-Boats Westward*.

It's 1943.

During the pre-Christmas season, the leaders of the District Jungmädel prepare a Christmas celebration at the Weinberg for convalescent officers and noncommissioned officers. Charlotte baked spice drops, Whiskers Grandma knitted wrist warmers. The tables are covered with white crepe paper. A pine tree with candles. Group singing of Christmas carols.

Nelly's dinner partner is a noncommissioned officer with a leg injury named Karl Schröder. He is the first man to introduce himself formally to Nelly, half rising from his chair, indicating a bow: With your permission. He has black hair, which grows in a dashing widow's peak, and pale cheeks with a bluish shadow. To Nelly's embarrassment he is the most eager participant in the charades which the Jungmädel play. He is first to call out the solution, snapping his fingers like a schoolboy. As a reward, he may ask for a song. He asks for: "I want streets so wide / that giant elephants / can take a stroll and not collide . . ."

He is from Brandenburg on the Havel. In spite of this he does, however, know how to yodel, he says, since he'd briefly served in a mountaineers' unit. He is asked to show off his art. He starts yodeling immediately and is loudly applauded. He was a happy-go-lucky sort of a fellow, he told Nelly, over cordials and schnapps, but still, he had little luck with the ladies. On the other hand, his superiors thought highly of him. You just couldn't have everything, although things did get hard at times, all by one's lonesome. He's already twenty-three.

His eyes are small, and extremely black. When his arm, which was resting on Nelly's chair back, touches her shoulder, he apologizes and takes it away. The likes of me always lose out, he says. Next week we'll all be shipped off to the eastern front; and then goodbye, home sweet home.

The senior officer allows his junior colleagues one hour's leave to escort their ladies home. Nelly warns her dinner partner that it's a long way to her house, but to him it's a matter of honor to see her to her door. Besides, it means a lot to him. Does she believe him? He asks as though his life depended on her answer. She couldn't possibly realize what this hour meant to him.

Nelly knows more or less what she is expected to feel. Her knowledge doesn't help her much. She concentrates on keeping pace with the limping man. She wonders if it's all right to draw her arm out of his, or if it's wrong to deprive a wounded soldier of his support. She has to keep him from kissing her; which turns out not to be overly difficult. It turns out that he is an idealist, and that he assumes the same of her. The moon so quietly up there in the sky, with the clouds drifting across it, that really does something to me. He asks if it does something to her, too. Yes, Nelly says, sure. He knew there was an affinity between their souls. That didn't happen often, she could take his word for it.

As expected, Charlotte Jordan is looking out her window, despite the cold, and sees to it that the parting scene is not unduly drawn out. Karl Schröder knows how to put feeling into a handshake. You'll hear from me, he finally says.

Charlotte informs her daughter that she is a mere fourteen, and that soldiers about to be sent to the front have no consideration for anything or anybody, with respect to certain things. Nelly's aware of that. In that case, she shouldn't see the noncommissioned officer again. Charlotte is willing to take responsibility for the refusal, but when Karl Schröder calls, it's Nelly who happens to pick up the phone. Her decision hurts him deeply, but he'd expected as much. He's always been unlucky. May he be permitted to wish her the very best on her future road through life. Might he hope that her thoughts will dwell on him every once in a while. Yes, he might hope. Well, then, goodbye forever.

(Recent newspapers—March 1974—published a photo of roll call on the Chilean concentration-camp island of Dawson. With a magnifying glass one can make out the expressions on the faces— grim, closed-off—and among them the expression on the face of José Toha Gonzales, Vice President under Allende. You try to imagine the people who will strangle him as he sits in the wheel-chair. They must have been average faces. But can one transfer one's European experience to other continents? Can one still recognize the torturer among ordinary faces in other parts of the world? And could one call that an advantage?)

The faces of the witnesses at the Auschwitz trial in 1963 in the historic town hall in Frankfurt am Main. In the factory-owned concentration camp—Monowitz—I. G. Farben calculated an average life expectancy of prisoners working for them to be from four to six months. The SS had promised them that all weak prisoners could be disposed of. The SS and I. G. Farben together worked out their economy interrelation, Farben participated in the perfection of the penal system. An expert appraisal recommended this particular location for the construction of a mill, because "soil conditions, water, and limestone, as well as the availability of labor— for instance, Poles, and prisoners from the Auschwitz concentration camp—were favorable to the setting up of a mill."

And in the evenings the questions of young people, students in their sparsely furnished apartments in Frankfurt, who became passionately involved in the course of the trial: they seemed to be looking for some horrible secret at the bottoms of your souls, or consciences. You were unprepared for their demand that you yield your secret. You were used to assuming that horrible secrets did exist, among older people who were unable or unwilling to reveal them. As though you could be relieved of the duty to lay a hand upon your own childhood. While the landscape of your childhood moved, as though by itself, into the shadow of the Auschwitz ovens.

But the secret we're looking for is the blatant lack of any secret. Which is perhaps why it can't be revealed.

In the fall of 1943, Nelly was crouching on the fields of the estate, digging up potatoes, together with a row of Ukrainian women. Her feeling toward these strangers wasn't pity, but rather a shyness, the strong notion that they were different, a notion which was not based on any secret, but on Julia Strauch's history lessons: her being different made her more valuable. Nelly wasn't allowed to put her potatoes into the same basket as one of the foreign workers. Did she think about the soup which was being dished out for the Ukrainians from a separate pot? Would it have occurred to her to get up and walk the thirty steps across the separating abyss, over to the foreigners, who were sitting along the same edge of the field, and hand one of them her own bowl, which had pieces of meat swimming in the soup?

The horrible secret: not that one didn't dare, but that the thought didn't occur to one. All attempts to explain stop at this fact. The usual thoughtlessness of the well-fed with respect to the hungry doesn't explain it. Fear? Certainly, if there had been such a temptation. But the temptation to do the natural thing no longer occurred to her. Nelly—innocent, so far as she knew, even exemplary—was sitting there, chewing her meat.

It wasn't Nelly, at any rate, who complained to Julia when the overseer of the estate, a one-legged veteran, scolded the German girls for doing sloppy work, in front of the Ukrainian women. It would have been up to her to inform Julia, because she was the leader of the work group. But she felt ashamed of the sloppiness, in front of the Ukrainians, whose eyes didn't give away whether or not they had understood what was going on. Instead, it was her friend Hella who informed Julia by telephone, and the overseer was made to apologize the next morning. Nelly felt ashamed, that was all.

One night, when Nelly's father was absent—a get-together of buddies from the district command—her mother was in urgent need of a doctor. Nelly had only the vaguest notions of the matter, which tolerated no delay. About 11 p.m. Nelly was awakened by her mother, whose pallor and expression frightened her to death. Would she please throw on some clothes and run to fetch Frau Blankenstein. Nelly flies. Frau Blankenstein seems to know what it's all about and asks no questions. Into the phone she says: But hurry, please hurry up; the woman is bleeding to death.

She's bleeding to death. But her mother hasn't been wounded.

She's carried out on a stretcher. She still has the strength to say to Nelly that she's a big girl and must behave accordingly. Frau Blankenstein adds the word "brave" before she leaves.

Nelly waits up for her father for one whole hour. It becomes apparent that words fail to communicate certain information from daughter to father. Her father seems to be as little surprised as Frau Blankenstein. Her mother had been right to complain that he was leaving her alone, even though he knew she wasn't feeling well. Nelly doesn't want to add a feeling of guilt to his embarrassment and concern. She can see that her father is not up to the situation. To ask him to explain is out of the question. Their inability to communicate becomes clearly apparent. (The scene happened at night: father and daughter in the bedroom door, dim light, her mother's bed rumpled, her father's bed untouched. Nelly in her pajamas, her father in his noncommissioned officer's uniform, without his cap. Half sentences.) The father's hand clasps the arm of his still-adolescent daughter. It'll be all right. Then he sends her off to bed.

The next day she finds out that what happened was for the best. Another child, the Lord have mercy, in these times. That's what Aunt Lucie said to Nelly's father, who thinks so, too. Her mother feels better, much better. Nelly is allowed to visit her. I know what was the matter, she says, a baby.

Well, if you know, then that's okay, says Charlotte.

That's all that will be said about it.

Nelly is finally allowed to go and have her hair cut. The women at the beauty parlor giggle about her awkwardness. The permanent has made her hair too frizzy. But that doesn't matter; it'll last longer that way. For a long time Nelly stands in front of the mirror, pulling at her hair. It makes the strands neither longer nor straighter. Before going to bed she ties a towel tightly around her head, to hold her hair in place. Lying in bed, she invents new hairdos that will make her look more beautiful. She no longer knows how to move her arms and legs so as to hide her awkwardness. She doesn't understand how other girls can show by their walk that they feel in harmony with their bodies.

Richard Andrack, Bruno Jordan's friend, a professional photographer, comes from the district command to photograph the Jordans in front of the bright wall of their house. Each of them separately, and then all of them together. As he hands Nelly her photo, he says: Well, this shows who's the prettiest in the family. Nelly rather likes Richard Andrack. The photo shows how the pleats of her blouse expand over her breasts. One thing that's not visible—the photo shows Nelly laughing—is a kind of wasting away, which is rapidly increasing and to which Nelly, who can't explain it to herself, responds with fits of depression. She can't stop damaging her cuticles. Must you hurt yourself, child! but she can't stop, although she feels that she is doing something reprehensible. She punishes herself by giving up sweets. Then, abruptly, and almost without taking any precautionary measures, she fetches the key to the storeroom and supplies herself with large quantities of chocolate, which she devours in bed. It makes her feel disgustingly good. She feels her self-esteem dwindling.

The next day she walks barefoot over the iron boot scraper in front of the entrance door ten times. God sees everything. It isn't true that punishment annuls the crime.

Lovelessness is a horrible secret.

12

Hypnosis.

Reaching for the dictionary that rests on a wooden stand to the left of the unfamiliar desk: an object which you see in use for the first time in this American house. *Random House Dictionary of the English Language.* The heading Hypnosis: "*An artificially induced state resembling sleep, characterized by heightened susceptibility to suggestion.*"

An objective description. Subjects are not involved. The realization of the ideal: *Nobody is involved.* But this isn't the kind of hypnosis we're going to deal with here, because it was not "artificially induced." Among the English and German books of the absent Professor C., in whose house you're living during your stay in the States, you find the *Kleine Deutsche Brockhaus*, a German dictionary which defines one point differently and better than its

American competitor: under the heading Hypnosis, it lists the same "state resembling sleep with heightened susceptibility to suggestion," but then it adds a modifying clause as an enlightening reference: ". . . into which a person is transported by another person, also occasionally by himself."

You pause at the word "transported." Exactly. A nine-hour flight toward the West, toward the time zone which has shifted six hours into the morning, to the latitude of Madrid and a coordinate system at whose points of intersection, as sure as hell, lies a dollar bill with the statement printed in small but clear letters: *In God we trust*.

End of page. American typewriter paper, with a shorter and wider format than the DIN sheets you're used to, cuts you short by two or three lines. Of course it doesn't matter, Mr. Random. It's only that one has to learn: it wasn't ordained by the good Lord that a typewriter sheet has to measure 210 by 297 millimeters. Or that water turns to ice at zero degrees. For the first time you realize the presumption of naming one's own measurements DIN, meaning Das Ist Norm—this is the norm. And yet a person who grew up measuring in Celsius will for some time find the Fahrenheit scale unnatural.

A word, Mr. Random: A visitor to America—whatever that may be—is forced to spend a good part of his energy on routine jobs, errands, the most primitive verbal communication, instead of being able to concentrate on his work. America is exhausting, Mr. Random.

Hypnosis was practiced at Nelly's confirmation. She didn't find it at all natural that she was to be confirmed. For instance, her friend Hella, who called herself "a believer in God," wasn't going to be confirmed. That's a long way from being a heathen, and Julia says it, too, incidentally. But it is sheer hypocrisy if you don't go to church all your life and then have yourself confirmed. Either-or, she thinks. Her father doesn't even see the problem, and her mother, knowing and fearing Nelly's stubbornness in questions of conviction, falls back on Whiskers Grandma: she just wouldn't get over it if Nelly weren't confirmed. It's true, she isn't exactly a churchgoer either, but she believes in God and all that. So please do us the favor.

Nelly, too, believes in God. But she'd be lying through her teeth if she claimed that she didn't mind going to the parish house every Wednesday morning from eight to nine for confirmation classes. After the third lesson with Pastor Grunau, she repeats her wish not to be confirmed, this time more urgently.

What happened?

Can she say that Pastor Grunau's hands, folded on his stomach, nauseate her? She realizes of course that the pastor's hands are no argument. Or that the candidates are supposed to bow their heads during prayer. His head high, Pastor Grunau controls the bowing of the heads of those to be confirmed. At least he finally gives up calling her name in a tone of disapproval. God, as Nelly imagines Him, wants no outward sign of subservience. The pastor doesn't realize that Nelly puts her hands side by side on the back of the chair in front of her, instead of folding them according to the rule.

Charlotte Jordan thinks one shouldn't feel above doing what everybody else does. Nobody has ever died of it yet.

"Thou shalt fear and love the Lord thy God . . ." Pastor Grunau has an oily voice that is capable of suddenly taking on a threatening tone in the same pious text. "I believe in God the Father, who hath made me, and all the world"—the length of this sentence permits the pastor a range of sounding humble, then astounded, disappointed, threatening, disapproving, until he reaches the benches of the primary-school pupils, until he has hit Lieselotte Bornow on the knuckles with his catechism; she was trying to clean her fingernails under the desk. Nelly is simply not able to make him explain to her that she's not supposed to commit adultery, and why.

Probably, by the way, she has judged him unfairly. What do you do when unfit words work themselves into the text: is it a warning? To pay closer attention or to quit? To wait until you'll have returned to the place where there's no exact equivalent of "fair"; where it may mean "impartial, honest, decent" (thank you, Mr. Random!), but surely not "beautiful, blond, light-skinned"? Where concentration on one's work will not be impaired by bewilderment about a language that doesn't hesitate to declare only the blond, the light-skinned, among its users to be impartial, honest, decent. And beautiful.

Irritation. A single word, never before part of your vocabulary, passes the board of control without objection. The filters, which at first strictly held back, for critical evaluation, all that was unfamiliar, now seem to have become more porous. Where will it all lead?

And what did you expect? That you'd not be affected by an ocean? That shifting your bearings that drastically wouldn't bother you while you pass various time zones? That they wouldn't trouble you at all on your way back, a way which couldn't be measured in miles or in kilometers but, in the end, only by European standards?)

It is a well-known fact that electric stimulation of the brain between the occipital, temporal, and parietal lobes will activate episodes of childhood which will supposedly run off in correct chronological order like a filmstrip, accompanied by optical and acoustical hallucinations. Olfactory hallucinations seem to be rarer. But for Nelly, the odor of lilies of the valley is forever tied to the image of a white, starched, and folded handkerchief placed on a black hymn book. To organ music. To a long aisle between pews, ending at the altar of St. Mary's Church. To an inhibited, reluctant walk—Walk! don't tramp! Pastor Grunau whispers—on a stone floor.

You didn't go into St. Mary's Church, by the way. You tried it twice, on the evening of July 10 and in the morning of July 11, 1971, from the east portal, where the candidates for confirmation, Nelly among them, had assembled on an April Sunday of the year 1943. But on Saturday the portal was closed, and on Sunday evening the crowd of the faithful, spilling over into the street, was blocking the way to idle onlookers who perhaps only wanted to refresh their memories. From inside the church came singing, and the people standing in the doors, whose backs were turned toward you, joined in, too. (In a black Methodist church in Philadelphia, all the parishioners turned their heads toward you, the three whites, as the pastor called out your names and country of origin from the pulpit, and asked your neighbors to welcome you. They stretched out their hands and laughed, and suddenly the softly murmured *"So glad to see you"* made sense.)

In the tightly packed pews of St. Mary's Church, all heads turned back as if pulled by a string as the procession of candidates for confirmation moved down the aisle toward the blood-red runner that covered the altar steps on which they'd kneel in pairs, the way they had rehearsed only yesterday. The organ plays, the congregation sings "How shall I receive Thee." The candidates worry about snagging their stockings while kneeling down, about choking on the dry wafer and the sour wine. With you, one has to be prepared for anything, Pastor Grunau had told them. For heaven's sake, behave like human beings as long as people can see you.

There they are, like lambs, treading lightly, singing, giving the appropriate responses, singly and in chorus: Yes, I believe, they step before the altar without stumbling, they kneel down, they don't choke on the body and blood of the Lord, they let Pastor Grunau's white hand rest in benediction on their heads, they rise and walk piously around the altar. But in back of it—as the panel with the passion of the crucified Christ, whose back is now turned toward them, hides them from the eyes of the pastor and the congregation—in back of the altar they suddenly throw their arms up in the air, they double up in soundless laughter, they make hideous faces at each other (without ever slowing down their steps), and reappear after ten, twelve seconds on the other side of the altar, their eyes lowered, innocence personified.

So there was still hope, says Lenka.

In the evening, the restaurant on the market square in G. was filled almost exclusively with local people, mostly younger men of the first generation born in this town, who were smoking and drinking beer, who stared at Lenka and offered to make room for her by sitting at the bar. You managed to find seats at the table near the window and ordered a few ham and chicken-salad sandwiches. You had an exchange of ideas about the spottiness of memory. You remembered the antics behind the altar, but Stalingrad—at that time no more than two months had passed since then—had not left a deep impression. ("The Myth of Stalingrad!" the General-Anzeiger wrote on February 4, and a little later: "The Sacrificial March of the 6th Army—A Sacred Example for Us All!") What Nelly did remember: that Miss Schröder, the sewing and needlework teacher, had rushed into the noisy, boisterous class and had torn into them: They should be ashamed of themselves. Our German soldiers are dying near Stalingrad and you are laughing and singing.

That is all. The total war, however, is anchored in your head acoustically: Goebbels's voice coming out of the radio, in howling screams: Now, my people, rise! Now, storm, break loose!

But not even the slightest indication that the names of Sophie and Hans Scholl (members of the Catholic resistance movement; executed in 1943) were ever mentioned in Nelly's presence. No mention ever of the uprising of the Jews in the Warsaw ghetto, which must have been at its height at the time Nelly was kneeling at her Christian altar. (And what if the blacks in their ghettos rise up someday, you ask a white American. He says regretfully: They haven't got a chance. Because of the very fact that they're black. They're sitting ducks. Every single one of them would be gunned down.)

Nelly's confirmation dress was black, according to custom, made by Whiskers Grandma out of silk taffeta. A white ruffle around the V neck: It's more becoming. When dinner with all the relatives was over—Nelly at the head of the table, her place decorated with green pine twigs, Whiskers Grandma had killed three rabbits—she was overcome with sadness. The men were sitting in the parlor, smoking, talking about the war. The women were doing the dishes and cutting the cake. Nelly's brother Lutz was in the playroom busily building an intricate structure with his Erector set. Nelly was sitting in the armchair in the dining room, her hands folded in her lap.

It's too bad, Whiskers Grandma said, anticipation is always the best part of the fun.

But her mother got on the phone and invited Cousin Astrid and Nelly's friend Hella over for coffee and cake. So she'll have some company. After all, it's her big day.

At the same time as Astrid and Hella, noncommissioned officer Richard Andrack, photographer, made his appearance.

Lutz, you do remember Andrack, don't you! Say, wasn't that the crazy character who made like the great magician at your confirmation? "Made like" is right. Do you remember how it started?

(In the evening it's noisy in the restaurant on the market square in G., especially on Saturdays, when the young men's girls come in and sit down at the tables by the windows, and smoke, and don't look over to the bar, where the young fellows begin to outdo each other at getting louder and louder. You can't even hear your own voice. But Lenka wanted to know all about it: Why "crazy character?")

Andrack did first what he had been called to do: he took pictures. With flashbulbs, of course. The Sunday was cold and overcast, no day for outdoor shots. Group pictures in the parlor on the couch, then the newly confirmed with parents, with grandparents, alone. Her hair had grown, it fell in a soft, inside curl. From out of the ruffle-trimmed puffed sleeve comes an arm like a wooden stick. Nobody could call this girl graceful. The expression on her face—one can see she's doing her best to say "cheese"—has always embarrassed and at the same time saddened you. The almost stupid grimace. The expression of the eyes, both startled and aloof. The awkwardness of her body, the slouched posture. But, above all, the unconscious sadness that hangs over the whole person. A fourteen-year-old who doesn't know in what words and in the name of which gods she is to express her sadness. Who has to punish herself for this secret sadness in the name of the gods to whom she is submissive.

Persistence of Memory. The famous painting by Salvador Dali that caught your eye, unexpectedly, in the Museum of Modern Art (New York). It shows what one wouldn't have thought possible: the landscape of memory. The clear, yet unreal colors. The islands rising from the sea. The direct, bright, yet eerie light whose source is not revealed. The continuous threat of darkness. Between the two, the unsharp boundary. Total stillness and motionlessness. The long-lashed sleeping eye that must belong to a creature whose glance you wouldn't care to meet. The naked, broken-off tree growing out of a sharp-cornered box. And above all, the four watches: one of them, its lid snapped shut, has ants crawling disgustingly all over it. The three others, bluish, deformed, are hanging, lying, clinging—as if they were wax, not metal—on the box, the tree, the sleeping eye, their three dials showing three slightly different times. An ironic commentary on its title. (Is there a connection between the deathly cold of the painting and the political cynicism its creator has displayed?)

The permanence of what is remembered.

The reliability of memory.

In the wide, comfortable American bed, under the electric blanket, you usually wake up without remembering a dream, even without astonishment at your dreamlessness. It seems to go without saying that sleep, too, is subject to laws here that are different from those at home. Only once, this morning, were you aware of having dreamed that you moved about in the scenery of your hometown. You went down Richtstrasse, in an unfamiliar house you were confronted with your former fellow pupil Christel Jugow, who was suffering terribly from an insect that sat under the lid of each large, bovine brown eye, and nobody was able to remove it; they had called you to ask for your advice. The scene was taking place in a room furnished in conventional upper-middle-class style, among self-satisfied people, while prisoners were languishing behind the bars of the courthouse windows across the street, and this fact was uppermost in your mind. You reacted—in your dream—to the suffering of your contemporary with a lack of feeling that was surprising even to yourself.

The dream took place within no time period, in a memory landscape that transmitted a deathly cold.

(For days you haven't been able to get an annoying word out of your head, it is as untranslatable as "fair," though one would think it could be translated. It is printed on most packaged foods; the word is *"flavor."* Taste, aroma, bouquet. *"The flavor of this juice makes your life delicious."* But the *flavor*, far from making life delicious, destroys the natural aroma of the juice . . .)

"The palping of eye movements in the absorption of information is steered by memory." Do eyes get less tired when they look at the familiar? Observations in supermarkets, based on films taken by hidden cameras, yielded an unexpected result: the shoppers, after entering the market, displayed reduced, rather than increased, eye blinking, contrary to expectation. The overwhelming masses of merchandise offered were conducive to a state akin to hypnosis.

One of the high points in Herr Andrack's demonstration of hypnosis—soon after coffee and cake he had begun with a few harmless tests—was the moment when Cousin Astrid, under the influence of the photographer's incantations and compelling stare, pushed away her lemon cream with disgust, because she believed it was something repulsive. But immediately afterward she enjoyed a glass of plain water with lip-smacking delight, thinking it eggnog. This was the signal for Pastor Grunau, who was making the rounds of some of his newly confirmed charges, to beat a hasty retreat. Uncle Alfons Radde gave a broad grin. To change water into wine, he said, that's a matter only for the pastor's boss.

But Uncle Alfons, too, was to have his comeuppance.

Hadn't he actually been the one to start the ball rolling by his display of doubt? Bruno Jordan had probably made it known that his comrade-in-arms Andrack was quite an operator, a dangerous character who could manage to make people spend the night in the coal bin without their even noticing it.

You don't say! said Alfons Radde. Don't give me any of that nonsense, I wasn't born yesterday.

Whereupon Richard Andrack turned to him directly with the polite question: Does Frau Radde suffer from headaches?

Aunt Liesbeth had always had a weakness for polite males, for gentlemen of refinement. Yes, indeed. She suffered from headaches, a neuralgia. Incurable, as Herr Andrack probably knew himself.

Well, now.

But extremely painful, Herr Andrack, believe me. There are days when I'm literally incapable of doing anything. But perhaps you can't even imagine what I'm talking about.

On the contrary, Herr Andrack assured her, he was quite capable of understanding her condition.

Stuff and nonsense, Alfons Radde said.

The men were about to retire to the parlor. Richard Andrack, who had come in civilian clothes—an unostentatious navy-blue, prewar single-breasted suit that he wore in his role as photographer at weddings, confirmations, christenings—Richard Andrack asked them politely to stay for another moment. Perhaps to sit down once more at the coffee table (which meanwhile had been cleared), if it was all right with the gentlemen. And just for the hell of it—you too, Herr Radde!—if you don't mind. Please place both hands on the table, the fingers spread, with the tips of both your thumbs touching each other, the tips of your little fingers touching those of your neighbors. That's it, Frau Liesbeth, so we'll have a closed circle. Excellent, ladies and gentlemen, excellent. It's not always the case, as you may well imagine, that my experiment meets with the necessary sensitivity on the part of the mediums.

It was the first time Nelly had heard the word "medium," and she immediately distrusted it. (You have left the restaurant on the market square and are walking in a part of the inner town which is built up with new houses, in order to look for traces of the old streets that were named Luisen, Post, Woll, and Bäckerstrasse. Your brother, Lutz, who hadn't been as lastingly impressed by Andrack as Nelly, remembers that he had sparse blond, slightly reddish hair, which he wore slicked back; that he had the round, basically insignificant, rather pallid face of the light-skinned type on which one could imagine freckles. Which doesn't necessarily mean, Lenka, that Herr Andrack did have freckles.

Nelly knows immediately: she doesn't want to be a medium.

Herr Andrack explains obligingly that among some twenty persons—at least that many were gathered at Nelly's confirmation —there were, rule of thumb, one excellent and two or three good mediums, and he was presently going to detect them, provided, of course, that he had their kind consent, which he admittedly had neglected to obtain. In fact, they, that is, the ladies and gentlemen sitting around the table in cosy hand contact, would soon experience the greatest difficulty in lifting their hands off this table. Even now they were feeling that their hands were becoming heavier and heavier from one second to the next, and now they were as heavy as lead. As if a hundredweight were pressing on each hand. As if heavy metal were coursing through their veins instead of thin blood. As if they were nailed to the table. And now it has happened: they can't lift their hands any more, even if they try with all their strength.

Go ahead, then, try it!

For quite a while, Nelly had secretly let her hands float fractions of a millimeter above the tabletop: Now she yanked them up, and others with her. But Heinersdorf Grandma, Aunt Liesbeth, and Aunt Trudy—long since divorced—and most of all Cousin Astrid, were sitting nailed down, no matter how much they were trying, their faces beet red from the effort to pry their hands loose.

Now you see, Herr Andrack said, polite and unperturbed, how correct my guess was: three good mediums, and one who's very good. He was keeping to himself whom he considered the "very good" medium. For the time being, he lightly stroked the four women's hands, and permitted them, in tactfully casual words, to loosen their hands from the table and to move about freely. He begged forgiveness for the little jest and asked for permission to withdraw.

But, Herr Andrack, please don't think of it! Charlotte, the hostess, voiced what they all felt. Of course they counted on his presence for supper, since he had been invited not only as a competent photographer but as a friend of the family. As for his other talents . . .

Herr Andrack, smiling a modest smile, bowed in all directions. Much obliged, ladies and gentlemen. All right, then, I don't mind if I do.

Richard, said Bruno Jordan, I didn't know you were a mind reader, too!

Well, now, that's what a layman might call it. The expert would express it a bit differently: he had the gift of deciphering thought-transferred instructions, and of executing them as far as it was possible.

Such as? Alfons Radde asked provocatively.

Insignificant little occurrences, Herr Radde. Nothing extraordinary, by any means. I could, for instance, in case you were to ask me for it in your mind, remove Frau Radde's necklace from her person and hand it over to you, if so desired.

I'd have to see it to believe it.

Uncle Walter, sufficiently impartial and in possession of all his faculties, is chosen to escort Herr Andrack as control. He swears to it that a person in the playroom won't be able to hear what's being said in the dining room. Uncle Walter Menzel—by now he is manager of the firm of Anschütz & Dreissig—considers games of this kind ill advised and refuses any responsibility for their possible consequences. Oh, come on now, Aunt Lucie says, and puts her arms around her husband in her "flirtatious" way (that's what the family calls it: Aunt Lucie just loves to be flirtatious), Don't be a wet blanket!

Richard Andrack doesn't seem any spookier when he does mind reading. One wouldn't even think of the word "demonic." True, he now has his eyes narrowed to a slit, and his right hand is lightly holding on to the wrist of Cousin Astrid, who has been instructed to pass the wishes of the celebrants on to Herr Andrack by way of thought transfer. Please concentrate, Fräulein Astrid! he begs. Think hard. Harder! Still harder! Aha . . .

No, Astrid didn't "lead" Herr Andrack. She had been urged to strain her mind, but to leave her body limp, so that Andrack has to drag her along as he sets out to execute their thought orders. To anticipate: the mind reader had to go to the armchair in which Aunt Liesbeth was sitting; he was to take a three-color braided silk ribbon out of her hand, go with it to the bookcase in the parlor in order to deposit it between the pages of a certain book, from which he was then to read a predetermined passage. A difficult, complex task, without a doubt, and Astrid of course had to dissect it into its component parts, which she gradually had to transmit to the photographer. For example, at first she thought of nothing but: Go right, go right, go right. Until Herr Andrack was on his way to Aunt Liesbeth, whom he then examined from top to bottom, his eyes still half closed, his free left hand executing somnambulistically searching movements—without touching her, of course— until Astrid, as she told it later, strongly and sharply thought: Stop!, when Herr Andrack's hand was close to Aunt Liesbeth's right hand. After that, Astrid thought: Ribbon, ribbon, ribbon, until Richard Andrack gently took the very ribbon out of Aunt Liesbeth's hand, who at that point couldn't help heaving a deep sigh.

Astrid testified later that it had been "very strenuous." The passage from the book, which Richard Andrack really and truly found and read out loud, to the speechless amazement of all those present, was from the novel *Der Löwe—The Lion*—by Mirko Jelusich, and may have gone something like this: "The lion stands on a high pedestal, seemingly staring straight into the Duke's chamber. His head is raised high, and every muscle of his forward-straining body is tense, as if he were about to pounce on an enemy. His eyes are flashing with fury, and his bearing manifests a will to fight and a proud awareness of his great strength."

Beautiful! says Aunt Lucie. But almost all of them feel it is not only beautiful, it's breathtakingly beautiful, and exciting to boot. Aunt Trudy even feels cold shivers running up and down her spine. It's just that she misses stimulating experiences ever since she's been divorced. Only Charlotte Jordan finds not only Trudy's remark but the whole performance highly inappropriate and would like to see it come to a speedy end.

But Herr Andrack—granted, he's a bit tired, but he doesn't feel worn out, thanks to his habit of concentrating—simply can't refuse Aunt Trudy's urgent request for another example of his "truly unbelievable" powers. He only asks to have Fräulein Nelly for a leader this time; he assumes that she has a vigorous, fresh mind. It's out of the question, he smilingly reassures Charlotte, that any harm will come to her.

Nelly's brother, Lutz, who'd been standing guard over Herr Andrack in the playroom, reports that they'd talked about different types of tanks the whole time.

Herr Andrack's warm hand is circling Nelly's wrist. She is instructed to think. She's thinking. The words are in danger of leaping from her head as if they were living beings. Bravo, Fräulein Nelly. I understand. Yes, I understand perfectly.

Herr Andrack pulls Nelly to the sideboard at the back wall of the dining room. He cuts a piece of the cream pie still standing there, lifts it carefully onto a gold-rimmed dessert plate, and hands it to Whiskers Grandma, bowing deeply. While she is eating the pie, Herr Andrack, still following Nelly's orders, recites a toast that's a favorite at the barracks and with the Hitler Youth: "We humans eat, pigs feed to burst, / today let's have the roles reversed!"

Even Uncle Walter must admit that this is an accomplishment. Congratulations. When asked, Nelly declares that, as far as she knows, she was no longer thinking in clearly defined words toward the end. It was more like a steady stream of thought between her and Herr Andrack. Herr Andrack is of exactly the same opinion. He must thank Fräulein Nelly. It almost came to the point where he would have kissed her hand if Charlotte, in a state of heightened vigilance, hadn't seen to it at the last moment that nobody made a fool of himself. Nelly dear, please be a good girl and get the lemon cream.

She won't let me have any fun, Nelly mumbled to herself in the kitchen.

(The purchase of a typewriter ribbon requires, as does every purchase here, an act of courage. For instance, what's the English word for "Farbband"? Typewriter ribbon. The owner of the big store on College Street, an Indonesian, comes to the rescue after your first fumbling attempt at finding your way among dozens of typewriter ribbons of various types. He asks the obligatory salesman's question: *Can I help you?* The sign behind the door reads NO PUR-

CHASE NEEDED!, but he won't give up until the right ribbon is found for the borrowed portable, trademark "Olympia.")

In summer 1971 (my God, it's almost three years ago!), on that unbearably hot Saturday, you weren't able to find out even approximately where those small streets north of the market square must once have run. Lenka wasn't familiar with the changes that towns undergo after their destruction: she flatly denied that there could have ever been any small streets. But you showed her the relics of the destroyed inner city as proof: the entrance to Poststrasse, for example, with the old post-office building, which is still the main post-office today. You secretly looked for the old store on Priesterstrasse—the street had almost completely disappeared—the store at whose windows Nelly used to stop for a long time every Wednesday when she came back from confirmation classes. She was always looking for a reason to go in. One could buy everything there. Stationery items, which had always fascinated Nelly, also cellophane pictures that curled up when you blew on them; sheets of colored paper, erasers; and besides, all sorts of seasonal stuff: carnival things in February, New Year's Eve tricks after Christmas. There were small toys, and even cheap dishes and housewares. Beside the window, a few stone steps led to the recessed store entrance; they were decorated with scrub brush, broom, and mop. The doorbell chimed three harmonious notes. A little gray woman appeared, as though she were materializing at the sound of the chimes out of the gray dust in the depths of her store, to be of service to her customers. She actually said it: Can I be of service? Nelly bought her first diary from the little gray woman, the diary that she later burned. Sometimes she had the urge to shock the woman, whose face was always impassive, by asking for something unheard of. But had she for instance asked for "moon dust," it would have been entirely possible that the little gray woman would have gone to one of the hundreds of pigeonholes that lined the walls, wordlessly got out a little box, placed it on the counter next to the scale, and asked, unruffled: And how much would you like, please?

"When memory breaks down, the new dies off before the old, the complicated before the simple. First forgotten are general concepts, then emotions and sympathies, finally actions—first voluntary, then automatic actions." The *Today* show on Channel 8 in Cleveland. The interviewer, a bright, famous woman, who proves her worth by the fact that she's making as many dollars per year as the highest-paid man, talks to an anthropologist who has just published his observations on certain African tribes that have been forced to exist for generations in a state of near-starvation. He found the social system of these tribes destroyed. A total loss of tradition: a disintegration of all social structures except for an occasional rallying of small groups to procure food; the researcher cannot call these groups "families." Three-year-old children are left to fend for themselves: live or die. The author wasn't able to detect even vestiges of "general ideas," of religious or cultic rites or concepts. Forgotten, too, are "feelings" and "sympathies": uninhibited food rivalry between husband and wife, mother and child, old and young. Like animals, says the bright interviewer. Did the researcher go to the starving tribe without taking any food? Of course. He wanted to study them under authentic circumstances. The interviewer draws the conclusion that human survival is possible without any social grouping. Immediately afterward one sees her doing an ad for a brand of gloves for Mother's Day: *Gloves that make your mother's hands young.*

Short people, Nelly's beloved teacher Juliane Strauch used to say, short people and short words have got what it takes. The short people were people like herself; the short words were the conjunctions with which one could do all sorts of interesting things, for instance, change the meaning of a subordinate clause into its opposite. Nelly was a past master at it. "Nobody loved him although he tried so very hard." "Nobody loved him because he tried so very hard."

And so forth.

Meyer's New Encyclopedia, 1962, gives the following definition of "idea": "The idea exists not independently, only in the consciousness of man as an abstract reflection . . ." Let's rely on short words: "only," according to Hermann Paul, the philologist, is a qualifying adverb, originally used in the sense of "if it weren't, unless it be." "Ideas would not exist, if it weren't (unless it be) in the consciousness of man." It's possible to imagine times that are less insecure, less cynical, less vulgar, but more reverent, than ours, in which the encyclopedia entry would say: Amazingly, magnificently, general ideas exist in man's consciousness. They reflect reality in the abstract, but they are also able to determine—either as the correct partial results of a progressive process of cognition, or, in unfavorable circumstances, as false projections of reality, even as the creations of insanity—the actions of individuals and of the masses.

One of Julia's unassailable postulates—one that was not to be tampered with—was: Teutonic tribes conquered the Roman Empire because the Teutons were hardened and inured to battle, but the Romans had become effete in a life of debauchery and gluttony. The President of the United States—who, afraid of losing office, does not criticize his people's worship of wealth—has just lately proclaimed the reverse: Despite the fact that the Romans were wealthy, their land was easy prey for the barbarians; the Romans lacked a great, general idea. He, the President, had come to give America its idea back. It seems to you that he believes it, regardless of Watergate.

The remainder of the old town wall of G., formerly L., has been carefully preserved. It is the landmark on the cover of the booklet of photographs that is sold at all newsstands. The background of the photo shows the former public swimming pool. The public pool was not for casual bathing; its overall purpose was to improve physical fitness and strength of character with the help of athletic coaches. Nelly's swimming is not at issue here, it goes without saying that water was her element, that in swimming contests she did her best, to the last ounce of her strength, even if afterward she was unable to climb out of the pool by herself. At issue here are Erna and Luise, both sharp-nosed, skin-and-bones, and incredibly awkward, unfit for any kind of physical exercise, and in mortal fear of swimming lessons. At thirteen, fourteen, they were barely able to swim, all the years of effort by Fräulein Kahn had been wasted on them, and she really had better things to do. Bucki, she said, go take care of those two starvelings fom India. Bucki was the best swimmer in the class. She was regional champion in the 100-meter breaststroke, she by herself was more solid than both Erna and Luise put together, and she was in this class because she'd had to repeat a year when she was thirteen. Bucki went over to the two miserable creatures and said in her rough way: Okay, go to it. Bucki was a trained lifesaver and kept dragging Erna and Luise, alternately, out of the pool when they became waterlogged. According to general opinion, the best way to learn to swim is by being thrown into the water, and it would doubtless have been to Erna's and Luise's advantage if they, too, had been able to swim. It's all fine and dandy, Fräulein Kahn said, but you simply aren't a full person unless you're able to swim.

Fräulein Kahn was popular because she was just. She wore her dark hair combed in a pixie hairdo, and never wore anything but her sweatsuit even in the teachers' room. A healthy mind in a healthy body, she said. Okay, then, shake a leg. Her favorite sentence was: After all, I'm not a monster! Her first name was Rosa. She herself gave flawless demonstrations of all the exercises that she demanded of her pupils. During a class trip on bicycles, she rode fifteen miles with Dorie—whose bike had broken down—on her luggage rack. Her second favorite saying was: Nothing ventured, nothing gained. And less frequently: No sweat! and sometimes: Let Rosa do it. She was a leader in the organization Faith and Beauty.

To her, comradeship came first. One thing she just couldn't stomach: being lied to. In the middle of the night she came into the dormitory of the youth hostel, just in time to see two girls from her class climb in through the window. A rendezvous in the middle of the night! Rosa Kahn said cuttingly. And they had given their solemn promise to be worthy of her trust. Well, since the ladies don't seem to be tired, report for a night march in three minutes! For weeks she didn't speak a word to Nelly's class.

What has remained: an oversensitivity to mass exercises, to roaring stadiums, to applause with rhythmic clapping. The empty streets, empty movie houses, at the time when the world championship soccer games are on television.

I can read your eyes, Fräulein Astrid, as if they were an open book. After a few intermediary attempts at magnetism (my hands are magnetic; while I stroke your hair, I'm pulling your hair backward), Richard Andrack concentrated on Astrid, the ideal medium.

The little jest with the lemon cream—may the lady of the house please forgive him—was one of the more harmless samples, although it was a great pity, of course, to have thus deprived Fräulein Astrid of the enjoyment of the delectable dish. But on the other hand, she mistook water for eggnog: Herr Andrack compensated her, you have to admit.

He himself realized that what he was asking of the young lady was of a somewhat delicate nature. Herr Andrack admitted it candidly after having induced a deep sleep in Nelly's cousin by means of three, four incantations, reinforced by the extraordinarily intense gaze of his pale-blue eyes. And while she was sitting in her chair, evidently asleep, he found the time to address his audience with a few words, especially Uncle Walter Menzel, who had a dark look on his face, and who had tried several times to distract the eyes of his orphaned niece—for whom he may have felt responsible—from her tempter and to draw them toward himself, in order to strengthen her willpower. Herr Andrack didn't feel offended at all. He fully understood the layman's reservations about his discipline. Nobody could be blamed, said he, for finding his art a little risky, a little shocking, even reckless, on first observation. He expressed candidly what Uncle Walter was thinking. But he was convinced that even skeptics would in time learn to appreciate the beneficial effects of hypnosis.

He then cited some truly amazing examples of healing that he himself had worked with hypnosis: not in order to boast, only to do justice to the gift that he had received from a higher power, and to assure everyone of the integrity of his motives regarding Fräulein Astrid.

First, though, he pricked Astrid's arm with a sterilized needle—an experiment that made not her, but her aunts, cry out loud. Because she, Herr Andrack asserted, did not feel pain. But he did cause—always in the spirit of keeping a balance—the slight redness of a burn on the back of her hand by cautiously touching it with a cold, blunt knitting needle which, however, he had declared to be "red hot." Perhaps the question should have been asked: Wasn't the medium about to become a victim? But those present—except Charlotte, her brother Walter and her daughter Nelly—were not in the mood or in a position to ask themselves such questions. Their role was to marvel and to wonder. It was Nelly's role to feel strangely attracted and repelled at the same time. And to be disdainful of the unrestrained admirers.

Astrid sang, in her sleep: "On the heath of Lüneburg, in the fair and lovely land." She went into the parlor and danced a schmaltzy waltz all by herself. She also recited, faultlessly, the Christmas poem "Out of the forest I have come"—all of this, as Herr Andrack made explicitly clear, from Fräulein Astrid's own repertory, although she would probably not have given the performance at this time and in this place without his inducement. He was willing and prepared, in case the ladies and gentlemen were agreeable, to coax his medium into achieving feats of an entirely different kind.

Please do! urged Aunt Trudy.

Whereupon Astrid went over to her and slapped her across the face.

Well—that was going too far, everyone agreed. Only it was difficult to react in an appropriate way. The perpetrator of this more than impudent action—Astrid—obviously was absent in a higher sense and couldn't be held responsible; her inspirer, Herr Richard Andrack, smiled as if he had to ask for indulgence toward a naughty child: I can guarantee you, she won't know anything about it when she wakes up. Besides, he was a guest in the house. It seemed advisable to take the incident in this sense, and to make light of it.

Then Cousin Astrid climbed on the table.

It wouldn't have taken much, only the fast action by many hands prevented the worst, and she would have swept every single glass off the table with one swing of her foot. The situation now called for a word that nobody had uttered so far: "shameless." Once a girl climbs on a table, Charlotte said, there's no limit to what she'll do. On the table, Astrid performed drill exercises like a recruit, obeying noncommissioned officer Andrack's commands. Right face, left face, about-face seemed to come as naturally to her as saluting with and without head covering, goose-stepping in place (My table! Charlotte said reproachfully, but not too loudly), and the present-arms routine, which she certainly had never practiced before.

Nelly saw that her cousin was able to do anything and everything. She saw that it was possible to climb on a table in front of everyone and, when Herr Andrack suggested it, to perform a belly dance. Cousin Astrid had always been different from her. But Nelly had stoutly and consciously resisted all Herr Andrack's attempts to gain power over her. She would have felt flawed had she been that easily seduced.

But she had to ask herself just the same—not exactly in plain words, but in a wordless dialogue—if it really paid to resist every temptation. If it wouldn't be quite amusing—oh, more than amusing: exciting, delicious—simply to let herself sink back under Herr Andrack's magnetic hands; he'd be sure to catch her. To climb on the table in front of everybody and to undulate, as her cousin was now doing.

At the same time she knew: it wasn't like her. Her role was to observe the one—her cousin—and to envy her a little, and to see through the other—Herr Andrack. And to hide it all—the secret longing, the envy, the feeling of superiority—from everybody.

Cousin Astrid was now pointing a broomstick—at Herr Andrack's command—with which she took aim, as with a rifle, at the crowd of relatives. The bullet, had it been fired, would have hit Uncle Walter squarely in the heart.

13

Thirteen means bad luck.

Ideally, the structure of the experience coincides with the structure of the narrative. This should be the goal: fantastic accuracy. But there is no technique that permits translating an incredibly tangled mesh, whose threads are interlaced according to the strictest laws, into linear narrative without doing it serious damage. To speak about superimposed layers—"narrative levels"—means shifting into inexact nomenclature and falsifying the real process. "Life," the real process, is always steps ahead; to catch it at its latest phase remains an unsatisfiable, perhaps an impermissible desire.

Late in the evening, when Astrid wanted to escape Herr Andrack at last, he latched the unlocked apartment door, addressing her with a single, pleasant sentence (But, Fräulein Astrid! You aren't seriously thinking of leaving us!), so she had to ask Nelly to let her out. Toward midnight, when almost all the guests— Andrack, too—had left, Nelly sat down on her Uncle Walter's lap and was reprimanded by her mother: She had to get used to the fact that she was no longer a child. It dawned on her what that could mean, and it saddened her.

In the evening of the terribly hot day in G., when you were returning to your hotel, walking through the red, violet, green lights of the neon signs, Lenka started a scuffle with her Uncle Lutz, on the street, in public. You said: Don't horse around! and Lutz stopped in his tracks: Say, isn't that what Whiskers Grandma used to say? You hadn't realized it.

Lenka, already taller than Nelly was ever going to be, was secretly comparing her height with that of the young men who passed by, who'd openly—barely minding their manners—turn their heads to look at her, which she, naturally, pretended not to notice. The game had begun. Lutz looked at you knowingly, you turned down the corners of your mouth—appreciation and resignation—and H. said: Now the whole thing is starting all over again. There was a little laughter. Even that far back—probably since earliest childhood—Lenka had mastered the art of playing deaf. She was displaying her notoriously impassive face.

(Now, three years later, in this changeable summer of 1974, Lenka comes home from the late shift spent with exhaustion. Within ten, fifteen minutes, while she sits in silence, unable to speak, color and life return to her face. Slowly eating a few strawberries, she at last starts to talk, single sentences followed by long pauses. She asks herself if it isn't an imposition that some people—me, for instance, she says—insist on finding work that interests them, which three-quarters of all the people can't do, she says: all the people in factories and in industry.

She describes how she's overcome with fear and rage when the machine which feeds her ten thousand resistors for coding per shift produces rejects with a monotonous, mean click: wrongly coded resistors—as if anything that dead could "resist"!—on which the colored rings appear in the wrong order, or are blurred beyond recognition. Sometimes, she says, she feels like smashing the machine with a sledgehammer. What do others do with their rage, she wonders—for instance, the intelligent young man who takes over after her, who has been standing at the automated machine for ten years. Somebody has to do the job, he says. Her pay is good, by the way. Shift workers can buy their lunch for fifteen pfennigs. That's socialism for you, says Lenka.

The others, she says, sneak out to the next room and look at the world championship soccer games on TV, and don't care if the machines ring desperately for help when they're in trouble. That's when Liebscher runs like mad to set them right. He wants to prove to himself that he's indispensable, because he has poor eyesight and won't be able to do this work much longer. So they all blame him when a batch of rejects is returned: That was Liebscher's fault, he's half blind, anyway.

It's shitty, says Lenka. Do you think people should be treated like that?

It makes Liebscher happy for three days if I shake hands with him when I leave. He always gives me half his milk; we get it free because we have to work with a poisonous solution that gives me a headache regularly. Maybe it's the heat, too: at least a hundred degrees, because of the drying ovens. That knocks you out. The fans have been out of order for a long time, but the women are compensated for it and so they don't insist that they be repaired.

Do you think that people can do that to themselves? All their lives? Eight hours a day?

She'd be crazy, she said, to do the same, just because of a guilty conscience. Still, she couldn't just quit. Although she knew that it would be on her mind for a few weeks, but then it wouldn't look so bad to her any more. Everything fades, she says. Why does it have to be like that?

There are things for which there's just no solution. And it doesn't have to be through any fault of your own, does it?

That's how it is, you say. Antagonistic contradictions.

Stop it, she says.)

That night in G.—formerly L.—the two of you were very tired and went to bed at 9:30; it wasn't completely dark yet. Lenka immediately curled up and turned toward the wall, without having touched the book *Job* by Joseph Roth. Each of the beds was against one of the long walls of the small room. The two bedside tables fitted between them exactly. In front of each bed was a gray-patterned bouclé runner. At the foot of the beds stood a little table with slanted legs, and two of those uncomfortable armchairs that we used to export to our Eastern neighbors in the late fifties. The wardrobe was to the right of the door. The bedside lamp, like all hotel bedside lamps: small, impractical, dim.

You closed your eyes and saw a clear and accurate image of the market square in L., as Nelly had known it, and you found it difficult to visualize it in its present state, as you had just seen it. Lenka—you thought she was asleep—suddenly asked if you had "any nostalgia." You were touched by her concern for your mood, and could answer truthfully: No.

You weren't able to fall asleep, although you couldn't have been more tired. The window was open. The roof edge of the low building in back edged the still-light sky. The moon had risen, but outside your field of vision. This is something I'll remember. Those are the things that will engrave themselves in memory. The others will fade.

Homesickness? No. It sounded good. But the answer had been ready long before Lenka asked to hear it. Meaning that it was no longer possible to determine whether you had told a lie or the truth.

During the night, in the foreign town with its foreign-language noises, you realize that the emotions which you have suppressed will take revenge, and you understand their strategy to the last detail: they apparently withdraw, taking related emotions with them. Now it's no longer just the sadness, the pain, that are non-existent but regret and, above all, memory, as well. Memory of homesickness, sadness, regret. Taking the ax to the root. Emotions are not yet fused with words: in the future emotions will not be governed by spontaneity but—no use avoiding the word—by calculation.

And now that words are used, harmless, unself-conscious, it's all over, innocence is lost. The pain—maybe it'll now be forgotten —can still be named but no longer felt. Instead, during nights like these, the pain over the lost pain . . . To live between echoes, between the echoes of echoes . . .

The lines—lifelines, work lines—will not cross at the point which used to be called "truth." You know only too well what you're permitted to find difficult, and what not. What you're permitted to know, and what not. What must be talked about, and in what tone. And what must be buried in silence forever.

You get up without turning on the light, very carefully, so as not to wake Lenka, and take a sleeping pill.

At night I'm a better person (a quotation). In these times, "better" means: more sober, more courageous, a combination which has become rare in the daytime. Sober and cautious, yes. Courageous and imprudent, yes. That night, until the pill began to work, you had been sober and discouraged—which is different from being cowardly—and endowed with the fleeting ability to see through yourself and to bear it.

You wouldn't be able to write the book, and you knew why.

To this day you know the reasons against it, and they're not unfounded. The inexplicable change occurred the next morning. The heat as early as 7 a.m. Feeling refreshed after only a few hours' sleep. Everything was different. The luxury of total candor —why should it be granted to you, of all people? This anachronistic, elitist happiness—the only one deserving of the name? You were relieved, once and for all almost rid of the burden of conscience.

Don't we all do what we are actually unable to do, knowingly and without talking about it, since it's our only hope?

That night's dream seemingly had nothing to do with the fantasies of the hours before falling asleep; only later, today, have the connections surfaced. You saw yourself as a man, with features and abilities which you lack in reality. It seemed that you could do anything you set your mind to. Three women of different ages were in the dream: all of them had been your friends, and all of them had died of cancer. They didn't pay any particular attention to you. But you could sense that they envied you in a completely unspiteful yet intense way, and you yourself knew, with a strong feeling of guilt, how very enviable your lot really was.

Monday, July 1, 1974. General Pinochet has appointed himself supreme leader of the nation. The names of the four recently murdered Chileans were in yesterday's paper: José, Antonio Ruz, Freddy Taberna, Umberto Lisandi. Forty years earlier, almost to the day, the *General-Anzeiger* printed the names of people whose German citizenship had been revoked for reasons of unworthiness: Bertolt Brecht, Hermann Budzislawski, Erika Mann, Walter Mehring, Friedrich Wolf, Erich Ollenhauer, Kreszentia Mühsam (who, it should be said, was later in a concentration camp in the Soviet Union, where she had fled, and only in the last years of her life was she able to resume her work as her late husband's literary executor). Forty years ago, people in other countries and continents would fold their newspapers and put them down next to their breakfast cups when they read German names in them. You have to think of this action while you're folding yesterday's paper and sticking it in the newspaper rack. It was yesterday that the sixty-nine-year-old mother of Martin Luther King, Jr., was murdered in a church.

On an old, slightly mildewed map of the province of Brandenburg, divided into the districts of Potsdam and Frankfurt (Oder) —an undated map still measured in German and Prussian miles, and which was printed and published by C. Flemming in Glogau— you find the hamlet of Birkenwerder, southeast of Seidlitz and Dechsel. The map was probably printed before the North German mile was introduced in 1868. Birkenwerder near Schwerin, then. The place itself won't play a role here. Only this: Uncle Alfons Radde's family, including Nelly, is spending a week at a hunting lodge owned by Otto Bohnsack, Alfons Radde's boss. In the pine forests, chanterelle mushrooms grow in vast numbers. Nelly is the only one who isn't mad about mushrooming. But the forest, child, the forest! Aunt Liesbeth isn't ashamed to intone "Who hath made thee, forest fair." Nelly is embarrassed, and her cousin Manfred, nine years old by now, is embarrassed, too. Nelly discovers that she no longer has to fake her affection for this cousin, they go off by themselves, they whisper and giggle.

The forest gives off a strong fragrance. Perhaps it had been raining in the morning; the afternoon of July 20, 1944, was all that a summer day should be. Was there a birch fence around the plain, dark-stained frame house? No matter: when they were eating their mushrooms, they already knew. Uncle Alfons had brought the news from the village, which must have been close by. Of course they'd go home immediately, the next morning. An attempt had been made on the Führer's life.

Half sentences which can't be made into whole sentences in Nelly's presence. Careful, you never know. Maybe there had been glances that were meant to say: This is the beginning of the end.

Or questions: Is this the beginning of the end? Nelly wasn't given the chance to see the glances, to hear the questions.

Two days later she stands in the market square, lined up in formation. Now more than ever! shouts the team leader. And the Führer, as one can see, is invulnerable. That makes sense to Nelly. For weeks, they all wear the Hitler Youth uniform to school, and at a time, as Charlotte grumbles, when one can't get ration cards for Hitler Girl blouses and it's practically impossible to always have one of Nelly's two white blouses ready. Nelly doesn't see any exaggeration in showing one's loyalty to the Führer in external ways too. Charlotte doesn't think blouses are necessarily the way to show one's loyalty. It upsets Nelly to see her mother judge sacred things by the exigencies of the laundry room.

Was there, among the people around Nelly, the slightest hint—with the exception of her mother's gloomy exclamation, which the Gestapo had investigated, and which had been kept from Nelly—that some considered the war lost? The question must be answered negatively. Thus Nelly learns for the first time, by her own experience, how long it takes until the unthinkable becomes possible. Nelly didn't dare draw the obvious conclusions from what she was seeing with her own eyes, for fear of losing her inner memory. External events, sure: the first transports of refugees arriving in town. But Nelly thought the strange look in the refugees' eyes was only a sign of exhaustion after a long, harrowing journey. It's as if a wall had been pushed between her observations and her attempts to interpret them.

Her fatigue is so great in these months that it can no longer be explained by the nightly enemy planes overhead. The bomber squadrons on their missions to destroy Berlin make a turn over L. and take off toward the west, unintercepted. Just the same, Charlotte conscientiously wakes her children every night, makes them put on their clothes and go down to the cellar, which is anything but bombproof. One mustn't tempt fate.

Another scene: Her father, in shirt sleeves, sitting at the dining-room table, talking with her mother about the French prisoners who are quartered in an old factory, and whose supervision has recently become his responsibility. They picked the thief to guard the store, he says. A guy who's been a prisoner himself can't be mean to other prisoners, that's for sure, he says. He can't forbid

the Frenchmen little stoves to secretly cook themselves something on, late at night. He can't subject them to being frisked every
time they get back to camp from their work. Although he's wise to
every nook and cranny where a prisoner can hide something. But
he also knows how much a slice of bread or even a little piece of
meat means to a prisoner. He can't punish them for theft. He
remembers—and he always has to think of it—that he himself one
day had involved his madame in a game of cards, while his buddies
raided her smoke house: *Oh, Monsieur Bruno, un filou!*

But we've heard that story before, Charlotte Jordan said wear-
ily.

True. But now he thinks of it all the time.

Nelly's external memory has preserved this scene the way a
piece of amber preserves a fly: dead. Her inner memory, which
forms opinions about an event, had to remain mute. Nothing
but mechanical notetaking.

Lenka should understand this in order to believe that Nelly was
subconsciously prepared for the exodus. Signals beyond language
had gotten through to her. One of the last was the look of a little
boy. He had come from Posen—now Poznan—with his mother,
who was in the last days of pregnancy. Nelly didn't go to school
any more. Like the rest of her class, she took care of refugees
instead. She was particularly concerned with the fate of these two
and couldn't get over the fact that the mother was to give birth in a
strange town, possibly without any help, and at the same time in
constant fear for her little boy. Nelly called the midwife, who
examined the woman briefly but thoroughly, then felt her feet
and declared: As long as her feet were that cold, her time hadn't
come yet. She shouldn't have any silly notions. Nelly tried to convince her mother to take in the boy so the woman could deliver in
the hospital without having to worry. Charlotte, who certainly
didn't lack compassion, was evasive. As cautiously as she could,
she mentioned as the last reason for her refusal the possibility of
their own departure in the near future. In that case, how would
the mother ever find her boy again?

In answer to that, Nelly could only laugh shrilly and contemptuously: shrilly, because this possibility was so absurd; contemptuously, because her mother, too, like all grownups, was using the
lamest excuses, just to avoid even the slightest risk in a case where

a human being was in desperate need of help. The thought of not having helped the woman and her boy tormented Nelly for a long time. It was these two people, complete strangers, whom she had to think of two weeks later when she herself was fleeing. She thought of them more often than of all her friends, who had been torn from her forever—she was certain of that—or rather, who had vanished from her life. When they learned from stragglers that there had been fighting at the hospital where the SS had entrenched themselves, Nelly had to think of the woman who might have been lying there (the shell marks, incidentally, are still visible in the front wall of the building; you showed them to Lenka when you were driving by). Her boy, though, might have been taken by a children's transport and ended up God knows where, and it wasn't at all certain whether his mother would ever be able to find him again. Even today, a Western station still announces missing-person appeals from the German Red Cross, and you wonder about the fate of the boy and his mother; but it is no longer a burden on your conscience after all these years.

It was Nelly's own body that ultimately signaled the fact that she actually knew without having been informed. Charlotte, capable of choosing unusual words in certain situations, called her daughter's state simply "a collapse"—meaning that she wasn't so sure about the effectiveness of the camomile tea with honey that she was administering to Nelly.

At first Nelly simply cried, and then she came down with a fever. "Nervous prostration," Charlotte declared. It had all been a little too much for her. But *what* had, come to think of it? The work in the refugee camps? Well, maybe she was overdoing it a bit; on the other hand, she was no hothouse plant that needed coddling. On that afternoon, as usual, she had gathered the refugee children around her in the Weinberg Inn, after the dishes had been washed, and had told them the fairy tale of *Fundevogel*, and had played and sung with them. Julia, Dr. Juliane Strauch, master of the situation as always, went from one refugee family to the next with her large Red Cross bag, crouched in the straw next to them, and gave them medication and good advice. She was obviously setting an example, and Nelly didn't hesitate to follow it.

Julia's nod was recognition enough for her, as they met at the entrance door when a new contingent of refugees was announced.

It had gotten dark. There was the usual hustle of unloading, but no real signs of despair, until an unforeseen event suddenly changed the general mood—especially Nelly's. An infant—a wrapped bundle that was handed to her from one of the covered wagons to be handed to its mother—was dead: frozen to death. The young woman knew it without having to open the bundle, by signs that Nelly hadn't noticed. The woman started to scream immediately, in a voice one doesn't hear very often, a voice which —in moments like these the truth of many an unbearable saying is experienced—"made your blood run cold." I have never heard anyone scream like that, was the last thing Nelly thought; after that her thinking stopped.

Black box is what these states were later called, quite aptly. The brain as a black box, incapable of taking in images, let alone forming words. Presumably—it can't have been otherwise—she dropped what she was holding in her hand, withdrew on stiff legs to the garden gate of the restaurant, turned, and ran off. To her home, where she could cry, but not speak, for a long time. The next image after the memory gap: the dining room, Nelly lying on the old sofa, her mother in front of her with the big teacup.

The next day, an excuse which satisfied everybody and had the advantage of not being entirely invented: Nelly had caught a cold and had to stay in bed. The sniffles, a headache, a fever, which are no longer called "nervous prostration," just as the exaggerated word "collapse" is relegated to where it belongs: to the store of unutterable words. Until a few months later, when it will be pulled out again for a larger, more general purpose, and will suddenly seem suitable to divide time into eras: before the collapse, after the collapse. The individual is thus excused from his own collapse.

Nelly has visitors. Nelly, sick, surrounded by her friends: one of the last images of the house on Soldinerstrasse, which we—it can only be a matter of days—will now have to leave in great haste, never to set foot in again. Nelly doesn't yet know it, but she has already seen Julia Strauch for the last time. Now begin the irrevocable goodbyes of the fifteen-year-olds. On this last afternoon they are in high spirits. They giggle and carry on without knowing why. Only when Dora tells about a rumor going around in the outskirts of town where she lives: Russian advance tanks had pushed forward beyond Posen, had even reached the Oder River south of Frankfurt—it becomes clear why there's laughter. Russian tanks at the Oder!

The friends' conversation took place around January 25, about two days after Marshal Konev's army had reached the Oder between Oppeln and Ohlau (today Opole and Olawa), while the troop units that affected Nelly and her friends—bypassing the town of L. on the north and the south, for the time being—had started out on their pincer movement toward Küstrin (today Kostrzyn), under the command of Marshal Zhukov. On the same day, the Führer personally made SS Reich Leader Himmler the supreme commander of "Army Division Weichsel" in charge of defense of the regions that interest us; the day on which General Guderian, the army's chief of staff, met with Foreign Minister Ribbentrop, in order to "open his eyes"—without result, of course —"to the critical military situation" (postwar publications by Guderian: *Reminiscences of an Old Soldier*, 1951; *Can Western Europe Be Defended?*, 1951); five days before Minister of Armaments and Munitions Speer announces in a memorandum to the Führer—without effect, of course—the impending total breakdown of the German war economy; seven days before the Soviet troops cross the Oder River north and south of Küstrin and establish bridgeheads on its west bank. Five days before Bruno Jordan— who has begun the march in the direction of Soldin-Stettin with his French prisoners—is taken prisoner in the village of Liebenau by the northern arm of the Soviet forces; four days before Nelly and her friends—although forever separated—cross the Oder at Küstrin at the last minute, before the pincers close. Five and a half days before Charlotte Jordan, passenger on the last bus to leave L. for the West, crosses the Oder Bridge, too, and has the opportunity to see those parts of Küstrin still intact which later will be completely destroyed during the battle for the town. (The pleasure of deploying language for once as a general deploys his troops: logically, forcibly. In rapid succession.)

The fact that Charlotte let her children leave for so-called points unknown, alone, even if in the company of relatives—her children about whom she worried almost too much—this fact has practically never been discussed within the family, whose history has been probed for years and has long since hardened into legend. And yet, one should have been more perplexed, had things taken their right and normal course—which they hadn't, that's just it—at her mother's crucial decision, than at the fact that the population was asked over the radio to evacuate the town. Of course there were no means of transportation. The scenes that took place at the railroad station—may they be described by those who witnessed them. On the evening of the same day, January 29, 1945, the last over-crowded refugee train was shelled and set on fire before Vietz by advance Soviet tanks that had bypassed the town to the south.

There is agreement on one point among all members of the family, now scattered in all directions, at odds with each other for personal and political reasons: it was thanks to brother-in-law Alfons Radde that they were able to flee in time. After an agree-ment by telephone in the early-morning darkness, he drew up in front of the Jordan house at 9 a.m. in a truck of the firm Otto Bohnsack, grain wholesaler, in order to "make a pickup," as it was called in truckers' lingo, of his parents-in-law, Hermann and Auguste Menzel, his sister-in-law Charlotte Jordan, and her two children, Nelly and Lutz.

It was his shining hour. Alfons Radde, who had had to fight all his life for recognition by his wife's family, now turned out to be the white knight and rescuer of defenseless women and children. The Jordans' baggage was loaded on the truck—everything: trunks, crates, firmly stuffed sacks of bedding, cartons of canned food from the Jordans' stock; even a small butter tub whose con-tents, of course, didn't withstand spoilage once the bitter cold winter was over; but even rancid, as rendered butter, it fed the family, and was used as a desirable object of barter.

The exodus from home calls forth a flow of tears. Charlotte was holding on to herself. Presumably her inner strength was used up by a decision slowly ripening within her while she was busy stowing away the baggage.. She had no time for weeping. For Nelly, tears in public were out of the question.

But not for Whiskers Grandma. She was crying shyly, to herself. Unlike the generation of aunts: Trudy Fenske, divorced; Olga Dunst, whose husband had "made off" with Frau Lude; Liesbeth Radde: they all sat in the semidarkness of the truck—except for Aunt Lucie, who had jumped off to help with the loading—and accompanied each new stop, each new goodbye, with their free-flowing and copious tears.

Today—it is August 31, 1974—on the thirty-fifth anniversary of the Führer's order that unleashed the Second World War, the newspapers offer commentaries appropriate to this date. No new war seems to have begun anywhere in the world. Although the hostile factions in the Middle East continue to arm themselves; although tens of thousands of Cypriots are suffering from the consequences of one of these "limited wars," which have become the fashion(among them an old Greek woman whose weeping on the TV screen reminds you of your grandmother's weeping); although the fighting goes on in Vietnam, the torturing in Chile: the greatest disasters of the day are the train wreck in the station of the Yugoslavian town of Zagreb and the flood catastrophe in Bangladesh.

Today, like any other day, is also the tip of a time triangle, whose two sides lead to two other, to any number of other dates—August 31, 1939: The shooting will begin before 6 a.m. January 29, 1945: a girl, Nelly, stuffed and stiff in double and triple layers of clothes (stuffed with history, if these words mean anything), is dragged up on the truck, in order to leave her "childhood abode," so deeply anchored in German poetry and the German soul.

Today, on this hot day, the open door to the balcony lets in the rustling of poplar leaves, the barking of dogs in the distance, the roar of a single motorcycle. Today—a rare joy—even unimportant things can only enhance the sense of living: the food, the wine at noon, the few pages of a book, the cat, the chiming of a clock in the room where H. is sitting among his pictures, the reflections of the sun on the desk. The nap after dinner, and the twilight-illumined dream. The poem you're reading: "Beware of the innocence / of your fellow wanderers." But above all, the five hours spent on these pages, the solid core of each day, the most real part of the real life. Without this, everything else: eating and drinking, love, sleep, and dream would lose reality with frantic, fearsome speed. It is right, and it is the way it's meant to be. Today you don't mind recalling that bitterly cold day in January.

Now it's time to leave, hurry up, quick, it's getting late. Nelly, already inside the truck, holds out her hand to help her mother climb in. But she suddenly steps back, shakes her head: I can't. I'm staying here. I just can't abandon everything.

Followed by an uproar inside the truck, shouts, beseechings, screams even—the grandmother, the aunts!—an uproar in which Nelly doesn't take part. What is happening is simply beyond belief. Followed by a short dialogue between Aunt Lucie and Charlotte, in which the children are entrusted mainly to the care of Aunt Lucie—a sensible choice!—while Charlotte promises in return to take care of her brother, Lucie's husband, who is "holding the fort" at his factory, the engineering works of Anschütz & Dreissig. Followed immediately by the starting jerks of the truck. Alfons Radde, rightfully annoyed, wasn't going to wait a minute longer. Whoever doesn't want to come along can stay behind. From the interior of the truck rose a shrill wail, which subsided as Charlotte quickly stepped out of view of the passengers. Nelly saw the house, the windows with the familiar rooms behind them, above the store windows the red letters: BRUNO JORDAN, GROCERIES, DELICATESSEN. Finally the poplar.

Years later, when the numbness began to dissolve, Nelly tried to visualize every minute her mother spent in her hometown. The moment when the truck had disappeared from view, she stood stock-still.

Now it's too late. She can't permit herself to think that she has lost her children. She rushes up the stairs, back into the ruined apartment. Straighten things, in any case, straighten up first. Put things back into chests, drawers, stack what was left behind and lying around. Take the Führer's picture off the wall (climb on the desk to reach it), hack it to pieces with the ax in the cellar, silently, and burn it in the furnace. Suddenly, on returning to the apartment, she stops, thunderstruck: she has nothing to do here any more. She must have been out of her mind to stay behind. She didn't even know where her children were going, how could she ever find them again. The reasons she had manufactured for staying were disintegrating at an incredible speed: to be the guardian of house and home, to be responsible to her husband for their goods and possessions, to preserve the children's inheritance. But that's insane, she may have said to herself. That's absolute insanity.

She realized that she needed information. The telephone was already dead, the situation seemed serious. An idea: Leo Siegmann, the book dealer, Bruno Jordan's friend, works in the administration of supplies at the General von Strantz Barracks. If there's anyone, it's he who can tell her what's going on. Ready to go to any length, she pushes her way in to see him. Siegmann, ashen, is in the process of destroying the last important papers; after that he's going to take off as fast as he can, even if he has to walk. The garrison has its marching orders. One look at the barracks square convinces Charlotte all is lost. Now she knows. The dream's over, she says to Leo Siegmann. And where is your final victory?

Now she flees, too.

Lenka comes in. She has something to tell you. Last night, when she came back from her youth tour to Živohošt' near Prague, she forgot something important: the songs our tourists sing when they are in socialist foreign countries. Can you guess what they sing at night when they get drunk on Prague beer?

"Why is our Rhine so fair," you guess.

Wrong, not that, this time. Two other songs. The first: "There's no beer in Hawaii, there's no beer."

I know that one, you say. And the second?

Lenka says: "In a little Polish town." Do you know it?

No.

Well, I do. "In a little Polish town, / there was once a maiden, / she was so fair, so very fair, / she was the fairest Polish lass / whose beauty no one could surpass. / No! said the Polish miss, / I'll never give you a kiss."

Is there more of it? you ask. You, too, know the rage and the urge to slap the singing faces.

The song has three verses. Lenka knows only snatches of the last two. She knows that "it" happens in the second. Whereupon the Polish girl hangs herself, a note around her neck, "which had the words: / I did give it a try / and I had to die."

Were those really our people, Lenka?

Well, who else?

How old?

Between twenty and thirty. But you haven't heard anything yet. Do you know how the last verse ends?

Tell me.

"You better take a German lass, / who's not afraid at the first stroke / that she might croak."

In this early fall, the evenings are beginning to turn cool. Today is the official end of summer. You know that one mustn't wish to age faster. Live within the meaning of the age! One has to give the meaning of the age a chance to reveal itself. Thirty-five years ago today, the seizure of a few little Polish towns by German soldiers started a great war. Suddenly you've lost interest in describing how some people—Germans—experienced the end of this war. Those people can go to hell, as far as you're concerned. A song, sung by Germans in the summer of 1974, has drained you of all sympathy for them.

How did the Czechs react to it, Lenka? They only stared and grinned.

The singers won't read a line of this book. They weren't looking at TV two years ago, when three Polish women told the camera their story, women who had been subjected to "medical experiments" in the German concentration camp of Ravensbrück. One of them had been unnecessarily operated on against her will. The other had received an injection in the breast, which afterward turned hard and black and had to be amputated. ("I always had to think that I'd never in my life have a husband. Nor children, nor a home. Nothing.") The third had been covered with abscesses for years from injections. In 1950 she had a child, Jadwiga. The horribly deformed face of the young girl suddenly appeared large on the screen.

Why did you want to have a child? the obstetrician, a woman professor, said to Jadwiga's father after the delivery. It's perfectly obvious that this deformity is a result of your wife's experiences in the concentration camp . . .

Jadwiga herself said a few words. She was crying. The twenty-two years of her life in this world had been one continuous nightmare. Her only consolation was that she was able to learn. She was studying mathematics at the University of Warsaw, but didn't attend lectures, that would be too hard on her. She said: I want to live a normal life, and do good to other people, be useful to them.

No more writing. It's evening. On TV, the song of a choir of old, black men: "Oh when the saints go marchin' in . . ."

Music by Bach.

The train crash in Zagreb was caused by human failure.

In G. (formerly L.), a little Polish town, you had breakfast on Sunday, July 11, 1971, in a milk bar on the market square.

"I have done much writing, in order to lay the foundation for memory" (Johann Wolfgang Goethe).

14

Verfallen—a German word.

A look into foreign-language dictionaries: nowhere else these four, five different meanings. German youth is addicted—*verfallen* —to its Führer. The bill drawn on the future is forfeited—*verfallen*. Their roofs are dilapidated—*verfallen*. But you must have known that she's a wreck—*verfallen*.

No other language knows *verfallen* in the sense of "irretrievably lost, because enslaved by one's own, deep-down consent."

Last night you set the alarm wrong, it rang at five. You lay awake tired, but not actually annoyed. You happened to think of a poem by Goethe, a poem that you hadn't thought about for at least twenty years:

The future conceals
From us fortune and sorrow,
Unknowns of tomorrow.
Yet without fearing
We're pushing ahead.

The thought might have been connected with this year's Goethe celebrations. But this particular poem had not been used anywhere. It was a pleasure to have it rise from memory line by line, almost undamaged; to bring forth the stanzas and to hear them as if for the first time:

And heavy and high
Hangs suspended a cover
Of awe. Stars hover
At rest in the sky,
And the graves rest below.

The poem would surely be in the small blue volume of poetry. You remembered, while the poem was continuing on another level of your dream-waking consciousness, that the little book was one of the two objects which you had salvaged and taken along from those early times. The second object is the spatula, indispensable for turning pancakes, which Whiskers Grandma inadvertently took from a farmer's wife in whose barn you had spent the night as refugees. Whiskers Grandpa's fit of rage when he discovered it: We aren't thieves! He demanded in all seriousness that we go back and return the spatula.

Okay, okay. Tomorrow, right after getting up, you'd look for the poem in the blue book.

Here, treetops will wave
In eternal calm,
Their abundance be balm
To the active and brave.

In your half-awake state, you began to add question marks to some lines. "Without fearing"? you thought. And what does "pushing ahead" mean?

It wasn't until you quickly wrote down the three stanzas after waking up for the second time that you noticed the gap at the end of the last stanza. One line was missing. Not until an hour or two later—a thorough search was delayed by daily chores—did the line suddenly appear to you, startlingly: We bid you to hope!

How was it possible, or rather what does it mean, if one "forgets" this particular line in an otherwise intact poem?

The poem, incidentally, was not in the small blue volume, which is now lying next to you; you can pick it up, turn its pages. Four hundred and sixteen thin pages, yellowed with age: *Goethe's Poems*, published in 1868 by G. Grote's Publishing House, Berlin. Brownish marbled endpaper, with your former name at the top on the right, written by Maria Kranhold—who gave Nelly the book— in her fluid, energetic hand. But in the middle of the page is an inscription written in brown ink with a thin-nibbed, shaky pen, in the old-fashioned Gothic script of the last century: From my brother Theodor. And the year 1870 in the right-hand corner, by the same hand.

The whole morning was spent looking for the poem. You finally called a learned friend, who gave it the title "Mason's Song," which wasn't correct, but at least it put you on the right track: under the title "Symbolum," it is the first poem in the section "Lodge," and it has—this was the greatest surprise—two stanzas which you didn't believe you knew: "The mason's roaming / Resembles life . . ." And so on. (Hence the futile search for the first line.)

One thing at a time, as Charlotte Jordan would say. Easy does it. What shall you tell about first, the blue book or the spatula? The spatula first, the trek through the villages. There are far more villages than towns in this world, a fact that Nelly hadn't quite realized before. Technically, the firm of Otto Bohnsack, grain wholesaler, had probably ceased to exist in February 1945. But its name is painted in large letters on the side of the gray truck which is being driven alternately by Uncle Alfons Radde and a professional driver, a man unfit for military service. First to Seelow, then via Wriezen, Finow, Neuruppin, Kyritz, Perleberg to Wittenberge on the river Elbe. It takes him a good two weeks, in the coldest winter in a long time. All along the route, people here and there notice the firm name, and Charlotte Jordan is able to ask them about it soon after, in her search for her children.

Nelly's seat was close to the loading door on one of the Jordans' sacks of bedding, which gradually turned as hard as a rock. She could see through the little cellophane window in the rear tarpaulin flap. A gray snow sky, the bare branches of cherry and apple trees along the road, and only from time to time a stretch of road. The crossing of the Oder was greeted with relief: to have the great river between them and the pursuing enemy; the Russians would certainly never be able to overcome this obstacle.

Late in the afternoon of the first day, they have to get off, lighten the load of the truck, help push. The road is snow-covered, icy, jammed with refugee vehicles. The damned truck, which would easily take the hill under normal weather conditions, won't budge an inch. Nelly woke up from her daze for a short while and saw what was happening on the road. The useless maneuvers which only wedged the cars more tightly into each other. The useless household belongings piled high on the farm wagons, an indication that everybody was on the verge of utter confusion, not to say madness. And in addition, the small army units that were coming toward them, tangling with the train of refugees. What on earth did they think they were going to accomplish at the Oder?

Nevertheless, it was the motor power of an army vehicle that finally helped them over the Seelow Heights. The signal was given to climb aboard, Nelly crouched on her sack of bedding. She just wanted to go on riding, no matter where it led. Not having to stop, not having to see anything. Later, the timing of Charlotte Jordan's route of flight was compared to that of the Otto Bohnsack truck, and it turned out that they had missed each other only by hours, as early as Seelow. Charlotte, back from the barracks, makes coffee on her stove one last time—she had a few real coffee beans in reserve—then her brother, Walter, comes, as agreed. Their last meal together at the kitchen table, sandwiches. They each take a few of them along in their briefcase, their only luggage.

Because now it means walking. The cigarettes—they're both nonsmokers—are useful in persuading the driver of the last mail bus to Küstrin. He lets them get on. They're already past Vietz. By then Charlotte has blisters on her feet. Both of them, independently, thought it possible that they wouldn't get across the Oder any more, and that they'd be cut off from their families. Later they admit to each other that they had seen the situation realistically.

The mail bus goes no farther than Küstrin. It's the middle of the night, yet there are people in the streets. Charlotte begins to ask the two questions: Had a troop of French prisoners marched by, and had a truck with the inscription Bohnsack Feed and Grain passed through. All answers to the first question were no (Bruno Jordan had been taken prisoner two days before), to the second question, after a while, yes. In the direction of Seelow.

That's where they—Charlotte and her brother, Walter—arrived in the morning; the truck they were looking for had left an hour earlier. They saw where their family had spent the night: underneath and next to the desks in the tax bureau. Now it would be child's play to find them, Charlotte thought, but she was mistaken . . .

That night, by the way, hadn't brought much sleep. The straw on the floor wasn't the worst. Much worse was the rapid disintegration of manners, which manifested itself in loud squabbles. Nelly and her kin were beginners as refugees; the first law of refugee life hadn't yet been engraved on their minds: Once you've gotten hold of a dry and warm spot, let nothing and nobody make you give it up. Whiskers Grandpa, with his easily upset digestive system—only too well known to his family—should have had a place right next to the door, within a short distance of the toilets. But these spots were occupied by fellow refugees from the eastern districts of the Reich—people not willing to negotiate—and he had to climb over them several times during the night, until they began to complain in their broad West Prussian dialect. Aunt Liesbeth resented having her father yelled at by some yokels from the hinterland—she yelled back. That's when Whiskers Grandpa made the mistake of directing a brusque word at his own daughter, thereby giving rise to the first of numberless major scenes which gradually were to lay bare the very innards of the family, and which caused Nelly—who witnessed them with anguish, but attentively—to think more than once: So that's how it is.

So that's how it was: Aunt Liesbeth refused to let herself be shut up by her father any longer. She no longer trembled, as she'd done when she was a child, when he came home plastered and then didn't know what he was doing (Liesbeth! Lucie Menzel implored her sister-in-law. For mercy's sake!). Liesbeth, for heaven's sake! that was Whiskers Grandma, half sitting up in her bed of straw. Now look who's talking—where did the little scar on her forehead come from? Yes, sir: from a broken piece of the kerosene lamp that her husband had thrown at her! Oh, for God's sake, stop your nonsense.

Nelly knew the scar well, she had often traced it with her finger: How did you get it? Well, child, the way one gets these things. So that's how it was.

They left Seelow in the direction of Wriezen. Her mother and her Uncle Walter—who miscalculated, or perhaps had been tempted, on the spur of the moment, by some means of transportation that came their way—turned toward the ruined city of Berlin, which Bohnsack's truck bypassed to the north.

When you lift your head, your glance falls on an old engraving of the town of L., a recent gift of a friend of yours. It shows the silhouette of the town as seen from across the river: the most flattering view. Important buildings, whose contours are visible, are marked with letters from A to L. A is the Public House; B, Mill Gate; D, Dye Works. Under C it says: Synagogue. The tall, spireless roof of the synagogue rises between Mill Gate and E, St. Mary's Church, in the silhouette of the town. You can figure out the location of the building, and you realize that you had been looking in the wrong place for the remains, or at least the site, of the synagogue, during your visit in July 1971. On Sunday morning —after getting up, after leaving the hotel—you had driven once more, very slowly, through the small streets between the station and market square, the streets where you expected to find the synagogue, but didn't.

The café at the market square, then, was all that was left. You stood in line for a few minutes with your tray, you got yourselves a glass of good coffee, also eggs, rolls. Lenka had a large mug of cocoa. It seemed to be the rule here that you started feeling good as soon as you sat down to eat. You praised the color of the walls—a light green—the practical, clean tables, the lightweight chairs. H. thought you were overdoing your praises, but you meant it. You meant everything you said. You finally even praised the sun. It's going to be beastly hot again, Lutz said. You were content to sit as a stranger at the foot of St. Mary's Church. All of it, you said, the whole house we're in, didn't even exist before. Of course the bells began to toll, the throng of the faithful was filling the church, later it was too crowded to get in.

Lenka wanted you to show her the route of your flight on the road atlas in the car. Lutz and you argued about which route you took: how could you have believed that you were bypassing Berlin to the south? Could Nelly have been that absentminded? Lutz, the younger, with the more reliable factual memory. He says, smiling: Less distracted by the inner life. It has its advantages, don't you think? But of course. Always.

In Wittenberge, Nelly's family—twelve people—occupied an entire classroom. That's something both of you remember.

And you? Lenka asks her father. His finger traces a different route, from south to north. From the Saale Dam, which he guarded as a Luftwaffe helper, to Berlin. To be exact: Berlin-Lichtenberg. Railway line. Because the flak guns and their crews were deployed at the Oder, in order to be used in the final battle. That's when we knew that things were desperate. Here, says H., Bad Freienwalde. In Altranft we lay over for a long time.

What does "lay over" mean? says Lenka. What does "deployed" mean?

"Deployed." That meant: again being transported in freight cars via Werneuchen, Tiefensee, Schulzendorf—in short, on a clogged, narrow-gauge railroad. It meant for the others: unloading artillery, further dispatch of gun carriages to the so-called front. Which was already this side of the Oder, at Neu-Lewin and Alt-Lewin. To us it meant switchboard operators and linemen, lugging the heavy cable drum overland, through the dead town of Wriezen, through the dead villages, and laying the lines to the frontline batteries. (Wriezen! says Lenka, electrified, but then disappointed: Your mother passed through the town seven days earlier, when it hadn't yet been evacuated. And anyway, a meeting would have been out of the question. Lenka is searching for the law that underlies chance.) "Lay over" meant: to sit for days at the switchboard, plugging, unplugging; now and then to call through to see if the line is still intact. If not, to go and mend it. Once a day—you could set your watch by it—to hear the burst of the 10.2-centimeter artillery trained on the wooden bridge at Neu-Lewin, where the Soviets had their bridgehead—and which inflicted heavy damage on the bridge each time, whereupon Soviet sappers immediately got to work and repaired it. (Lenka says, you'll probably think I'm dumb, but what's a bridgehead?) Once—we were calling the neighboring place from a post at a deserted village—we suddenly had a Russian voice at the other end. We dropped the receiver like a hot potato. We spent the nights in abandoned bedrooms and conjugal beds, still covered with sheets, of owners who had fled.

All of this together, Lenka, means "deployed" and "lay over." Lenka's mind has been wandering: Without all of this, you wouldn't have met each other. Perhaps both of you, with someone else, would now have a daughter my age, but the daughter wouldn't be me. Pretty weird, isn't it?

No comment, says H.

But Lutz, your brother, Lutz, of all people, took it upon himself to drag his niece away from the perilous approach to nihilism, by means of logic and the law of probability. Yes, indeed, he thought it inappropriate to get hung up too early on nonsensical speculations; he didn't like to see a young person reduce the mystery of his origin to a stupid coincidence.

That's what he told you when you were walking back to the car on the market square in G. So what do you propose? you asked. Providence? The higher principle once again? That wouldn't be at all bad, said Lutz, if it were still possible. But those times are past. And so you spread out your net of mathematical formulae in order to arrest the plunge into the big black hole. Lutz said: Have you ever heard of "white dwarfs"? Are you interested in fairy tales? Of course not. A white dwarf is a star with a small diameter and low absolute luminosity, but high effective temperature. So? White dwarfs represent a late phase in the development of stars. Lately it has become known that star matter may collapse when its core deteriorates due to the absence of hydrogen. You, with your notions, could also talk about a collapsed horizon of events.

Meaning what?

That nothing can leave a black hole, not even light. That neither space nor time can exist in the center of such black holes, not even the laws of physics. For instance: an astronaut who got close to a black hole would be squeezed out of time, would become a dot. Well?

Excellent, you said.

See what I mean? said Lutz. Now I can see my sister's brain waves rev up into high gear.

Above all, it's kind of a shock. Not of fear. More like the shock

one gets when one recognizes something where one least expects it.
You ponder: Does this super-heavy nothingness create a suction?

Before you start speculating, said Lutz, so far there's no physical proof of the existence of black holes. Half of all astrophysicists consider them a fallacy due to the fuzziness of a theory. A miscalculation, if you will.

If you were an astrophysicist, you'd belong to that half.

Right you are. And you'd join the other half.

And you'd have no compunction, you asked Lutz, about preventing the recognition of black holes?

No, said Lutz. None. Because you considerably overestimate the number of people who are willing and able to live with black holes. I find no fault in catering to the many others who aren't able or willing to.

What about the ersatz word "hope"?

Suit yourself, said Lutz.

You asked: But, then, shouldn't deception—self-deception, too—be allowed only at the very end of our experiments? Way after the loss of faith?

You said it, Sister. But how will you know that we aren't at the very end of our experiments?

Now listen, you said, reversing your position is against the rules.

In the car it was quickly decided, in the terrible heat that had started to rise again, to turn toward the eastern part of town (Concordia Church, hospital) and its northerly outskirts along the former Friedebergerstrasse and Lorenzdorferstrasse.

"Collapsed horizon of events"—that's what stuck in your mind. Nelly's state in those months couldn't have been described more aptly. She believed that she wouldn't return home ever again, yet at the same time she still considered the final victory possible. Better to escape into absurd thinking than to give in to the unthinkable. She hissed at her grandfather, who declared in his mumbling, toothless way, that the war was "a lost game."

What she saw, smelled, tasted, felt, heard—distorted faces, people dragging themselves along, the reek of the different overnight quarters, the lukewarm, thin coffee served by Red Cross helpers from their tin coffeepots, the sack of bedding that had turned into a solid rock from her sitting on it, the curses and invective over the distribution of places to sleep—it all registered, but she was by no means allowed to convert it into emotions, such as despair, discouragement. She knew from then on, and didn't forget, that emotional numbness can look like courage, because that's what she was now being praised for: She's really courageous for her age.

Months later, in May, she read in the eyes of a U.S. Army officer that he seriously thought she was insane, but she understood only years later that his almost shocked look meant nothing more than that.

That the suffering of the old differs sharply from the suffering of the young: this, too, one could have learned in those days. But nobody was exempt from suffering then, and that's why there are no reliable witnesses today. For the old—for those who had babbled about death for years, just to hear the young contradict them—the time had come to keep silent; because what was going on now was their death, and they knew it. They aged years in weeks, and then died, not neatly one after the other, for a variety of reasons, but all at once, for one and the same reason, be it called typhoid, or hunger, or simply homesickness, which is a perfectly plausible pretext for dying. However, the real reason for their dying was that they had become totally superfluous, a burden to others, a burden whose weight sufficed to dispatch them from life to death. Especially when they suspended this weight—as Nelly's great-grandfather Gottlob Meyer did—from a solid nail in the wall by means of a rope around the neck. He didn't want to go with his daughter and son-in-law, the Heinersdorf grandparents, when they were forced to leave in May 1945. Neighbors found him and reported the news of his death. Thank God, Heinersdorf Grandma is supposed to have said.

Great-grandfather's watch, you said to your brother, Lutz, on the way to Lorenzdorferstrasse, now that's another one of those things you didn't inherit. That's true, said Lutz. You know, I was sorry about it for a long time. I would have loved to have carried it behind his coffin at his funeral, since he had no medals. I would have loved to hang it on my wall, to give it a place of honor. I remember exactly what it looked like, and what sound it made when he let the lid snap open. So do I, you said.

No good will come of it, the great-grandfather supposedly said to Heinersdorf Grandma, when she—herself way over sixty—left

her home. And of course he was right. She, Nelly's other grandmother, died in June 1945 near Bernau, of malnutrition, according
to the death certificate, and that meant that she had starved to
death. Nevertheless, she was given a grave that is still tended and
on which a wreath is placed once a year.

Things are different with the scattered graves of the three other
grandparents. Whiskers Grandpa was the next to die, of typhoid,
he was buried at the cemetery wall in the village of Bardikow in
Mecklenburg. His grave is unmarked. Lutz claims to have identified
it recently in the Bardikow cemetery by unmistakable signs. In
Magdeburg, in a neglected grave, lies Auguste Menzel, his wife,
Whiskers Grandma, from whom Nelly learned the meaning of
self-denial and kindness. A simple attack of flu had been enough
for her. Charlotte Jordan cut a gray strand of hair off the thin braid
that rested on the shriveled body's right shoulder, and kept it God
knows where.

Heinersdorf Grandpa, Gottlieb Jordan, was the only one with a
goal that kept him alive: he wanted to live to be eighty. He succeeded, although under difficult circumstances, in a hole-in-the-
wall in a village of the Altmark. He then said: Now it's enough,
and died. Nothing is known about the present condition of his
grave. A color photo exists, snapped by Aunt Trudy, his daughter,
which shows Heinersdorf Grandpa's grave planted with flowers
and surrounded by white gravel paths. The tombstone shows the
epitaph he had chosen: Vengeance is mine, saith the Lord.

A blanket crocheted by Whiskers Grandma of good wool is the
only object in the family's possession that recalls the grandparents'
generation. Sometimes you think—Lutz and you—of the two
stories that Whiskers Grandpa used to tell his grandchildren: the
story of the snake and the story of the bear. Sometimes the taste of
pudding reminds you of the blancmange with raspberry syrup that
Nelly used to eat in summer at Heinersdorf Grandma's kitchen
table. Sometimes someone will say: Lutz is so tall because he takes
after his grandfather. Sometimes—but not for long any more—
Auguste Menzel's expression appears in one of her descendants.

In those days, the old people, who knew how soon they'd be
gone and forgotten, were acting childish or keeping quiet. Their
sons and daughters were the ones who felt they were truly cheated,
the real losers, and that made them think they had the right to take

it out on everybody, particularly on the old, who had lived their lives, and on the young, whose lives were still ahead of them. But they themselves, they had worked hard for a decent life, from which they were now being expelled. Aunt Liesbeth, who was given to dramatic outbursts, yelled out, throwing up her hands: My life is ruined! Uncle Alfons Radde, her husband, suffered less, because he hadn't been deprived of the basis of his existence: he continued to serve Otto Bohnsack, be it without wages. He admonished his wife. Nobody understood her! lamented the aunt. Aunt Lucie reminded her that she should be thankful for having her husband with her. Oh, you! said Aunt Liesbeth contemptuously. The other aunts, Trudy Fenske and Olga Dunst, sat huddled in the straw of the school at Wittenberge, silently observing the quarrel. We, too, they said to each other, have lost everything, whether it was much or little.

Nelly was suddenly severed sharply from her elders. She saw that possessions and life meant one and the same thing to them. She began to feel ashamed of the comedy they were acting out, at first in front of the others, in the end for their own benefit.

One day—a dark morning in the middle of February—a voice calls from the schoolyard inquiring if people by the name of Jordan are sheltered here. That's when Nelly knows that her mother has found her; she throws herself on the straw and begins to sob.

In the first hour of their reunion—which some of them didn't hesitate to call a miracle (consider the circumstances!)—after the first tearful embraces, the first short reports back and forth, the great feud began between the two sisters Charlotte Jordan and Liesbeth Radde. A feud that continued from then on, day after day, starting with needling and bickering, and swelling into a grand scene, a feud that was to poison the two and a half years the families were forced to live together. Dozens of eruptions of hate, vituperative tirades, fits of crying, silent meals in an oppressive atmosphere. Two sisters who can't give an inch either way.

Nelly didn't know at the time that it wasn't in their power to deal dispassionately and courteously with each other. That they had to enter the battlefield anew each day God gave them—that's how Charlotte put it—because in the distant past of their childhood the question of questions: What are you worth? had been asked the wrong way: Which one is worth more than the other?

And because since then the battle—up to now kept in check by separation and mitigating circumstances—had been waged back and forth between them, forever undecided. (Only when Charlotte lay dying did a stream of desperate sister-love break forth from Liesbeth Radde. The death of one of the sisters had decided the battle, the other was finally free to love.) Sometimes, when they began to quarrel, it was as if they were undertaking a job which they found annoying, even hateful, but which simply had to be done, and who was there to do it if not they?

Charlotte, to give an example, just had to be unwise enough—as she was during the first hour of their reunion in the school at Wittenberge—to mention the exertions she'd had to endure: those hikes through the ruins of Berlin, those bombing raids, those wanderings when they were lost. That was enough for Liesbeth to use her irritated tone of voice, trying to outdo her sister by talking of her own sufferings. Either side would then come up with disparaging remarks about the other, introduced by "never ever." Never ever had Charlotte taken the accomplishments of her younger sister seriously. Never ever did Liesbeth stop trying to get into the good graces of her mother, at the expense of her older sister. (Walter, the brother, had always been out of the competition; now he reacted to his sisters' deportment with silence and neutrality.) Then came the moment when one of them would tell the other to shut up, without result, of course. Finally they'd quit in a rage, walk away from each other, stiff-necked, heads high, heels clattering, slamming doors.

It sometimes happened that Whiskers Grandma, huddled quietly in her corner and secretly wiping away tears, would say in the lull: Now all the trees stand silent. Whereupon both daughters would turn on her. When she died, both thought that they hadn't paid enough attention to her. Uncle Walter, who lived in West Berlin and refused to set foot behind the Iron Curtain, sent a wreath. Its streamers had the inscription in gold letters: TO DEAR MOTHER, A LAST GOODBYE. Liesbeth saw fit to malign her brother's conduct. There was nothing to inherit. Some of Auguste Menzel's worthless clothes were given to the rag collector, some to the People's Mutual Aid.

This summer, too, is past. The rustling of shriveled poplar leaves on the balcony, a sad sound, no matter how one may love autumn. So this is to be the autumn—you think, and in Charlotte's words: Knock on wood!—in which the flow of this narrative shall come to an end: an error, as it later turns out. Charlotte would knock on wood, or on her own forehead. 1974. The sixth autumn after her death. Her death became an indisputable fact when she returned the small transistor radio to you, and the books that you had taken to her in the hospital, and said in a tone that no longer allowed contradiction: There are more important things. After that, she turned completely inward.

Autumn, which presents us with our weaknesses one by one, and which uncovers, more relentlessly than other seasons, the web of habits in which we are caught. You begin to question yourself about all the things you'll never know, because you're not equipped to learn about them. When these conversations start, Lenka pushes her chair back and leaves the table. She won't tolerate it when her parents speak about getting older, which intimates that she, too, perceives aging as an impairment. She just doesn't wish to know that the impairment progresses even if one doesn't acknowledge it. She asks if the two of you really succeed in thinking everything through to the end, every condition in the world. If those people who don't rack their brains about it aren't better off, shouldn't one let them be?

Charlotte Jordan was as old as you are now when she moved with her children and parents into a room at a hotel in the village of Grünheide near Nauen. She must have been absolutely certain of one thing: in the months ahead, there would be dying in great numbers. And she must have made up her mind: Not my children. I'll pull them through. That's what she did, and nothing else.

Why are you crying now? It must be the autumn, the enfeebled autumn, which causes a single line of poetry, which you read as you're standing by the window, to fill your eyes with tears: "Alas, brave brothers, off into exile!" Veiled with tears, you see the yellow poplar leaves, while the birch still perseveres, green. "There is neither pure light / nor shadow in one's memories." Neruda, the poet, dead for one autumn, one winter, one spring, and one summer. "Up to the empty ledges / through broken doors the wind had come / and caused oblivion's eyes to dance."

But you don't weep for him. You weep for everything that will one day sink into oblivion—not only after you and with you, but from you yourself while you're still here. For the gradual but inexorable loss of that magic which used to enhance things and human beings, freeing them from aging. For the waning of the excitement derived from exaggeration, which creates truth, reality, fullness. For the shrinking of curiosity. The weakening of the potential for love. The impairment of eyesight. The choking of the most ardent desires. The strangulation of unrestrained hope. The relinquishing of despair and rebellion. The muting of joy. The inability to be surprised. For the failing of the senses of smell and taste, and—incredible as it seems—for the inevitable decline of longing. And ultimately, acknowledged with hesitation, for the fading of the eagerness to work. Late-summer decline.

Once you took a side trip to Grünheide to survey certain localities from the period of the past which is being dealt with here: Grünheide near Nauen, the place to which the Bohnsack truck had been directed, for the time being, from Wittenberge on the Elbe. One leaves the main road a few miles past Nauen. The exit is marked correctly. A drive over a poor dirt road. It struck you as more and more incomprehensible that these places should be accessible to you today, places that belonged to "those times." Those early places existed for you not only in a different time, but also in a different country. Though you hadn't thought of it for a long time, you had actually walked after the war only through towns whose Lenin and Stalin Boulevards you hadn't known as Adolf-Hitlerstrasse and Hermann-Göringstrasse. You wouldn't have liked to have run into a teacher, while taking a walk, whom Nelly used to greet with the Hitler salute, and to whom she'd now have to say good day. And when the local people—in the new towns to which you moved every few years—showed you the cooperative department store with the remark "Formerly Wertheim," you couldn't help feeling superior, secretly and unjustifiedly.

Grünheide is a dilapidated village. It's obvious when you see the front of the hotel ZUR GRÜNEN LINDE—the Linden Hotel—which is closed nearly all the time now. You couldn't even get a glass of apple juice there. The linden trees in front are still disfigured by the same spherical clipping that kept them from darkening the windows in the room on the second floor in which Nelly and her mother, brother, and grandparents were "accommodated." It still seems strange that Liesbeth and Alfons Radde had again sought quarters in the same house. Evidently each of the two sisters, Liesbeth and Charlotte, secretly considered the other incapable of coping without her, in these times. Which each could then, on occasion, blame on the other.

The room must have been spacious. The floor, which Nelly often had to scrub—you may be poor, said Charlotte, but that doesn't mean you have to live in a pigsty—the floor consisted of rough boards that absorbed water and splintered along the edges. The five beds were set up all along the walls. In the middle was the big, crude wooden table on which the meals were served to the family, including Aunt Liesbeth, Uncle Alfons, and Cousin Manfred, who had their own, smaller room next door. In the corner by the window stood the box of canned milk and the butter tub for the family—and for strangers, provided they had something of value to offer in exchange.

Nelly found her situation oddly familiar. She knew from way back that one can be under a magic spell, but she was a little surprised—as anybody would be—that this could happen to her. At that time she had no doubts, deep down, that luck was with her, that she was bound to be lucky in the long run. She took it unemotionally that the school in Nauen—to which Charlotte had sent her children right away as a sign that order had returned to their lives—had been bombed on the very day when they couldn't attend because of a breakdown in railroad traffic. No it wasn't her fate to be buried under the debris of a school.

At this moment the fire sirens have been sounding for a long time in the neighboring village; shortly after, the horns of several fire engines can be heard from the main road. It goes without saying that you—people of your age—are still petrified at the sound of a siren. Again—paler, of course, than in the first years after the war—again you go down the cellar steps, half asleep, where the dank coolness of the air-raid shelter, the onetime beer cellar, constricts your chest. Again the vicious motor noise of the bomber formations, and—Uncle Alfons Radde measured the time on his stopwatch: Now!—the detonation in nearby Berlin, where, according to Charlotte, only debris and dead bodies were left to be whirled about. (Lenka says that this is what she can imagine least of all: to be faced with one's own death night after night. This may be the ultimate generation gap: the experience that one can be threatened with death and still not die, not commit crimes, not go mad.)

Nelly, just sixteen, is to have another scant two months in which she is allowed to believe in her invulnerability. Then it's high time for a low-flying American to put an end to this twilight state, once and for all, with a few well-aimed—but then again not too well-aimed—volleys from his aircraft's machine gun. Up to then, Nelly spends her evenings sitting at the end of the table in front of her diary, and puts down in writing—there can be no doubt about it, even though the diary is lost as a document—her decision to keep absolute, lasting faith in the Führer, even during hard times. With Eve, an evacuee from Berlin of the same age, who has lived in the Grünen Linde for a longer time, she crouches at night in a corner of the air-raid shelter, and enters the first lines of songs in a green notebook, songs that are dear to both of them and that they don't want to forget, even if there's no opportunity to sing them right now: battle songs, Hitler Youth songs. They sing in harmony: "The moon has now arisen."

The Western Allies have now crossed the Rhine. ("The Rhine, Germany's river, not Germany's border!") The Führer had given the order—about which Nelly had not been informed—that every single installation concerning traffic, news, industry, public utilities had to be destroyed upon retreat. Nelly would have been hurt to the quick had she known about the Führer's pronouncement, which equated the loss of the war with the downfall of the nation: since the best had fallen, there was no need to show consideration for the inferiors who were left. Meanwhile, Nelly was wondering how she could join a Werewolf group, about which she had heard rumors: an indication that she was wishing to escape the grim reality by acts of desperation.

About this time, Charlotte Jordan took her daughter, Nelly—for protection and companionship—on a somewhat dangerous trip to search for Bruno Jordan, husband and father.

How much of your present experiences will be worth remembering in twenty years? Which of today's images will be impressed on the memory, as indelibly as the layout of the army barracks under the Brandenburg firs, where Nelly learns that the most commonplace can be so menacing as to take your breath away?

Stalag stands for "Stammlager"—main army camp. Charlotte was familiar with the name of the sergeant major from whom she could expect to get information about her husband's fate. They asked for him and found him quickly. It seemed ominous: the overly hasty friendliness of everybody—from the captain on down. Hastily, with exaggerated courteousness, they were passed from one unqualified person to the next, until they were sitting on two wooden chairs in an orderly room, and the lance corporal, a gray-haired man with a heavy limp, had hurriedly and obligingly left the room to call for the sergeant major. What was wrong with Charlotte and Nelly that made people run from them?

No room that you might enter today could instill such a feeling of ominousness as the drab barracks where Nelly and her mother sat in silence, for minutes, until Charlotte, who could never keep her hunches to herself, put into words what Nelly, too, was thinking: Your father is dead.

That's what the sergeant major, a portly, jovial man, believed too, it was only too obvious. But he had—which could hardly be expected under the circumstances—no official killed-in-action certificate in his possession, let alone the identification tag, the paybook, and the watch of the deceased. He did have a watch on his person? the sergeant major asked, and Charlotte Jordan, as if it mattered, answered truthfully: "Yes." Only too understandable that the sergeant major preferred to contact war widows in writing, instead of dealing in person with a comrade's wife—that's what he called Charlotte several times—whose status, war widow or no, was still uncertain, and from whom one could expect any minute that she'd become aware of her situation and start to cry.

What he could do for her was produce the witness. The office lance corporal was already bringing him. He was a private of the detachment which had guarded the French prisoners, and which had been under the command of noncommissioned officer Bruno Jordan. The man was the only one who had managed to escape on that early morning in the village of Liebenau, when machine-gun fire strafed the main street and drove all of them, prisoners as well as their guards, who would themselves be prisoners in the next minute, into the nearest village houses. The fast Russian advance in the north, you know. The soldier had last seen her husband, his commanding noncommissioned officer Bruno Jordan—whom he called a "great guy"—running into a house. Doubled over, like that (he demonstrated), his arms folded over his stomach.

As if he'd been hit in the stomach, Charlotte said.

And the soldier: That's about it.

From then on, Charlotte Jordan considered her husband dead; at least that's what she claimed, what she blurted out, crying, to the young daughter-in-law of the Linde hotelkeeper, who let them in late at night: Frau Krüger, my husband is dead! Oh, my God, Frau Jordan, come in and sit down.

Nelly saw the two women embrace, saw the older one, her mother, rest her head on the shoulder of the younger, and she, Nelly—as had become the custom at catastrophes—was the mute bystander, unable to show emotion. She knew her mother didn't really believe that her father was dead. But she, Nelly, did. And that was reprehensible. It was possible he was still alive, the sergeant major had said so, too; there was a fifty-fifty chance, they should always keep that in mind. Nelly clung to the darker fifty. A father who had first thrown away his belt, then—the fleeing soldier had seen this, too—one of the French prisoners had ripped the noncommissioned officer's insignia from his shoulders in one jerk (that was Jean, the teacher, he may possibly have wanted to save your husband, Frau Jordan!); a father who had raised his hands, and then, suddenly doubling over, raced into the nearest farmhouse, his hands pressed to his stomach: such a father had to be dead. On one level, beyond thought yet penetrated by a feeling of self-suspicion, Nelly was realizing that he had to be dead, and why. She slept long and soundly. Her mother cried all through the night and the following day, but she, Nelly, sat down in the afternoon with a book by the window, slurped sweet condensed milk by the spoonful, and read. She was disgusted with herself, but she was completely calm, the way one is calm when one has reached the end of one's misdeeds and can go no further. She learned that it's a sin to be a bystander, and how sweet this sin can be. A lesson she never forgot, nor the temptation.

It was more than a year later, in a different place, when she received, as if by a miracle, the first postcard from prisoner of war Bruno Jordan, from a forest camp near Minsk. Only then does she break down and sob inconsolably, only then does she realize that she had been mourning, and how deeply. And that it should be possible to forgive oneself.

It had, in fact, been Jean the teacher who had ripped off Bruno Jordan's shoulder insignia when the first Russian commands could be heard from the edge of the village, after the surprise machine-gun attack. Officer, run! he's supposed to have shouted, and later, in the cellar of the house into which they had run, bent over but not hit, Jean, the teacher from a little village near Paris, had posted himself in front of the German, the former noncommissioned officer who had commanded the guard detachment in charge of the prisoners of war, and who therefore was to be killed on the spot by a Soviet commando. Nicht! said Jean, who knew a little German but no Russian. Guter Mann! he said. The Russian understood the little word "gut"—good—of all words in the whole German vocabulary, and lowered the machine gun. Or else he knew how to read the Frenchman's face.

A strange series of coincidences had saved Bruno Jordan's life, among them, in the first place, the fact that he himself as a young man had experienced the sufferings of a prisoner of war and that this experience had rendered him incapable of mistreating other prisoners.

What remains to be reported, to round off the picture, is that Bruno Jordan—perhaps only this one time in his life—was given the opportunity to experience something like tragedy. He himself would never call it that, the word wasn't part of his vocabulary. He said: Just try to imagine: you're driven past your own house in a truck, as a prisoner! You crane your neck to get a glimpse of your family, but you can see nobody, and for the next two years and seven months you don't know where they are. Whether they're even alive. Then you're being kept a prisoner in the factory where you yourself had to guard prisoners before. Just try to think what that means.

Toward the end, before their transport east, the prisoners were housed in the barracks of I. G. Farben, which had previously been occupied by the Volhynia Germans. On that Sunday morning in 1971, Lutz said: Let's drive toward I. G. Farben. You had shown Lenka the Concordia Church, also the hospital, which in Nelly's memory had been large, white, and threatening, and which in reality was an insignificant gray building still sprinkled with shell holes.

I. G. Farben meant: up the former Friedeberger Chaussee in the direction of the Old Cemetery, in the direction of the State Hospital for the Insane. In a few sentences, without too much detail, you told the story of mad Aunt Dottie. It turned out that Lutz didn't know how she had been put to death. What, after all, had Aunt Dottie meant to him? A rumor, an ambiguous whispering among adults. Now, thirty years later, she became for all of you an unfortunate human being, the victim of a verdict which she hadn't been able to escape.

Pretty insane, the whole thing, said Lenka. Or don't you think it is?

15

What are we to do with the things that are engraved in our memories.

That is not a question but an exclamation, perhaps a cry for help. The things for which we require help tell more about us than other things.

A few days ago—after you'd read Chapter 11 at a public reading in Switzerland—a man came up to you, a German: I just wanted to tell you, I belong to your generation and I can't cope with the guilt from those days. He had trouble finding the sleeve of his overcoat, trouble controlling his face—a robust man, there was nothing soft about him—and his young companion, a foreigner, looked at him with a mixture of pity and fear. A few days later someone stood up in the audience, also a contemporary, from Southern Germany, to judge by his accent, and asked if the writing profession shouldn't finally abandon dutiful exercises on Auschwitz and instead acquaint the youth with the subtler methods and dangers of Fascism. He was vehemently contradicted by an almost white-haired man with a still youthful face, another contemporary.

It was this man who later told you in private that he had left Germany with his Jewish parents when he was seven. He had a business in the medium-size Swiss town, where coincidence had now brought the two of you together. He said he never again wanted to set foot on German soil. However, at one point, at the suggestion of friends, he had nonetheless taken a train to the Netherlands which passed through West Germany. Even the way in which the train waiter had called out the word "Beer!" in the corridor had seriously disturbed him: something about the man's intonation; he couldn't explain it. He had gotten off at Cologne, his hometown, and walked through the streets. He kept waiting for some kind of emotion, a pain, a feeling of loss, perhaps. He had felt nothing whatsoever. He had carefully avoided shaking hands with people of a certain age, since he wasn't sure what they might have done with their hands. Now his decision was final: he'd never set foot on German soil again, if he could help it. This was, incidentally, the first time he had told his decision to a German. You tell him that people like him had been as indispensable to you as daily bread during the years after the war. I know, he said. I know. You shake hands: you'll never see each other again. You catch up with him at the door. You tell him that, where you live, nobody could have called writing about Auschwitz a "dutiful exercise" in public. I hope not, he says. I hope not, at least not in public.

It was obvious that they were surrounded, but Nelly didn't see that at all. She had her reasons for believing the armed-forces news bulletins and the Führer's sentence: Berlin will remain German, Vienna will become German again, and Europe will never turn Bolshevik. In your probably deceitful memory this sentence came over the radio on the same Sunday that the Jordan family sought cover under their dinner table because bombs were exploding nearby—bombs which were, at this point, being transported to Berlin, above their heads, "shamelessly," according to Charlotte Jordan, in broad daylight.

To this day you're unable to remember the names of military figures and commanders of battles, or to understand their strategy.

It may perhaps be a sign of a reprehensible lack of interest, considering that, in those days, our private lives were bound up with the strategic maps of the general staffs and military leaders, and that the minutest deviation from roads marked as "escape routes" (which were, of course, unknown to the refugees) meant certain death. The Twelfth Army, under General Wenck, Hitler's last attempt, was unable to carry out its orders: to take the pressure off the Reich's capital. There is no indication that Nelly had, at the time, ever heard the general's name, not any more than the names Heinrici, Tippelskirch—the alternating commanders of the Army Group Weichsel in the north of Berlin. Their decisions cut directly into Nelly's life: the first, by trying to stop the Soviet divisions which had broken through at Prenzlau; the other, by trying to lead the troops and the "fleeing members of the population" back behind the closed "front-line" Bad Doberan—Parchim—Wittenberg, by May 2.

It must have been near Parchim then, and not near Neustadt-Glewe (as you had long thought, based on a 1959 road atlas), that the chaotic last crossing of a river—the Elde—took place. This, more than anything that had happened before, deserved the term "flight." Those were the weeks when one had to expect that bridges would blow up and everything on them would fly into the air, to avoid their falling into enemy hands. The bridge at Parchim was in immediate danger of being occupied by the Russians, which would have cut off the escape route to the Elbe, not only for the totally disintegrated military units, but for the fleeing civilian population as well. Herr and Frau Folk's two mares, brown Rosa and the almost coal-black Minka with the white forehead, had foaled shortly before the hasty departure from the Herminenaue estate; the foals had been shot, despite the objection of the Pole Tadeusz, called Tadde, who took care of the horses. The two mares soon appeared to be showing signs of blindness after being whipped through the swampy terrain that led to the bridge (the driver's hideous screaming while he forced the mares to strain against their harness until their veins protruded arm-thick from their necks). This is not your memory, but that of your brother, Lutz, who had just begun to learn how to groom horses and discovered that he "had a feel" for them. He felt sorry, therefore, that the two beautiful mares were going blind, and the detail stuck in his memory.

You're comparing dates. In Lutz's opinion, the second departure of the Jordan family, i.e., the flight from Grünheide, took
place on the evening of April 20, in other words, on the Führer's
birthday. That would be an ironic coincidence. But after you told
Lutz that the Americans hadn't occupied Schwerin and Wismar
before May 2, he didn't exclude the possibility that the Jordans
might have taken to the road one or two days after April 20, but in
any case, before April 25. Because on April 25, the front units of
Generals Zhukov and Konev met in Ketzin near Nauen. This also
entailed the occupation, by Soviet units, of the hamlet of Grünheide
—whose remaining inhabitants were to fare badly—and the closing of the circle around the German capital.

You talk about the second flight as you take a wrong northeast
turn onto a street behind Concordia Church which leads into the
main street (it seems to be new; you come upon Polish soldiers
engaged in street construction, lively young faces, bare brown
torsos). Today, toward the end of 1974, you couldn't recall that
hot Sunday in July 1971 without the notes you took then. You find
yourselves in the back of the former plant of a branch of I. G.
Farben, today a synthetic fiber plant which has been considerably
expanded. You compare memories before you ask H. to make a U-
turn. That wasn't the street you'd had in mind. You find the correct street that leads into the former Friedeberger Chaussee, which
runs northeast at a steeper angle than you had assumed; a kind of
sunken road at first—it cuts through the southern sweep of the end
moraine—and after one reaches the plateau, it offers an open view
to the left and to the right. Gnarled cherry trees on both sides.
Before Friedeberg, which neither of you ever set eyes on, there
used to be two equally unfamiliar villages: Stolzenberg and Alten-
fliess, today called Rózanki and Przyłck, names which you spell out
from the map and which prompt no association. Now, you said.
Now you can see the former guesthouse of I. G. Farben on the left,
and on the right the red brick building of the plant. Drive slowly,
please. Yes, the old cemetery over here on the right, and immediately next to it the park in which the old houses of the former State
Hospital for the Insane can be seen through the trees.

The Führer's proclamation which prophesied to the Soviet
troops that they would run into "the old fate of Asia" outside the
walls of the German capital, and that "the Bolshevik assault would

be drowned in a bloodbath," didn't reach the Jordans. That same evening they had loaded a pushcart with a couple of suitcases and sacks of bedding, and taken to the road once more. Five of them, Nelly, her mother, her brother, and her grandparents; on foot this time. Aunt Liesbeth and Uncle Alfons Radde with Cousin Manfred followed with a pushcart of their own. Uncle Alfons Radde's truck was no longer at their disposal, one evening he had come back without it: roadblocks, intended for the first Soviet tanks, had also stopped his vehicle. It's madness, he said, outraged, how am I to explain that to Bohnsack? At any rate, for their second flight, the Raddes themselves had to make do with a pushcart; local people who didn't want to leave traded it for butter from Charlotte Jordan's little tub.

They set out toward evening. Lutz convincingly informs you all that he no longer believed in Germany's victory then. A feeling for facts can already be developed in a twelve-year-old. You of course —he said to his sister—needed stronger medicine. You ponder that, trying to remember. If Nelly had ever been in danger of going off the deep end, it must have been that night. Desperation was not the proper expression for it, because, to be able to despair, indicates a connection with the cause of the desperation. Nelly was no longer connected with anything. The road on which she was walking—in the dark, the sky flared red to the east and the south, in the direction of Nauen, leaving only two directions open to them, if open was the word for it—the road on which she was walking, stumbling, getting stuck, was the outermost edge of reality. The circumference of the thoughts she was still allowed to think had shrunk to a dot: to get through. She realized, with her body more than with her brain, that if that dot ceased to be, she would plunge over the edge. Since all outside commands had broken down, she had to adhere even more strictly to something within, which perhaps prevented her from going stark raving mad on the spot.

You had to let your brother's statement pass.

The only German names one finds in the once-German town of L. are the names of the dead. Lenka would rather not venture into the thicket which the old cemetery has become. What for, she says. But there are footpaths, although they're overgrown with nettles and other weeds. All things grow lush in cemeteries, Lutz says. And you all try to convince Lenka that she shouldn't miss out on the opportunity of visiting a cemetery in which no human being has been buried in twenty-six years. She says she isn't the least bit curious.

You know what she's afraid of: you might be annoyed (or, more accurately, hurt), not only because the cemetery has been neglected—which is natural—but because it has been destroyed. Neither of you says a word, but what kind of words are forming inside you? You watch yourself closely and discover that you're slightly upset, and that you're grieving, a feeling you'd like to trace.

All the tombstones on which the words "Rest in Peace" or "Faith, Hope, Charity, these three. But the greatest of these is Charity" have been cut into the sandstone or chiseled into marble, and gold-leafed: all of them, almost all, have been tipped over. The swords of the sandstone angels outside the family vaults are broken off, as are their wings, their noses. The mounds of the graves are at a level with the ground, and overgrown. People whose ancestors aren't lying in this cemetery use the paths which run through this wilderness as shortcuts to their jobs. You meet no one. It's a Sunday morning.

You'll never again find the grave of the only relative who lies buried in this cemetery, your great-grandmother, a certain Caroline Meyer. Nelly visited the grave only once or twice, with her paternal grandmother, Heinersdorf Grandma. You remember that even then it was completely overgrown with ivy, and on the simple tombstone the almost illegible line: Yet is their strength then but labor and sorrow. Each time, Heinersdorf Grandma would read the line in a soft voice, sigh, and say: Remember that, my daughter. It's the truth.

You think that Caroline Meyer's peace will not be disturbed, even if her stone has been tipped over and is now lying alongside her head. Fortunately, there is no risk of the dead being resurrected. If there were, you thought, you wouldn't want to be the one to explain to them why the deeds which the living committed against another people should have been avenged on their own dead: because they had driven another people into gas chambers and fueled ovens with them and forced them to kneel down in mass graves by the thousands, graves which they had dug themselves, so that the blood oozed from the earth when everything was finally covered over, and the soil began to move in certain spots, because not everyone was completely dead.

Now you understand the reason for your upset and your grief: it was not for the dead in this cemetery with their German names, but for those living, those survivors, who had felt compelled to come here and uproot the stones, and trample on the graves; because a hatred such as the one that had been kindled within them cannot be contained, doesn't stop at a grave. You were rarely as conscious of the complete turnabout of your feelings as during that half hour in the old German cemetery in L., today G.; it must have taken years of the greatest effort to accomplish this turnabout (which took so much out of us that we no longer had the strength to look back): free, unforced empathy for the "others." You could see by Lenka's face that she needed no help to understand.

It was probably you who discovered the opulent and, incidentally, perfectly preserved tombstone of baker Otto Wernicke. Did Lutz remember the name of the baker on Soldinerstrasse? Wasn't his name Wernicke? Lutz asked. You both remembered that he had died during the last years before the end of the war, the tombstone said 1943. My God, Baker Wernicke! He was rarely seen in his shop. His wife had dyed auburn hair. Now, in front of his tombstone, we think of those two people. We never bought bread from them, only cake. Bruno Jordan sold bread in his own store.

You don't know if Nelly used to dream during those years; you know even less what kind of dreams. (Lenka reported that, during the night in the Polish hotel, she had dreamed that she had smuggled herself into a distinguished party at court, clad in her faded jeans and shirt, that she had been the first to eat the exquisite cold buffet, casually, before the arrival of the royal family, and that her offense against this taboo had given her power and prestige, both of which she had used to introduce a young man and his girlfriend, simple people, into the august society from which she herself had fled when she noticed pieces of a rococo costume on her body, and caught herself behaving according to etiquette.) Nelly may have dreamed dreams of annihilation or of omnipotence, perhaps in alternation.

(You would like to be able to report about this more than about other things, because it occupies a most intimate region, a region which cannot be conquered with one determined leap over the hedge. The unadmitted hope that, after an appropriate number of years, the thorny hedge would one day transform itself into a sea of flowers, through which one strolls unimpeded, in order to awaken truth from its "one-hundred-year-long enchantment." Your only alternative is to continue your report as faithfully as possible.) The figures with whom Nelly and her family found themselves face to face on the first morning after their second flight were Herr and Frau Folk.

You can still see them, you can describe them, which is risky, because they seem too much like the image we have today of estate owners east of the Elbe: he, apoplectic, completely clad in loden, a hat with a tuft of mountain-goat hair stuck to the band, and a cane; she more distinguished, with a pursed mouth, her hair in a plain bun, with a female dachshund named Bee-Bee constantly wagging her tail against her mistress's legs. For all these years you had been convinced that the estate belonged to the Folks . . . on whose grounds you had found shelter for a night—in Herminenaue, named after a Prussian court lady who had retired to this place at one point in her life. In the morning, the Folks had the refugees line up, sleepy, unwashed, and of course hungry, and checked them for their potential usefulness. Nelly was aware of the look in their eyes, to which she immediately responded with rebellion. She wasn't used to being inspected for her value as a worker. But the Folks had only this cold-blooded scrutiny for persons of lower rank. The assumption that they had been the owners of Herminenaue turned out to be false.

Only recently did the agronomists in charge of the Herminenaue Research Institute for Fodder Plants tell you the name of the former owner of the estate, who had known the Folks, who had come from farther away and had found shelter in Herminenaue for a couple of days, together with their household. The shots which they all heard that morning, and which spurred them to extreme haste, were indeed rifle shots, but not from Soviet troops, as you all had assumed, but from a Polish unit which had been trying for days and with heavy losses to push through the German units that were still massively concentrated in this spot. With Soviet reinforcement the Poles eventually succeeded, though there were continued heavy losses on both sides. The laying of foundations for the two-thousand-head dairy farm, which now occupies the grounds of the former estate, unearthed masses of skeletons, all unidentifiable. A peasant from the village, whose name you're told, had walked across the battlefield at the time and taken the identification tags off all the corpses, regardless of their nationality, and sent them to the International Red Cross. Until 1949, the estate was under Soviet administration and served as the supply base for the occupation troops. Then it became public property; today it is a well-known center for the raising of meat and dairy cattle, and crossing breeds. The brood cows in the pastures are named Diet, Carnation, Flame, while the two thousand dairy cows inside the plant are identified only by the final digit of a four-digit number; because of the risk of infection, you're allowed only a brief peek through the door, and you see them standing dully in their rotating milking stalls.

The agronomists showed you the spots where the refugee barracks had stood. The mansion is light stucco, that's accurate. Nelly probably never saw it from the front, with its full-length porch; she and her family had reached the house from the back, and in pitch-dark night at that.

The Folks were looking for a driver for their fodder wagon. Uncle Alfons Radde was being considered. Of course he knew how to drive a vehicle, provided the eight persons who composed his family found space on it. (For the second time, he became the savior of his relatives.)

The inspecting glances appraised the situation.

Bon, Herr Folk finally said, but no baggage.

With our bare skin, Nelly thought, and it gave her a touch of incomprehensible satisfaction.

Impossible, said the grownups.

After a hasty, vehement discussion back and forth, the lighter luggage was stowed in the wagon on which the sacks of fodder lay, the heavy suitcases on one of the two pushcarts, whose shaft was tied to the rear axle of the large wagon by a strong rope. The picture was ridiculous, but that wasn't the issue. In times such as these, a sense of comedy is sheer luxury. Besides, they would slowly follow the Folks' trek, together with the ox cart, which was transporting more fodder and the seven members of farm worker Grund's family.

The one at the end'll be a sitting duck, Whiskers Grandpa said. They asked him for God's sake to be quiet. They had entered Herminenaue during the night and were leaving it at dawn; it had hardly left an impression.

Nelly's brother Lutz had begun to show an interest in horses. Nelly sat in the back of the open wagon on a feed sack. It seems to you that the weather must have been mostly beautiful, although the soggy terrain before the bridge would appear to contradict that. (It may have been the thawed ground.) One always remembers the quality of the sky. Nelly told herself that she would remember this kind of sky: delicate and blue. Also, the evening when a shot was aimed at her for the first time, as she carried a basin with washed dishes from a farmhouse across the street to the barn in which they were spending the night. Her mother dragged her inside the nearest house. You remember Nelly's pride when it turned out that not a single plate had been broken: she wasn't one of those who simply dropped whatever she was holding, just because there was shooting going on. Precisely for that reason she was severely reprimanded by her mother: the next time she should never mind the dishes, or whatever else, and run for cover. As if Nelly had cared about the dishes. (Most reluctantly she begins to learn: every human being is vulnerable, including herself. A lesson which has a lasting effect.)

Route 5 runs northwest, via Friesack, Kyritz, and Perleberg. The Folks' trek must have gotten off the road at Kyritz, and taken Route 103 as far as Pritzwalk, and from there side roads (Triglitz, Lockstadt, Putlitz, Siggerkow), in order to reach Parchim, the bridge across the Elde, the dividing line between hell and heaven, life and death.

The many times you've driven along that road since, even in the spring you've never recognized anything. One quickly learns to see a landscape as a terrain, to look at a bush, a tree, a hedge, as objects behind which to seek shelter in an emergency. That may be why the road at which Nelly had looked with different eyes later seemed unfamiliar to you. As a matter of fact, the road looks less and less favorable for hiding as you continue in a northerly direction, since wooded areas which are ideal for cover became rarer and rarer and were set farther back from the road.

You say to Lenka (who seems to think that things were "really happening" then, unlike today): What happened was that one's inner sense of time stopped. Yet Nelly maintained her outward appearance. Of course nobody noticed how she felt, since she was behaving in keeping with the circumstances, and nobody is curious about another's inner life when his own life is in danger.

Nelly lost interest in herself, since she felt nothing. Everything that happened to her was covered with a gloss of eerie strangeness. She, the motionless observer, cast an impenetrable shadow onto herself which, as shall be seen, was harder to dissolve than the pale furtive shadows of enemy planes overhead.

Anything that lasts long enough acquires the privilege of being called "chronic." Chronic conjunctivitis. Chronic fatigue. A chronic tendency to sadness in the evening. The chronic compulsion to work. (A full life: a life filled with work. Lenka shrugs, unable to understand.)

The chronic dependence on the flickering screen. The faces of three men, placed one beside the other, without any particular characteristics, Greeks. Torturers in the service of the fallen regime. They speak. What they're saying is something new: they've been turned into torturers by torture. The methods they were to use on others had first been tested on their own bodies. When, crazed with pain, their only wish became to ram the rifle that was hanging on the wall into the belly of the little sergeant who was beating them, then they themselves knew that they were ready, that they were ripe. Only the face of the one who couldn't bear the pain, who "collapsed" and was expelled from the army, shows traces of grief. The wife of one of the men who ordered the torture says (she is standing in the door to her house in her apron, behind her a half-dark hall, the entrance to the kitchen, the stove): I'm sure of one thing: he's a good man. What the newspapers say about him is a bunch of lies.

Chronic blindness. And the question cannot be: How can they live with their conscience?, but: What kind of circumstances are those that cause a collective loss of conscience?

It will be just about thirty years ago, this end of January 1975, that Soviet troops liberated the Auschwitz extermination camp. At the end of April 1945, Nelly—who is most probably heading in the direction of Neustadt-Glewe, on Route 191, after the successful crossing of the Elde at Parchim, since the crossing of the Elbe

at Boizenburg is the goal of all refugees—Nelly has not yet heard
the name Auschwitz. On April 21, the SS guard unit drove thirty-
five thousand prisoners from the Sachsenhausen concentration
camp, on a march that current history books call a death march.
On the road to Mecklenburg, almost ten thousand prisoners were
shot by the guards. Nelly's group preceded these marchers, who
were dragging along different roads, but in the same direction. She
didn't see any of the corpses; she doesn't know whether the inhabitants of the towns and villages, along whose roads they may
have lain, or the refugees who found them, gave them a hasty burial
or let them lie. Later, she saw survivors of the death march. But
her first corpse was the farm worker Wilhelm Grund.

Herr Folk says: Losses are of course unavoidable. The Grunds
in their slow ox cart always had to get on the road ahead of the
others. Lately, the low-flying planes had begun their activity in the
early-morning hours. Nelly was in the barn with the horses, she
heard machine-gun fire close by and pressed herself against the
wall. The horses hadn't been taught to control their fear and
reared. Horses' hooves and horses' bellies close to her eyes. She
probably screamed, like everybody else. Horses never needlessly
step on a human body, supposedly, but she didn't doubt that this
kind of rule belonged to a different life. These horses wouldn't
hesitate to trample her to death in their terror.

Suddenly an unnatural silence fell outside the door of the barn.
And it was Gerhard Grund, the son of the farm worker who drove
the ox cart, no older than Nelly, who was, incredibly, causing the
silence. Whoever looked in his face fell silent. Then he spoke, in a
changed voice. My father, he said. What have they done to my
father?

Losses are unavoidable. Nelly didn't see Wilhelm Grund's
corpse—a shell had apparently torn his chest. When she reached
the road, a blanket had been spread over him. For the first time,
Wilhelm Grund had, by his death, caused his master's affairs to
come to a halt instead of keeping them going, and this halt wasn't
allowed to last longer than half an hour. A shallow grave was dug
for him, at the edge of the woods. Two Polish laborers carried him
in a fodder tarpaulin, his body almost brushing the ground. He
might at least have deserved a coffin, whispered Frau Grund. Frau
Folk rested her delicate wilted hand on the shoulder of the field

worker's wife: It can't be helped. Frau Grund's eyes were water-clear, and stricken. It was a very beautiful day. A first shimmer of green on the trees and a "limpid" sky. A piercing scene.

The death of Gerhard Grund's father instilled in Nelly a feeling for which she found no expression, as though she had been wounded.

Last night you dreamed that H. tells you outright that you aren't able to describe a stack of corpses in every detail. You agree instantly, without thinking. He says that's the least an author of this century ought to be able to do. You aren't qualified for your profession.

Nelly saw stacks of corpses only in photographs or in films. As they were being doused with gasoline and burned, or else shoved together by a bulldozer, starved skeletons. In German newsreels only the enemy died.

A chronic tendency to have a guilty conscience. A writer's conscience—so it would seem—need concern itself solely with "the truth, the whole truth, and nothing but the truth." But since communication is inherent in the character of truth, he, often hesitantly, produces a truth that is bound in many respects: bound to himself, the reporter, and to the ever restricted freedom of outlook for which he has struggled; it is bound to the person about whom he reports and, not ultimately, to those at whom his report is aimed and who must be forewarned. The truth which reaches them cannot be "unadulterated," and they themselves will adulterate it further with their judgments and their prejudices. Only in this way is it useful.

For instance, few descriptions exist of "the flight." Why? Because the young men who later wrote books about their experiences had been soldiers? Or because there's something dubious about the subject? The term itself later disappeared. Refugees became relocated persons, an expression which accurately defines people who moved out of Polish and Czech areas in June 1945, but who had not fled (Nelly's Heinersdorf grandparents among them). Whereas Nelly and her relatives were fleeing toward Schwerin (and still called themselves refugees, years after the war) and thought they knew what they were fleeing from. If only we don't fall into the hands of the Russians, Whiskers Grandma said. She'd never seen a Russian in her life. What image did she have when she said "the Russians"? What did Nelly think? What did she see? The blood-dripping monster on the jacket of the book *Socialism Betrayed*? The filmstrips with herds of Soviet prisoners—shorn heads, emaciated numb faces, tatters, torn rags on their feet, a dragging step—people who didn't seem to belong to the same species as their strapping German guards?

Or had she no image at all? Was the sinister-mysterious word "rape" enough to turn her ready fears into sheer terror? (The Russians rape all German women: an undoubted truth. A girl who is not able to preserve her innocence. A dark struggle of bodies, and certainly: pain and shame, and after that: inescapable death. No German woman lives through that. Another link in the chain that ties physical love to fear.)

As a matter of fact, Nelly is lucky. She's not crouching in a cellar, in a parlor among stylish furniture; she can't crawl into a hideout or stick her head in the sand. She has to be out in the open, to see and hear with her own ears and eyes. She's forced to see the soldier who's washing his torso at the pump, beside one of the red Mecklenburg farmhouses, to hear him call out to the passing refugees, in an unconcerned tone: Have you heard? Hitler's dead.

Another limpid day that made no attempts at shrouding itself in darkness. A new thought. The end of the world didn't mean one's own death. She was alive. It was surely shameful, but also interesting. But it wouldn't be decided for a long time whether she would destroy herself with depression—grieving for her worst enemy—or if she would succeed in developing her atrophied faculties to interpret experience properly and survive. For a long time, for years, the struggle wavered, undecided, even after she herself thought that it had been decided in her favor. (How did we become what we are today?)

The road as a classroom. Once, Nelly saw dreadfully emaciated women in prison clothes squatting along the roadside, relieving themselves, their bare buttocks turned to the road, indifferent to whoever might be passing by. They've lost all shame, Whiskers Grandma said, betraying a horrible understanding by the word "lost." Nelly keenly felt the shame those women had lost. Why didn't the guards—men—turn away at least? she asked herself. They, too, seemed to have lost all shame, but not in the same way as the women. Could it be that there existed two types of shame, from the beginning?

Nobody said a word about the women, whom they passed (forever passing) as though they didn't exist. Their eyes had been trained to look the other way, they hastily withdrew. It's easier to forget what one didn't see, almost didn't see. The stockpile of the forgotten was growing.

Shortly thereafter Nelly herself saw the Polish drivers lay down the reins—it was rumored that the Americans were close in front and the Russians close behind—jump from the wagons, and walk off in the opposite direction: east, forward for them, because it was the direction of their homeland. She watched Herr Folk burst into a rage, and lift his arm as though to strike, by force of habit. She saw one of the Poles take hold of his arm. She saw that the Germans, farm workers most of them, didn't come to Herr Folk's aid. The remarkable thing about the incident was the calm in which it took place. Nelly couldn't help feeling that what was happening was right. Only later did it surprise her that the Poles had shown so little triumph. At the time it didn't strike her as strange that the victors weren't shouting for joy. In her own depressed state, the fact that those people had survived hardly seemed a cause for their rejoicing. The tone in which her mother spoke of survival held no happy prospects: Out of the frying pan into the fire, she said.

In opposition to the persistent meteorological order, an unbelievable disorder was spreading on the roads: the chaotically fleeing Germans rid themselves of their ballast. For years afterward, Nelly dreamed of landscapes that were choking under thick layers of paper; from office paraphernalia to machine guns, all the equipment of a modern army was tossed, placed, discarded along the roadside. A laying bare of the innards. Nobody looked. All our tax money, said Whiskers Grandpa, who had become very quiet. Don't talk about what you don't know! Alfons Radde, his son-in-law, yelled at him.

If that had been the criterion for conversation, everybody would have had to shut up.

It was bright noon when they ran across the concentration-camp men. To the left of the road lay a sparse wood, on the right a low grass slope. How they knew that these men were from Oranienburg can no longer be established. The former inmates were not joyful; some were standing, crouching, or lying in the wooded area at a certain distance from the road, others had taken up positions on the grass, holding rifles pointed toward the road. Those on the grass must have been the stronger ones, those who were still able to carry a rifle and stand with it. They either couldn't speak or didn't feel like it. When Nelly later asked herself about the expression in their eyes, she thought it had mostly been indifference, coldness actually, and also vigilance. At any rate, neither hatred nor joy.

You're not in a position to make any other statement about the attitude of those men, except that it surprised Nelly. However, surprise was a trifling progress, a tiny ray of light, compared to the darkness of total otherness ("Those people aren't like you or me") that had been Nelly's feeling up to then.

Lenka can't understand why nobody, not a single person among the refugees, went over to the almost completely starved figures and held out a piece of bread. Why nobody called out to them. Why they remained silent and didn't stop. They were afraid. Not fear due to guilt: guilt is not what one feels when one's own life is in danger. They first had to feel saved before they could be ready to pay a certain price for their skins. (Not everybody, naturally. It soon became apparent that all nations have their good and their bad people. To quote Uncle Alfons Radde, Uncle Walter Menzel, Aunt Trudy, the Aunts Liesbeth, Lucie, Olga: Everybody is always blaming the Germans. To quote Charlotte Jordan and Bruno Jordan, the only two among all their relatives who remained in the Soviet-occupied zone, the eventual German Democratic Republic, even after the division: "Those people will never learn.") Old people, your brother, Lutz, says. Don't ask too much of them. You're sitting on a bench on the side of the road between the Polish town of G., which you just visited, and Bruno Jordan's place of birth, which is a few miles away; you're eating cherries. You realize that that particular village is one of those rather prosperous roadside villages which are typical of this region. Rather lovely, actually. It's late Sunday morning, July 11, 1971, as has been said. You bought the cherries from a young blond fellow who was standing behind a plank table at the side of the road—jeans, open white shirt—the price was sixteen zloty, not according to weight but to bag size. No other place could have been more desirable. It may seem an exaggeration, but you still haven't forgotten the taste of those cherries. The word "refreshing" is appropriate, although mainly used for water and sleep. Those delicious fruits, which bestowed unimagined strength and magic powers upon the legendary heroes. You told no one what strength you longed for, or what magic powers.

At that moment, the whole trip was worthwhile.

A list of blessings: it was Lenka who started it. Everybody should name the blessings in his life. You immediately proposed placing the cherries at the top of the list, but your idea was rejected as being too "conditioned by the moment." You were, however, at liberty to place cherries, or whatever else you might fancy, on a personal list, at any spot you wished. "Eating" ranked high on the general list, as did "sleeping," "loving." (Lenka requested that loving be placed at the top, loving as an attitude not as an activity! And that it be followed by "hating." Hating as a blessing? Yes, indeed. Well, she was free to put that on her personal list.) Lenka wanted to include "living," at all costs. She quarreled with her uncle about whether "living" in the sense she had in mind added up to more than the sum of all activities, emotions, thoughts, conditions taken separately; in her opinion, these activities, emotions, thoughts, conditions didn't always prompt a person to "live." Lutz found that above his head.

He wanted to place "work" on the list of blessings. That was fine with H. and you, but Lenka protested vehemently. She preferred to enumerate types of work: painting, singing, playing with kids, but that would lead too far afield. She abstained. Then she proposed putting "music" very high toward the top, in giant letters, and all the seasons of the year, with the exception of November. But not to forget nature in general: rain! and the ocean, and swimming. And books. And her old worn-out plastic slippers. And theater, but only certain plays. And dancing, but only to certain bands (you made a fool of yourself, using the old-fashioned term "orchestra"). And her faded top. And her bed. And pictures. And, for heaven's sake, all the way at the top: friends.

It was getting out of hand. But at least one more, the most important of all: joy. Being friendly. By all means.

Lutz had dropped his attempts at categorizations. In June 1946 he was exactly Lenka's age, he went to school in a Mecklenburg village named Bardikow, and watched Farmer Freese's cows in the afternoons; at that time he'd have placed "bread" at the very top of his list, right after the longed-for return of his father. In January 1943, when Nelly was Lenka's age, she would have placed the favor of her teacher Julia Strauch at the top—that's not certain, but probable; and H.'s top blessing, when he was Lenka's age, in August 1943, would have been the forest. And being allowed to be alone. And reading.

Well, somehow you started talking about progress. Can progress be measured by such a "list of blessings"—a game, after all—as you all seem to be about to do? Your brother, Lutz, warned you not to ignore technical and scientific progress. He accused you of intellectual snobbery. In what way? Insofar as you're trying to make somewhat eccentric needs seem normal and don't give sufficient importance to the normal needs of average people. As though it were a disgrace to prefer a financially secure existence in a comfortable apartment with icebox, washing machine, and car to other things. As though all governments didn't try to take this need of the majority into account—they're better mass psychologists than the rest of you, said your brother, Lutz. (Perhaps Jehuda Bakon, who was in Auschwitz at the age of fourteen, would have started his list with being allowed to warm himself at the cremation ovens, a favor the guards sometimes granted to the children's column after they had finished work on the campgrounds.)

How did your conversation shift from the blessings of civilization to the Germans?

They weren't the only ones, said your brother, Lutz; all people could potentially be oppressed, kept in check by a system of terror, incited to war, driven to commit inhuman acts. He enumerated examples from the last fifty years of history. Heroes were scarce in all nations, a heroic conduct meant more than rising to the human norm. The masses keep silent, or play along. And the Nazis kept their worst horrors—the "euthanasia" program, the mass extermination of Jews—secret from their own population as much as possible. (That was true.) And why, did we think, had they taken the trouble?

Yes, why? you asked. Because they feared uprisings? A general strike? Or a gigantic campaign to rescue the Jews, as in Denmark?

Or passive resistance? At least the refusal to do duty in the extermination camps? (Jehuda Bakon, at fourteen—he could already draw—warmed himself at the extermination ovens, which had the nameplate of the German manufacturer durably fastened to one side, perhaps with a guarantee: I. TOPF, ERFURT.) Not that. None of that. But it would have caused a depressed mood, maybe also a certain shock, and of course fear. Don't imagine that all Germans were sadists, Lutz said.

(An Auschwitz survivor is asked his opinion of the character of the SS guards. He replies: It's hard to say anything about them. Only a few sadists, who stood out, of course, because it permitted them to indulge their tendency to the utmost. The others, some seven thousand altogether, I'd say: interchangeable.)

Do you by any chance believe, said Lutz, while you were finishing your bag of cherries, that our industrial civilization with all its comforts—which you, too, appreciate, unless I'm totally mistaken—is possible, that the conveyor belt—still the basis for it all—is possible, and that on top of everything, it's still possible to have "good human beings" as a mass phenomenon? Don't kid yourselves.

Charlotte's utterances, which became darker and more numerous after their encounter with the liberated concentration-camp inmates, may possibly have been the brimming over of an uneasy conscience. In Nelly's environment, Charlotte was almost the only person equipped with the prerequisite for a conscience: the possibility to be sensitive toward people who didn't belong to her own narrow circle. What were the things she said? She'd say: Blessed be he who, free of guile, retains the pure soul of a child. Or she'd say: Do not unto others . . . She was losing weight. She fastened her skirt with a large black safety pin, she no longer wore her hair in a stylish twist, she wasn't dyeing it any longer, it rapidly turned gray, and she pulled it straight into a bun at the back of her head; thick veins stood out on her bony legs. Thus she strode darkly beside the wagon.

Nelly felt her mother becoming estranged from her by the fate she categorically refused to share: a good-looking vivacious woman of forty-five changed into a withered gray-haired hag in the span of a year. (Hyperactive thyroid was the medical explanation for the disastrous change, of which there exists no photographic proof, of course, only precise images of memory; but the medical explanation didn't explain the most important thing: what it was that made the thyroid hyperactive. The old folk saying was more to the point: It's grief that's eating the flesh off her bones.)

The categorical refusal of the children to participate emotionally in their mother's drama. The mother's outbursts of despair at tiny misdeeds which the children commit daily, not intentionally—thoughtlessly. The enemy is at our heels, and the girl is picking flowers! Daisies, the meadow was dappled with them. Didn't you hear? The Americans! What are they going to do to us?

First they ordered them off their wagons, an order that was passed on down the long train. They stopped in a sunken road in the vicinity of Schwerin, which you've looked for many times but have never been able to find again. You're not sorry. Actually, that particular spot deserves to have been swallowed up by the earth; in your memory it is steeped in a sinister twilight, despite the glorious May weather. The sites of events that weigh too heavily in one's life must not be preserved on the surface of the earth. They drop to the bottom of memory and leave pale, unrecognizable imprints at the spots where they actually took place.

Nelly wanted very much to rebel. Not to get off the wagon, not to take her hands out of her coat pockets, not to pass through the extremely narrow hedge between two relaxed six-foot-tall American sergeants. This unacceptably narrow gap through which they pushed themselves one by one, to be frisked for weapons, was the only exit. Nelly felt it keenly. Charlotte, who was keeping an eye on her daughter, pulled her along by one arm: No nonsense now. Losers can't be choosers. They're the ones to give the orders now. Better get used to that, and fast.

That was out of the question.

What the others did was on their own conscience: the burning of army papers on small, brief, brightly flaming fires along the roadside, also rank insignia, sometimes whole officer's jackets; the eager saluting of the three American officers who were rolling along the sunken road in a jeep, unapproachable and silent, surveying their prisoners. Nelly didn't move a finger. She looked away. Her pride was unbroken. With an inscrutable face, on which she tried to express contempt, she let herself be frisked; she had put her watch into her coat pocket—the first Americans in her life were after German watches—they didn't find it. A minute triumph. Abruptly the order: Let's move. Hurry up, hurry up, back onto your wagons. Get your horses moving. Some Americans were throwing German army blankets onto the refugee wagons: For night! one of them called out, which meant that they would be sleeping out in the open. The next gathering place was near a locality called Warsow. The civilians were to camp on the left of the road, on a vast, gently sloping meadow, while members of the German Army were driven into a hastily erected barbed-wire pen.

A comparison of memories with films taken by Soviet cameramen shows the expected result: the memories have been distorted by emotion (shame, humiliation, compassion); they didn't allow the German prisoners to look as run-down as the enemy prisoners had; the objective strips of film record the various stages of the Soviet advance on the German capital; one sees German soldiers at the time of their surrender, and then again after one, two, three days of captivity: the rapid deterioration of the faces, due to growth of beard, loss of weight, but most of all to the numbness which dulled the features. Whiskers Grandpa, whose infrequent utterances grew increasingly unpleasant, says about the prisoners on the other side of the road: Like cattle put out to pasture. Good Lord, when will the old man finally learn to shut up.

The May evening was cold. They had to do their cooking outdoors. They had to go in search of kindling in a park-like wooded area, of stones to build a hearth, of water. Water? The villas on the hill were occupied by the Americans. That couldn't be helped. Charlotte grabbed a bucket, pressed a second bucket into Nelly's hand. Let's find out if they're inhuman. If something happens, you just run, never mind me. Nelly is grimly determined not to leave her mother's side.

All the doors stood open in the small house. Charlotte and Nelly stepped into the unfamiliar hall, in which American military overcoats hung on the coat rack as though they belonged there. A foreign, blaring music could be heard from the upper floor. Somebody was singing along with the unintelligible lyrics. Outside the kitchen door, a pile of empty cans. The foreign, unpleasant smell. Those people are living it up.

As they turned around, a small dark-haired officer was leaning against the door, which probably led to the living room. He must have been watching them for quite some time. Charlotte, who was used to launching attacks, held up her bucket. Wasser, she said. The man said nothing. He doesn't understand us. You tell him in English. Nelly, in the impeccable English she had been taught by Professor Lehmann: *Water, please.*

The officer's face remained expressionless. He detached himself from the door frame and opened the door to the bathroom: Help yourselves, he said in accent-free German. They filled their buckets over the tub; they avoided looking around in the unfamiliar room which was being occupied by the enemy. The officer carried their buckets for them as far as the garden gate. Charlotte said: Thank you very much. Don't trouble yourself any further.

The officer looked at Nelly. Perhaps he was expecting her to thank him also, but she didn't. Where have you come from? he asked.

Charlotte told him. He nodded, as though he were familiar with German place names. He asked Nelly how old she was. Her mother answered in her stead. He repeated the number sixteen as though he had to try it out. Grim, he finally said.

It was strange that the sadness in his eyes didn't seem to be new, didn't seem to be caused just by her. Then he asked, hesitantly as before, but still in his impeccable German, if they needed anything. Nelly feared for her mother's pride, but Charlotte Jordan knew what she owed her self-respect. She thanked him. Any medicine perhaps? he asked again. Fortunately, none of them happened to be ill at the moment, Charlotte said. He couldn't bring himself to let them go. He pushed himself, and then said in a voice that didn't seem to suit him: Things will get better again for you, too.

Charlotte didn't want to hear that sort of thing. The fatherland is finished, she said, and so are we. Such is war. You're the victors, we the losers. We have nothing to hope for.

The little officer replied softly, as though he were ashamed: It's Hitler who finished Germany.

Of course, said Charlotte, that's your opinion. You'll permit me to stick to mine. I don't kick a man who's down.

She picked up her bucket. The officer's sad eyes were fastened on Nelly's face. Shortly before they arrived at their cooking hearth, Charlotte softly said to Nelly: That was a Jew, did you notice? Probably a German emigrant.

Nelly hadn't noticed anything. The American officer who was supposed to be a Jew and from Germany gave her the creeps. They never went back to that particular house to fetch water.

Pea soup was cooking on the fire in the scrubbed-out washbasin. Nelly had to think far back to remember when she had last seen open fires in the falling twilight: campfires before the outbreak of the war, solstice fires still longer ago, in the ravine. That had happened in another life, she thought, and felt strangely satisfied with her precise division. Lutz, who was twelve, couldn't remember lights being permitted to burn in the dark, let alone open fires, without an air-raid warden immediately yelling: Lights out! He ran from fire to fire like a young dog, he was as excited as though he were being allowed to take part in a forbidden game. Charlotte was beside herself with worry. The boy's going nuts.

How had the concentration-camp inmate come to the fire? Somebody must have invited him, probably her mother. She had probably seen him meander alone among the wagons and the cooking hearths, stopping every now and then and looking at the people, not belonging anywhere. Charlotte had an eye for people who wandered around like that. May I invite you to share our modest meal? she said, as though a guest were coming into her parlor. He stared at her, until he realized that he was not being mocked, that this politeness was sincere. He sat down on a tree stump. Charlotte gave him one of her carefully guarded, least-chipped plates. She ladled the soup for him first. He ate in a way that made Nelly think that she'd only now discovered what it meant to eat. He had taken off his striped round beanie. The ears stuck out from his square shaved head. His nose was a huge bone in the fleshless face. It was impossible to imagine his real face, especially when he closed his eyes, which he did often, due to exhaustion. Then he swayed, although he was seated; Nelly had never seen anyone do that. Tin-framed glasses with thick lenses were tied behind his ears with a dirty string. Whenever he opened his eyes behind the thick lenses, one caught a hint of his face, one didn't know if it was his former or his future face. Nelly saw that he was unable to laugh. That was the first minute point of contact between them.

Her mother apologized about the soup being so thin. Oh, my good woman, he said, we're not choosy. It was the first time that

Nelly heard anyone call her mother "my good woman" and speak to her in such a tone of superiority. Charlotte seemed to think his tone natural, and said: Not choosy, I can well believe that. They obviously put you through hell. In case it's no secret, what did they accuse you of?

I'm a Communist, said the concentration-camp inmate.

Nelly was to hear all kinds of new sentences that day. How important were the fires burning in the dark with impunity compared to this man who openly accused himself of being a Communist?

I see, her mother was saying. But that wasn't reason enough to put you in a concentration camp.

Nelly was surprised to see that the man's face was able to change expression. Although he was no longer able to show anger, or perplexity, or mere astonishment. Deeper shadings of fatigue were all that remained accessible to him. He said, as though to himself, without reproach, without special emphasis: Where on earth have you all been living?

Of course Nelly didn't forget his sentence, but only later, years later, did it become some kind of motto for her.

The nights were cold, out in the open. You've finished your cherries and are back in the car, driving back in the direction of L., half inclined to end your stay in that town. That's when H. tells his daughter, Lenka, how they lay in tents on a vast, softly sloping meadow, as prisoners of war—to the west of the Elbe, which he had to cross by boat, later, in order to escape, in a homeward direction—how they developed an aversion to American canned meat, which they were forced to eat without bread, and how a fellow prisoner from another tent higher up the slope used to step outside and call out across the camp every single morning, in a drawn-out howl: German people, everything is shit!

H. imitated the howl that had rung in his ears for over twenty-six years. Lutz said, surprisingly: The man wasn't wrong, you have to give him that much. H. continued to tell how his first attempt to cross the Elbe had failed, how the second one had succeeded, how he had walked home, in several day-long marches, hiring himself out to farmers along the way, for a day's food and provision for the march. He had managed to pick up some civilian rags, which made him look like a kid. The military patrols let him pass. Thus he managed to escape the terrible starvation camps.

Lenka realized that new coincidences kept turning up, which either had to occur or else had to be prevented, to bring her parents together later and produce her. She didn't know: should she no longer consider herself important or, on the contrary, all the more important? In case of doubt, always choose the point in between, said her Uncle Lutz. Not too much, but not too little, either.

The camp near Warsow was dismantled on the third day. The refugees were able to stay on the road only for a couple of miles, then military posts directed them onto rural roads which led to remote villages. They were to look for shelter there. Herr Folk, who studied his map, set their goal: Grossmühlen. Grossmühlen belonged to Herr Folk's fellow officer Gustav von Bendow, old Mecklenburg aristocracy. The Bendows wouldn't close their door on their friends in need.

Charlotte, who was becoming more and more rebellious, asked loudly: What have the Bendows to do with us? But she could not, after all, throw her suitcases and her bedding from the wagon and stand in the middle of the forest at the crossing of two sand paths.

Liesbeth and Alfons Radde thought they ought to be grateful to the Folks for taking them along.

You're full of shit, Charlotte said.

Liesbeth, her sister, reproached her for becoming more vulgar by the day. She could have been right. Because, upon arrival at Grossmühlen, after a mile and a half on a brief but bad road— meadows on both sides, lined with sloe bushes—after taking a look at the low, decaying houses of the farm workers, and at the dogs that were leaping up against the wire fences of their cage in the center of the courtyard, with hellish barking, after inspecting the castle proper—a box inside which nothing stirred for the longest time—Charlotte opened her mouth once more and said: Well, my dears, here we are in the asshole of the world.

It was the truth.

16

Lot's wife.

To be inconsiderate—without looking back—as a basic requirement for survival; one of the prerequisites that separate the living
from the survivors.

Question from the audience: And do you believe it's possible to
come to grips with the events that you write about?

Answer: No. (The deaths of six million Jews, twenty million
Russians, six million Poles.)

In that case—follow-up question—what's the use of bringing it
up again and again?

(Survival syndrome: the psychosomatic pathology of persons
who were exposed to extreme stress. As studied in patients who
had to spend years of their lives in concentration camps or under

other conditions of persecution. Main symptoms: severe, lasting depression, with increasing difficulty in relating to others, states of fear and anxiety, nightmares, survivor's guilt, disturbances of memory and recall, increasing fear of persecution.

A doctor's remark on the results of his research: The world of the living and the world of the survivors are infinitely far removed from each other, they are light-years, or rather, shadow-years apart.)

Who would dare to say at any particular time: We have come to grips with it? The friend who was sent from Theresienstadt to Auschwitz when she was sixteen, who escaped two years later from a "transport," which would have meant certain death: Reality, for her, she says, has been hidden behind a veil since then. A veil that lifts only momentarily, only on rare occasions. She has become strangely indifferent to herself, although she is suffering from nightmares and persecution mania. Death is her fate; the fact that she survived is accidental. One cannot ascribe the same value to accidental survival as to a life that has never been contested. Shadow-years.

In August 1945, Nelly walked around the cemetery of Bardikow with Volkmar Knop, the pastor's thirteen-year-old son, to look for a spot for Herr Mau, who lay dying. She asked the boy if he didn't feel strange, picking out a burial site for a person who was still living. The boy, blond, blue-eyed, tall and lanky, answered gravely, No. He himself, for instance, imagined that he'd like to rest under the weeping willow alongside of the cemetery wall. Did he think about his death, then? Oh yes, often.

Nelly suddenly knew that she wanted to live a long time. It was as if there had never been the person within her who'd thought that she'd die of despair as recently as three months ago; those things happen. From a great height she saw herself walking with the boy, down below, in the old part of the cemetery, where the tombstones had partly sunk into the ground and were standing lopsided, and where ivy had grown over the names of the dead. She thought that somewhere, someday, a stone bearing her name would sink into the ground, like those others. Never before had she felt the impact of time; now she sensed it in her body, which had aged toward death within seconds. She didn't ask how she would spend the time which separated her from that stone. She was amazed at the lust for life that she found in herself. The fragrance, Volkmar! Don't you smell it? Sure, Volkmar said seriously. Wild roses.

The horizon around the village of Bardikow was low, the Horsemen of the Apocalypse stayed right below its edge. The village was crammed with people who had survived their catastrophes, and with others who hadn't noticed any catastrophe. This increased their bitterness toward each other.

Nelly sat at a desk by the window of the mayor's office and observed the two groups fighting. She found that most human beings were evil, and only hesitantly did she get involved on the side of the survivors, because she was one of them. Life in the village was her salvation, but it wasn't to her liking.

No doubt the room in the so-called Castle of Grossmühlen—an ugly, box-like building with an equally ugly, squat tower on its south side—was, for the time being, the final but also the only spot in the world that was available to them. Straw was spread on the parquet floor and covered with a tarpaulin. There must have been at least one chair with a curlicue back, its seat covered with Gobelin tapestry. Perhaps several of them. No table, as far as you know. (Charlotte Jordan's comment: We're going down in style. Nelly thought that she'd never again be able to read a fairy tale which said: "And he brought her home to his castle . . ." without bursting out laughing.)

Whiskers Grandma, sitting on the elegant chair, legs apart, a pail between her knees for the skins of the potatoes she was peeling. An unforgettable picture.

When does a person stop picturing things? (Does everyone stop doing it?) Bardikow is the last place preserved in your memory as a series of images. If it's true that the good Lord is to be found in details—and the devil, too, of course—then both withdraw more and more from memory in the years to come. (A memory without God and the devil—what would be the use?) Not that there are no more pictures: flash photos, also sequences. But their luminosity has diminished, as if the colors of reality no longer had the same quality as before. Instead, other mementos—flashes of perception and insight, conversations, states of emotion, thought processes— are becoming noteworthy. What does it indicate: aging? Perhaps a change in the material that must be remembered? No longer the sense organs which set the memory in motion ("Dreaming eyes of wonder"), but more and more frequently the manifold impressions of the vast world of the unseen, the impalpable? A store of experiences from which God and the devil have disappeared, and in which only you yourself continue to exist? It's all bunk! according to Charlotte. We're nothing but little chessmen moved about by the fingers of the high and mighty. Yet she was the one who always had her fingers in the pie, because of her children. Naturally she considered her children intelligent, even "gifted," although she couldn't have said what their gifts were. The material foundation for a "secure future" had vanished; one therefore had to grab any, even the most unlikely opportunity to find an occupation for the children that matched their abilities; Nelly first. Charlotte never regarded a girl's education as less important than a boy's. No, she said to Herr von Bendow's sister, the "Fräulein," who was way over sixty, with gray skin, hair, and dress—known to the children as the "Mummy"—and in charge of the female personnel on her brother's estate: No, my daughter is already committed elsewhere. (She, Charlotte, had long since made herself indispensable in the kitchen.) She took Nelly to the mayor of Bardikow (1.1 miles away), and succeeded, by boldly praising Nelly's intelligence and ability, and by glancing repeatedly at the mayor's messy papers, in convincing Richard Steguweit, a haggard, bony man of sixty, to hire Nelly as a "clerk." But with "no salary whatever," he said in his almost unintelligible Mecklenburg dialect. The community treasury was empty. Breakfast and lunch, that was all.

The way from Grossmühlen to Bardikow is one of the most beautiful paths you know. A rutted, seasonal road—to this day—with hedges on one side, on the other a view over wide fields and paddocks. Early in the morning, at seven-thirty, Nelly met no one on the road; in the distance she saw people in the fields who began waving to her after a while. Because it didn't take long before everyone in the village, local people and refugees, knew the mayor's "new Fräulein."

You certainly don't have a surveyor's memory, but you could still draw the map of Bardikow by heart. Nelly thought that the village was beautiful. H. said later, when the two of you visited Bardikow, that Nelly, at the time, had probably been overcome by the village romanticism city people are prone to. There might be some truth to it; but the village was changed in ways that are hard to describe: by a few utilitarian buildings of the cooperative, which is now specializing in the industrial production of milk and beef, by the razing of a few barns which had become superfluous, by the new ten-grade school at the edge of the village. The village pond across from the inn—it used to be choked with mud—has been dredged and reshaped, and is surrounded by small individual garden lots. The layout of the village, which Nelly took to be its unchangeable nature, has been improved. It's functional all right, but the improvements haven't beautified the village.

You leave the old cemetery of L. at about 11 a.m. Coming from the former Friedeberger Chaussee, you drive into G. again, just as the service in the former Catholic Concordia Church is over. The name of this church is meaningless today, since all churches are Catholic: functional buildings that are useful as long as human beings feel obliged to believe. You drive through the rebuilt inner city—you must admit, it's no beauty—and you ask yourselves why the conviction that man should be guided by his knowledge, rather than by his faith, has thus far produced so little beauty. You find no answer, because the question is posed wrongly. It doesn't cover the type, the extent, the direction, and the goal of this knowledge. Lenka suggests substituting the term "people-oriented" for the term "functional" until the time when town planning is no longer solely devoted—just to give a for instance, she says—to securing a place to sleep for every inhabitant. That'll be too expensive, says Lutz, while you are thinking: One would first of all have to find new purposes for man, something beyond the part he plays in the production of new material goods. Suddenly nothing would be too expensive, you think, because wealth would not be a word for money, and because a person who'd be wealthy in the new sense wouldn't have to lose his heart to a new car in order to feel like a human being . . .

Come off it, your brother, Lutz, says. What you're indulging in now is nothing but wishful thinking.

You're a well-coordinated team, says Lenka. Or did mind reading happen to be part of the curriculum, way back?

Lutz says: Your mother is thinking of a world in which people develop only needs that are beneficial to their growth—mental as well as physical. You understand?

Lenka understands. Perfectly, she claims. She herself sometimes thinks of such a world. What does her uncle have against it?

Lutz says: Me? Nothing at all. I only want to call to your attention, my dear little niece, that the growth process takes a different course: toward the steadily increasing gratification of needs that aren't all "people-oriented." But that are developed by people as a substitute for the real life which the production-oriented economy, the way it still works and has to work, withholds from them. Anyone who sticks his hand into this mechanism, in sheer provocation, will have his hand torn off. That's all. Because here we're in the realm of harsh laws, not of considered opinion.

Perhaps not the whole hand right away, you say. Stick the little finger in. A few reflections. And not in provocation. It's only because the end may be self-destruction.

Be my guest, says Lutz. Your personal risk. Besides, all of you can think what you will, you're out of it, anyway. No offense intended. But where these things are decided, your thoughts are unimportant. It's the domain of the experts. The suffering soul doesn't enter into the picture.

When Lutz was right, he was right.

You wonder why now, as you're writing down your conversation—the distillate of many conversations—you think of the statement of a physician of former concentration-camp inmates. His patients taught him that the survival of many of them was possible only in a state of total automatism.

Heroes? It would be better for us, it would be more bearable, if we could think of the camps as places where the victims necessarily turned into heroes. As if it were contemptible to break down under no longer bearable pressure. One should also, you think—again unrealistically—talk in the schools about those millions who gave themselves up, and who were given up by their comrades: "zombies." One should also, you think, teach the horror of the results of man's hatred of man; it would only increase the admiration for those who resisted.

(When you lift your eyes, you see a small, colorful ball hanging from the window handle. A Chilean woman prisoner had shaped it out of tiny roses which she made from bread and then painted. She gave it to a woman whose country had given her asylum. According to her request, it was to be passed on to persons who, at one time, had given hope to others. How you would love to be able to send it to the Spanish woman, Eva Forest, who wrote to her children from the prison of Yeserias: "Why should I keep it from you that I wept much? Tears are human, more so than laughter. It is a great effort for me merely to survive . . . I know that history runs in phases, and we are living in a phase that forces us to acquire technical knowledge. But one must always be aware of the great danger that lies in exclusive specialization . . . It is equally important to develop sensibility, and the best means to that end is art—the way it describes, pictures, and gives testimony to life." This woman gave you hope from prison.)

The new Fräulein at Mayor Steguweit's—his small property was the first when you came from Grossmühlen—was just, and she rarely laughed. She guarded her date of birth as a deep secret, for she understood that all her successful attempts at looking older wouldn't help her if it became known that she was sixteen. She pinned her long hair up in a bun, she practiced a self-assured demeanor and a stern look. You must be able to command respect. If you lose the people's respect, you're lost; keep that in mind once and for all. Those who came to the mayor's office with petitions and applications met a person who commanded respect.

Nelly never learned what it meant to be sixteen. She didn't ever have a chance to be sixteen or seventeen. Her ambition was to look at least twenty, to show no vulnerability, no weakness. Later on, her true age painfully made up for the headstart that she had gained by force. But the years are gone for good. Your children are dealing with parents who were never young themselves. Ruth, Lenka, without knowing it (perhaps even knowingly), enlighten their mother about the foreign word "youth." They teach her to be envious, but they ease this feeling by giving her the opportunity for vicarious joy.

(When H. and you come home late at night, you find a piece of paper outside Lenka's door. She's made a drawing, a self-portrait, as she sees herself in the mirror, very sober-faced. On the back it says: Well, I didn't do my math, as usual; I didn't straighten my room, as usual; I didn't take a shower, as usual. Can't you understand that other things are more important to me? Sure, they don't write "University Material" on my report card. So what. Are you going to disown me for it?)

Mayor Steguweit was impeded in matters of justice, for reasons that only gradually became clear to Nelly. He wasn't at all well, almost wasted away by a stomach ailment. He exuded a sourish smell. The blows of the past months had left him frail. Least of all was he up to dealing with the various occupation forces. He'd crawl into bed fully dressed, even with his shoes on, and in his quavery old-man's voice he'd call for the hot brick which his daughter-in-law Rosemary Steguweit, née Wilhelmi, had to keep in readiness on the stove. The brick was wrapped in towels and placed on the mayor's stomach. Meanwhile, in the next room, the office, Professor Untermann was showing the clerk Nelly Jordan how to run the show and how to deal with the local people.

Professor Untermann, a refugee from Dresden, assigned Nelly her place at the little table by the window, with the ancient type-writer, which she had to learn how to use. Untermann himself was enthroned at the end of the center table. He had a disgusting way of stressing the "professor," and intimidating the people. Besides, he spoke with a Saxon inflection which the Mecklenburg people didn't understand, while he himself never called the farmers' Plattdeutsch anything but "Hottentot language." In a short time, Nelly learned to understand or guess both dialects, and therefore had to act as an interpreter, a triumph which Untermann didn't forgive her.

Professor Untermann also recommended to Nelly the study of the so-called village list, a compilation of all landowning community members, written by Richard Steguweit himself in pale ink, in a slanted, shaky, Gothic script. The local population of the village was divided into "farmers," "landholders," "cottagers." The heads of household of every family were entered, each with the number of hectares he owned. Untermann asked Nelly to find out in which category "our boss," the mayor, was listed.

The record showed Richard Steguweit as cottager with eight hectares of property. That makes, said Untermann, how many acres? Well? Right: all of twenty acres. That's nothing. And among it, to boot, is that piece of sour meadow that you can see from the kitchen window, and on which our dear Dulcinea— Steguweit's cow was named "Bessie," but Untermann never called her anything but "our dear Dulcinea"—is about to croak. And now please read me what it says under the name "Pahlke." Under the name Pahlke, Wilhelm, it said: 74 hectares, and the designation "farmer." There you are. First-grade soil, by the way. Maybe now it'll dawn on you why our dear Steguweit will crawl out of bed when Herr Pahlke enters this room, and why he'll happily stay flat on his back when Herr Forster gives us the honor. Mr. Forster from Wisconsin will leave. Wilhelm Pahlke stays. Yep, my child— Untermann couldn't refrain from calling Nelly "my child" in his Saxon inflection—there's still a lot for you to learn.

Mr. Howard Forster, an American sergeant, was in command of the "Ami Troop" (Untermann's expression) in Bardikow, consisting of a dozen men at most. He came to the mayor's office in order to make requests for the needs of his soldiers, or to sign permits, and to offer cigarettes to Professor Untermann, who'd stuff his pipe with them.

The house in which the Americans "camped" was landowner Johann Theek's place, which had been evacuated for this purpose. It was located on one of the slightly rising side roads which all end in the Ringweg, the road that circles the village. Sergeant Howard Forster was a dark, sturdy type with a string of hair falling in his face; he didn't enforce strict discipline among his scant dozen equally sturdy, or else gangling, men. Loud raucous music (nigger jazz: Professor Untermann) came from the "Ami house" day and night, also other noises, and a mound of tin cans and empty bottles was rising in the front garden. Not to mention the American cans and cigarettes and coffee which found their way into many a village house. In return for services that Herr Untermann didn't think he'd have to elaborate on.

No, he didn't have to, in his pinched, whiny voice. But neither did it enter his mind to interfere when Mayor Steguweit ("In many respects he's already beyond good and evil") sent the new Fräulein to Mr. Howard, with a paper that she had first laboriously typed out from Untermann's draft, and which asked to have the mayor himself, as well as his "deputy," Untermann, exempted from handing in their radios. For urgent administrative reasons. The text had been translated by Untermann into an English Nelly didn't wish to pass judgment on.

So she reluctantly went to the "Wild West," the name her mother had given to the Americans' house, and found her expectations confirmed.

All the doors were open in the Ami house. It's one of the

American customs one gets more easily used to than to many others, but it's better suited to an oil-heated, fully automated American one-family home than to a Mecklenburg farmhouse, which is "as drafty as the Windward Islands" (Charlotte Jordan), even with the doors closed. Music, of course, out of portable radios. (What do they need the German sets for? Professor Untermann: As a prelude to the mental despoliation of the German people.) From the room to the right of the brick-floored hallway came hooting and whistling after Nelly had entered. Not "vulgar," by the way, as Charlotte would have interpreted it; not dangerous, either. Cheerful rather, even appreciative. A look into a barracks. Mecklenburg farmers' beds, on which half-naked youths were lolling around (Charlotte's words) in the middle of the day. Most of them wearing a piece of clothing that Nelly later learned to call *shorts*. Bare, hairy men's torsos. *Hello, baby,* and so on.

Nelly, with impeccable pronunciation, asks for the "commander." A noisy answer: The other door. Across the hall. Sergeant Forster wears a T-shirt with his shorts, his feet are resting on a caned chair with an intricate wooden back, he's chewing gum, listening to music from his portable radio. He reads Nelly's paper, writes a word underneath, and returns it to Nelly with his signature.

The word, which Nelly reads immediately, is "No."

Nelly says: Thank you. Goodbye.

The commander says: *Bye-bye.*

Professor Untermann, after reading the word "no": Infamy of the victor. Nelly gloats. Although she shares Untermann's views about "our fatherland" (Thus we shall witness how they run our fatherland into the ground), she still wishes him personally "all the best." (Charlotte Jordan; she, too, thinks the professor is "some catch.")

The wagon for transporting the confiscated radio sets out of Bardikow, including those of Professor Untermann and the mayor, has to be provided by Farmer Pahlke, with clenched teeth of course, as Untermann assumes. A simple box wagon will do. Whatever gets broken on the way, that's not our problem. The wagon stops at every house. Nelly has to knock on the doors, ask for the registered sets, cross them off her list as they're handed over. Professor Untermann stands on the wagon, stows them away.

All in all, it's a humiliating affair. In this case she has to agree with him.

Richtstrasse once more (St. Mary's Church, last glimpses). Once more the former Soldinerstrasse, once more past the former Jordan house. It gets repetitive. And what now? Turn around, or what? Turn around. The former Jordan house in the rearview mirror now, getting smaller. Nobody is tactless enough to say: Look back once more. Nobody admits his lack of emotion.

Someone asks whether or not you should stay longer. (Lenka said reluctantly, No, not as far as she was concerned.) You stopped at the small Old Cemetery, at the foot of the mighty stairway that connects two streets of different levels and then, dividing, leads steeply up to the former General von Strantz Barracks, where, in those days, in the forties, a man by the name of Gottfried Benn was officer and army surgeon. At the foot of the stairway, which Nelly had once climbed with Julia (Dr. Juliane Strauch), you suddenly remembered what they were talking about. If Nelly would tutor a nine-year-old butcher's son with great gaps in his learning, to prepare him for the entrance exam to a secondary school. She, Julia, couldn't think of anyone in all her classes who was better qualified than Nelly. Of course for a fee, five marks an hour; she shouldn't be bashful. Nelly's surge of happiness, right here, on this stairway. The shy, thin, blond butcher's son. Klaus— that's right: Klaus. Has difficulties with spelling. The white envelope at the end of the month, contents: twenty reichsmarks. The large bouquet of flowers from the butcher's wife—thin, blond, shy—when her son Klaus passed his exam . . .

No, you hear yourself say, not as far as I'm concerned, either. Let's go on.

The town as an incentive, as a motive, as a sign, not as a town. You believe you understand.

Professor Untermann's days at the mayor's office were numbered, incidentally. Lutz, who had begun his career as a stableboy in Herr von Bendow's stables, has no memory of Felix Untermann, almost none of Mayor Steguweit, only a vague recollection that he was a Nazi. Nazi, you said, I'm not so sure. Member of the National Socialist Party, in any case; hence he was apprehensive.

And his son? Wasn't he in the SS?

Fighting SS.

Nevertheless. He didn't come home.

Not as long as we were in Bardikow. His wife, Rosemarie, waited for him with their children, Dietmar and Edeltraut, but he didn't come. His father feared more than he hoped that he'd come back.

Your brother, Lutz, still knows the names of some of the horses, he still knows what they were being fed, and he sees himself squatting in the hayloft, with Gerhard Grund, the son of the farmhand who had been shot, and talking about their mutual ambition to become engineers. They succeeded, both of them.

Off we go, says your brother, Lutz. Home.

You didn't use the word "Nazi" for many years after the war. It wouldn't have occurred to Nelly to call Professor Untermann a "Nazi." The word was used by the American captain who appeared one afternoon in the mayor's office with two military police and the ubiquitous Sergeant Howard Forster; Nelly heard the word for the first time. The captain spoke a strongly American-flavored German, therefore she heard "Nayzec," and it was only later that she could interpret to herself what the captain had called the professor from Dresden. In front of the mayor's house stood an American Army truck with a white star on its door and a black driver who laughingly distributed chewing gum to the village children who were crowding around him.

The most remarkable part of the short scene of the arrest—the first that Nelly witnessed—was the fact that Professor Untermann knew what was up before the captain had gotten off the truck, walked through the front garden and the entrance hall with his escort, and entered the room after a short, sharp knock. As soon as the truck had stopped, Professor Untermann rose from his dominating place at the center table; he turned white and murmured with actually trembling lips: Now they're coming! Whereupon Richard Steguweit, who happened to be in the room just then, had nothing to say but: What will be will be.

The captain, after taking a quick look at the personnel of the mayor's office, addressed Untermann with the sentence that contained the word "Nayzee." Untermann immediately stepped forward from his table; he made a pitiful attempt at an incredulous smile, whereby a thin thread of saliva ran down the left corner of his mouth; he still managed to speak of denunciation (A malicious denunciation, *Mr. Captain*, I implore you!), but an indignant person looks different from a fearful person. Untermann was afraid. He stepped—in back of Nelly's chair, as usual—to the door where two MPs were posted, one on the right and one on the left; he tripped, as usual, over the chair legs, and went, finally indignant: Tsk, tsk, tsk! As usual.

It made Nelly laugh. Against her will, she burst out laughing, while the two MPs gripped Untermann's arms with white-gloved hands. That's when Untermann showed that he was an educator through and through, because in the door he turned around and punished Nelly with the epithet: Immature! It was the last word she heard him say.

Through the window she watched him shuffle to the truck, whose tailgate was lowered. Two other male figures were crouched on the loading platform; they resembled Untermann only in their common fear. They grabbed Untermann from above, pulled, while the MPs—white belt, white shoulder straps, white pistol pouches —shoved from behind and then swung themselves up to the three prisoners. Sergeant Forster bolted the tailgate. The captain climbed in and gave the order to start to the uniformed black man at the wheel, who stared ahead, unmoved and immovable, chewing all the time. He took off with a jerk, and everyone crouching on the loading platform was thrown topsy-turvy. And that was the last Nelly got to see of Professor Untermann: on the bottom of the American truck, a once fat man in his late fifties, dressed in his only, formerly best, gray suit, which hung loose on his body, his jowls wobbling in his once fat face. A bundle of misery.

There he goes, said Mayor Steguweit. It hits where it hits.

Nelly was promoted to Untermann's responsible position, without changing her place in the office.

She never knew, said Lenka, and she found it hard to believe, that any member of the National Socialist Party wasn't also an out-and-out Nazi. Your mayor, she said, he certainly must have had dirt on his hands. You said: Yes. He was poor. It's twelve noon, a Sunday in July 1971, still the same heat; the former Friedrich-strasse, the village of Weprice, are behind you. What remains is the road home. Lenka asks about Richard Steguweit, who has been lying under Mecklenburg soil now for twenty-five years, about whom nobody asks any more. How come he became a Nazi because he was poor?

How long had it taken Nelly to find out? The two years in Bardikow supply her only with the material for later conclusions: year after year, Cottager Steguweit, eight hectares, borrows tractors from Farmer Pahlke, seventy-four hectares. When the mayor's position becomes vacant—anno 1937—Pahlke himself doesn't want to take it. He isn't keen on joining the party. Steguweit isn't keen on it, either, but then he does join and becomes mayor. Pahlke is in fine shape. The Nazi label gets stuck on Steguweit, who is poor.

Just as in trashy novels, says Lenka. How's that? Exactly the way one imagines it. It isn't always possible to keep fictional reality from conforming to current concepts of reality. Besides, most bad books aren't even characterized by this partial conformity. What are they characterized by, then? By an attempt to correspond completely to the current concepts of reality.

What does that have to do with Steguweit?

With the fact that Steguweit, Nazi against his will, is taken seriously by his son Horst, who becomes what his father only pretends to be. And Horst was a beautiful man. A radiant demigod. Nelly slept for weeks next to Rosemarie Steguweit, under his picture in the couple's bedroom. Nelly saw every night that Rosemarie adored the photograph; there is no other word for it. She saw that Rosemarie Steguweit's first look, every morning that God gave her, was devoted to the photo; little Edeltraut promised to take after him, while Dietmar seemed to be just like his mother. Nelly heard Richard Steguweit curse his son during a quarrel with his daughter-in-law: He was the death of his mother, he'll bring disaster on all of us if he comes back. I curse the day he was born. And then Rosemarie: You're sinning against your own flesh and blood, and at your age!

Biblical scenes. Lenka has no opinion, she stays out of it. You drive through Sunday villages, all of them built alongside the road, groups of young people, separated according to sex, strolling shortly before noon along the only street. Are they bored? They crane their necks after the few cars that pass by. They wear white shirts and jeans, or short skirts and colorful blouses. When boys and girls are together, it's in groups, not in pairs. Like in our village back home, Lenka says.

Nelly was the last to realize that she was in a position of power. It was her job, for instance, to requisition the vehicles of the village for public duty, wagonloads of sand from the gravel pit for repairs of the worst tank damage to important roads. Nelly was just. Her principle was: One vehicle per farm, at regular intervals. On this basis she drew up a list and informed those eligible for public duty. In the afternoon, shoemaker Sölle came in without knocking, yanked off his cap, tossed it in front of his feet on the scrubbed floorboards, and lit into Nelly. She knew the Mecklenburg dialect well enough to understand that he was yelling at her because of unfairness about the public-duty question. He, Sölle, was no longer the authorities' doormat. Those times were over. Sölle was known to her as the village's only Communist, and an irascible character. She felt she had the strength to hold her own with irascible characters, especially when she was so obviously in the right, as in this case. That's what she told him, and was rewarded with scorn. Sölle was angry because Pahlke and Freese and Laabsch, each with four to six horses in his barn, were not required to do more public duty than he with his one half-starved nag.

One vehicle per farm, said Nelly.

Sölle said she could wipe her ass with that list of hers, and left.

Mayor Steguweit appeared from his bedroom, fully dressed, stepped, without a word, to Nelly's table with the telephone that had lately been in operation again—Bardikow had seven connections—turned the crank, chose a number, and informed Farmer Pahlke of changes in Nelly's public-duty list, which were to the advantage of Sölle, to the disadvantage of Pahlke. Oddly enough, no objection came from the other end. Nelly was to take the new list to Sölle.

No, she said. She didn't see it. Then everybody could come.

Sure, said Richard Steguweit. But everybody doesn't come, Fraülein. That's the difference.

One of the rare dreams in recent dreamless weeks: you sit facing a crowd that is friendly to you, and you're to read from a thin book, but it's written in Polish. (The languages of others stymie you.) The thin book, whose text you can't decode, whose meaning you can't transmit to the crowd. The fat book into which years of your life are entering. Which you want and at the same time are unable to want. To drive with the brakes on. Bad for the motor.

To think that you didn't understand what was happening when

the heartbeat was irregular, but you understood immediately why it happened. The organ was signaling a severe, inner state of being hunted, which you couldn't acknowledge in other ways. The language of our organs which we can't decode because we're doggedly determined to separate the physical from the spiritual. The insights that occur to you while the physicians suspect fear of death, never thinking that the word should be "relief." Immense relief, although the injections still haven't taken effect. Relaxing—no longer a forbidden longing, but a command. The exhaustion. No more reason for embarrassment, it's legal now. The weakness, so what. You even have to laugh at your body's cunning. (A body will remain in a state of inertia, or of unvarying motion on a straight course, as long as it isn't compelled by a force to change this state. Which force? asks the physics teacher, a severely ailing man, evacuated from the bombed-out city of Berlin. Well: the force of gravity. Well: the friction resistance of the base. Well: the air resistance. Or do you think that what you can't see can't offer resistance?)

From exhaustion to exhaustive? The serious temptation to break off. After all, it isn't a story that must necessarily lead to a precise end. Or to what conceivable point would it have to be pushed forward? In the hospital, with no inclination to work, under the first, still misunderstood attacks of fear, you believe you see clearly: the final point would be reached when the second and the third person were to meet again in the first or, better still, were to meet with the first person. When it would no longer have to be "you" and "she" but a candid, unreserved "I." It seemed very doubtful to you whether you could reach this point at all, whether the road you've taken would ever lead to it. Nevertheless, you didn't want to die before finishing the book, that was something you couldn't even speak about. Secret speculations which come up only in times of lack of faith: lack of faith in the inexhaustible nature of certain abilities or incentives. Or compulsions.

Revulsion for the word "creative."

The unlived is the important influence, and at the same time it's something that is hard to talk about. Deep in the cave of the narrative. A faint glimmer from the exit. The unknown nature of the light that awaits you on the outside.

Is there any sense any longer in the question Who are you? Isn't it hopelessly antiquated, outstripped by the cross-examiner's question: What have you done?, which provokes in you the weak counter-question: What did they make me do? The sense of being accountable, worn thin by the things for which there is no accounting, which stop the flow of the narrative. (Lenka remembers that you once sat by her bed for a whole night when she was sick, that she saw you whenever she woke up; she believes that this is how you saved her life, because her fever started to go down in the morning. She doesn't accept your reminder that her illness had been severe but not fatal; it was enough for her that she'd believed it, and that you had taken her belief seriously. You understand. She furnishes you with material for exoneration.)

Nelly, then. A case of emergency maturity, of being quite unfamiliar with herself. Trained and used to pulling emergency brakes: strictness, consistency, responsibility, diligence. No record of what she may have dreamed in those days. Dreams meant nothing to her. On the other hand, she took herself seriously to the point of tragedy, a habit she learned to overcome only much later.

The new administration in the district capital sent the order to take a census of the communities' residents. Nelly went from house to house and counted every person, classified as to local residents and refugees, grouped as to sex and age. She climbed on the ancient two-seater wagon next to Mayor Steguweit, presented her lists in the district capital, gravely affixed her signature next to the mayor's on the census ("checked and found correct"), and then returned to the village with a briefcase full of food ration cards: her life was at stake for their safe delivery. On the way back, she discussed with Richard Steguweit what they should do in case of armed robbery, which was by no means to be ruled out. I'll stay where I am, I'm an old man. You, Fräulein, grab the briefcase and run into the woods. If we come back to the village without the cards, they'll kill both of us, anyway.

Nelly was the first to learn about the change of occupation forces, by phone. British occupation forces were to take over Bardikow. Sergeant Forster and his troop disappeared. Landowner Theek moved back into his house, buried the empty bottles and cans behind his garden fence, and started a business with cans of Nescafé, which had been left in his attic in a torn-open carton. Among other, more perishable goods, the business netted him a set of silver tableware, a floor lamp with a green silk shade and bead fringes, an oil painting on which a forest brook—crossed by a little wooden bridge with handrails—flowed down to a valley, but, above all, a black, sequin-spangled wrap for his twenty-year-old daughter, Ilselore, who looked a little consumptive, and whom he adored.

The British occupation force in the lanky, reddish-blond figure of a single soldier on a bicycle, who appeared one fine day in June, in his yellow-brown uniform, with his beret, at the mayor's garden gate, leaned his bicycle against the hedge, then decided to lock it, and knocked at the office door a few seconds later. After the correct greeting, his first question was, in English: Did she speak English? And Nelly, in whom two kinds of pride were struggling, finally said: Yes.

The Englishman—he was the epitome of an Englishman—formed a one-man patrol, according to his own statement. He was instructed to take care of his own board among the farmers, for payment, of course. He showed his occupation money. Nelly had forgotten the English word "daughter-in-law," when she introduced Rosemarie and the Englishman. Rosemarie was willing to serve breakfast. Nelly was left alone with the victor, both were taciturn. He looked over every piece of furniture in the room, almost without moving his head. That's how he'll always picture a German mayor's office, Nelly thought. But she saw no sense in explaining to him what a sheer accident it was that the wall between the stove and the pendulum clock was decorated with the hand-embroidered motto: Faith in the Lord is its own reward.

A shock: the unfortunate Rosemarie Steguweit brought breakfast for two. Ham and canned liverwurst. The Englishman and Nelly sat diagonally across from each other at the big table, on which the papers had been pushed out of the way. After some time, the inquiry: Did the (uninvited) guest enjoy his food? *Oh yes, thank you.* Silence. After a while, from his side, the memorable sentence: Field-Marshal Montgomery wouldn't like it if he knew whom the Englishman was sitting with at the table. Why? Any social contact with the German population was strictly prohibited. No fraternizing permitted.

What does the representative of the German population do in a case like this? She takes plate and cup, rises from the center table, and sits down at her window seat, her back to the victor (our

Germanic cousins). The Englishman, who doesn't want to have it understood that way, doesn't eat much more, pays Frau Rosemarie, nods a brief goodbye, and leaves. Nelly saw him mount his shiny new bicycle. He disappeared for good. For her, it had been a sublime pleasure to follow the order of the enemy Field-Marshal Montgomery.

For quite a while she thinks she's done the right thing. For quite a while longer—as you understand it today—it's not a question of right or wrong. Unfortunately, no one yet can speak the redeeming, or at least the enlightening, words. Still, the five hundred people of the village of Bardikow, the one hundred of Grossmühlen, don't want to know anything about world history except that it has led them into misery. Almost all are in a panic when the British occupation forces one day post the notice—bypassing the German authorities—that they will be relieved at midnight by Soviet occupation forces, on the basis of certain agreements. (Between July 1 and 3, 1945, the Allies withdrew to the agreed-upon zones of occupation.) All roads will be out of bounds for civilians, to allow for troop movements. The population is requested to keep calm.

The Russians arrive. Around two in the morning there is loud and continued knocking at the heavily bolted main door of Bendow Castle in Grossmühlen. Charlotte says: It could only happen to us. Just when the Russians are coming, we would have to live in a castle of all places, like royalty. Aunt Liesbeth thinks it makes absolutely no difference where one lives when the Russians come.

Charlotte orders her children to get dressed in the dark. She was going downstairs to see what was what.

Mamsell flees into their room, panting hard, begging them to hide her. Mamsell was a rotund woman of about fifty, with eyes like pinheads and frizzy, colorless hair full of tiny clips. Nelly had heard that her little attic room was spick-and-span. Now she threw herself down on Charlotte's bed, in her clothes, muddy shoes and all.

Downstairs the knocking had stopped. Movement, running. Foreign, very foreign, rough voices. Fear was shooting up in Nelly.

It was a long time before Charlotte came back. Her brother-in-law Alfons Radde meanwhile prophesied several times that "nothing good" would come to her. Several times, Aunt Liesbeth broke into nervous tears.

When Charlotte came in, she brought a foreign odor with her. The first thing she said was that the Bendows were "downright idiots": The occupation forces are knocking at the door, and they sit in their salon and pee in their pants instead of going and opening it and handing over the house to them.

How on earth did she know what to do when the victor knocks at the door? So it was she who opened? Who else? And? And, and! They had women with them, in uniform. One of them, who knows German, asked me: You owner? Women carrying rifles? Then I took them through the lower floor. Nice little rooms, let me tell you. They picked the rooms where they were going to stay. And? You want to know something funny they asked for? Towels.

There was a silence. Then Alfons Radde said: They're going to use them as socks.

Nope, said Charlotte. They sure won't.

The door opened. Mamsell shrieked. A very young Russian soldier stood there with a flashlight. He shone the light through the room, the ray flickered across Nelly's face. Charlotte lit into Mamsell: Pull yourself together, for God's sake!, and to the soldier she said, as if to a person hard of hearing: Re-fu-gees, understand? Ah, goott, said the soldier, and left. The straw on the floor may have impressed him more than Charlotte's explanation.

The castle was declared commandant's headquarters, and cleared of all Germans. Nelly made room for her large family in the parsonage of Bardikow. The straw on the floor was the same, the rooms into which they were crammed got smaller and smaller. Slanted walls, a dormer for a window. No doubt, it was a step down, even if the pastor's wife, Hermine Knop—she was taking care of her husband's obligations as long as he was a prisoner of war—received her new housemates with a "God bless you." She asked Charlotte please to call her "Frau Pastor," even if she, Charlotte, was possibly not a believer. The Lord is not on good terms with us, said Charlotte. I'm sure you know what I mean, Frau Pastor.

Frau Pastor Knop believed—there was no doubt, she believed— that Jesus Christ had been serious, dead serious about His commandment "Love thy neighbor." Never a bad word came from her lips. But one can't eat friendliness, and where there's nothing, nobody gets anything, neither the king nor the good Lord. One day Aunt Liesbeth simply had to give up fighting with the other refugee women over a corner of the large parsonage stove for her frying pan. They had to make up their minds to cook outside, which meant building a fireplace in the parsonage courtyard, using bricks from an old field barn. Now the family had to admit: they were on a level with the Volhynia Germans, who had been camping outside for a long time. They had to learn that one can always sink lower. The most humiliating sign: Whiskers Grandma ate meatballs made of horsemeat, and acted as if she didn't know what she was eating. At home she had refused to let the children use her casserole for warming up some horsemeat sausages left over from the fair. Nelly saw her grandmother eat the horsemeat.

Meanwhile, next door, in the attic room on the left, Herr Mau, ecclesiastic councilor from Posen, lay dying. As recently as two weeks ago, one could still see him—he must have been an imposing presence at one time—as he walked, bent over, through the house and across the yard. He was one of the refugees who had access to Frau Pastor's living room. She discussed liturgical questions with him, he was a great comfort to her. His wife, an elderly, shriveled-up little mouse, flitted about, lamenting, and weeping over the set of Rosenthal dishes in her breakfront in Posen. The children—Nelly too—never called her anything but Frau Meow. Every day Frau Mau washed her piqué cuffs and collar and basted them into her only, mouse-gray dress. Nikolaus, her husband, loved everything prim and proper.

Now he was dying. Hard to tell of what. Martha, the community nurse, guessed that his heart was not the strongest. It never was, Frau Mau lamented. But her husband had always been as strong as an ox, she said it several times a day: Isn't he as strong as an ox? The children stopped crying "Meow." Frau Pastor Knop took up secret negotiations with the village carpenter. None of her housemates was to be put under the earth like a dog, if she could help it. Nelly, then, went to the cemetery with Volkmar Knop, to choose a grave site. The dignity of death became quite apparent to her, since the dying man was given a room all to himself: the men's quarters, seven by ten feet large. Whiskers Grandpa, Uncle Alfons Radde, Nelly's brother, Lutz, and Cousin Manfred made do with part of the attic. Frau Mau's place in the women's chamber stayed empty, since she had to watch over her husband's dying. She quit lamenting. It was Herr Mau's turn, with his death rattle and his moaning. In the night, Nelly's brother, Lutz, moved from the attic to the women's chamber and quietly lay down on Frau Mau's spot, but the thin wooden door didn't do much to muffle the sounds of death. They all lay on their backs quietly and looked up into the darkness. Nelly was wishing that Herr Mau wouldn't feel anything.

Lenka claims that death is different from what the living imagine it to be. (You're driving through the place that used to be called Vietz. The streets are almost deserted now, in the country one eats at twelve noon, on the dot. You are thirsty, the taste of the cherries is gone. H. says: Wait until Kostrzyn.) Lenka had listened to a radio program. People who'd been clinically dead and had come back to life, reporting on their memories of the road to death. As if on a screen, they had seen the most important events of their life, had then left their body, which they saw lying on a bed. The way Herr Mau, you say, would have seen his emaciated body lying on a bed of straw, covered with a white sheet of Frau Pastor Knop's—sheets, a privilege not granted to the living? Presumably, says Lenka. And next to it he saw a prostrate woman whom he recognized as Frau Mau, and whom he serenely left in her bereavement? Next to the body from which he separated without regret? Supposedly without regret, says Lenka. Those who had survived their death spoke of a suspension of our habitual perception of space and time, and of an overwhelming awareness of music and light. So that now they were expecting their unavoidable death in complete serenity. Without fear. Sounds nice, said your brother, Lutz. If you can believe it, more power to you. He remembered Herr Mau's dying very clearly. You kept talking for a while about the strange urge of human beings to see their body and their soul as separate entities, in life and in death. The conversation petered out because of the heat and your tiredness.

When it had become still in the death room, everybody got up and gathered in the attic. Frau Pastor Knop came upstairs, fully dressed, with a candle. Her prayers had accompanied Herr Mau's soul in its transition to the new state. She opened the door. Frau Mau, crouching on the floor next to the body, looked up at them. Frau Pastor Knop pulled the sheet over Herr Mau's face. The sheet was too short and didn't cover the feet. Nelly had to keep looking at the feet of the dead body, while Frau Pastor Knop recited the prayer for the dead. Thou, O Lord, in thy infinite mercy . . .

For a long time, Nelly was haunted by the question of how one can tell with certainty the feet of a dead body from those of a living person. And to this day, when you think "death," you see in front of you the wax-like feet—toes turned inward—of the dead Herr Mau.

Having died—having survived—living, how can you tell one from the other? One cannot speak of the dead. The survivors can look neither forward nor backward. The living are in free command of the past and the future. Of their experience, and of the conclusions it enables them to draw.

17

A chapter of fear—a sparing dosage.

Why don't you simply eliminate all fear from your life, who's stopping you? Present fears, past fears: that might be the desired existence (as others desire it). The putty of the century melted away. Everything broken up into anecdotes, with the advantage of being "workable."

The commandment: Thou shalt produce! prevents, you think, the capacity for suffering from gradually taking over other—all other—capacities. You want to say: The commandment has no influence on the nature of my writing, but you come to realize that is wrong. You're taken aback when you keep forgetting it is the special nature of the suffering called "fear" which brings forth that special type of product in which you recognize yourself. Why deny it?

The hope to free yourself.

Liberation as a process with no specific deadline. To work at making fear retreat by writing.

There are areas that are still not liberated, that are still occupied by fear: prehistory.

As exemplified by the stranger, named Nelly, who is made to supply details nobody could invent. In August 1945, she and her family move once more, the next to last time during that year. One third of the village of Bardikow is being evacuated to make room for a Soviet unit; the parsonage among other sites. The soldier who tries to deliver the evacuation order to the mayor's office finds a locked door; from her seat at the window Nelly had seen him coming. She's alone in the room, fear shoots through her like lightning, fear of the foreign uniform, of this foreign young man, who is rather tall and looks like a peasant, with a moustache on his upper lip. Fear stops all thought, gives her legs independent motion. Nelly rushes to the door of the office, through the outer hall to the front door, which she locks an instant before the soldier presses the handle. For seconds the two faces, separated only by a pane of rippled glass, distorted by fear and perplexity. Then rage, on the Russian's side.

A banal incident, which, in a film today, would prompt laughter —an example of progress. The amused spectators would watch the panic-stricken girl run out the back door, climb over fences, run across pastures behind the village, while the soldier rattles the mayor's door so vehemently that the rippled glass falls out and breaks in the hall. While Rosemarie Steguweit flees to the cow shed, and the mayor has to lift the hot brick off his stomach, climb into his brown corduroy pants, and open the door for the Russian soldier. A comedy, at best, in which pure misunderstanding is, after all, permitted to further the action.

You don't laugh while you're sweating blood. The news spreads through the village like wildfire, faster than Nelly can run. By the time she arrives, panting, at the parsonage, her mother is beside herself: the Fräulein in the mayor's office has been threatened and raped by a Russian.

A big, tearful scene.

The next day, the unavoidable argument with the mayor about the broken pane, which Nelly considers totally immaterial, while the mayor insists that she must receive anyone, without exception, who comes to the office. Moreover, she has to explain to the inhabitants of the western sector of the village that they have twenty-four hours to evacuate their houses. And to those who may stay in their houses, to expect more people to move in with them.

K.L., your Moscow friend, who is the first Russian you tell the Bardikow stories to, thinks the evacuation of the village cannot be presented as a comedy. You agree. Although, you say, there were certain moments . . . Frau Knop, for instance, the pastor's wife, who appeared before the future commandant of Bardikow flanked by her two sons, her head erect, asking that the parsonage be declared a neutral zone, exempt from the evacuation order. Her performance had been meant to look tragic, but it collapsed before Lieutenant Pyotr's total lack of comprehension; she did, however, manage a dignified exit. Unlike an old woman named Stumpen, a few days later; she had done the commandant's laundry, and taken her leave from him with "Heil Hitler!", whereupon she fled and stayed in hiding and had to be brought before him by two soldiers a week later; she was convinced that she was going to be executed. Instead of shooting her personally, the dead-serious commandant handed her a bag of dirty laundry, with which she ran through the village as if she'd hit the jackpot, telling everybody that the commandant was a great man.

She was probably alone in her opinion.

Does memory prefer to store anecdotes? Something about the structure of memory seems to lend itself to a story with a point. A structure is a composite—of points and so on—which clarifies certain connections. The transformation of difficult chapters in history—in which certain connections are as yet unclarified—into newspaper anecdotes, prompted by anniversaries ("thirtieth anniversary of the Liberation"). Erasing, selecting, stressing. What may be told boils down to what the editor in chief of any given newspaper deems acceptable; Salvation Army stories. (The saying of the taxi driver, Herr X: Spare me those Salvation Army fairy tales!) Soviet soldiers doling out soup, saving children, taking women in labor to the hospital.

All of which shall not be denied.

What on earth do you expect? No army in the world could survive this war as a salvation army. The effects of war are also devastating for those who didn't start it. This to the taxi driver, Herr X, who has been living in the area for thirty-five years and has "seen it all with his own eyes." Who lets you know that he's aware of your profession, which is his only reason for speaking up: But if you're only interested in what the papers tell you, then never mind.

He assures you convincingly that he didn't enjoy being a soldier; he'd even been locked up for two years for undermining the morale of the armed forces, which was why he witnessed the end of the whole mess at home, no longer fit for service. He says that his neighbor denounced him to the Gestapo near the very end, because he'd cut short the latter's Führer-faith fantasies about the miracle weapon. The atom bomb? Forget it, we blew that one! Later, the same neighbor was shot in his cellar, in front of all of us, believe it or not, because he refused to take off his leather jacket. After a week of all this, my wife wanted to tie a rope around her neck. I couldn't protect her, or else it would have been all over for me, too. But I told her she could make it, it couldn't last forever. It lasted two weeks, then the second wave arrived, the fighting troops were relieved, the commandant's office was set up, and we had quiet and order. I don't know how you feel about it all, young lady, but you just don't forget that kind of thing. Yep, if we Germans had committed similar crimes . . . but let me tell you, we didn't have the time for that sort of thing. And besides, that's not in our nature.

That happened between Teltow and Mablow. The drive to Schoenefeld would take another fifteen minutes. Fifteen minutes versus thirty years. You realized that a show of anger would do no good, indignation would only drive him back into his silence. But then, what did do any good? Hoping to prove Germany's war guilt in a taxi . . . Your first sentences were clumsy. Herr X didn't deny that Germany had been guilty of starting the war, he didn't doubt a single one of the millions of Soviet dead, of whom you started speaking. He didn't even say: War is war. Sure, we started it. Most people around here were wearing blinders, they were completely nuts over their Adolf. However, what those people did to us afterward, that's quite another story.

In thirty years it has not been possible to make the two texts which run parallel in Herr X's head fit on one and the same page. He starts telling you details which are gruesome, you admit that:

gruesome, but you add, and feel almost ashamed to inform Herr X of, things that must have found their way into his living room in thirty years of newspapers, radio, and TV, things which he has blocked out for thirty years. It can't be possible, you think, that he didn't read certain descriptions, that he didn't see certain films and photos. That he has not once been seized with horror. Nausea. Shame. He's even listening to you, but one can feel when one's listener does or does not believe what he hears. He won't accept the possibility of the German debt being greater, if it ever came to a settling of accounts. Considerably greater. What does he say at the end? Never mind, he says again. No offense intended. But we all have our opinion. And everybody looks out for his own.

Herr X almost prompted you to tell the Bardikow stories as a series of newspaper anecdotes. (I'm sure you don't know what it means to be afraid, young lady.) Just in time you remember one of the main themes of your conversations with the history professor from Moscow: the accursed falsification of history into a moralistic tale. He has now been dead for ten years. You knew each other for at least six years, as can be ascertained from the dates of letters in your Moscow correspondence file. He had greater and greater difficulty breathing, more and more of his letters were sent from sanatoriums. Your visits to him in hospitals: in Berlin, in Moscow. (He said that Stalin's daughter, whom he had known, used to live in a world that didn't exist. The sentence made a lasting impression on you.) Moscow, as you'd never seen it before, and have never seen it since. The hospital on the hill. The garden in which the patients move slowly, alone or in groups. The unexpected view of the silhouetted city, dark against the pale golden edge of the sunset.

The professor who thought that each goodbye was the last. Who was not given to self-pity. His sad eyes, his sad smile. During the war, he had been a major, the editor of an army newspaper. He had been allowed to take part in the Potsdam Conference as an observer. You sometimes thought that he had perhaps been made to see too much. Then he'd smile again, and give you his articles to read. He had faith in reason. He'd quote Montesquieu, who thought that "reason possessed natural power . . . 'people resist reason, but this resistance is reason's triumph; sooner or later we shall have to go back to reason.' "

Your last visit—he died soon after—in the dark car in the park of the Cecilia Court, where he had attended a meeting, at the site of the Potsdam Conference. You no longer know how it came about, but you started telling him about the village of Bardikow. About the "Ark," about Pyotr, the commandant, about the raids. He wanted to hear more, hear everything. Sometimes he'd laugh, at other times he was silent. At the end, he said if ever he envied you for something—he never complained, he never felt that he had missed out on anything—it would be the following: You'd live to see the day when one would be able to speak and write about everything, openly and freely. That time will come, he said. You'll live to see it, I won't.

Today you know that the honest word doesn't exist in the age of suspicion, because the honest speaker depends on an honest listener, and because the person who hears the distorted echo of his own words eventually loses his honesty. There's nothing he can do about it. We can no longer tell exactly what we have experienced.

Nelly spent the August nights in the barn of a farm woman named Laabsch, Erna Laabsch, who had three daughters, Hanna, Lisa, and Brigitte, and only the middle one, Lisa, was remotely pretty. The stars flickered through the holes in the roof, Nelly would lie awake between her mother, who'd also be lying awake, and her brother, Lutz, who'd fall asleep the instant he stretched out, tired as he was from working in the fields. They'd hear "the Russians" sing; meanwhile, they'd found out that there were also non-Russians among the Russians. The singing sounded sad, but also threatening, she felt, and she was afraid in their unlocked barn. Every night, the widow Laabsch, a bony, hard-working, sharp-faced woman, bolted and barricaded her three daughters away like the gold treasure of the Aztecs, Charlotte Jordan said, who couldn't stop worrying because she wasn't able to pull a bolt on her daughter. The Russians had no Nescafé cans to offer the girls in the village. They ate heavy black bread and ran through the village in faded, sweat-stained soldiers' blouses. Sometimes they'd snatch a bicycle and do acrobatics in the main village road. They marched with a rapid step, which the Germans poked fun at. A man, known only as Concentration Camp Ernst, said to a couple of women in the mayor's office that the Germans were probably the only nation in the world that judged other nations by their march step. Nelly thought: That's just what I was doing. Suddenly it seemed ridiculous and embarrassing to her. The songs which the Russians sang on their marches differed strongly from those that could be heard in the village at night. The children ran alongside the column, imitating the soldiers' step, singing: Liverwurst, liverwurst, tam-ta-ta, liverwurst!

It was about this time that the Red commandant appeared in Bardikow. His name was Fritz Wussagk. Before he appeared in person, his existence had been a village rumor. One fine morning the legendary dogcart pulled up outside Nelly's office window. His permanent escort was with him, a character by the name of Franz (What's in a name: call me Franz. But the boss is called Herr Wussagk, if you don't mind), and Manne Banding, the onetime leader of the Bardikow Hitler Youth, who had lost his left arm at the eastern front. Nelly knew him because he was after her. One of his brown eyes had a white spot in the iris. Charlotte Jordan thought him an "unsavory character," and Nelly had to agree with her. Now he was wearing a red band around his arm, with a white K.

The K stood for Kommandant, as Nelly was personally informed by Herr Wussagk. Because the new occupation force had named him commandant of five villages, he declared, enumerating the villages, and had, among other exceedingly far-reaching authorizations, empowered him to appoint a representative for each of these villages, to enforce law and order, to protect the population against bandits, and to execute the orders of the chief commandant. Was all this clear?

Wussagk was like a person constructed of thin flexible steel wires. He inspired instant fear, and the simultaneous question: Why fear of this thin little man with the sparse blond hair? With his beret at a slant? Then he'd turn on his chair, flashing a strange look, one of his small delicate hands cramped nervously on the table: one knew once more why one was afraid.

Everything clear, Herr Wussagk.

It was known in the villages that the commandant liked his breakfast, and he didn't refuse the little piece of ham Rosemarie Steguweit went to get from the smoke chamber, or the little jar of lard. He had a way of receiving the offerings with such lightning speed that Nelly thought he was a magician rather than a commandant. For Saturday, he ordered two chickens—killed, cleaned, and plucked. The Fräulein here was to go and requisition them, in his name, together with Manne Banding. Manne Banding grinned in precisely that fashion Nelly couldn't stand. She managed to have two chickens ready by Saturday, without having to go requisitioning with Manne Banding. All she'd had to do was whisper to Widow Laabsch's youngest daughter, Brigitte, and to Rosemarie Steguweit, that the commandant, Herr Wussagk, had an incredible memory for people who'd done him a favor. The chicken from the Laabsch woman was, however, plumper than the mayor's chicken. No wonder, said Rosemarie Steguweit, that woman can feed them grain.

Nelly thought: The village was smarter than the town. Just by being there, she had acquired a little of that smartness. Without that, she'd just be washed up, and nobody would give a damn. She didn't want that. She shouldn't have cared what those peasants thought of her but, strangely enough, she did care. She wanted to keep her position with the mayor for reasons she didn't admit to herself: she enjoyed her work. She kept a blank face when one of the farmers told another in her presence: Our little Fräulein here wasn't born yesterday, either! But she did enjoy it.

Which is to say that fear and enjoyment aren't mutually exclusive, as long as there is no real fear of actually existing objects. Nelly lost her fear of the Russians in the village—because she learned to know them not as heroes but as slightly comical men. (Lenka says: Please, not the egg story again.)

One day, the Soviet commandant's orderly appeared in Nelly's office. He had mottled, stubbly blond hair, pale-blue eyes, and a face covered with freckles, and he painstakingly explained to Nelly: Every third day, the village had to supply twenty eggs, for which they would receive payment. Egg—understand? Hen—understand? Money—marks—understand? (This occurred before the time when Nelly called the orderly simply Seryozha, and long before she called the commandant simply Lieutenant Petya.) The orderly's stern tone contrasted sharply with the expression on his face, and Nelly let him understand that she noticed the contrast. That needed no vocabulary.

The mayor, who knew that his days in office were numbered, considered it Nelly's job to round up the eggs. Consequently, Nelly set out with a basket on her arm, and begged, threatened, and forced the farmwomen to give up eggs at the price of thirty pfennigs apiece: Richard Steguweit said that that was the maximum price an official could pay. On the black market, an egg was worth up to two marks. Nelly described what would happen to the village if the commandant, whom she portrayed as extremely stubborn, didn't get the eggs. The farmwomen sighed, and gave her two or three. Still carrying the egg basket, she walked up to the barricade that separated the Soviet-occupied part of the village from the rest. The eggs and the password "commandant" prompted the sentry to open the barricade for her. (Later, the sentries merely waved, and she'd unceremoniously walk around the barricade.) She was directed to an inn, the Greening Tree, in whose kitchen the Soviet company's food was being cooked. Five cooks, two of them with high white hats. The taller of these two, the head cook, was qualified to transact the egg business. Nelly pushed her basket across the counter; he pulled a bundle of bills, occupation money, from the pocket of his army trousers under his white apron. Nelly said, as though standing behind the counter in her father's store: six marks, please. The cook placed a fifty-mark bill on the counter. Nelly said: Too much. The cook said: Enough. They repeated this three times. Nelly showed six fingers. The cook became disgruntled and said: Now leave. Nelly took the fifty-mark bill. On her way out, she started laughing. She was no longer afraid of the head cook.

The mayor, who was spending almost all his time in bed, wanted no part of the Russian money. Didn't Nelly know that the village was hardly able to pay her for all the work she had been doing. Thirty marks a month, the price of half a loaf of bread.

Nelly kept a conscientious ledger of the egg money and its use, the number of collected eggs, which she, incidentally, kept in the stove pipe in the office, but in the midsummer heat they couldn't be kept for more than four or five days. On the other hand, it was smart to have a small stock, because the results of her collection efforts fluctuated. The eggs which became too old had to be eaten. By whom? The mayor believed that this was also Nelly's responsibility. Nelly's family of eight had no trouble eating twenty scrambled eggs for supper. Nelly conscientiously paid for the eggs with the extra money from her transactions with the head cook. Those were not small sums. Richard Steguweit said: Now the Russians are paying you your rightful salary.

And that was that.

The widow Laabsch said to Charlotte Jordan, whom she couldn't stand, because Charlotte wouldn't let herself be intimidated: It seems that your daughter is quite friendly with the Russians. Going in and out as if she belonged there.

What about it? said Charlotte. Why don't you send your daughters, if you've got the guts. My Nelly knows how to handle them. The Russians are human, too.

Then, the other cook at the Greening Tree entered Nelly's life for a number of weeks. Every afternoon around 3:30 he'd appear in the mayor's office. Apparently his kitchen duties were over at that hour. At first Nelly hardly recognized him without his white hat. He must have been from the Caucasus, a dark-skinned man with black eyes and curly bluish-black hair. He'd enter, greet her, take off his cap, and sit down in the worn-out visitor's chair, where he had a good view of Nelly. There he'd sit, and look at her. It gave her the creeps. She tried to find out what he wanted. He kept silent, and she gave up. He'd usually stay for an hour, play with the crank of the old telephone, then get up abruptly, put his cap back on, say goodbye in Russian, and leave.

When he came for the third time, she understood. She certainly needn't be afraid of him. Let him sit and stare at her, while she calmly—at least outwardly—wrote, typed, dealt with visitors who, incidentally, seemed to prefer to come between 3:30 and 4:30 and weren't sparing with remarks about her taciturn visitor. Charlotte said: You're being talked about. Now it was Nelly's turn to say: What about it? It's possible that she did move a little more provocatively than usual when the cook was around. But maybe not. The villagers soon began calling him "her Russian." Perhaps she could have made better use of the situation. He'd sit and look at her. The structure of their relationship was clear.

Once, after three or four weeks, he unscrewed the crank of the telephone, dropped it beside the phone, quickly got up before his usual time, left without a greeting, and never came back.

He got scared because of the busted telephone, said Uncle Alfons Radde. Nelly tried to believe him, despite her doubts. She'd see the cook when she took the eggs to the Greening Tree, every three days, but he'd keep in the background and not look at her. Nelly didn't ask herself in what way he had disappointed her.

(Twenty-three years later, in a city on the Volga, after the second bottle of champagne in the Culture Center, before the beginning of the film, the man who offered the champagne—a Russian journalist—asks you if you know a village named D. Somewhere in Mecklenburg. You've never heard of the village. But he had spent forty-five months there, as a sergeant. There had been a young refugee girl, Anna B., who was beautiful. It might just be possible that she still lives in that village, the man said. You offered to write to the mayor's office. The man thought for a while. Yes, he finally said. Please do that. And if you manage to get in touch with her, please ask her if she has a child that is now twenty-two years old. And write to me about it. The mayor's office of D. answered your inquiry by return mail, no woman by the name of Anna B.—or with the maiden name Anna B.—was known in the village. Sorry. You found it absurdly hard to write this information to the man with whom you had drunk champagne.)

Fall had come. October. As had been long expected, the politically undesirable mayor, Richard Steguweit, was replaced; the community shingle was removed from the Steguweit house and fastened to the fence of shoemaker Sölle, who had no need for Nelly, because his own daughter would help him with the office work.

Nelly no longer had any reason to go to the Greening Tree. But she was asked to perform one last official task. She had to make up a list and be present for two days during which a young Soviet woman doctor examined all the women in the village for venereal disease. A room had been cleared in cottager Stumpf's house on the Ringweg: a sofa, a kitchen table for Nelly, a wooden chair, a living-room table with chair for the doctor, a washbasin with disinfectant in a corner, on a nail a towel, which Frau Stumpf had to change frequently. The nurse Nadia was boiling tea on the potbellied stove in the corner. The women, summoned in alphabetical order, stood in line outside the house. The village men walked past, grinning. Nelly drank tea with the woman doctor and the nurse, they talked together as well as they could; she called the women inside, confirmed their identity, checked their names off on her list, and learned to enter certain medical terms into the respective column. She pledged to honor the Hippocratic oath, which she had not taken, and to reveal to no one the names of the six or seven women who were under suspicion of infection and who would have to go for a more thorough checkup in the district capital.

It was a significant experience. For the first time Nelly saw how women were made to pay for the things men did to them. Several women cried, the pastor's wife, for instance. Nelly tried, in vain, to persuade the woman doctor to make exceptions. She offered to vouch for the pastor's wife, Frau Knop. The doctor said sternly: *Nyet*. She made her understand that Nelly wouldn't even be able to vouch for herself. That was obvious. The woman doctor's job was certainly necessary and right. But Nelly thought it was superfluous to ask each woman before the examination if she was married.

On the first evening the woman doctor said: German women, pigs. It became apparent that she expected unmarried women to be virgins. The vehemence with which Nelly opposed this concept taught her that she believed differently. But since when? And how? She no longer seemed to know herself. She loathed the oilcloth-covered sofa on which the women lay down, one after the other, as though on a conveyor belt. She didn't know what to do with her rage.

When Nelly was staying on with the Steguweits, as their maid, without pay, just for meals, she came across a box of books while sweeping under the conjugal bed of Rosemarie Steguweit and her absent husband. Among them were several titles which she had once borrowed from Julia Strauch at the school library. All the other inhabitants of the house were out in the fields, digging pota-toes, including the ex-mayor, whose loss of office had worked an instant cure. Nelly gave the two children, Edeltraut and Dietmar, toys to play with while she spent hours, entire mornings, reading in the former visitor's chair in the former office. Once more she read *The Wagon Fortress* by Friedrich Griese, she read *Sacrificial Pil-grimage* by Rudolf Binding, *Gion, the Physician* by Hans Carossa, and thought that she was suffering as she read. Only now did she experience—not surprisingly—the pain you'd call "phantom pain," the type amputees are supposed to feel in the limb they lost. The things she no longer had and the person she no longer was hurt her violently. The books supplied her with the poison of self-pity.

(Interview question: Do you believe in the influence of litera-ture? Certainly, though probably not as you do. I believe that the mechanism which deals with the absorption and processing of reality is formed by literature; in Nelly's case, this mechanism was severely damaged, although she was not aware of it. How did we become what we are today? One of the answers would be a list of book titles.)

You decide to tell only amusing stories for the time being, to tell about the tricks and pranks which abound in uncontrolled times. The wedding of the Red commandant, Fritz Wussagk, divided the population of his five tributary villages into two camps: the outraged farmers and the laughing refugees. Because it was the farmers who had to supply the stuff for the banquet, and without being stingy about it, either, as Charlotte gleefully said. For the preparation of the feast a large-scale campaign to round up farm produce was taking place under the very eyes of the occupying force, although without the latter's knowledge. Fritz Wussagk's bride was a pale refugee from Barkhusen, who had three outstanding characteristics: colorless frizzy hair, two red circles on her cheekbones, and a squeaky voice. Her name was Ilse Wiedehopf, and Wussagk called her Ilsie in front of everybody. Marrying these two was the last official act of Mayor and Registrar of Vital Statistics Richard Steguweit. On this occasion Nelly saw him for the first and only time wearing a white shirt, a thick black cloth coat, and a black tie. Of all the sweating participants, Richard Steguweit sweated the most.

Will you, Fräulein Ilse Wiedehopf, be faithful to your betrothed, Herr Fritz Wussagk, as long as you both shall live? Yes, squeaked Ilsie.

Ilsie wore a white bridal gown. And she was given to tears. But that was to be expected. Whereas Nelly had hardly expected to see Franz, Wussagk's bodyguard, whom Charlotte Jordan called "a tough customer" (as tough as they come), bursting into uncontrolled sobs, nor to see Wussagk himself (as cold as a dog's nose) giving the ceremony the greatest importance and strictly observing all formalities. It was rumored that he had offered to give a calf to the pastor's wife, Frau Knop, if she would marry him in the church (a calf which she might have traded for a new altar cloth, because the old one had recently been stolen from the Bardikow church). But Frau Pastor abhorred the dance around the golden calf and, for the first time, pleaded lack of official authority.

Some hundred people had been invited to the Red commandant's wedding. It took place in a barn that had been cleared out and freshly whitewashed and scrubbed by ten Barkhusen women. There was said to have been an abundance of meats of all kinds, and the booze, hardly watered down, was said to have flowed in rivers. At the height of the festivities the ladies, it was said, had to prove themselves by doing certain dances (on the tables!) and the gentlemen by shooting at empty bottles. Wussagk might be the most crooked of crooks, but he sure knew how to throw a party. You had to hand it to him. The children and teenagers of Barkhusen crowded around the open barn door, were generously fed, and given a powerful desire for what they took to be "living." That Wussagk guy sure knows how to live.

Then he disappeared. The drama of those years produced its effect: the sudden appearance of people who recognized him, who couldn't keep their mouths shut and started a rumor that reached the ears of the new authorities, which led to his being unmasked. He had indeed been jailed "before the changeover," but not for political reasons. Besides Ilsie Wiedehopf, two other women in different German towns could claim to be his legally wedded wives. In other words, as Charlotte Jordan expressed with satisfaction, he was just your run-of-the-mill bigamist. It was obvious that no one in all of God's creation had appointed Wussagk to be the Red commandant. Lieutenant Petya, who had a fit of rage when he heard the details, appeared in the mayor's office with his orderly Seryozha to inquire in the sternest of tones why he had not been informed of Wussagk's carryings-on. Nelly told him the truth: Because of fear, understand? The lieutenant roared: *Nyet!* and slammed the door behind him.

Unfathomable as people are, the five villages respected Ilsie Wiedehopf highly when she swore to remain faithful to her husband. A man who gives a woman that kind of a wedding—she's supposed to have said—such a man doesn't deserve to be left in the lurch. He wasn't all bad, said Charlotte. She'd had long conversations with him, about mystical subjects mainly, which particularly interested the Red commandant. During her overland forage expeditions, she had often depended on his protection. He tolerated no banditry inside his realm. When others make it that easy for a man to become a crook, commented Charlotte, they shouldn't be surprised when he turns into one.

On the road between Vitnica and Kostrzyn—on Sunday, July 11, 1971 (a date that lies discouragingly far in the past: this is March 1975)—at noon, as you drive through the now deserted villages, you ask your brother, Lutz, when everybody started calling the Frahm house the Ark. Lutz knows nothing about it. He never called the Frahm house the Ark. Although he thinks the name most fitting.

The Frahms were the only people who were willing to take in refugees at the beginning of winter; for instance, refugees who had spent the summer in a barn, exposed to the inclemencies of the weather. Nobody liked to move to the Frahms unless he was forced to, the house was too isolated: over a mile from the village, over a mile from the Black Mill, at the crossing of two rural lanes, not far from the edge of the woods. Its scenic beauty, however, didn't matter. What mattered was a safe location. (It's hard to believe that only four, five people are living in the Frahms' house today. Young Frau Frahm is alone with her son as you arrive. She's the only one you hadn't met before. She married Werner, who's responsible for the crop production of the cooperative. She takes you on a tour of the house and laughs when you remember which whole family used to live in which room.)

Lutz, too, remembers who used to live where, in the various rooms of the Frahm house. (During your visit in 1974, you sit with young Frau Frahm in the very room in which Nelly's family lived. Today it's a modern living room, just like any living room in any city apartment. As the young woman leaves to fetch the old photo album, you show H. where the large wooden table used to stand at which the family took their meals, and where the old tile stove and the beds used to be.

You found the new arrangement irritating, it overshadowed your memory. You had to close your eyes to see the shabby room again clearly, the worn armchair Nelly used to push to the window to see the three fir trees on the opposite side of the road, which made a deeper impression on her than had any other tree. You couldn't believe that they had been cut down; you had described them to H. as an unmistakable landmark for finding the house. They had been cut down because they were dangerous to the overland power lines, young Frau Frahm explained.)

Lenka claimed that no one could possibly remember the names

of twenty-eight persons for twenty-six years, persons with whom one had, at one time, happened to share the same house. (You had reached the number twenty-eight when you counted the occupants of the Ark.) Oh, you said, not only the names! You can still see them, every single one of them. They had come from Mecklenburg, Brandenburg, Pomerania, Silesia, West Prussia, Berlin. Frau Mackowski, the wild-haired, emaciated woman who lived in the room next to the Jordans, separated only by a thin door, with her five children and her invalid husband. She'd curse in Polish when she stepped out into the hall at night, and gave Fräulein Tälchen hell. Lydia Tälchen, who received a variety of male visitors in the single room which she shared with her innocent son, Nicky; she was so disorganized that one visitor frequently walked in on another; and they all got in the way of Heinz Kastor, who lived in a garret above the stable and who considered himself Lydia Tälchen's steady boyfriend. The situation often led to blows during the night, despite the thin walls and the presence of all the children, especially the children of shoemaker Mackowski, an ailing, limping man who kept quiet and was satisfied with being able to put up with his wife; who could repair almost any damage that occurred in the rambling house.

Lydia Tälchen became a security risk only later, during the dark winter nights, when it was vital to barricade doors and gates and not open them for any reason, not even to let a lover slip out. But before that, there were the days when beet syrup had to be cooked in the laundry room, when Concentration Camp Ernst, a Berliner, who lived in the attic with his German shepherd, Harro, and who was an old hand at ruses, had to kill a cow. They were all going to celebrate Christmas together in the Frahm living room, which gave everybody the opportunity to contribute to the entertainment. Irene, the twenty-two-year-old daughter of Ludwig Zabel, a teacher from Glogau in Silesia, sang, as she often did, "Every day is not Sunday," and everybody knew that she was thinking of Arno, her fiancé, who was missing in the West and for whom she displayed exemplary love and fidelity; she also sang the last verse: "And when I'm dead / please think of me / before you go to sleep / but do not weep for me." (Your brother, Lutz, by now thirteen, never took his eyes off Irene while she sang. Yes, he says, I liked that girl a lot.)

Then the four girls had to sing a round: "Evening calm upon the world." The four girls were Irene's younger, blonder, and shorter sister, Margot; Frahm's fifteen-year-old daughter, Hanni; the maid Herta, and Nelly. But only Lydia Tälchen's contribution was unbeatable, unique. Lydia, who thought nothing of practically sitting on the knees of this Kastor person, this poker-faced hick, gaping at him with her big brown cow eyes; but who rose with a spiral movement of hips and shoulders when her turn came, and after a brief dramatic pause performed "Mamatchi, give me a pony" with such depth of feeling that almost everyone's eyes filled with tears. For the first time Nelly experienced art triumphing over morality.

Nelly tried to sit next to teacher Schadow, a pale young man who was the first new teacher in the village of Bardikow, and for whom Lutz has words of respect to this day: He wasn't the worst by any means. He was more than okay. He'd go hungry—he'd really starve himself, rather than let the farmers bribe him with bacon and sausages to give their sons better marks than they deserved. He can't have been more than twenty, twenty-one years old. Where had he come from, how come he wasn't a prisoner somewhere? Maybe he was ill, maybe he had been wounded. Nelly thought, deep down, that he was "pure" (Good Lord, pure! That was a must for her). She didn't actually use the word, but that was how she felt. Naturally, Armin Schadow didn't try to sit close to Nelly, but to Hanni Frahm, who was wide-hipped like her mother, cheerful and upright and hard-working; she was going to marry the teacher, as it soon turned out, and she certainly deserved him. Meanwhile, Nelly had added a warning to the sayings next to her bed, written on white paper and tacked to the crumbling wall: "Maturity means to bear pain's test / to lay your cherished dream to rest / and still wish others all the best."

On the other hand, she was learning the unforgettable lesson: When food is scarce, food becomes the only goal. She learned once and for all about cooking syrup: about the smell of precooked chips of beet, which used to drift in layers over the Frahm courtyard for weeks, a disgusting smell. That's why we never have syrup sandwiches, Lenka, which is probably ungrateful and unfair. Nelly never experienced greater joy in eating than when she saw the first spoonful of the gooey, dark, brownish-red syrup trickle onto the whole-grain bread, which the Frahms baked themselves and which no regular knife was able to cut. (Not to mention that this was the same syrup that later hastened the cure of her right lung. Her father, who had meanwhile returned, brought it to her in the TB sanatorium; Nelly would eat whole cupfuls of the syrup in the afternoons. Syrup, rather than badger fat or one's own urine, which other patients swore by.)

Other images: Charlotte, who couldn't possibly get any thinner, nothing but skin and bones. It's now her chore to go scouring for food in the countryside. She ties the heavy brown skirt, made from a blanket, around her waist with a rope, places several layers of newspaper into her worn-out shoes, pulls a clean sack over her head against the rain, the way millers do. In this way she runs along the unsafe roads, fearlessly, for hours, and when she comes home, often in the dark, she places a bag of flour on the table, a little piece of butter, a tiny chunk of lard. God only knows how Charlotte does it. Yes: God and I both! Always her accursed arrogance, which Aunt Liesbeth can't stand. She makes a nasty remark. Everybody knows what's in store: a scene. The boiled potatoes in mock gravy number 2 (low fat) are eaten in complete silence in the dim flicker of a kerosene lamp. In gloomy silence. And still without electricity, the dishes are washed in the hall which Nelly's family uses as a kitchen; taciturn and embittered, each withdraws to his sleeping quarters: the Jordans and Whiskers Grandma in an attic room, with a bucket in the center, which everybody has to use at least three times a night, since their diet consists mainly of half-frozen potatoes.

Lutz knows the cow story in all its intricate detail (you ask him over the telephone; he laughs: You're going to write that?), details which only a person like Concentration Camp Ernst could think up and carry out: a man who seems to come right out of a prankster tale. He kept his concentration-camp rags downstairs in his chest, but he didn't tell anyone when, where, or why he had been in the camp. In his opinion, sadness didn't do humanity much good, and eating and drinking kept body and soul together. He walked to the neighboring village with Harro, his dog. According to a rumor, a farmer in that village had taken in a stray ox. Ernst managed to convince the suspicious farmer that it was his ox. When he came back, he managed to persuade farmer Frahm, who usually wanted no part in shady deals, to give him four days' worth of fodder to pay the farmer back for feeding "his" ox. The ox was pitifully emaciated, but farmer Frahm traded Ernst a well-fed calf for it, which Ernst instantly slaughtered in order to give a feast for all the inhabitants of the Ark. Everybody had an enormous piece of meat on his plate. The large Frahm kitchen could barely accommodate the crowd. The Mackowski children, whose uncombed heads were most probably the breeding ground of the lice with which the house had become infested, were benignly tolerated: at the high point of the meal, teacher Ludwig Zabel from Glogau in Silesia, a solemn man, rose to his feet, clutching a calf's shank, and intoned: "Drink up, my love, let's drink all night, drinking makes your eyes shine bright." Then they toasted the calf by clinking its bones together. Farmer Frahm and his wife sat at the head of the table, happily eating their own calf. Nelly noticed that one could get drunk on eating.

In the night, after feasting on Melusine the calf, Lydia Tälchen opened the attic door to let one of her lovers out. The lover was Farmer Voss's slightly lame son, who could afford to bring Fräulein Tälchen an egg and a sip of milk—not like Heinz Kastor, who slept in Herr Ernst's attic room, totally drunk and destitute—but was incapable of defending her against physical violence. At any rate, neither he nor the delicate Lydia were able to push the half-opened door shut against someone who was pushing hard from the outside. Russian sounds, which also startled the Frahm family from their sleep. Four Russian soldiers were giving orders to the shaking Lydia in Russian, and were communicating with each other in low voices. This first time everything went very quickly: Lydia, who didn't understand Russian, instantly understood the orders, hurriedly opened the door to the smoke chamber, each of the four grabbed as many hams and sausages as he could carry, and before the Frahms had gotten out of bed, and before Charlotte and Nelly emerged from their attic room and came downstairs, it was all over. All that could be heard was the sound of a horse-drawn vehicle disappearing wildly into the darkness.

Heinz Kastor appeared and beat Lydia black and blue. Nobody intervened. Maybe it would teach her a lesson.

The next morning, Frahm himself informed Lieutenant Pyotr, the commandant of Bardikow. That afternoon the lieutenant sat in the Frahms' kitchen. Frau Frahm served him crumb cake, he spoke at great length, and sometimes with great anger, while Seryozha translated laconically: Commandant say not good. Bandits. Lock door. Call commandant.

The location of the house was a problem. It became known that there were hiding places in the woods for groups of soldiers who had deserted the regular troops. Most of the fourteen attacks that were perpetrated against the Frahms' house during the next eighteen months had worse consequences than the first one: an extensive course in fear. Details have become legends in the families who lived through them. One night, Charlotte heard the young women screaming in the house, and poured a bottle of Lysol over her threshold, shouting: Typhoid! to the soldier who demanded entry. A word that is understood in any language and which has the effect of an exorcism. That time, nobody entered her room except Herta, the Frahms' maid, who slipped and fell near the door: Frau Jordan, what are they trying to do to me . . .

Lieutenant Pyotr had the telephone line between the Frahm house and the village repaired. Now there was an army telephone in the living room with a direct connection to the commandant's office. Twice, the commandant came riding over, wildly shooting into the air, and drove the looters off without catching them. The third time, the telephone didn't function: the line had been cut.

During that night Nelly understood that one should never think that one had experienced a sensation to the fullest: neither fear, nor therefore joy, nor despair, nor what she called "happiness" in the few poems she wrote in secret during those days. You asked young Frau Frahm to show you the tiny attic room in which Nelly had crouched during that night, with the twelve women who lived in the house, while people rummaged through the wardrobe, which had been pushed in front of the thin door, and heavy steps and curses in a foreign language could be heard from the next room. The little room is no longer in use. It no longer has the cot in it. Everything is light, functional, clean. You looked at it without emotion.

One morning—the morning after that night—Nelly's only clothes were her pajamas and a coat. She stood outside the Frahm house, with a blanket wrapped around her shoulders, and watched the sun come up. She felt indescribably good. (A feeling of well-being that occurs in extreme situations.) Expressions like "by the skin of our teeth" didn't occur to her. Later she understood what was meant by it.

It's the truth: she felt a touch of disappointment when she got her clothes back a couple of days later. Charlotte Jordan had been asked to come to the Russian commandant's office in the district capital. There was a room that looked like a storage room, except that the merchandise that was stored there was not new. Charlotte said she'd felt embarrassed seeing the other women throw themselves upon the things. She'd felt like walking out. That's when she's seen her old battered suitcase standing in a corner. From out of a mound of clothing she'd pulled Nelly's sweatsuit, which was irreplaceable, and a few blankets. She declined the offer made by the young soldier leaning against the door frame to take more. In the hall, men in Soviet uniforms had been lined up. An interpreter of officer's rank asked the women—politely but coolly, Charlotte said, an educated person at any rate—if they could identify any of the men as the night raiders.

Charlotte did recognize the tall dark one with the high fur cap, who had been standing at her door when she'd yelled "Typhoid." Incomprehensibly she didn't turn him in. He'd had such a desperate look in his eyes. She'd felt sorry for him.

Uncle Alfons Radde tapped his forehead. You're the one to feel sorry for, he said to his sister-in-law.

There wasn't a subject that didn't lead to a fight between them.

Did Lutz remember how Alfons Radde insulted Whiskers Grandma that day in the Frahm house? Lutz doesn't know what you're talking about. Well, he called her a "Polack." You no longer remember why. Polack. A deadly insult, and Nelly immediately protected Whiskers Grandma. (Don't you dare insult my grandmother! Something like that. And his possible answer: You're still wet behind the ears!) The deep satisfaction of utter hatred.

The memory surged shortly before Kostrzyn, after Lenka declared that she liked Polish people. For what reason, Lutz and you wanted to know. (H. was concentrating on his driving, in the heat.) They were livelier, Lenka thought. More spontaneous. They didn't seem to use order, cleanliness, and discipline as weapons against each other. Unlike us.

In what respect?

Well, they don't seem to be killing each other with efficiency.

I don't know what you mean by kill, Lutz said to his niece. But, he said, if they want to improve their living standard, they'll have to recognize the value of efficiency. At any rate, that's what I believe.

What *do* you believe, anyway? Lenka asked. (She must have been interested in confessions of faith at that time.)

Is that the proper subject for almost 100-degree heat?

Tell me, anyway.

I believe, said Lutz, for example: taking specific laws of physics into account, and the reaction of certain materials under specified stress conditions, that it's possible to construct a machine with a predictable overall efficiency.

I thought as much, said Lenka.

H. never took part in this kind of discussion. Consequently, Lenka relied on you. At first the usual evasions: what had made her ask that kind of question, etc. Oh, stop fiddling around, she said.

You're embarrassing your mother, said H. A little hint.

What do you mean?

The substance of faith varies according to generations.

It occurred to you that Lenka had never had to use the term "believer" with regard to herself. You remembered the totally different confessions of faith which you renounced every few years. You thought that the demands that had been made on your generation might perhaps be unique—a thought that unburdened you somewhat.

For instance—you said, and instantly stopped, because a confession of faith shouldn't start with a for instance—for instance, I believe in the significance of communicating what you consider to be the truth.

Lenka never doubted that. Your answer was of no use to her. Whereas H., who'd recently become fond of attacking especially those utterances of yours which you considered the most truthful, H. said: Forgive me, but without communication the kind of truth you have in mind cannot exist. So what's the point?

The truth, Lutz said. My goodness me, you do aim high.

I said: What I *consider* the truth. Or do you think I'm absurd enough to ask that everybody "tell the truth," like children? We're talking about truth as a relative reference system among people. What's going on all of a sudden? said Lenka. Could somebody please tell me what you're talking about?

We're talking about the fact that there are other kinds of truth, you said, still angry, besides 2 times 2 equals 4. And I ask myself why these truths are always recognized so late, and why it's so difficult to discuss them.

I see, said Lenka. But that wasn't my question. I only wanted to know, do you believe that a person can make a complete change?

Holy cow, said Lutz.

You drove into Kostrzyn in search of a restaurant. The town had been almost completely destroyed. But it had been rebuilt. You drove into a dreary, newly built-up section: a few rows of concrete houses in a desolate landscape. The only restaurant was hot and crowded, and didn't serve food as early as noon. You drank some juice and left. Lenka's question remained unanswered, and she didn't insist. One of those instances when embarrassment kept you from understanding the subject she had raised. The sequence of thoughts that passed through your mind would have been of no use to her: to make a complete change. To become a "new person." You've seen films in which the "new person" didn't act at ease. Was this supposed to be the new person? Aspiring toward a vision of the new being is as hopeless as it is essential. The new layer of fear that covers the old: again failure seems to be your fate. Older people who shrug: How oversensitive, how weak this younger generation . . .

Lenka remained alone with her doubts about herself.

The role of time in the dissolving of fear.

K.L., your Moscow friend, insisted that you describe to him the alarm system that had been put in at the Frahm house to the last detail. He had you draw it for him. You realized: its invention was based on concentration and the need for it to succeed; its functioning required the flawless collaboration of man and technology. To begin with, the upper floor of the Frahm house was hermetically sealed off from the ground floor by a thick trapdoor, made by the village carpenter; it had to withstand axes and crowbars. Then, a guard schedule was established to assign the men to alternating nightly outdoor shifts and the women to the telephone. The third installation—Lutz's original invention, for which the entire household outdid itself in praise—anticipated the break-down of the telephone and consisted of three empty oxygen bottles and iron clappers suspended in the enormous ancient chestnut tree in the Frahm courtyard, connected by ropes with one of the attic windows of the Frahm house. They made an incredible racket when the ropes were pulled at a certain rhythm.

K.L., who asked precise questions, trying to discover a gap in the system, roared his appreciation: *Molodiets!* Well done! which kept you laughing for the longest time. You told him that later raids had followed a specific pattern: for instance, the man who is on outdoor watch hears—usually between 1 and 2 a.m., when the night is darkest—a vehicle approach. He gives a loud signal with his whistle and crawls into a prepared hiding place. The woman who has the indoor telephone watch opens the living-room door and yells: Alarm! as loud as she can, in order to wake the entire house. After that she rushes back to the telephone and informs the commandant's office. All the Ark inhabitants who sleep on the ground floor move rapidly and soundlessly to the upper floor, where the luggage is stored every night. It is Nelly's responsibility to see to it that all inhabitants are upstairs before the trapdoor is closed. She issues the command: Close the door, to Uncle Alfons Radde and teacher Zabel. The trapdoor falls into place, twice the key is turned in the heavy iron lock, the bolt is pushed.

At the same time, a deafening noise fills the air. It's your brother, Lutz, in the attic window, activating the ropes, which set the clappers beating against the oxygen bottles. One and a half miles away, the whole village wakes up. Commandant Pyotr jumps into the saddle, followed by Seryozha; he shoots a whole magazine from his machine pistol into the air as he rides; later he sits in the Frahms' kitchen, sweating and cursing.

While you told all this to K.L.—in whose living room one photo among many shows him as a captain of the Soviet Army during the war—you laughed so hard, you sometimes couldn't go on with your story.

Write that down, he roared, you've got to write that down!

The nights spent in the Frahms' kitchen after the thwarted raids. The black bread, hard as a rock. The knife with its razor-thin blade. In the middle of the table a jar of preserved liverwurst, whose taste has never been equaled by any other sausage. The fire in the stove. Hot soup from the day before. Hot barley coffee. Excited conversation. Everyone tells everyone else how cold-blooded and smart he's been. The outdoor guard is praised. Teacher Zabel draws the route of his flight from Glogau on the kitchen table so Lieutenant Pyotr can determine if and where his unit almost ran into Zabel. Irene Zabel reads the last letter from her fiancé, Arnold: it's from an American POW camp. My dear girl, the letter starts, and Irene says: That's what he's always called me.

In the back room Frahm's grandmother lies dying. Soon it'll be daybreak. More and more of the gray sky shows above the stables, since they are no longer necessary and have been pulled down. Farmer Frahm claps his hands and says: Well, folks, another day. The commandant says: *Rabota!* Work! And gets up and bids everybody goodbye. A few people, Nelly, for instance, who has by this time contracted TB and should have constant rest, crawl back into bed.

Fear describes strange and unpredictable curves. It grips you, it lets go. Fear in the form of pincers.

Now only self-discipline can help you. A regulated day, a strict working schedule. H., who doubts your efforts to gain perspective. Who doesn't know that you'd pay almost any price to get rid of your fear. The problem is contained in the word "almost," you're aware of that. (What, for instance, is the price of perspective?)

You'd like to know what's going on. The search for the perfect expression as one of the deepest satisfactions. Days when every promise of satisfaction dissolves into the acid of self-knowledge: The expression is false even before it has been formed.

The Plague, Hunger, War, Death: the old-fashioned Horsemen of the Apocalypse. You're acquainted with three of them, if ty-phoid fever may be substituted for the plague. (Typhoid fever makes the blood gush from Nelly's nose, topples her, forces her down on a bed, which rocks throughout the night as though on heavy seas. Which throws her out of time—timelessness as a milky river—into a region where authority has no say. She survives the news of her own death, which terrifies her mother—who is in the village—for three hours. When she's able to decide to get well, she's well. She hadn't been afraid.)

Why is Fear lacking among the Horsemen of the Apocalypse?

(Paul Fleming, "To the self": "Your sorrows and your joys, take them as what was chosen / Accept the fate that's yours, leave everything unrued." Emotional involvement, but no envy toward the ancestors who lack the experience of our time: The inability to accept the self; not to know what "To the self" is supposed to mean.) "In the heaven of self-denial," it says in a letter, "fear is unknown." But so is love. Has fear been placed as the watchman at the gates of the hell of self-knowledge?

(A news item: Vast offensive of North Vietnamese forces which now occupy the northern part of South Vietnam.)

Late afternoon. The drive into the district capital on the new highway. On your left, the blood-red horizon as a backdrop for the silhouette of the town, bare branches, turrets. "In this light, any landscape looks beautiful." You know it, but you don't feel it. The same thoughts keep spinning in your head. You say: Perhaps it's the fear of tearing myself apart as I try to detach myself from what I am now. Is there an alternative? No, you say. But it's a choice, nonetheless.

H. says: Why must we always imagine that we're in control of everything? And feel devastated when we realize that we're not?

The darker, still-red horizon is in back of you now, the full moon in front, a cold light over the town. That night you dream that you're writing a postcard to H., and after you wake up, you can read the text on the card, word by word, from a film strip in your head: Dear H., you wrote, now I'm no longer the old Adam but a new one. Now everything has dropped away from me. Your old Adam.

You both laugh, since fear can reveal humor as it dissipates. It was the first day with a smell of spring in the air. "And in the chasm lies the truth," H. says with irony. Do you know who said that? You won't believe it: Friedrich Schiller.

18

Time is running out. We're often not really alive.

Something within you affirms that these two sentences belong together. One might be the exclamation of a radio sports commentator, the other the complaint of a hypochondriac. The different stuff sentences are made of; the different stuff of eras.

It's gotten so that you have to concentrate in order to remember last night's film on television. Pale, very pale. Whereas you remember the Steguweit kitchen with the utmost clarity, the stove on which Nelly stirs the daily gruel—without sugar or salt—the cast-iron pan in which she learns to make home fries without burning the onions. You've taken to jotting down the daily events, sometimes even the weather and its changes, hoping that: "Unseasonally cool, occasional sunshine" might later open up a vista on life. You don't imagine when the "time" will come for you to remember, which means: reliving the unlived life, "wearing it out." The way one wears out old clothes, or clears out a stack of papers. (The temperature drop, this spring 1975, after another unreal winter, the drop in people's morale; the drop in the national health picture—the outbreak of flu: supposedly even younger people died of it.)

You suspect that we're living in times that are forgotten more quickly than those resilient good old days. (Throwaway times.) Different times that pass at a different speed. The present time, which seems to expand, which is measured by minutes, whose hours drag but whose years fly, taking life along with them on their flight. And compared to that, the time of the past, compact, vehement, concentrated, as though melted into time ingots. It is describable. Whereas the naked everyday time of the present cannot be described, it can only be filled in.

It is humanly impossible, people say, to become emotionally involved with every war in the world. (The NLF rockets are striking the outskirts of Saigon.) When people buy imported shoes (when we buy imported shoes), there's a collection box beside the cash register, sometimes it's transparent, usually half full, even with bank-notes: for Solidarity with Vietnam, with Angela Davis, with Chile. Today's notion—that money can redeem everything—leads to the assumption that we're paying for not having been hit. A conclusion which once again presupposes an irrationally guilty conscience: that one actually ought to take part in it. Another assumption: the imagination of the donors is unrelated to the donation.

The imagination of the citizens of America, the world power, who haven't learned to read the faces of the populations they have bombed or bribed, must be based on the assumption that every child on this earth can deem himself fortunate to grow up in the American civilization. This explains their lack of understanding about why other people think their South Vietnamese child-adoption program is obscene.

You were singing, in the car, between Kostrzyn and Slubice, despite the heat. "The mighty generals betrayed us," you sang, "betrayed us, betrayed us." And "In the valley of Rio Jamara." And the Song of the Faithful Comrade, the text of which had been rewritten to fit the occasion of Hans Beimler's death—Lenka didn't know it. "A bullet had come flying / From his homeland, with his name. / It caused the good man's dying, / if not we would be lying, / German guns have perfect aim."

Lenka wasn't in tears. She said: Shit.

Throughout 1945 Nelly didn't learn a single one of these songs. She continued to write first lines of songs into her green imitation-leather notebook, but they were different songs. ("A drum can be heard in Germany," "When everyone deserts the cause" . . .) Another two, three years and she'll sing—walking in the streets of a town whose name she hadn't even heard in 1945: "Rebuild, rebuild." And she'll try to forget the songs in the green notebook. Which has been lost, incidentally. It never works, overlapping eras of songs.

Death is a reliable contemporary who has assumed the task of dividing the narration into segments. When Nelly comes out of the hospital after her bout with typhoid fever, Whiskers Grandpa lies dying. Nelly's mother seems more horrified by the fact that her daughter has come back with lice than by her father's impending death. Her daughter has head lice. In the hospital everybody had lice, but that's no consolation. Charlotte scrubs Nelly's scalp, dusts it with lice powder, wraps her head in a white cloth. Thus bandaged, insensitive to the ridiculousness of her appearance, Nelly goes to see her grandfather, Whiskers Grandpa. Hermann Menzel, seventy-one years old.

He's been given a narrow room to himself to die in. Nelly is familiar with it. As she enters, the room is filled with his death rattle. (Today, the little room is empty, clean and tidy, like all the attic rooms in the Frahm house.) Whiskers Grandpa is lying on his back—people always seem to die on their back when they die a so-called natural death—his chin angrily pointed at the ceiling. His yellowish-white beard, grown wild, sprouts from his death's head. Restless hands on the bedcover: death hands. Nelly thinks of the calluses on his right thumb and fingertips, caused by the use of the shoemaker's awl. Do calluses melt when people die?

The rasping and gasping doesn't sound as though it were coming from his throat. Nelly stands, leaning against the door frame. She doesn't touch her grandfather—although she later touches her dead grandmother, her dead mother—it seems impossible to her. After a few minutes she leaves, pursued by the gasps that can still be heard on the stairs. She sits down on the top step and forces herself to think: My grandfather is dying. Of his entire life, which she tries to imagine, she can think only of the desperation he must have felt in Bromberg, when "Gussie" turned down his marriage proposal. When he, a young shoemaker's apprentice, threatened to go and hang himself in the forest. Whereupon she (Whiskers Grandma) ran looking for him in the forest, with several girl-friends: because he was the type, a maniac, who might just have gone and done what he'd said he'd do. For the first time, now that their life is drawing to an end, Nelly thinks of her grandparents as young people, running through forests, nimble, slender, driven by passions.

It wasn't the first time that Nelly was surprised at how naturally all stories seemed to develop once one knew their ending: as though they had never had the choice to develop differently, to lead to a different fate, to different persons. She didn't weep for Hermann Menzel's death, but for the fact that he hadn't found the chance to know himself and to be known by others.

Whiskers Grandma didn't leave her dying husband's bedside. On the third evening she walked into the room when they were all eating supper. Everybody knew what that meant. She went to wash her hands and sat down in her chair. Charlotte served her some soup, Nelly pushed a couple of peeled potatoes toward her. Nobody said a word. After a few mouthfuls she laid down her spoon and said: You wouldn't think so, but after living together for so long, it isn't easy.

This was the only epitaph Nelly heard for the onetime shoe-maker and subsequent railroad conductor and ticket puncher Hermann Menzel. She wasn't allowed to go to the cemetery, not in this cold weather, not in her condition. For one morning the stretcher with her grandfather's body stood in the Frahms' hall, which Nelly's family used as a kitchen. When the sheet was lifted, she saw his face one more time for a few seconds. She saw that her grandfather's face had never been as severe as it looked in death. Her mother had an outburst of despair and hammered her fore-head with her fists because Nelly had lost her lice cap and now the "nits" might spread all over the apartment. Nelly thought bitterly: As though this were a reason to be so desperate. A good reason might have been the thought of a man who'd once been young and stubbornly greedy for happiness, but who'd stayed poor and far below his expectations, who'd taken to drinking then, and to beating the woman for whom he had once almost hanged himself: that such a man was now lying there like that.

Nelly didn't want to admit that her mother might perhaps be beating her forehead for those very reasons.

Love and death, illness, health, fear and hope left a deep impression in your memory. Events that have been run through the filter of a consciousness that is not sure of itself—sieved, diluted, stripped of their reality—disappear almost without a trace. Years without memory which follow the beginning years. Years during which suspicion of sensory experience keeps growing. Only our contemporaries have had to forget so much in order to continue functioning.

Reopening of the so-called secondary schools toward winter. Charlotte insists that her children complete their education. She had saved their report cards. She also saved her desire for her children to have a higher education. Nelly wants to be a teacher, and that's what she shall be. A Frau Wrunk, a distant relative of the Frahms, who lives in town, is willing to rent Nelly her couch, provided Nelly keeps an eye on her children and lends a hand with the housework. Frau Wrunk works at the food-rationing office, and her husband—but she doesn't know that yet—works in a mine in Siberia. Once again Nelly is exposed to the head of the household only through a photograph: a thin blond man. The two boys, aged eight and ten, take after him. Cool, as is the North German temperament, but decent and extremely clean, the whole bunch of them, and most of all honest.

From the first hour on, Nelly realizes that she is out of place in this unused drawing room, a situation she finds unnatural. Drawing-room laws no longer have anything to do with her. She helps herself to the pudding in Frau Wrunk's pantry. She cuts thin slices off the hard country sausage and eats them without any guilt. She brazenly counters Frau Wrunk's glances, first questioning and later piercing. Sullenly she sweeps the living-room carpet in the morning. Her relationship with the actually very nice and decent Frau Wrunk gradually deteriorates, mainly because of Nelly's way of looking around the apartment. Frau Wrunk doesn't need that sort of behavior in exchange for her kindheartedness.

The school was on the edge of the Pfaffenteich (church pond), where it stands to this day. The classes were taught in shifts, the boys in the mornings, the girls in the afternoons, then vice versa. Letters were left lying under the benches: If the young lady who occupies this seat has no objections . . . That was how marriages came about. That was how Ute Meiburg, who sat behind Nelly— she was from Stettin—met her future husband. Holding hands, they'd walk past the Bürgerstuben—today one of those popular rustic-style restaurants with wooden benches—where Nelly would sit—always at the same table—and mash four bluish potatoes into her mock gravy number 3. She couldn't fathom how an unapproachable, proud girl like Ute could meet a boy on the basis of such an advertisement. She discussed the case at great length with Helene from Marienburg—who had long black hair and deep blue eyes, a rare and attractive combination—who shared her opinion, which did, however, not interfere with their friendship for Ute. All three agreed that Germany's defeat had taken the joy out of their lives. They'd never get used to the nonsensical, red-bannered slogans in the streets, or the green fences around Soviet displays, or the hammer and sickle all over town. They could only laugh loudly and sardonically as they watched the new films in the Schauburg, to which their embarrassed teachers had to take them. Less than a year earlier they had stood in line in their respective towns to see Kristina Söderbaum in *The Golden City*.

Helene's beautiful eyes grew larger and larger as the winter wore on. On one of the first warm days in March she ran to the water faucet in the middle of a German composition and let cold water run over her wrists. Maria Kranhold, the teacher, expressed surprise, since the classroom was barely heated and all were sitting in their coats. But she felt hot, said Helene, and keeled over. During recess, her mother brought her a slice of bread from the new ration. They learned that Helene had three younger brothers and sisters, and that she had taken to eating less and less.

The subject of the composition was Marquis Posa in Schiller's *Don Carlos*. Maria Kranhold affirmed to their faces that this play —as well as *Wilhelm Tell*—had not been taught in German schools during the final years of National Socialism because of a single sentence: "Give us freedom of thought, Sire!" Everybody, but especially Ute, Helene, and Nelly, bitterly denied her statement. It was slander to say that their schools hadn't been teaching all of Schiller.

Nelly took great pains to write a most ambiguous composition: the special longing for freedom of every nation, which other nations can neither share nor understand in the past or today. She was furious that Kranhold had given her a B, not because of the content, but for her "stilted style." Toward the end of class, Maria Kranhold said in a different context: The high point of freedom to her, during the "brown period," was that she'd been able to avoid saluting the "spider flag." Whether openly, deviously, or by ruse, she had never raised her arm to the swastika. When using the word "freedom," one should at least realize that some people's freedom might mean a lack of freedom for others.

Nelly was hearing such talk for the first time from someone who had not been in a concentration camp. She didn't want to like Kranhold. Kranhold never said "the Nazis" the way other people did. Before the changeover she used to say "the Nazis," but now it disgusted her how everybody was suddenly using the pejorative. Maria Kranhold was a devout Christian. Come and see me if you feel like it, she said to Nelly.

She lived only two blocks from Nelly. You drove slowly along the street the other day. You still remembered the house number, but then you weren't sure that you were looking at the right house. Maria Kranhold had gone to the West long ago.

It's a secret source of pride to Nelly that she doesn't know anyone in this town—except the twenty-four girls in her class and a dozen teachers—and that no one knows her. She rehearses the game: strange, stranger, strangest. A little cheating at the housing office—Herr Wrunk's allegedly imminent return—nets her a small room of her own in Widow Sidon's apartment on Fritz-Reuterstrasse. This severs her last tie with the village of Bardikow.

Fritz-Reuterstrasse was ostentatiously ugly, but Nelly didn't care. She didn't care that every building in the project on this street looked alike. She'd disappear into the doorway of her house—which stank to high heaven—as though into a hideout. Widow Sidon's total indifference to everything in life—except the fact that her sixteen-year-old son, Heiner, stole every bite of food from her pantry, without any concern for his mother, who could starve to death for all he cared—fascinated Nelly. She'd hear widow Sidon chase her son around the table with the carpet beater, in the ice-cold room next to hers. The son would pretend to be running from his mother, shaking with laughter, until he got fed up; then he'd wrest the carpet beater from her hand and throw it out the window, five flights down into Fritz-Reuterstrasse.

He sure didn't use to be like that. A sign of the times.

The sentence hooks itself into Nelly's mind, for one whole day and one whole night she can't get rid of it: He sure didn't use to be like that, he sure didn't . . . In the morning, she steps up to the window that goes down almost to the floor, she holds on to the window frame and looks down into the street, which is milling with people running to work. She isn't scared by the thought that suggests itself, but she knows that she's not going to do it. She'll go to school as she does every day and quarrel with Kranhold.

Kranhold repeats her invitation. That afternoon Nelly goes to see her for the first time, despising herself for it.

It's the first warmish day of the year, a March day. Maria Kranhold lives with her mother in the former parsonage, the official residence of her father, who had been a minister. As an explanation for her visit, Nelly says she simply couldn't make head or tail of the new math problems. She'd never been able to understand geometry. She'd never been able to visualize a space on the basis of a formula. Maria Kranhold teaches the rare combination of mathematics and German. Nelly informs her that she's actually never liked her math teachers. Unmoved, Kranhold offers her her other half to like, the German-teaching half. Tea just happens to have been made. Blackberry-leaf tea, which comes closest to real tea. And a kind of pastry, oats with dark flour, sweetened with saccharine. Her mother, who appears at one point in the background, white-haired and hunched over, is an expert at economy recipes.

It is exactly one year and three months since Nelly ate oatmeal cookies in the house of a different teacher, Julia, on Schlageterstrasse in L. Julia's room had been just as lined with books as the former study of Maria Kranhold's father. Kranhold says that the books may have been the same, at least to some extent. She is twenty years younger than Julia, her hair is brown instead of black, and she, too, wears it in a bun. She has large teeth. Julia, too, might have worn a blue linen dress with a white belt. Suddenly Nelly asks if she, Maria Kranhold, really thinks that people like her teacher Julia Strauch knowingly lied to her all those years. She's instantly angry with herself because of her question.

Maria Kranhold took her time with the answer. She may have cautioned herself to be extra careful. Carefully she first repeated the word "lied," with a questioning intonation. Lied? That would be too simplistic, she then said. Are you lying to others when you yourself believe lies—at least to some extent? This, she thought, had most probably been the case.

But of course believing was no excuse, Kranhold then said. You had to look at what you believed. Nobody had ever been lied to about the most important issues. Hadn't Hitler demanded more Lebensraum for the German people from the very beginning? To any thinking person, that meant war. Hadn't he repeated over and over that he wanted to exterminate the Jews? That's what he had done, as much as he could. He had declared that Russians were subhuman, and that's how they had been treated, by people who wished to believe that they were. And people of her old teacher Julia Strauch's caliber had fallen into the trap themselves, with their belief in everything. Who can absolve them for having sent their minds on a vacation?

Julia couldn't have killed anybody, Nelly said, she was sure of that.

That's possible, Kranhold said. But she gave you a guilty conscience if you're forced to tell yourself that she couldn't have killed anybody.

Nelly said nothing.

She has made your conscience turn around, against yourself, Kranhold said. She's made it so that you can't be good, that you can't even think good thoughts, without feeling guilty. Because how can you reconcile the commandment: Thou shalt not kill, or the request: Love thy neighbor as thyself, with the doctrine of other people's inferiority?

And what about you? Nelly asked. How did you manage to reconcile the two?

Poorly, said Maria Kranhold, very poorly. Constantly with one toe in prison, constantly on the edge of betraying God and the persons entrusted to my charge. But I didn't adore those alien gods. That way, of course, I haven't the excuse of having believed in them.

Nelly was surprised that she understood what Kranhold was

talking about. Kranhold asked her if she knew Goethe's *Iphigenia*. No? Really not? One of those strange grown-up looks, which Nelly was to experience more and more in the years to come. Kranhold made her a present of a small paperback volume. Take it home. Read it.

Nelly lay on the bed in Widow Sidon's cold narrow room. She read: "Out into your shadows, lively treetops . . ." She felt nothing as she read the heretofore unknown words. Her Goethe was the one whom her teacher Julia Strauch had recited to her with her vibrant voice: "Cowardly weighing / fear-ridden swaying / womanish faints / anguished complaints / won't avert sorrow / won't set you free. / All force and all might / to defy is your right, / never to cower / to show your own power / will open the arms of the gods to thee."

Time runs out. Nelly must fall ill, break down. The structure which strictly governs coincidence is evident here. In January— such are the laws of coincidence—she was given a seat next to a new girl, Ilsemarie from Breslau.

Ilsemarie has large features, but they look transparent, slightly curly, medium-blond, streaked hair, braided and pinned up. She has deep shadows under her eyes and strong hands with delicate wrists. Her manner is unnaturally lethargic. Nelly is both attracted and repelled by the way Ilsemarie combines things that don't fit together. Her voice is slightly hoarse and her speech hesitant, which Helene and Ute think is "affectation."

In the spring Ilsemarie starts coughing dreadfully. Or, more accurately, her constant cough, to which everyone had grown accustomed, enters a new, horrifying phase. Maria Kranhold emphatically advises that she consult a doctor. Ilsemarie shrugs. Nelly can't understand why her eyes have taken on a mocking expression, as though despite herself. Her eyes are brown. Brown eyes aren't meant to look mocking. Something about Ilsemarie grows more irritating by the day. Nelly and Ilsemarie do their homework together. Sometimes Nelly thinks it's simpler to copy a Latin text from the book and to translate it at home. *Vedetis nos contenti esse. Certo vos dignitatis esse. Postulo ut diligentia sitis.*

Nelly wrote these sentences into a yellow-brown notebook with the words "Notes/Diary" printed on the cover in black script, which she must have bought for 75 pfennigs—according to a small sticker—at W. Klee Succ., G. Schepker Prop., in Hagenau, Mecklenburg. Most of the pages are covered with Rilke poems, interspersed with sentences uttered by Maria Kranhold, without comments. On the last pages she kept accounts for several months of her monthly budget of 100 marks. Not all items can still be identified today. It seems quite impossible that she spent 10 marks 55 in the lending library in January 1946. There probably had been a registration fee. But where was that library? What books did Nelly take out to read? Theater: 4 marks—what play did she see? The movies: 1.10 reichsmarks. Basic expenses: rent 30 marks, weekend trip to Bardikow, 2.80 marks. (The delousing center on the station square. The scrabbling fingers of the nurse on scalp and neck. The small white delousing certificate without which one could not purchase a train ticket. The short ride in the drafty boarded-up cars. Her mother waiting for her at the station, or coming to meet her in the forest. The best hour of the week: the walk through the forest, which is beginning to turn green.)

In March, a visit to a doctor cost 3 marks. Hadn't she caught a rash on her hands in the train? But what vaccination could one buy for 70 pfennigs? Toothpaste cost 13 pfennigs, and once the rare word "meat" appears in front of the incomprehensible amount: 48 pfennigs . . . In February, Nelly spent 5 marks at the hairdresser, to have her hair cut; she wanted to look young again. Later, she spends 2 marks 75 a month at the hairdresser. Oatmeal—with which she cooks a watery gruel for herself in the evenings—cost 10 pfennigs. She must have been giving private lessons to have earned the strange amount of 18 marks 75. What kind of lessons? To whom?

No idea.

Unfortunately, the photo for which she paid 3 marks has been lost.

Dinner conversation. In biology, Lenka's class discussed the problem of famine that is threatening humanity, and weighed possible countermeasures, from birth control to total, worldwide disarmament. The girl who is first in her class, and maintains a legendary A+ average, who is active in a number of social clubs, and who has been accepted with flying colors to study medicine—this particular student wonders toward the end of the class if one shouldn't first deprive old people and terminal patients of food, when confronted with the unsolvable task of distributing too little food among too large a population.

Lenka will probably forget the details of the one-gene–one-enzyme hypothesis. But she'll remember the class during which a fellow student suggested selecting the old and the sick for preferential death by starvation. A moral memory? Just as you remember nothing of Maria Kranhold's math classes, but clearly know the moment and the place when Nelly met her weeping teacher in the street. Months later, Maria Kranhold wrote the reason for her tears in a letter to the TB sanatorium: she had again been unable to find potatoes to feed her mother, who was gravely ill. From the moment her teacher had wept in front of her, Nelly stopped calling her Kranhold and started calling her Maria, and she began listening to Maria's thoughts on the subject of dictatorship. Nelly discovered that she'd been living under a dictatorship for twelve years, apparently without noticing it.

The city of Phnom-Penh has "fallen"—that's how the others describe it. We say "has been taken," "has been liberated," and hardly realize that what you say depends on coincidences that took place thirty or twenty-five years earlier. The thirtieth anniversary of the liberation. Without quotation marks. Quotation marks would move this sentence one hundred and twenty-five miles farther west. The schools of the industrial district, which includes three communities, marching toward the stadium with red and blue flags. Delegations of the people's army and Soviet forces in gala uniform. Brass bands. ("Of all our army buddies / none was so sweet and dear / as our Red Guard comrade / the little trumpeteer.") Snatches of speeches from the assembly field nearby. Prefabricated sentence fragments strung together. Loudspeaker music, all too loud. "Wake up, ye damned of this earth," as a song.

You're almost the oldest persons in the small even-sided square in front of the grandstand with the two groups of singers. Nobody else seems to mind that the loudspeaker on the left distorts the sound unbearably. Young people in groups, in shirts and jeans. Here and there, a girl wearing one of the new little knitted hats with wavy brims. People's Army members and Soviet soldiers in small separate groups. Rapprochement in one spot: together they look at postcards. A lively young blond Soviet soldier arranges group pictures, takes photos. Soviet soldiers with members of the People's Army, mixed rows, the back row arm in arm, the front row kneeling. Three Soviet pilots who've just arrived in the square quickly and silently join the second photo. The choir of the expanded secondary school sings about Our Pastor and His Cow. People are crowding around the knackwurst stands. Firemen have driven up to watch the campfire, the wood is stacked and ready. The setting sun shines red behind the sparse little birch forest.

April 21, 1975. It's the thirtieth anniversary of the eve of the liberation of these localities in the Potsdam area. A veteran with snowy-white hair and decorations on his chest smiles blissfully as he limps to the edge of the square, where the leaders of the local party are lined up. Two girls, one blond, one dark, with bouffant hairdos and patent-leather jackets, are surrounded by Soviet soldiers, and are engaged in lively conversation, in Russian and in German, with a young officer. Nearby on the concrete square the band is tuning up. The young people's dance begins at 7 p.m. Lenka says she'll go and check it out, although the music will probably be a drag.

Quite a beautiful afternoon, you say to H. Yes, he says, quite beautiful actually.

Ilsemarie from Breslau did go to the doctor, eventually. She would be sick for a long time. Her worried mother appears at school, the class can see her talking with Maria in the hall, she is crying. A week later, the health department shows signs of functioning again: the whole class is summoned for X rays. Nelly, without premonition, for the first time behind the machine which she'll learn to fear. After three days the postcard with the invitation to stop by again. An elderly X-ray specialist with gold-rimmed glasses and wavy gray hair holds her upper arms, turns her from side to side behind the X-ray screen, makes her lift her arms sideways above her head, inhale, exhale. Lights on. You can come out now.

Well. How old are you? Seventeen? (Two motherly nurses form a chorus: She's really brave, considering . . . Again the misunderstanding: numb is not brave.) An explanation follows: how highly contagious her friend Ilsemarie had been; she's already in a TB sanatorium. As for your condition, Fräulein Jordan, unfortunately, the first suspicion has been confirmed. It would really have been a miracle if she hadn't caught the disease, considering her state of malnutrition, and the close contact. It's an infiltrate, I'll explain to you what that means. The size of a one-mark piece, by the way. We'd have preferred it the size of a cherry pit, but on the other hand, it could have been a cavern, couldn't it. The prognosis is favorable, quite favorable.

And the nurses again: She's really very sensible, considering her age.

Nelly spits into the blue glass container with the screw top. A diet rich in fats would of course be best. You'll even get a small supplementary ration card. In the country? But that's perfect. Just stay flat on your back and take it easy. We'll notify your school.

How well she's taking it, the nurses say sympathetically.

The TB Institute is still on the same street, in the same house as it was then. (You tentatively touch the cast-iron door handle.) The interior has been modernized. Nelly clearly remembers a few gray house walls on her way home. In the middle of May, the list of expenses in her Notes/Diary breaks off with the item 50 pfennigs for the rental library. Nelly does her last homework in the afternoon—numb, not brave—while in her shoulder blades she feels the growing need to lie down. A need that's going to stay with her. Composed—this is her resolve—composed and sensible, she'll say goodbye to Maria the next day. She'll not subject others to her handshake, nor to a whiff of her breath. She's supposed to withdraw, that's the way an accident of fate should be. The motherly nurses would have been amazed at the turmoil within her, the non-acceptance of this damned accident of fate, the self-pity.

But she never thought to succumb to the illness that wasn't meant for her. Her greatest worry was that her mother didn't share her secret knowledge. Charlotte let herself sink into the grass next to the sandy path from the station to the village, devastated—as was to be expected—by the new blow; she covered her face with her hands, and only after a long while did she come out with the question: Why did this have to happen to her? (Children as fate's weapons against mothers, Nelly knew this role and hated it.) But when the Frahm house came in sight, Charlotte had already figured out the necessary practical measures.

Everything was done the way she wanted it. A cot was set up behind the lilac hedge in the Frahms' apple orchard, that's where

Nelly lay down on fair days. Her mother made an arrangement with Frau Frahm, who was a sympathetic soul. In exchange for Charlotte's remaining two golden bracelets and rings, the farmer's wife furnished a daily pint of sour cream, which Nelly ate in the afternoon with sugar and crumbs of rye bread. Nelly was obliged to lead a drone's life in the midst of busy, hard-working people. It gave her at last the opportunity to study the books Maria Kranhold was sending her (among them the small blue volume of Goethe's poems); at last she fell into the hands of the poets. She didn't talk about it, but she sometimes thought it was for this that she had fallen ill. Most of the lines of poetry that you know by heart are the ones Nelly absorbed in those years.

In August there was the performance of the play *The Return of the Father*. (The mail as the herald of fateful changes. The first, a dirty-gray postcard from a forest camp near Minsk with the message: "I am alive" had—almost a year ago—brought her mother to the brink of a breakdown. This time there was the telegram with the plain notification of the time and place of Bruno Jordan's arrival. Bruno Jordan, believed killed: the assumption of those years.)

The day was very hot. From early morning on, Whiskers Grandma cried at every opportunity. Nelly was unable to read, and wandered aimlessly around the house. Aunt Liesbeth, transfigured by unselfish happiness, baked a potato cake. All during the past years, whenever Nelly could make a wish while blowing off an eyelash, she had wished for only one thing: Let him come back. Now he was coming, and it would be foolish to call the emotion she felt by any other name than "joy."

He came in the carriage that Werner Frahm, the farmer's son, had gotten ready for him. Why was it that Nelly only hesitantly went outside when Irene Zabel called through the house: They're coming!? The scene that awaited them would certainly be excruciatingly embarrassing. Her father should have come in the dark, unannounced and alone. At least the crowd scene in front of the house should have been avoided, and most of all, the painful blunder perpetrated by the three girls—Irene and Margot Zabel and Hanni Frahm—who sang from Herr Ernst's attic window, in harmony, "No fairer land in our time," to welcome the homecomer.

Then, with the appearance of the main character—the moment Nelly saw "the Father"—the scene maliciously slid into the absurd. Strangely enough, Nelly had foreseen it. Fairy tales prepare us for it from childhood on: The hero, the king, the prince, the lover, falls under a spell in foreign lands; he returns a stranger. Maybe those who stayed home don't notice the transformation, and he is faced with the difficult task of having to reveal himself as somebody different, a person who is loved for what he no longer is. The bewitched "father" had at least been provided with an out-and-out change of exterior while he was in foreign lands.

The apparition that climbed down from the carriage, supported by Werner Frahm and Charlotte Jordan, was a wizened little old man with a small mustache, ridiculous steel-rimmed spectacles fastened behind the ears with strips of dirty cloth, a close-cropped, hoary round head, whose ears were sticking out; dressed in a uniform many sizes too large for him, and much-too-big, horribly useless boots. When a stranger arrives, the idea of a "return" is out of the question. So is that of a "happy reunion"; at best there's embarrassment and pity. Compassion. But that isn't what the seventeen-year-old wants to feel for the returning father.

In the silence that descended—except for the persistent singing from the attic window, "The silv'ry moon has risen"—Nelly was being nudged and pushed, to make her do what a dutiful daughter does: go up to her father, embrace him, put her arms around his bony shoulders, see his twitching, unfamiliar face close by, the gap between his teeth. Breathe in the sour smell that he exuded.

Her mother, Charlotte Jordan, was distraught. She kept repeating, always with the same foolish expression on her face, that they hadn't recognized one another. Several times they had passed each other on the station platform. Only now—since she rarely looked in a mirror—only by her husband's vacant glance, which went right through her, did she learn of her own transformation into an unrecognizable person, together with the realization that the one whom she expected, whom she had described to others as somebody special, whose picture she had shown around, that this person would not return. With a single blow she had lost herself and her husband. Her conduct in the weeks to come can be understood only in light of the losses she had suffered. She was forty-six years old, he was forty-nine. Bruno Jordan was given a place next to his wife in the wide farmhouse bed in the attic room, and it's true that

Nelly was sometimes awakened by her mother's impatient, rejecting words and the disappointed, bitter words of her father.

Aunt Liesbeth was the only one who rose to the occasion. Nelly wouldn't have expected it: Aunt Liesbeth understood. When everybody was standing around Bruno Jordan at the Frahms' kitchen table, watching shamelessly as he slurped Frau Frahm's soup from the battered tin spoon he had pulled out of his dirty satchel, deaf and mute with ravenousness, when Nelly was sitting alone in the worn armchair in her room, it was Aunt Liesbeth, Liesbeth Radde, who came in to look after her. Against her nature, she dispensed with any ostentatious display, she touched Nelly's shoulder lightly and said: You'll see, your father's going to snap right back. We'll feed him until he's his old self again. For this moment, Nelly has preserved a feeling of indelible gratitude to her aunt.

Nelly observes her father unlovingly, horrified at herself: her father, who is still imprisoned, still shackled by the needs of his body. Not only does he refuse no plate of food, no crust of bread from the farm kitchen—the others, no matter how ravenously hungry they may be, cannot imagine the hunger of a man who weighs a hundred pounds. The look on his face when he fetches his soup, when he takes the crust of bread, offends Nelly, as does his anxious-obstinate way of fighting for his tin spoon, for the absurd tin bowl that Charlotte has pulled out of his satchel, for the piece of rock candy wrapped in a dirty rag, for the tattered foot wrappings.

Nelly doesn't understand that she no longer lives in that time and place where the poet rhymed "finality" with "personality" and had the arrogance to emphasize it with an exclamation mark. Nelly applies the wrong standards to her father, who has come very close to starving to death.

Nelly didn't mind being given a bed in the sanatorium when the weather got colder. She wanted to be among people on all occasions. Her inquisitiveness—that much she knew—was directed more toward the depths than toward the "high points of life," as others called them. This, perhaps, was the basic reason for the strange satisfaction she derived from her illness. (Through the bacillus, she had caught an infection that was incurable: the secret knowledge that one must die in order to be born.)

She therefore had to laugh when the beautiful white modern

hospital in town (the two-bed room in which Ilsemarie was already waiting for her, she as the superior one, initiated and at home in the habits and the language of TB patients), when this building—she had hardly moved in—had to be evacuated within three days to make room for a Soviet military hospital. Deep down she was amused by the doctors' resignation, the nurses' panic, the slightly feverish excitement of the patients, while she ostensibly played the game. She fluttered with the others, lamented with the others, stole with the others: a complete set of cutlery and a thick, white woolen blanket. A knife is left over from the set, the hospital's initials engraved in its handle. Its blade—razor-thin, flexible, slightly curved at the tip, a bit nicked—has cut all the bread and all the sausages in the house for years. The blanket was made into a three-quarter-length coat for Nelly: for a full-length coat it lacked exactly that end piece which had had to be cut off because of the hospital's name woven into the edge in large letters. Without the short coat Nelly wouldn't have survived the winter in Winkelhorst—a fact that they, Nelly and her mother, reiterated to each other, even later—because the winter of 1946–47 was again excessively cold, and Nelly had to take daily walks in the open air, in addition to her rest cure, according to doctor's orders. Outside, a sharp wind came whistling from the Baltic Sea, which was only a few miles away, but the patients never got to see it. But on clear evenings they could see the lights of Lübeck across Dassow Lake, when they climbed up a hill behind the castle park.

Nelly often went up this hill, but you forgot to look for it when you revisited Winkelhorst. First you wandered around at the wrong site, close to the village (where the castle was in your memory); you kept telling yourself that it was the right spot, you wasted half a roll of film, despite your doubts, until two old men on the road cleared up your mistake and directed you to the castle, which lies a mile and a half outside the village, and which has become a mental hospital. It was hard to understand how you could have forgotten, how you could have confused the two buildings. The wonderful, ancient trees on the castle lawns alone should have been indelibly engraved in your memory. (Although Nelly never saw them in foliage: she was there from October to April.) You slowly walked around the castle. It was a murky, foggy day, not cold. Patients and nurses were sitting on the landing of the stairs that led to the main entrance of the house. A young girl, leaning against a pillar, kept putting her hands to her head in a gesture of despair, at ten-second intervals, without stopping. Hundreds of times every day.

The park, located in an unhealthy, swampy area, is falling into decay. Even back then, everybody agreed that it was a bad place for TB patients, who delighted in talking about their unfavorable location during their long walks. Nelly went with the girl from her room, or with Herr Löbsack, who made regular dates with her. She knew that he was a sarcastic, cold person—homely besides—and severely ill, very contagious as the head nurse warned her, yet she dutifully went to their meetings, she dutifully felt a little excitement when they met in the house, when he gave her a sign across the table in the dining hall, felt a little ashamed when he kept her waiting. But it gave her no pleasure to walk by his side, to meet other couples at the stagnant castle pond; she felt no need to touch his red hands with the prominent wrist bones, or to be touched by his pouting, usually sarcastically twisted lips. She could see his Adam's apple move when he talked, and she knew that he had no inclination to touch either her hair or her face. They met with the tacit understanding that it didn't matter, and that an illusion of pleasure and love had to suffice for them, for the time being. That the only pleasure open to them was abandonment to their dangerous pseudo-existence. Nelly felt the enticement of seduction and saw no reason to resist it.

A crackling, bitter cold that went gradually to one's very marrow, that came from without and within and made the patients sarcastic and indifferent, subject to hasty, unstable alliances. Always those men, said the head nurse to the women in the large corner room, which they had dubbed the "Ice Palace" because the temperature never went above freezing.

The head nurse was a rotund, stern person, a battle-ax, but she knew what was what, who would get well and who would die, she knew it sooner and more accurately than the two M.D.'s—the X-ray specialist, Dr. Brause, who had diagnosed Nelly, who came once a week from Boltenhagen, gloomy with impotence, and the lady doctor, unmarried, long-haired, who had missed out on too much in her life, who'd invite a few colleagues from the villages for an evening of drinking and singing (orgies, said the head nurse, that's what's called orgies in my book), who'd puke over the balcony railing early in the morning, and make her calls at noon with bleary eyes.

You really should gain some weight, Dr. Brause said, and then he burst out laughing sardonically, as though it were an obscene joke. Occasionally, however, he'd use the pneumothorax treatment, as for instance in the case of blond Fräulein Lembcke, who had caverns and lesions in her left lung and was completely bedridden after several hemorrhages, whose voice was hoarse—which was noted with apprehension in this place—and who suffered most from the fact that she hadn't been able to wash her beautiful blond hair for months, whereupon her sad mother brought some witch hazel and rubbed her scalp with moistened cotton balls. When Fräulein Lembcke was moved from the Ice Palace into one of the rooms for the severely ill, Nelly read regularly to her before supper Gottfried Keller's *Romeo and Juliet in the Village*, until the head nurse, tactless as usual, called her out into the hall and forbade her, in an audible whisper, to visit severely ill, highly contagious patients. That's how Nelly learned that the head nurse didn't include her among those who would die (strangely enough, she never forbade Ilsemarie's new friend Gabi—a delicate, pale girl whose X-ray evidence was negligible—to visit the severely ill in their rooms, even to sing for them), but neither was she one of those who could tempt God with impunity. Nevertheless, Nelly continued her visits, not only because Fräulein Lembcke cried over the head nurse's evaluation, which she had guessed quite correctly, but also because Nelly wanted to play with fire. She did, however, stay closer to the door from now on, and she read shorter sections, now from *The Pennon of the Seven Upright Men*. What she read in books seemed more real to her than her pale, cold life in this house, among these people.

Fräulein Lembcke survived and is perhaps, to this day, still working as an insurance clerk.

Gabi died.

A hundred times Gabi sang to the sick in the wards, in her clear, pure voice, "Oh, my dad is a beautiful clown" and "The carousel turns round and round and round." "So please get on," she sang, "and ride with me, I'll ride one time, two times, three times around our fate with thee."

Her bed stood between Ilsemarie's and Nelly's beds. In the night she told how she and her delicate, slender mother had gotten the news, during the war, that her father, a first lieutenant, had been killed. That they had to flee from a small Pomeranian town, and on their way they had been laid up with typhoid in the house of a malicious woman who bullied and robbed them. That her mother had died, and that she now had nobody in the world but an old aunt in Grevesmühlen.

Dr. Brause, who usually seemed indifferent toward the incurably sick, became rude to Gabi, ruder after each new X ray. Then he decided on the pneumothorax treatment, although he could barely find a spot—as he said irascibly—to insert the needle on that skin-and-bones body. Gabi, in her inflated state, had trouble breathing for two days; then she sang again, "My heart is like a pigeon cote." Evenings one could see her in the semidarkness of the cold corridors, with a red-haired youth named Lothar, a fact which, contrary to the usual house rules, was overlooked and never mentioned to her. Only Fräulein Schnell, an old spinster who had the habit of plucking her facial hair, sitting up in bed in the morning, found it appropriate to speak, to no one in particular, about the proven fickleness of redheads, which made Gabi cry under her blanket and prompted Nelly and Ilsemarie to hold a long, loud, and uninhibited conversation about sour grapes.

To be affected, but not seriously endangered—that, too, can become a formula for living. Nelly tried it out. (To live in the third person . . .) It seemed easy to her to keep her distance. Never again would she let herself be seriously hurt by anyone.

Slubice. Here one should be able, all of you thought, to get a bite to eat somewhere. You slowly drove through several streets. Cobblestones, willows clipped in spherical shape. A vain search for a restaurant. To go on, then, to the border. The Oder in the heat of high noon, glistening. A quick border clearance on both sides. You look out the side window while your credentials are being checked by the GDR border guard. A young naked bird has fallen from a nest in the eaves of the border station, in front of the guard's feet. He pushes it aside with his boot. You say: But you're cruel. He asks: Do you expect me to take care of every dead bird, as well as my duty? Do you think I should stand here holding my cap to catch any that fall out of their nest?

He's right, of course he can't do that.

At the Interhotel in Frankfurt (Oder) you are served an excellent meal, although you have to wait a long time for it, since a tour group from the West is occupying almost the entire place, keeping all the waiters busy. You can't make out the language of the expensively and garishly dressed people, most of them elderly. Portuguese, the waitress says, contemptuously. They act as if they owned the place. The men have heavy eyelids and flabby features, the women's faces are brightly painted, sharp, irritated. Much gold on hands and necks.

Do they think they're beautiful, Lenka wonders. Her uncle, your brother, Lutz, gives her the good advice to make use of this rare opportunity to observe the living specimens of a ruling bourgeois middle class. That means nothing to me, says Lenka. Today, less than four years later, there are discussions about the results of the first election after the defeat of Fascism in Portugal.

The dead in Winkelhorst were taken to a small chapel in the castle park. There were always patients who saw to it that a body was carried out feet first, so it wouldn't pull anybody else after it. Some patients would always bet they had the nerve to sneak to the chapel at midnight and touch the body's feet: others would go along as witnesses, and still others would pay five marks to the winner. When Frau Hübner, the mother of Klaus and Marianne, died (Nelly had seen the notorious death roses on her cheeks bloom and wilt), Herr Manchen, an elderly East Prussian, thwarted any kind of bet in the men's ward by dint of his authority. But during the three nights when the deceased was still above ground, there were knocks against the window of the Andreas Hofer men's ward—it was on the second floor—in which the ten-year-old Klaus slept between Herr Manchen and Herr Löbsack. And on the last night, there were three heavy blows against the boy's bed, rousing everybody from sleep. Now your mother has said goodbye to you, said Herr Manchen.

Gus. Gus from near Pilkallen. One day he informed Nelly that he had chosen her for his protectress. He was ten years old, a pudgy, stocky, awkward boy. The expression in his brown eyes— "doggie eyes"—made other children, and adults, feel like tormenting him. His letters (the oldest of those you've kept): "Now there isn't anybody I can wash the knives and forks for," he writes after her discharge. The spelling in the letters proves that Nelly's attempts to teach him the three Rs had failed miserably. His gawky, pushy wooing, his jealousy of the other, more handsome, brighter children.

"After I find my aunts, and when I'm living with them, and when I'm grown up and a tailor, I'll sew you a warm coat, and I'll send it to you so you'll always think of your dear Gus." (In 1947, his aunts from the West claimed him, and Gus went to live with them. He must be forty years old by now. Perhaps he did become a tailor.)

"Hannelore has been dead now for a long time, and Herr Löbsack, too, and Grandma Radom, and my sedimentation rate is worse again, and I lost 500 grams in one week, but my sputum is negative."

Hannelore was the little five-year-old girl whom Nelly took care of when the nurses, one by one, left this remote area, this distressing house. Hannelore's favorite expression was: What's up? five candies in a cup! She sang, "Buy me a bouncing balloon, but soon," and there were days when she'd let people address her only as "Princess." The women in the second women's ward said they couldn't take Hannelore's nightly coughing any longer, but the head nurse threatened to quit if the lady doctor had the child moved to a single room.

When little Hannelore began to whimper as soon as Nelly took her temperature; when Nelly—in spite of her experience—could no longer find the child's pulse; when she barely felt any weight when she lifted Hannelore in order to smooth her sheets; when the sedimentation rate, which Nelly had learned to read, remained the highest in the entire house; when no ruse, no begging, would succeed in getting one spoonful of soup behind her teeth: that was the day Nelly didn't want to go to her any more. That's when she simply stayed in bed while everybody else went for a walk. She put on her heavy knit sweater and gloves, covered her feet with her white coat, and read Dante's *Divine Comedy*. The head nurse came in, Nelly kept reading. The head nurse smoothed the blankets, complained that people had again been toasting bread on the pot-bellied stoves, and asked, Was it possible that pigeon-chested Elisabeth had lately been carrying on with the severely ill Herr Heller. Always those men. Then she turned to leave. Nelly called after her: Anyway, why should I get involved! The head nurse, in total surprise, raised her eyebrows, which gave her a foolish expression, and said she certainly didn't know, Nelly would have to figure it out for herself.

Nelly got up, ran to the washroom, bawling, wiped her tears, went on bawling, dried her face, and went to little Hannelore, who said in a weak voice: I thought maybe you weren't coming. What's up, Princess, said Nelly, three candies in a cup! Five, said little Hannelore. She died a few nights later.

Nelly was working toward her discharge. Every afternoon she ate a large cup of the syrup which her father, who was getting to be more like himself again, brought her in a little pail. It made her gain weight, she became shapeless, thereby increasing her chance of being ready for discharge. At the beginning of April, Dr. Brause gave the longed-for okay, and Nelly left, all 165 pounds of her. An ambiguous but necessary accomplishment.

This seems to be the end. All the notes have disappeared from your table. Strange that it should be today, May 2, 1975. The day on which the brown leaf sheaths dropped off the poplar all at once.

It's almost four years since the July trip to Poland. You got home between four and five in the afternoon. Lenka declared she was pleased to be "back" again as she walked upstairs, while H. put the car in the garage, your brother, Lutz, carried the bags up, and you took the Sunday papers from the mailbox, realizing that your trip had taken no longer than forty-six hours. You had a premonition of the emotions—although not of their full impact—the work would evoke in you.

The closer you are to a person, the harder it seems to say something conclusive about him; it's a known fact. The child who was hidden in me—has she come forth? Or has she been scared into looking for a deeper, more inaccessible hiding place? Has memory done its duty? Or has it proven—by the act of misleading—that it's impossible to escape the mortal sin of our time: the desire not to come to grips with oneself?

And the past, which can still split the first person into the second and the third—has its hegemony been broken? Will the voices be still?

I don't know.

At night I shall see—whether waking, whether dreaming—the outline of a human being who will change, through whom other persons, adults, children, will pass without hindrance. I will hardly be surprised if this outline may also be that of an animal, a tree, even a house, in which anyone who wishes may go in and out at will. Half-conscious, I shall experience the beautiful waking image drifting ever deeper into the dream, into ever new shapes no longer accessible to words, shapes which I believe I recognize. Sure of finding myself once again in the world of solid bodies upon awakening, I shall abandon myself to the experience of dreaming. I shall not revolt against the limits of the expressible.